AWAKE

Stories of
LIFE-CHANGING
EPIPHANIES

Edited by Thomas Dyja

ILLUMINA™

A BALLIETT & FITZGERALD BOOK

MARLOWE & COMPANY
NEW YORK

An Illumina Book ™

Published by
Marlowe & Company
An Imprint of Avalon Publishing Group Incorporated
161 William St., 16th floor
New York, NY 10038

Distributed by Publishers Group West

Book design: Jennifer Daddio

Special thanks to assistant editor Nathaniel Knaebel for leading us to *Siddhartha,* "Revelations" and *The Death of Ivan Ilyich,* and to assistant editor Lauren Podis for unearthing "The Pot of Gold."

Manufactured in the United States of America

Library of Congress Catalog-in-Publication Data

Awake: stories of life-changing epiphanies / edited by Thomas Dyja
p. cm.— (Illumina)
ISBN 1-56924-583-5
1. Life—Fiction. 2. Epiphanies—Fiction. I. Dyja, Thomas. II. Series.

PN6120.95.L6 A95 2001
808.83'935—dc21

CONTENTS

LETTER FROM THE EDITOR

Many believe that literature cannot change the world, that it should be content to live between its covers, on the shelves, as a decoration to our lives.

But at the most difficult, challenging, complex moments, again and again we reach up to those shelves, finding guidance and solace and drive among the words of great writers. While a novel may not topple a government, it can change hearts, stiffen resolve, light fires, dry tears or cause them to flow and so affect the world along with the millions of other small motions, the seed-carrying breezes and rivulets, that make our planet work.

We have created Illumina Books in hopes of changing your life. Maybe not in earth-shattering ways, but in ways that comfort and inspire, in ways that help you to continue on.

Each Illumina anthology is a careful collection of extraordinary writing related to a very specific yet universal moment. With the greatest authors as your guides, you'll read the stories of those who have traveled the same road, learn what they did, see how they survived and moved on.

By offering you the focused beauty and wisdom of this literature, we think Illumina Books can have a powerful, even a therapeutic effect. They're meant not just to work on the mind, but in the heart and soul as well.

—The Editor

from

THE SEVEN STOREY MOUNTAIN

THOMAS MERTON

The Intellect alone rarely takes us into the light. In fact, the tides of theories and isms *often pull us farther and farther away. In this selection from his autobiography, Catholic philosopher Thomas Merton explains how he finally overcame his intellect to find God in a small church on New York's Morningside Heights.*

By the time I was ready to begin the actual writing of my thesis, that is, around the beginning of September 1938, the groundwork of conversion was more or less complete. And how easily and sweetly it had all been done, with all the external graces that had been arranged, along my path, by the kind Providence of God! It had taken little more than a year and a half, counting from the time I read Gilson's *The Spirit of Medieval Philosophy* to bring me up from an "atheist"—as I considered myself—to one who accepted all the full range and possibilities of religious experience right up to the highest degree of glory.

I not only accepted all this, intellectually, but now I began to desire it. And not only did I begin to desire it, but I began to do so efficaciously: I began to want to take the necessary means to achieve this union, this peace. I began to desire to dedicate my life to God, to His service. The notion was still vague and obscure, and it was ludicrously impractical in the sense that I was already dreaming of mystical union when I did not even keep the simplest rudiments of the moral law. But nevertheless I was convinced of the reality of the goal, and confident that it could be achieved: and whatever element of presumption was in this confidence I am sure God excused, in His mercy, because of my stupidity and helplessness, and because I was really beginning to be ready to do whatever I thought He wanted me to do to bring me to Him.

But, oh, how blind and weak and sick I was, although I thought I saw where I was going, and half understood the way! How deluded we sometimes are by the clear notions we get out of books. They make us think that we really understand things of which we have no practical knowledge at all. I remember how learnedly and enthusiastically I could talk for hours about mysticism and the experimental knowledge of God, and all the while I was stoking the fires of the argument with Scotch and soda.

That was the way it turned out that Labor Day, for instance. I went to Philadelphia with Joe Roberts, who had a room in the same house as I, and who had been through all the battles on the Fourth Floor of John Jay for the past four years. He had graduated and was working on some trade magazine about women's hats. All one night we sat, with a friend of his, in a big dark roadhouse outside of Philadelphia, arguing and arguing about mysticism, and smoking more and more cigarettes and gradually getting drunk. Eventually, filled with enthusiasm for the purity of heart which begets the vision of God, I went on with them into the city, after the closing of the bars, to a big speak-easy where we completed the work of getting plastered.

My internal contradictions were resolving themselves

out, indeed, but still only on the plane of theory, not of practice: not for lack of good-will, but because I was still so completely chained and fettered by my sins and my attachments.

I think that if there is one truth that people need to learn, in the world, especially today, it is this: the intellect is only theoretically independent of desire and appetite in ordinary, actual practice. It is constantly being blinded and perverted by the ends and aims of passion, and the evidence it presents to us with such a show of impartiality and objectivity is fraught with interest and propaganda. We have become marvelous at self-delusion; all the more so, because we have gone to such trouble to convince ourselves of our own absolute infallibility. The desires of the flesh—and by that I mean not only sinful desires, but even the ordinary, normal appetites for comfort and ease and human respect, are fruitful sources of every kind of error and misjudgement, and because we have these yearnings in us, our intellects (which, if they operated all alone in a vacuum, would indeed, register with pure impartiality what they saw) present to us everything distorted and accommodated to the norms of our desire.

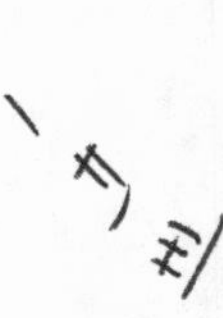

And therefore, even when we are acting with the best of intentions, and imagine that we are doing great good, we may be actually doing tremendous material harm and contradicting all our good intentions. There are ways that seem to men to be good, the end whereof is in the depths of hell.

The only answer to the problem is grace, grace, docility to grace. I was still in the precarious position of being my own guide and my own interpreter of grace. It is a wonder I ever got to the harbor at all!

Sometime in August, I finally answered an impulsion that had been working on me for a long time. Every Sunday, I had been going out on Long Island to spend the day with the same girl who had brought me back in such a hurry from Lax's town Olean. But every week, as Sunday came around, I was filled with a growing desire to stay in the city and go to some kind of a church.

At first, I had vaguely thought I might try to find some Quakers, and go and sit with them. There still remained in me something of the favorable notion about Quakers that I had picked up as a child, and which the reading of William Penn had not been able to overcome.

But, naturally enough, with the work I was doing in the library, a stronger drive began to assert itself, and I was drawn much more imperatively to the Catholic Church. Finally the urge became so strong that I could not resist it. I called up my girl and told her that I was not coming out that week-end, and made up my mind to go to Mass for the first time in my life.

The first time in my life! That was true. I had lived for several years on the continent, I had been to Rome, I had been in and out of a thousand Catholic cathedrals and churches, and yet I had never heard Mass. If anything had ever been going on in the churches I visited, I had always fled, in wild Protestant panic.

I will not easily forget how I felt that day. First, there was this sweet, strong, gentle, clean urge in me which said: "Go to Mass! Go to Mass!" It was something quite new and strange, this voice that seemed to prompt me, this firm, growing interior conviction of what I needed to do. It had a suavity, a simplicity about it that I could not easily account for. And when I gave in to it, it did not exult over me, and trample me down in its raging haste to land on its prey, but it carried me forward serenely and with purposeful direction.

That does not mean that my emotions yielded to it altogether quietly. I was really still a little afraid to go to a Catholic church, of set purpose, with all the other people, and dispose myself in a pew, and lay myself open to the mysterious perils of that strange and powerful thing they called their "Mass."

God made it a very beautiful Sunday. And since it was the first time I had ever really spent a sober Sunday in New York, I was surprised at the clean, quiet atmosphere of the empty streets uptown. The sun was blazing bright. At the end of the street, as I came out the front door, I could see a burst of green, and the blue river and the hills of Jersey on the other side.

Broadway was empty. A solitary trolley came speeding

down in front of Barnard College and past the School of Journalism. Then, from the high, grey, expensive tower of the Rockefeller Church, huge bells began to boom. It served very well for the eleven o'clock Mass at the little brick Church of Corpus Christi, hidden behind Teachers College on 121st Street.

How bright the little building seemed. Indeed, it was quite new. The sun shone on the clean bricks. People were going in the wide open door, into the cool darkness and, all at once, all the churches of Italy and France came back to me. The richness and fulness of the atmosphere of Catholicism that I had not been able to avoid apprehending and loving as a child, came back to me with a rush: but now I was to enter into it fully for the first time. So far, I had known nothing but the outward surface.

It was a gay, clean church, with big plain windows and white columns and pilasters and a well-lighted, simple sanctuary. Its style was a trifle eclectic, but much less perverted with incongruities than the average Catholic church in America. It had a kind of a seventeenth-century, oratorian character about it, though with a sort of American colonial tinge of simplicity. The blend was effective and original: but although all this affected me, without my thinking about it, the thing that impressed me most was that the place was full, absolutely full. It was full not only of old ladies and broken-down gentlemen with one foot in the grave, but of men and women and children young and old—especially young: people of all classes, and all ranks on a solid foundation of workingmen and -women and their families.

I found a place that I hoped would be obscure, over on one side, in the back, and went to it without genuflecting, and knelt down. As I knelt, the first thing I noticed was a young girl, very pretty too, perhaps fifteen or sixteen, kneeling straight up and praying quite seriously. I was very much impressed to see that someone who was young and beautiful could with such simplicity make prayer the real and serious and principal reason for going to church. She was clearly kneeling that way because she meant it, not in order to show off, and she was praying with an absorption which, though not the deep recollection of a saint, was serious enough to show that she was not thinking at all about the other people who were there.

What a revelation it was, to discover so many ordinary people in a place together, more conscious of God than of one another: not there to show off their hats or their clothes, but to pray, or at least to fulfill a religious obligation, not a human one. For even those who might have been there for no better motive than that they were obliged to be, were at least free from any of the self-conscious and human constraint which is never absent from a Protestant church where people are definitely gathered together as people, as neighbors, and always have at least half an eye for one another, if not all of both eyes.

Since it was summer time, the eleven o'clock Mass was a Low Mass: but I had not come expecting to hear music. Before I knew it, the priest was in the sanctuary with the two altar boys, and was busy at the altar with something or other which I could not see very well, but the people were praying by themselves, and I was engrossed and absorbed in the thing as a whole: the business at the altar and the presence of the people. And still I had not got rid of my fear. Seeing the late-comers hastily genuflecting before entering the pew, I realised my omission, and got the idea that people had spotted me for a pagan and were just waiting for me to miss a few more genuflections before throwing me out or, at least, giving me looks of reproof.

Soon we all stood up. I did not know what it was for. The priest was at the other end of the altar, and, as I afterwards learned, he was reading the Gospel. And then the next thing I knew there was someone in the pulpit.

It was a young priest, perhaps not much over thirty-three or -four years old. His face was rather ascetic and thin, and its asceticism was heightened with a note of intellectuality by his horn-rimmed glasses, although he was only one of the assistants, and he did not consider himself an intellectual, nor did anyone else apparently consider him so. But anyway, that was the impression he made on me: and his sermon, which was simple enough, did not belie it.

It was not long: but to me it was very interesting to hear this young man quietly telling the people in language that was plain, yet tinged with scholastic terminology, about a point in Catholic Doctrine. How clear and solid the doctrine was: for behind those words you felt the full force not only of Scripture but of centuries of a unified and continuous and consistent tradition. And above all, it was a vital tradition: there was nothing studied or antique about it. These words, this terminology, this doctrine, and these convictions fell from the lips of the young priest as something that were most intimately part of his own life. What was more, I sensed that the people were familiar with it all, and that it was also, in due proportion, part of their life also: it was just as much integrated into their spiritual organism as the air they breathed or the food they ate worked in to their blood and flesh.

What was he saying? That Christ was the Son of God. That, in Him, the Second Person of the Holy Trinity, God, had assumed a Human Nature, a Human Body and Soul, and had taken Flesh and dwelt amongst us, full of grace and truth: and that this Man, Whom men called the Christ, was God. He was both Man and God: two Natures hypostatically united in one Person or suppositum, one individual Who was a Divine Person, having assumed to Himself a

Human Nature. And His works were the works of God: His acts were the acts of God. He loved us: God, and walked among us: God, and died for us on the Cross, God of God, Light of Light, True God of True God.

Jesus Christ was not simply a man, a good man, a great man, the greatest prophet, a wonderful healer, a saint: He was something that made all such trivial words pale into irrelevance. He was God. But nevertheless He was not merely a spirit without a true body, God hiding under a visionary body: He was also truly a Man, born of the Flesh of the Most Pure Virgin, formed of her Flesh by the Holy Spirit. And what He did, in that Flesh, on earth, He did not only as Man but as God. He loved us as God, He suffered and died for us, God.

And how did we know? Because it was revealed to us in the Scriptures and confirmed by the teaching of the Church and of the powerful unanimity of Catholic Tradition from the First Apostles, from the first Popes and the early Fathers, on down through the Doctors of the Church and the great scholastics, to our own day. *De Fide Divina.* If you believed it, you would receive light to grasp it, to understand it in some measure. If you did not believe it, you would never understand: it would never be anything but scandal or folly.

And no one can believe these things merely by wanting to, of his own volition. Unless he receive grace, an actual light and impulsion of the mind and will from God, he cannot even make an act of living faith. It is God Who gives us faith, and no one cometh to Christ unless the Father draweth him.

I wonder what would have happened in my life if I had been given this grace in the days when I had almost discovered the Divinity of Christ in the ancient mosaics of the churches of Rome. What scores of self-murdering and Christ-murdering sins would have been avoided—all the filth I had plastered upon His image in my soul during those last five years that I had been scourging and crucifying God within me?

It is easy to say, after it all, that God had probably foreseen my infidelities and had never given me the grace in those days because He saw how I would waste and despise it: and perhaps that rejection would have been my ruin. For there is no doubt that one of the reasons why grace is not given to souls is because they have so hardened their wills in greed and cruelty and selfishness that their refusal of it would only harden them more . . . . But now I had been beaten into the semblance of some kind of humility by misery and confusion and perplexity and secret, interior fear, and my ploughed soul was better ground for the reception of good seed.

The sermon was what I most needed to hear that day. When the Mass of the Catechumens was over, I, who was not even a catechumen, but only a blind and deaf and dumb pagan as weak and dirty as anything that ever came out of the darkness of Imperial Rome or Corinth or Ephesus, was not able to understand anything else.

It all became completely mysterious when the attention was refocussed on the altar. When the silence grew more and more profound, and little bells began to ring, I got scared again and, finally, genuflecting hastily on my left knee, I hurried out of the church in the middle of the most important part of the Mass. But it was just as well. In a way, I suppose I was responding to a kind of liturgical instinct that told me I did not belong there for the celebration of the Mysteries as such. I had no idea what took place in them: but the fact was that Christ, God, would be visibly present on the altar in the Sacred Species. And although He was there, yes, for love of me: yet He was there in His power and His might, and what was I? What was on my soul? What was I in His sight?

It was liturgically fitting that I should kick myself out at the end of the Mass of the Catechumens, when the ordained *ostiarii* should have been there to do it. Anyway, it was done.

Now I walked leisurely down Broadway in the sun, and my eyes looked about me at a new world. I could not understand what it was that had happened to make me so happy, why I was so much at peace, so content with life for I was not yet used to the clean savor that comes with an actual grace—indeed, there was no impossibility in a person's hearing and believing such a sermon and being justified, that is, receiving sanctifying grace in his soul as a habit, and beginning, from that moment, to live the divine and supernatural life for good and all. But that is something I will not speculate about.

All I know is that I walked in a new world. Even the ugly buildings of Columbia were transfigured in it, and everywhere was peace in these streets designed for violence and noise. Sitting outside the gloomy little Childs restaurant at 111th Street, behind the dirty, boxed bushes, and eating breakfast, was like sitting in the Elysian Fields.

from

TAKE ME TO THE RIVER

AL GREEN
WITH DAVIN SEAY

If you visit Memphis on a Sunday, you can attend services at the church of the Reverend Al Green, who after this dramatic, joyful revelation turned from a life as the world's greatest soul singer to the robes of ministry. That the moment took place at Disneyland only makes it that much more wonderful.

Creativity is a strange and fickle thing, sometimes flowing like a river and sometimes trickling down to a dry creek bed. For me, Willie, and the whole Hi Records' crew, a flood of pure music was pouring out of us all throughout 1972 and right into 1973. I can't account for it exactly, other than to say that, once we were in that particular groove, we rode it all the way, never knowing when we'd run out of inspiration and have to pull over to the side of the road.

We had our recording routine down cold. Usually Willie and Al Jackson would work out the fundamentals of a song, then give it to me to write the lyrics. Once we had something we were all happy with, Leroy and Al—or sometimes Bulldog Grimes—would put down a rhythm track. That's what I'd sing my vocals to, and Willie rarely altered the way my voice came through on his funky double four-track system. The most he'd add was a little echo chamber, and I never even heard of EQ until years later. After I sang the song, my job was pretty much done. Willie and the rest of the musicians would get to work adding their bits and pieces and when it was finished, it would be presented to me for approval. Once in a while I'd have a suggestion or a second thought, but by that time, I'd learned to trust Willie's ear as completely as my own and would let him have his way.

I've sometimes heard it said that Willie just made the

same record over and over again. But I don't agree. Just like anybody else, we had a sound and, within that sound, we played around as much as we liked, changing things up and mixing them around. If some of it ended up sounding the same, it was because that was what naturally occurred when we came together. There was no use pretending to be something we weren't.

Especially when what we were was working so well. Within six months, we rolled right out of *I'm Still in Love with You* into my fifth album, *Call Me*, which would earn me my first Grammy nomination, and another number-one single, "You Ought to Be with Me," followed up in short order by the title track and "Here I Am (Come and Take Me)," both jumping into the number 2 slot on the charts. We had a sure sense that we could do no wrong by this time, and we were starting to play around with the musical formula that was serving us so well. I took on country music for the first time with a rendition of Hank Williams's "I'm So Lonesome I Could Cry" and Willie Nelson's "Funny How Time Slips Away." "Stand Up" was a tune I wrote by myself that gave me a chance to reflect my feelings about all the social and political upheaval that was going on at the time, while "Have You Been Making Out O.K." was one of those ballads we could now do in our sleep. In fact the song itself has a sleepy, lazy feel to it, as if I was trying to describe a beautiful dream.

And in a way, that's what my life had become . . . a

dream. After a lifetime of work, I'd become an overnight sensation, and in a little more than two short years, I'd racked up five million-selling singles, sold-out concert halls around the world, and sent soul music spinning off in a whole new direction.

God knows, I'm not bragging. It was just a fact. What was coming out of Hi Records was different from anything else the competition could put together and, as a result, some of the big hit-making factories of soul music in the sixties were starting to falter and lag. Stax, another staple of the Memphis music scene, couldn't keep its hard-core soul sound selling, and Motown was looking for a new formula once their big productions started getting a little top-heavy. In fact, some of the A&R ears from Motown came down to the Royal Studios shortly after we cut "Let's Stay Together" and threw down a bunch of cash to rent the place for a week. Willie was only too happy to oblige and turned the place over to them. They went through it with a fine-tooth comb, making notes on everything from the way he miked the drums to the crazy angle of that slanted floor. In the end, they brought in a dozen session musicians, just to try the place out and see if they couldn't get close to the sound we had. But what they couldn't duplicate or manufacture was the chemistry that Willie had achieved between me, his musicians, and that intangible asset that can only be called genius.

Who knows how long things might have kept up if

they'd been allowed to run their course? *Call Me* was every bit a big hit as what came before and there was no reason to expect that whatever came after wouldn't make every bit as big a splash. We were on a roll.

But God had something else in mind, and it was getting to be time for Him to make a move. I think I must have known that something was coming to an end and something else was about to start, even if I couldn't have put that feeling into words.

Yet, what I couldn't express one way came out another. The last cut on *Call Me* was a song I had written without even really knowing why. It was called "Jesus Is Waiting," and when I listen back to it today, I can clearly hear what was only a still small voice back then. Jesus was waiting. For Al Green. And the time had come to heed His call or turn away, one last time.

"I've been a fool," I sang in "Jesus Is Waiting," "disregarding your love . . ." I sang those lyrics with feeling, even with conviction, but it was a fervor that I could only remember once knowing. I could recite the words of repentance, the formula for forgiveness, and the attitude of saving grace. But behind that knowledge was spiritual ignorance. I had forsaken the faith and, in the process, sold my birthright.

It had been a long time since I had felt the power of the Holy Spirit move through my life and my music, a long time since I'd given glory to God for the gifts He had bestowed. I had played out the age-old drama of the prodigal son, turning my back on my father's house to pursue the world and all its passing pleasures. And while it's true that, in Scripture, there is the clear promise that if you train up a child in the way he should go, he will not depart from it when he is old, that's no guarantee that the road back won't be twisted and curving and full of danger. I knew God was real, knew it as well as I knew I needed air to breathe and water to drink. But *knowing* is not enough . . . it's never enough. You've got to believe and, believing, walk out your faith, one step at a time. Somewhere down that road I'd traveled, I'd thrown away the map God had given to mark my way. It's no wonder I found myself lost in a wilderness of my own vain imaginings.

So if I had fallen so far away from the love of God, how is it I could see my way clear to write and sing a song like "Jesus Is Waiting" on a album that was supposed to be about nothing more than flirtation and romance and the hot passions that spring up between a man and a woman?

I've asked myself that question and I've never found the answer. But if I had to guess, I'd say that the meaning behind the words of "Jesus Is Waiting" is somewhere between an invitation and a challenge, a test and a tease. A part of me, deep down inside, cried out, and the hunger I felt so powerfully I didn't even know it sought to be satisfied. Was it Jesus that was waiting or was it me? He says He stands at the door knocking, and for Al Green, the rhythm of that knock beat out a gospel tempo that I couldn't ignore.

If Willie and the band thought anything about us doing dyed-in-the-wool church music, they never said it to me. Of course, we all had a connection to the gospel sound and its message of Good News—you can hardly be a black man in the South playing music without having those songs stuck in your head. Still, while there was nothing unnatural about singing outright to Jesus, I'm sure most of them, Willie most especially, were hoping it was just a phase I was going through.

I never gave it a second thought. At their best, the songs I wrote and the music I sang were the expressions of what I was feeling at the moment they arrived. And at the moment "Jesus Is Waiting" arrived, I was in what you might call an expectant mood. After a trip to the top that pretty much took my breath away and more than I could imagine of the kind of success that was supposed to matter. I was already beginning to ask a question that has come to haunt more than one rich, famous and fabulously happy celebrity: *Is this all there is?* And although I hadn't quite put it to myself in exactly those words, the uneasy feeling that followed me around like a hungry dog was getting harder and harder to ignore. Jesus *was* waiting . . . for the right time to make His move.

That time finally came in the summer of '73, in the middle of a nonstop tour to promote *Call Me*. At that point,

I was booked up with solid shows for better than a year and, as a result, my life was suddenly no longer my own to control. I was answerable to promoters and producers and bottom-line box office numbers and in case I ever forgot why I was doing it all in the first place, all I had to do was look around the Hi Records headquarters, or the Royal Studios, or the office Willie and I had set up to take care of business. Everywhere I turned there were people who were depending on me to make their living, to keep the whole bandwagon rolling and meet the payrolls week in and week out. We had secretaries and accountants and janitors and engineers and bodyguards and roadies and publicists and . . . well, you get the idea. I wasn't just a singer, or a songwriter or even a star. I was an enterprise: Al Green and Company.

And most of the folks that worked for me I'd never met and couldn't call by name. And because I got tired of being surrounded by strangers all the time, I decided to add a few familiar faces to the entourage. I brought both my dad and my brother Bill out from Grand Rapids and put them on the security detail because that was the best way to have them next to me on a regular basis.

It was great having family around again, talking about old times and sharing that comfortable feeling you can get with kin. Bill and I had slept in the same bed growing up, and you just don't get much closer than that.

But it wasn't just family I had the yearning to draw close

around me. More than anyone else, I wanted to keep Laura Lee close by. At that point in my life, I felt as if she was the only one who really understood me, knew where I was coming from, where I was going, and why it sometimes felt like I was stuck in between the two. It wasn't just that we both had careers in music and knew the pressures and problems that come with that territory. We connected at a deeper level altogether and shared a common longing to fill an empty place inside that we couldn't describe but only recognize, each one within the other. It was what bonded us as friends, but more important than that, it made us both pilgrims together, traveling down the same dark path.

As I said, we came to the crossroads of that journey in the late summer of '73 in a hotel room with the Matterhorn rising up outside the window. No, I wasn't in Switzerland. It was Disneyland and the spotlights that lit the fake snow on the ride shone into my room with a pale and ghostly light. I was feeling a little ghostly myself, as a matter of fact. Earlier that day, I'd met Laura at the airport in San Francisco, where I had an matinee scheduled at the Cow Palace. I hadn't seen her for a few weeks and, since we weren't on the same bill anymore, the only way we could grab any time together was when she was off the road, back home in Detroit, and I could send for her to spend a day or two with me while I was touring. For some reason, I felt a special need just then to see her, talk with her, and let her gentle presence soothe my mind, and she must have heard the urgency in my voice because she caught the next plane out, even though she'd just come off a heavy schedule herself.

We spent the afternoon hidden away in the hotel room until it was time for the show and rode out together in the limo. After the concert, we headed straight back to the airport. I was booked to play another date that same evening at Disneyland and had about three hours to get to the gig. It was all a blind rush, but, back then, *everything* was a blind rush until you actually got there and then, more often than not, they'd keep you cooling your heels backstage for no good reason. Whoever came up with the expression "hurry up and wait" surely spent time on a concert tour.

It must have been about one o'clock in the morning before we finally got checked into the hotel the Disney promoters had reserved for us. I made sure Laura had her own room whenever we were together because it was important, to both of us, that folks on the tour understood that we weren't just in the middle of some hot and heavy love affair and that they should respect and honor her as much as I did.

We kissed good night and, after taking a shower to wash the stage sweat away, I got ready for some well-deserved sack time. I remember as I passed into sleep feeling strangely serene and at peace with myself and the world. In the midst of all the craziness that surrounded my life, I had Laura in the room right next door to mine and my father and brother just down the hall. It was a little like having a home on the road.

I couldn't have been asleep more than an hour or two when I was suddenly awakened by the sound of shouting. I sat bolt upright in bed, frightened that some crazy fan had broken into the room. The shouting continued and as I listened, I realized that the voice wasn't threatening so much as excited and happy, as if someone had just walked into a surprise party with all his oldest and dearest and friends in attendance. There was something oddly familiar about the voice, as well. Where had I heard it before?

It was then that I realized that the voice was my own! And while the words I shouted were of no earthly tongue, I immediately recognized what they meant. I was praising God, rejoicing in the great and glorious gift of salvation through His son, Jesus Christ, and lifting my voice to heaven with the language of angels to proclaim His majesty on high.

People who have had such an experience, when the power of God and the presence of the Holy Spirit fall so heavily that they drip like sweet honey from the rock with the very oil of gladness, will tell you that their memories of the moment are always from the outside, looking in. And the same was true for me. There I was, rejoicing at the very top of my lungs, and yet at the same time, I could watch myself, hear myself, and wonder to myself, *Now, what is this fool shouting about? Doesn't he know folks are trying to sleep?* But as much as I understood that if I kept up all that hollering for too much longer I was sure to get arrested or worse, there was nothing in either earthly or spiritual realms that could have shut my mouth. A different spirit had taken charge, even while it left me free to watch and marvel at how the power of God can move a man with a sovereign touch. I believe to this day that two different events were coming to pass in that hotel room at the very same time. First, a man was being quickened and called to a new life in Jesus. Second, that same man was allowed to be witness of his own salvation, that forever after he could speak of the power of the Holy Spirit from firsthand experience. God didn't take away my mind. He gave me a new one, even as he left my senses free to marvel at the transformation.

Suddenly the shouting and celebration stopped and I heard a voice, calm and clear coming from inside me, but rattling the walls like a ten-point earthquake all the same. "Are you ashamed of Me?" was the question it asked and the words pierced me like a knife. I might have been ashamed of myself, for all the years I had let the love of God languish as I pursued my own lusts and desires. But ashamed of Jesus? Ashamed of the Lamb of God, the Alpha and the Omega, sitting at the right hand of the Father in glory and majesty. Never!

I began shouting out praises in tongues once again and, jumping out of bed, ran into the bathroom. The part of my mind that was still tethered to the world was starting to panic. If I didn't shut myself up pretty soon, there was sure to be an embarrassing scene, and then what would I tell the police: *I'm sorry, Officer, but I can't seem to contain the abundant grace of God within this mortal frame of flesh and blood.* I wondered how *that* would look on the arrest report.

I couldn't think of another thing to do but grab an armful of towels off the rack and bury my face in them. I remember biting at the cotton nap, trying to muffle myself when I suddenly heard that voice again, asking one more time, "Are you ashamed of Me?"

"Lord, no!" I shouted into the towels and threw them off myself, as if I was holding a fistful of poisonous snakes. "No!" I screamed again as I heard a pounding from the door connecting Laura's room to mine own.

"Al!" she was saying from the other side. "Are you all right? What's going on in there?"

I rushed back into the room and flung the door open. "I am not ashamed of the Lord Jesus Christ!" I yelled into her wide-eyed face. "I am not ashamed of His Gospel?"

"Al," she said, a look of fear clouding her big brown eyes. "What's happened to you. Should I call a doctor?"

For an answer, I grabbed her and half-dragged, half-pulled her with me out the hotel door and into the hallway. A little ways down the corridor another door opened and I could see Haywood Anderson, my chief security guard, rush into the hall, ready to take on whoever was assaulting his boss.

But no one could have overcome my attacker that night. Jesus Himself had laid in wait for me and picked that moment from out of all eternity to reveal Himself in all His glory and splendor. Whatever it was that I knew of God and His love up until that moment—all the sermons I'd heard preached and all the gospel songs I'd sung, and all the times I seen folks weeping and wailing as they made their way to lay down their lives at the altar of Mother Bates's revival tent—all that faded into insignificance. I was in the middle of a personal encounter, one on one with my Creator and now, at last, I understood what all the words and all the songs and all the tears had really meant.

As Haywood rushed up to me, he was joined by my brother Bill, who, as I recall, was still dressed in just his underwear. Other guests had started to poke their heads out to see what all the commotion was, but I didn't care. In fact, I wanted them all to know exactly what was going on. "I am not ashamed!" I shouted again and started hammering on my dad's door.

When he opened up, a robe around his shoulders and his eyes like saucers, I thrust out my hands right under his nose. "Look, Daddy!" I cried, wiggling my fingers at him. "Look at my hands!" I pointed down at my feet. "And my feet, Daddy," I said as tears began to drop from my eyes.

"What is it, son?" my daddy asked. "What's wrong with your hands and feet?"

"Can't you see?" I answered, the tears nearly blinding me now. "They're brand-new! All of me . . . is brand-new!"

Daddy turned to Laura with a terrified look. "What are we going to do?" he said. "What's wrong with him?"

But Laura just smiled and in that sublime moment I knew that she understood. "Nothing to do," she said softly. "Al's in God's hands now." She put her arm around me. "Come on, honey," she said. "Let's go back in the room and let these good folks get some sleep." She waved down the hall. "It's fine," she said to the bewildered guests. "Everything is just fine." And, along with Haywood, Bill, and Daddy, she led me back into my suite.

It took me the rest of that early morning to come back to myself, weeping and praying and holding on to my friends and family like a lost child found safe again. We all sang songs I remember, the old gospel gems I'd grown up with, and one by one those around me offered up their thankgivings for so great a salvation of so great a sinner. And when dawn finally broke over the Disneyland Matterhorn, the freeway began to fill up with morning traffic and all along the boulevard, the shops and stores and little souvenir stands that sold Mickey watches and hats with Goofy ears began to open up, and I passed into a deep and untroubled sleep. My head was cradled in Laura's arms. My daddy held my hand. And my Savior dwelt within, never to leave me nor forsake me.

from

ZEN IN THE ART OF ARCHERY

EUGEN HERRIGEL

Eugen Herrigel's brief classic recounts his path towards Zen through the discipline of archery. In this excerpt, he shows not just how he broke through to oneness with his practice, but also the crucial role his Master played in guiding him.

Day by day I found myself slipping more easily into the ceremony which sets forth the "Great Doctrine" of archery, carrying it out effortlessly or, to be more precise, feeling myself being carried through it as in a dream. Thus far the Master's predictions were confirmed. Yet I could not prevent my concentration from flagging at the very moment when the shot ought to come. Waiting at the point of highest tension not only became so tiring that the tension relaxed, but so agonizing that I was constantly wrenched out of my self-immersion and had to direct my attention to discharging the shot. "Stop thinking about the shot!" the Master called out. "That way it is bound to fail." "I can't help it," I answered, "the tension gets too painful."

"You only feel it because you haven't really let go of yourself. It is all so simple. You can learn from an ordinary bamboo leaf what ought to happen. It bends lower and lower under the weight of snow. Suddenly the snow slips to the ground without the leaf having stirred. Stay like that at the point of highest tension until the shot falls from you. So, indeed, it is: when the tension is fulfilled, the shot *must* fall, it must fall from the archer like snow from a bamboo leaf, before he even thinks it."

In spite of everything I could do or did not do, I was unable to wait until the shot "fell." As before, I had no alternative but to loose it on purpose. And this obstinate failure depressed me all the more since I had already passed my third year of instruction. I will not deny that I spent many gloomy hours wondering whether I could justify this waste of time, which seemed to bear no conceivable relationship to anything I had learned and experienced so far. The sarcastic remark of a countryman of mine, that there were important pickings to be made in Japan besides this beggarly art, came back to me, and though I had dismissed it at the time, his query as to what I intended to do with my art if ever I learned it no longer seemed to me so entirely absurd.

The Master must have felt what was going on in my mind. He had, so Mr. Komachiya told me later, tried to work through a Japanese introduction to philosophy in order to find out how he could help me from a side I already knew. But in the end he had laid the book down with a cross face, remarking that he could now understand that a person who interested himself in such things would naturally find the art of archery uncommonly difficult to learn.

We spent our summer holidays by the sea, in the solitude of a quiet, dreamy landscape distinguished for its delicate beauty. We had taken our bows with us as the most important part of our equipment. Day out and day in I concentrated on loosing the shot. This had become an *idée fixe*, which caused me to forget more and more the Master's warning that we should not practice anything except self-detaching immersion. Turning all the possibilities over in my mind, I came to the conclusion that the fault could not lie where the Master suspected it: in lack of purposelessness and egolessness, but in the fact that the fingers of the right hand gripped the thumb too tight. The longer I had to wait for the shot, the more convulsively I pressed them together without thinking. It was at this point, I told myself, that I must set to work. And ere long I had found a simple and obvious solution to this problem. If, after drawing the bow, I cautiously eased the pressure of the fingers on the thumb, the moment came when the thumb, no longer held fast, was torn out of position as if spontaneously: in this way a lightning loose could be made and the shot would obviously "fall like snow from a bamboo leaf." This discovery recommended itself to me not least on account of its beguiling affinity with the technique of rifle-shooting. There the index finger is slowly crooked until an ever diminishing pressure overcomes the last resistance.

I was able to convince myself very quickly that I must be on the right track. Almost every shot went off smoothly and unexpectedly, to my way of thinking. Naturally I did not overlook the reverse side of this triumph: the precision work of the right hand demanded my full attention. But I comforted myself with the hope that this technical solution would gradually become so habitual that it would require no further notice from me, and that the day would come when, thanks to it, I would be in a position to loose the shot, self-obliviously and unconsciously, at the moment of highest tension, and that in this case the technical ability would spiritualize itself. Waxing more and more confident in this conviction I silenced the protest that rose up in me, ignored the contrary counsels of my wife, and went away with the satisfying feeling of having taken a decisive step forward.

The very first shot I let off after the recommencement of the lessons was, to my mind, a brilliant success. The loose was smooth, unexpected. The Master looked at me for a while and then said hesitantly, like one who can scarcely believe his eyes: "Once again, please!" My second shot seemed to me even better than the first. The Master stepped up to me without a word, took the bow from my hand, and sat down on a cushion, his back towards me. I knew what that meant, and withdrew.

The next day Mr. Komachiya informed me that the Master declined to instruct me any further because I had tried to cheat him. Horrified beyond measure by this interpretation of my behavior, I explained to Mr. Komachiya why, in order to avoid marking time forever, I had hit upon this method of loosing the shot. On his interceding for me, the Master was finally prepared to give in, but made the continuation of the lessons conditional upon my express promise never to offend again against the spirit of the "Great Doctrine."

If profound shame had not cured me, the Master's behavior would certainly have done so. He did not mention the incident by so much as a word, but only said quite quietly: "You see what comes of not being able to wait without purpose in the state of highest tension. You cannot even learn to do this without continually asking yourself: Shall I be able to manage it? Wait patiently, and see what comes—and how it comes!"

I pointed out to the Master that I was already in my fourth year and that my stay in Japan was limited.

"The way to the goal is not to be measured! Of what importance are weeks, months, years?"

"But what if I have to break off half way?" I asked.

"Once you have grown truly egoless you can break off at any time. Keep on practicing that."

And so we began again from the very beginning, as if everything I had learned hitherto had become useless. But the waiting at the point of highest tension was no more successful than before, as if it were impossible for me to get out of the rut.

One day I asked the Master: "How can the shot be loosed if 'I' do not do it?"

" 'It' shoots," he replied.

"I have heard you say that several times before, so let me put it another way: How can I wait self-obliviously for the shot if 'I' am no longer there?"

" 'It' waits at the highest tension."

"And who or what is this 'It'?"

"Once you have understood that, you will have no further need of me. And if I tried to give you a clue at the cost of your own experience, I would be the worst of teachers and would deserve to be sacked! So let's stop talking about it and go on practicing."

Weeks went by without my advancing a step. At the same time I discovered that this did not disturb me in the least. Had I grown tired of the whole business? Whether I learned the art or not, whether I experienced what the Master meant by 'It' or not, whether I found the way to Zen or not—all this suddenly seemed to have become so remote, so indifferent, that it no longer troubled me. Several times I made up my mind to confide in the Master, but when I stood before him I lost courage; I was convinced that I would never hear anything but the monotonous answer: "Don't ask, practice!" So I stopped asking, and would have liked to stop practicing, too, had not the Master held me inexorably in his grip. I lived from one day to the next, did my professional work as best I might, and in the end ceased to bemoan the fact that all my efforts of the last few years had become meaningless.

Then, one day, after a shot, the Master made a deep bow and broke off the lesson. "Just then 'It' shot!" he cried, as I stared at him bewildered. And when I at last understood what he meant I couldn't suppress a sudden whoop of delight.

"What I have said," the Master told me severely, "was not

praise, only a statement that ought not to touch you. Nor was my bow meant for you, for you are entirely innocent of this shot. You remained this time absolutely self-oblivious and without purpose in the highest tension, so that the shot fell from you like a ripe fruit. Now go on practicing as if nothing had happened."

Only after a considerable time did more right shots occasionally come off, which the Master signalized by a deep bow. How it happened that they loosed themselves without my doing anything, how it came about that my tightly closed right hand suddenly flew back wide open, I could not explain then and I cannot explain today. The fact remains that it did happen, and that alone is important. But at least I got to the point of being able to distinguish, on my own, the right shots from the failures. The qualitative difference is so great that it cannot be overlooked once it has been experienced. Outwardly, for the observer, the right shot is distinguished by the cushioning of the right hand as it is jerked back, so that no tremor runs through the body. Again, after wrong shots the pent-up breath is expelled explosively, and the next breath cannot be drawn quickly enough. After right shots the breath glides effortlessly to its end, whereupon air is unhurriedly breathed in again. The heart continues to beat evenly and quietly, and with concentration undisturbed one can go straight on to the next shot. But inwardly, for the archer himself, right shots have the effect of making him feel that the day has just begun. He feels in the mood for all right doing, and, what is perhaps even more important, for all right not-doing. Delectable indeed is this state. But he who has it, said the Master with a subtle smile, would do well to have it as though he did not have it. Only unbroken equanimity can accept it in such a way that it is not afraid to come back.

"Well, at least we've got over the worst," I said to the Master, when he announced one day that we were going on to some new exercises. "He who has a hundred miles to walk should reckon ninety as half the journey," he replied, quoting the proverb. "Our new exercise is shooting at a target."

What had served till now as a target and arrow-catcher was a roll of straw on a wooden stand, which one faced at a distance of two arrows laid end to end. The target, on the other hand, set up at a distance of about sixty feet, stands on a high and broadly based bank of sand which is piled up against three walls, and, like the hall in which the archer stands, is covered by a beautifully curved tile roof. The two halls are connected by high wooden partitions which shut off from the outside the space where such strange things happen.

The Master proceeded to give us a demonstration of target-shooting: both arrows were embedded in the black of the target. Then he bade us perform the ceremony exactly as before, and, without letting ourselves be put off by the target, wait at the highest tension until the shot "fell." The slender bamboo arrows flew off in the right direction, but failed to hit even the sandbank, still less the target, and buried themselves in the ground just in front of it.

"Your arrows do not carry," observed the Master, "because they do not reach far enough spiritually. You must act as if the goal were infinitely far off. For master archers it is a fact of common experience that a good archer can shoot further with a medium-strong bow than an unspiritual archer can with the strongest. It does not depend on the bow, but on the presence of mind, on the vitality and awareness with which you shoot. In order to unleash the full force of this spiritual awareness, you must perform the ceremony differently: rather as a good dancer dances. If you do this, your movements will spring from the center, from the seat of right breathing. Instead of reeling off the ceremony like something learned by heart, it will then be as if you were creating it under the inspiration of the moment, so that dance and dancer are one and the same. By performing the ceremony like a religious dance, your spiritual awareness will develop its full force."

I do not know how far I succeeded in "dancing" the ceremony and thereby activating it from the center. I no longer shot too short, but I still failed to hit the target. This prompted me to ask the Master why he had never yet explained to us how to take aim. There must, I supposed, be a relation of sorts between the target and the tip of the arrow, and hence an approved method of sighting which makes hitting possible.

"Of course there is," answered the Master, "and you can easily find the required aim yourself. But if you hit the target with nearly every shot you are nothing more than a trick archer who likes to show off. For the professional who counts his hits, the target is only a miserable piece of paper which he shoots to bits. The "Great Doctrine" holds this to be sheer devilry. It knows nothing of a target which is set up at a definite distance from the archer. It only knows of the goal, which cannot be aimed at technically, and it names this goal, if it names it at all, the Buddha." After these words, which he spoke as though they were self-evident, the Master told us to watch his eyes closely as he shot. As when performing the ceremony, they were almost closed, and we did not have the impression that he was sighting.

Obediently we practiced letting off our shots without taking aim. At first I remained completely unmoved by where my arrows went. Even occasional hits did not excite me, for I knew that so far as I was concerned they were only flukes. But in the end this shooting into the blue was too much for me. I fell back into the temptation to worry. The Master pretended not to notice my disquiet, until one day I confessed to him that I was at the end of my tether.

"You worry yourself unnecessarily," the Master comforted me. "Put the thought of hitting right out of your mind! You can be a Master even if every shot does not hit. The hits on the target are only the outward proof and confirmation of your purposelessness at its highest, of your egolessness, your self-abandonment, or whatever you like to call this state. There are different grades of mastery, and only when you have made the last grade will you be sure of not missing the goal."

"That is just what I cannot get into my head," I answered. "I think I understand what you mean by the real, inner goal which ought to be hit. But how it happens that the outer goal, the disk of paper, is hit without the archer's taking aim, and that the hits are only outward confirmations of inner events—that correspondence is beyond me."

"You are under an illusion," said the Master after awhile, "if you imagine that even a rough understanding of these dark connections would help you. These are processes which are beyond the reach of understanding. Do not forget that even in Nature there are correspondences which cannot be understood, and yet are so real that we have grown accustomed to them, just as if they could not be any different. I will give you an example which I have often puzzled over. The spider dances her web without knowing that there are flies who will get caught in it. The fly, dancing nonchalantly on a sunbeam, gets caught in the net without knowing what lies in store. But through both of them 'It' dances, and inside and outside are united in this dance. So, too, the archer hits the target without having aimed—more I cannot say."

Much as this comparison occupied my thoughts—though

I could not of course think it to a satisfactory conclusion—something in me refused to be mollified and would not let me go on practicing unworried. An objection, which in the course of weeks had taken on more definite outline, formulated itself in my mind. I therefore asked: "Is it not at least conceivable that after all your years of practice you involuntarily raise the bow and arrow with the certainty of a sleepwalker, so that, although you do not consciously take aim when drawing it, you must hit the target—simply cannot fail to hit it?"

The Master, long accustomed to my tiresome questions, shook his head. "I do not deny," he said after a short silence, "that there may be something in what you say. I do stand facing the goal in such a way that I am bound to see it, even if I do not intentionally turn my gaze in that direction. On the other hand I know that this seeing is not enough, decides nothing, explains nothing, for I see the goal as though I did not see it."

"Then you ought to be able to hit it blindfolded," I jerked out.

The Master turned on me a glance which made me fear that I had insulted him and then said: "Come to see me this evening."

I seated myself opposite him on a cushion. He handed me tea, but did not speak a word. So we sat for a long while. There was no sound but the singing of the kettle on the hot coals. At last the Master rose and made me a sign to follow him. The practice hall was brightly lit. The Master told me to put a taper, long and thin as a knitting needle, in the sand in front of the target, but not to switch on the light in the target-stand. It was so dark that I could not even see its outlines, and if the tiny flame of the taper had not been there, I might perhaps have guessed the position of the target, though I could not have made it out with any precision. The Master "danced" the ceremony. His first arrow shot out of dazzling brightness into deep night. I knew from the sound that it had hit the target. The second arrow was a hit, too. When I switched on the light in the target-stand, I discovered to my amazement that the first arrow was lodged full in the middle of the black, while the second arrow had splintered the butt of the first and plowed through the shaft before embedding itself beside it. I did not dare to pull the arrows out separately, but carried them back together with the target. The Master surveyed them critically. "The first shot," he then said, "was no great feat, you will think, because after all these years I am so familiar with my target-stand that I must know even in pitch darkness where the target is. That may be, and I won't try to pretend otherwise. But the second arrow which hit the first—what do you make of that? I at any rate know that it is not 'I' who must be given credit for this shot. 'It' shot and 'It' made the hit. Let us bow to the goal as before the Buddha!"

The Master had evidently hit me, too, with both arrows: as though transformed over night, I no longer succumbed to the temptation of worrying about my arrows and what happened to them. The Master strengthened me in this attitude still further by never looking at the target, but simply keeping his eye on the archer, as though that gave him the most suitable indication of how the shot had fallen out. On being questioned, he freely admitted that this was so, and I was able to prove for myself again and again that his sureness of judgment in this matter was no whit inferior to the sureness of his arrows. Thus, through deepest concentration, he transferred the spirit of his art to his pupils, and I am not afraid to confirm from my own experience, which I doubted long enough, that the talk of immediate communication is not just a figure of speech but a tangible reality. There was another form of help which the Master communicated to us at that time, and which he likewise spoke of as immediate transference of the spirit. If I had been continually shooting badly, the Master gave a few shots with my bow. The improvement was startling: it was as if the bow let itself be drawn differently, more willingly, more understandingly. This did not happen only with me. Even his oldest and most experienced pupils, men from all walks of life, took this as an established fact and were astonished that I should ask questions like one who wished to make quite sure. Similarly, no master of swordsmanship can be moved from his conviction that each of the swords fashioned with so much hard work and infinite care takes on the spirit of the swordsmith, who therefore sets about his work in ritual costume.

Their experiences are far too striking, and they themselves far too skilled, for them not to perceive how a sword reacts in their hands.

One day the Master cried out the moment my shot was loosed: "It is there! Bow down to the goal!" Later, when I glanced towards the target—unfortunately I couldn't help myself—I saw that the arrow had only grazed the edge. "That was a right shot," said the Master decisively, "and so it must begin. But enough for today, otherwise you will take special pains with the next shot and spoil the good beginning." Occasionally several of these right shots came off in close succession and hit the target, besides of course the many more that failed. But if ever the least flicker of satisfaction showed in my face the Master turned on me with unwonted fierceness. "What are you thinking of?" he would cry. "You know already that you should not grieve over bad shots; learn now not to rejoice over the good ones. You must free yourself from the buffetings of pleasure and pain, and learn to rise above them in easy equanimity, to rejoice as though not you but another had shot well. This, too, you must practice unceasingly—you cannot conceive how important it is."

During these weeks and months I passed through the hardest schooling of my life, and though the discipline was not always easy for me to accept, I gradually came to see how much I was indebted to it. It destroyed the last traces of any preoccupation with myself and the fluctuations of my mood.

"Do you now understand," the Master asked me one day after a particularly good shot, "what I mean by '*It* shoots,' '*It* hits'?"

"I'm afraid I don't understand anything more at all," I answered, "even the simplest things have got in a muddle. Is it 'I' who draw the bow, or is it the bow that draws me into the state of highest tension? Do 'I' hit the goal, or does the goal hit me? Is 'It' spiritual when seen by the eyes of the body, and corporeal when seen by the eyes of the spirit—or both or neither? Bow, arrow, goal and ego, all melt into one another, so that I can no longer separate them. And even the need to separate has gone. For as soon as I take the bow and shoot, everything becomes so clear and straightforward and so ridiculously simple . . . ."

"Now at last," the Master broke in, "the bow-string has cut right through you."

from

TRAVELING MERCIES: SOME THOUGHTS ON FAITH

ANNE LAMOTT

Enlightenment is, after all, the business of ascetics. For those of us, like Anne Lamott, who live in the day-to-day world, coming awake is a harder business, but it is no less sweet and transforming when it happens.

From the hills of Tiburon, Belvedere Island looks like a great green turtle with all of its parts pulled in. It's covered with eucalyptus, cedars, rhododendrons, manicured lawns.

I had come back to live in Tiburon. It was 1982, I was twenty-eight, and I had just broken up with a man in a neighboring county. He was the love of my life, and I of his, but things were a mess. We were taking a lot of cocaine and psychedelic mushrooms, and drinking way too much. When I moved out, he moved back in with his wife and son. My dad had been dead for three years. My mother still practiced law in Hawaii, my oldest brother John had moved even farther away, and my younger brother had, in the most incongruous act of our family's history, joined the army.

When my boyfriend and I split up, I had called a divorced friend named Pat who'd lived in Tiburon for twenty years; I had baby-sat for her kids when I was young. She had loved me since I was eleven. I said I needed a place to regroup for a couple of weeks. Then I stayed for a year and a half. (Let this be a lesson.)

She worked in the city all day so I had the house to myself. I woke up quite late every morning, always hungover, the shades drawn, the air reeking of cigarettes and booze. The whole time I stayed at her house, I kept drinking from her one bottle of Dewars. Most nights I'd sip wine or beer while she and I hung out, eating diet dinners together. Then after she'd gone to bed nice and early every night, I'd pour myself the first of sixteen ounces of Scotch. I'd put music on the stereo—Bruce Springsteen, Tom Petty—and dance. Sometimes I would dance around with a drink in my hand. Other times, I would toss down my drink and then sit on the couch in reveries—of romance, of seeing my dad again, of being on TV talk shows, chatting with Johnny Carson, ducking my head down while the audience laughed at my wit, then reaching demurely for my glass of Scotch. My self-esteem soared, and when the talk show ended in my mind, I would dance.

I took a sleeping pill with the last glass of Scotch every night, woke up late, wrote for a couple of hours, and then walked to one of four local liquor stores to buy a pint of Dewars. Back at Pat's, I would pour the whiskey back into the big bottle, raising the level back to where it had been before I started the night before. Then I'd put the empty in a brown paper bag and take off for the bike path to dispose of it.

There were many benches along the way with beautiful views of Richardson Bay. Some of them had trash cans next to them, but others did not, and I'd be frantic to get rid of my empty bottles. Certainly someone might interpret them as a sign that I had developed some sort of drinking problem. But sometimes I'd be forced to leave the bag on a bench where there was no trash can, and I lived in terror of someone running up to me holding out the paper bag, calling, "Oh, Misssss, you forgot something." Then they'd drop it, and it would shatter inside the brown bag, and the jig would be up.

I was scared much of the time. There were wonderful aspects to my life—I was writing, I loved my friends, I lived amidst all this beauty. I got to walk with Pammy several times a week, along the bike path or over in Mill Valley where she was living happily ever after with her husband. Every night I'd swear I wouldn't hit Pat's Scotch again, maybe instead just have a glass of wine or two. But then she'd go to bed, and without exactly meaning to, I'd find myself in the kitchen, quietly pouring a drink.

Life was utterly schizophrenic. I was loved and often seemed cheerful, but fear pulsed inside me. I was broke, clearly a drunk, and also bulimic. One night I went to bed so drunk and stuffed with food that I blacked out. When I awoke, feeling quite light, I got on the scale. Then I called Pat at work with my great news: "I lost five pounds last night!"

"And I found it,' she said. It seemed she had cleaned up after me.

I made seven thousand dollars that year and could not afford therapy or enough cocaine. Then my married man called again, and we took to meeting in X-rated motels with lots of coke, tasteful erotic romps on TV like *The Bitch of the Gestapo*. But it was hard for him to get away. I'd pine away at Pat's, waiting for her to go to sleep so I could dance.

I was cracking up. It was like a cartoon where something gets hit, and one crack appears, which spiderwebs outward until the whole pane or vase is cracked and hangs suspended for a moment before falling into a pile of powder on the floor. I had not yet heard the Leonard Cohen song in which he sings, "There are cracks, cracks, in everything, that's how the light gets in." I had the cracks but not the hope.

In pictures of Pammy and me taken then, she weighs a lot more than I. I'm skinny, insubstantial, as if I want to disappear altogether and my body is already starting to, piece by piece like the Cheshire cat. Pammy looks expansive and buttery and smiling. I look furtive, like a deer surprised in a heinous act.

I'm always squinting in these pictures, too, baffled, suspicious—get this over with, my eyes say. Pammy's hair is no longer wild blonde hippie-girl hair. Now it falls in soft waves to her shoulders. My hair is in a long fuzzy Afro, a thicket behind which I'm trying to hide. Pammy gives off natural charm, like someone who is dangling a line with something lovely attached, saying, Come play with us—we're worth it! While I'm saying, Go away! Stop bothering me!

I kept the extent of my drinking a secret from her. And in a show of control, played to an often empty house, I'd try to wait until five for the first beer. But this other person inside me would start crying, Help me. So I'd get us a little something to tide us over.

It was so frustrating to be in love with an unavailable

married man that of course I found a second one. He was a dentist, who met me in fancy hotels, with lots of cocaine and always some Percodan to take the edge off. He was also doing nitrous oxide after hours, but he wouldn't share. I tried everything to get him to bring me a little soupçon of nitrous, but never got it. When he reported one night that his wife had torn at one of her eyes in despair over our affair and that he'd taken her to Emergency four days before, I thought, *God*, is your wife a mess.

But a feather of truth floated inside the door of my mind that night—the truth that I was crossing over to the dark side. I still prayed but was no longer sure anyone heard. I called a suicide hot line two days later, but hung up when someone answered. Heaven forbid someone should think I needed help. I was a Lamott—Lamotts *give* help.

I kept walking into town on the bike path to dispose of my bottle and buy another; the path was where the railroad tracks used to be. I'd turn right on Beach Road and walk along the west shore of Belvedere Island, passing below the big concrete Episcopal church on the hill. I'd actually spent some time at St. Stephen's as a child. My mother and I would go there for Midnight Mass on Christmas Eve every year, and I went with assorted friends every so often. It looked like a PG&E substation. I'd heard from family friends that there was a new guy preaching, named Bill Rankin, an old civil rights priest who had gotten this stolid congregation mobilized behind issues of peace and justice. I wasn't remotely ready for Christianity, though—I mean, I wasn't *that* far gone.

Still, I had never stopped believing in God since that day in Eva Gossman's class. Mine was a patchwork God, sewn together from bits of rag and ribbon, Eastern and Western, pagan and Hebrew, everything but the kitchen sink and Jesus.

Then one afternoon in my dark bedroom, the cracks webbed all the way through me. I believed that I would die soon, from a fall or an overdose. I knew there was an afterlife but felt that the odds of my living long enough to get into heaven were almost nil. They couldn't possibly take you in the shape I was in. I could no longer imagine how God could love me.

But in my dark bedroom at Pat's that afternoon, out of nowhere it crossed my mind to call the new guy at St. Stephen's.

So I did. He was there, and I started to explain that I was losing my mind, but he interrupted to say with real anguish that he was sorry but he had to leave. He literally begged me to call back in the morning, but I couldn't form any words in reply. It was like in the movies when the gangster is blowing bubbles through the bullet hole in his neck. There was this profound silence, except for my bubbling. Then he said, "Listen. Never mind. I'll wait. Come on in."

It took me forty-five minutes to walk there, but this skinny middle-aged guy was still in his office when I arrived. My first impression was that he was smart and profoundly tenderhearted. My next was that he was really listening, that he could hear what I was saying, and so I let it all tumble out—the X-rated motels, my father's death, a hint that maybe every so often I drank too much.

I don't remember much of his response, except that when I said I didn't think God could love me, he said, "God *has* to love you. That's God's job." Some years later I asked him to tell me about this first meeting. "I felt," he said, "that you had gotten yourself so tangled up in big God questions that it was suffocating you. Here you were in a rather desperate situation, suicidal, clearly alcoholic, going down the tubes. I thought the trick was to help you extricate yourself enough so you could breathe again. You said your prayers weren't working anymore, and I could see that in your desperation you were trying to save *yourself*: so I said you should stop praying for a while, and let me pray for you. And right away, you seemed to settle down inside."

"What did you hear in my voice when I called?"

"I just heard that you were in trouble."

He was about the first Christian I ever met whom I could stand to be in the same room with. Most Christians seemed almost hostile in their belief that they were saved and you weren't. Bill said it bothered him too, but you had to listen to what was underneath their words. What did it mean to be saved, I asked, although I knew the word smacked of Elmer Gantry for both of us.

"You don't need to think about this," he said.

"Just tell me."

"I guess it's like discovering you're on the shelf of a pawnshop, dusty and forgotten and maybe not worth very much. But Jesus comes in and tells the pawnbroker, 'I'll take her place on the shelf. Let her go outside again.' "

When I met him for a second time in his office, he handed me a quote of Dag Hammarskjöld's: "I don't know Who or What put the question, I don't know when it was put. I don't even remember answering. But at some moment, I did answer Yes." I wanted to fall to my knees, newly born, but I didn't. I walked back home to Pat's and got out the Scotch. I was feeling better in general, less out of control, even though it would be four more years before I got sober. I was not willing to give up a life of shame and failure without a fight. Still, a few weeks later, when Bill and I met for our first walk, I had some progress to report: I had stopped meeting the love of my life at X-rated motels. I still met him at *motels*, but nicer ones. I had stopped seeing the man with the bleeding wife. I felt I had standards again—granted, they were very *low* standards, but still . . .

Slowly I came back to life. I'd been like one of the people Ezekiel comes upon in the valley of dry bones—people who had really given up, who were lifeless and without hope. But because of Ezekiel's presence, breath comes upon them; spirit and kindness revive them. And by the time I was well enough for Bill even to *consider* tapering off our meetings, I had weaseled my way into his heart. I drank, he led a church, and together we went walking every week all over Belvedere Island, all over the back of that great green turtle.

In the dust of Marin City, a wartime settlement outside Sausalito where black shipyard workers lived during World War II, a flea market was held every weekend for years. In 1984 I was living in a mother-in-law unit on a houseboat berthed at the north end of Sausalito, on San Francisco Bay. I was almost thirty when I moved in, and I lived for the next four years in a space about ten feet square, with a sleeping loft. I had a view of the bay and of Angel Island. When it was foggy, San Francisco across the water looked like a city inside a snow globe.

I got pregnant in April, right around my thirtieth birthday, but was so loaded every night that the next morning's first urine was too diluted for a pregnancy test to prove positive. Every other day, Pammy, who still lived in Mill Valley with her husband, would come by and take a small bottle of pee to the lab that was near her home. I did not have a car. I had had a very stern conversation with myself a year before, in which I said that I had to either stop drinking or get rid of the car. This was a real no-brainer. I got around on foot, and by bus and friend.

The houseboat, on a concrete barge, barely moved even during the storms of winter. I was often sick in the mornings. On weekdays, I put coffee on, went for a run, took a shower, had coffee, maybe some speed, a thousand cigarettes, and then tried to write. On weekends, I went to the flea market.

Marin City is the ghetto in this luscious affluent county, built in a dusty bowl surrounded by low green hills on the other side of the freeway from where my houseboat was. The town is filled with families—lots of little kids and powerful mothers. There are too many drugs and guns, there is the looming and crummy government housing called the Projects, and there are six churches in a town of two thousand people who are mostly black. On the weekends, the gigantic lot where the Greyhound bus depot used to be was transformed into one of the country's biggest flea markets. Many years before, I used to sit on my mother's lap on the exact same site and watch black men drink coffee at the counter while we waited for a bus into San Francisco. Now every square foot was taken up with booths and trucks and beach umbrellas and tables and blankets and racks displaying household wares and tools and crafts and clothes, much of it stolen, most of it going for a song—hundreds of sellers, thousands of buyers, children and dogs and all of us stirring up the dust.

You could buy the most wonderful ethnic food here, food from faraway places: Asia, India, Mexico, New York City. This is where I liked to be when I was hungover or coming down off a cocaine binge, here in the dust with all these dusty people, all this liveliness and clutter and color, things for sale to cheer me up, and greasy food that would slip down my throat.

If I happened to be there between eleven and one on Sundays, I could hear gospel music coming from a church right across the street. It was called St. Andrew Presbyterian, and it looked homely and impoverished, a ramshackle building with a cross on top, sitting on a small parcel of land with a few skinny pine trees. But the music wafting out was so pretty that I would stop and listen. I knew a lot of the hymns from the times I'd gone to church with my grandparents and from the albums we'd had of spirituals. Finally, I began stopping in at St. Andrew from time to time, standing in the doorway to listen to the songs. I couldn't believe how run-down it was, with terrible linoleum that was brown and overshined, and plastic stained-glass windows. But it had a choir of five black women and one rather Amish-looking white man making all that glorious noise, and a congregation of thirty people or so, radiating kindness and warmth. During the time when people hugged and greeted each other, various people would come back to where I stood to shake my hand or try to hug me; I was as frozen and stiff as Richard Nixon. After this, Scripture was read, and then the minister named James Noel who was as tall and handsome as Marvin Gaye would preach, and it would be all about social injustice—and Jesus, which would be enough to send me running back to the sanctuary of the flea market.

You'd always have to shower after you got home, you'd be so covered with dust, the soles of your shoes sticky with syrup from snow cones, or gum, or one of those small paper canoes that hot dogs are served in.

I went back to St. Andrew about once a month. No one tried to con me into sitting down or staying. I always left before the sermon. I loved singing, even about Jesus, but I just didn't want to be preached at about him. To me, Jesus made about as much sense as Scientology or dowsing. But the church smelled wonderful, like the air had nourishment in it, or like it was composed of these people's exhalations, of warmth and faith and peace. There were always children running around or being embraced, and a gorgeous stick-thin deaf black girl signing to her mother, hearing the songs and the Scripture through her mother's flashing fingers. The radical old women of the congregation were famous in these parts for having convinced the very conservative national Presbytery to donate ten thousand dollars to the Angela Davis Defense Fund during her trial up at the Civic Center. And every other week they brought huge tubs of great food for the homeless families living at the shelter near the canal to the north. I loved this. But it was the singing that pulled me in and split me wide open.

I could sing better here than I ever had before. As part of these people, even though I stayed in the doorway, I did not recognize my voice or know where it was coming from, but sometimes I felt like I could sing forever.

Eventually, a few months after I started coming, I took a seat in one of the folding chairs, off by myself. Then the singing enveloped me. It was furry and resonant, coming from everyone's very heart. There was no sense of performance or judgment, only that the music was breath and food.

Something inside me that was stiff and rotting would feel soft and tender. Somehow the singing wore down all the boundaries and distinctions that kept me so isolated. Sitting there, standing with them to sing, sometimes so shaky and sick that I felt like I might tip over, I felt bigger than myself, like I was being taken care of, tricked into coming back to life. But I had to leave before the sermon.

That April of 1984, in the midst of this experience, Pammy took a fourth urine sample to the lab, and it finally came back positive. I had published three books by then, but none of them had sold particularly well, and I did not have the money or wherewithal to have a baby. The father was someone I had just met, who was married, and no one I wanted a real life or baby with. So Pammy one evening took me in for the abortion, and I was sadder than I'd been since my father died, and when she brought me home that night, I went upstairs to my loft with a pint of Bushmills and some of the codeine a nurse had given me for pain. I drank until nearly dawn.

Then the next night I did it again, and the next night, although by then the pills were gone.

I didn't go to the flea market the week of my abortion. I stayed home, and smoked dope and got drunk, and tried to write a little, and went for slow walks along the salt marsh with Pammy. On the seventh night, though, very drunk and just about to take a sleeping pill, I discovered that I was bleeding heavily. It did not stop over the next hour. I was going through a pad every fifteen minutes, and I thought I should call a doctor or Pammy, but I was so disgusted that I had gotten so drunk one week after an abortion that I just couldn't wake someone up and ask for help. I kept on changing Kotex, and I got very sober very quickly. Several hours later, the blood stopped flowing, and I got in bed, shaky and sad and too wild to have another drink or take a sleeping pill. I had a cigarette and turned off the light. After a while, as I lay there, I became aware of someone with me, hunkered down in the corner, and I just assumed it was my father, whose presence I had felt over the years when I was frightened and alone. The feeling was so strong that I actually turned on the light for a moment to make sure no one was there—of course, there wasn't. But after a while, in the dark again, I knew beyond any doubt that it was Jesus. I felt him as surely as I feel my dog lying nearby as I write this.

And I was appalled. I thought about my life and my brilliant hilarious progressive friends, I thought about what everyone would think of me if I became a Christian, and it seemed an utterly impossible thing that simply could not be allowed to happen. I turned to the wall and said out loud, "I would rather die."

I felt him just sitting there on his haunches in the corner of my sleeping loft, watching me with patience and love, and I squinched my eyes shut, but that didn't help because that's not what I was seeing him with.

Finally I fell asleep, and in the morning, he was gone.

This experience spooked me badly, but I thought it was just an apparition, born of fear and self-loathing and booze and loss of blood. But then everywhere I went, I had the feeling that a little cat was following me, wanting me to reach down and pick it up, wanting me to open the door and let it in. But I knew what would happen: you let a cat in one time, give it a little milk, and then it stays forever. So I tried to keep one step ahead of it, slamming my houseboat door when I entered or left.

And one week later, when I went back to church, I was so hungover that I couldn't stand up for the songs, and this time I stayed for the sermon, which I just thought was so ridiculous, like someone trying to convince me of the existence of extraterrestrials, but the last song was so deep and raw and pure that I could not escape. It was as if the people were singing in between the notes, weeping and joyful at the same time, and I felt like their voices or *something* was rocking me in its bosom, holding me like a scared kid, and I opened up to that feeling—and it washed over me.

I began to cry and left before the benediction, and I raced home and felt the little cat running along at my heels, and I walked down the dock past dozens of potted flowers, under a sky as blue as one of God's own dreams, and I opened the door to my houseboat, and I stood there a minute, and then I hung my head and said, "Fuck it: I quit." I took a long deep breath and said out loud, "All right. You can come in."

So this was my beautiful moment of conversion.

And here in dust and dirt, O here,
The lilies of his love appear.

I started to find these lines of George Herbert's everywhere I turned—in Simone Weil, Malcolm Muggeridge, books of English poetry. Meanwhile, I trooped back and forth through the dust and grime of the flea market every Sunday morning till eleven, when I crossed the street from the market to the church.

I was sitting through the sermon now every week and finding that I could not only bear the Jesus talk but was interested, searching for clues. I was more and more comfortable with the radical message of peace and equality, with the God in whom Dr. King believed. I had no big theological thoughts but had discovered that if I said, Hello?, to God, I could *feel* God say, Hello, back. It was like being in a relationship with Casper.

Sometimes I wadded up a Kleenex and held it tightly in one fist so that it felt like I was walking hand and hand with him.

Finally, one morning in July of 1986, I woke up so sick and in such despair for the umpteenth day in a row that I knew that I was either going to die or have to quit drinking. I poured a bottle of pinot noir down the sink, and dumped a Nike box full of assorted pills off the side of my houseboat, and entered into recovery with fear and trembling. I was not sure that I could or even wanted to go one day without drinking or pills or cocaine. But it turned out that I could and that a whole lot of people were going to help me, with kind eyes and hot cups of bad coffee.

If I were to give a slide show of the next ten years, it would begin on the day I was baptized, one year after I got sober. I called Reverend Noel at eight that morning and told him that I really didn't think I was ready because I wasn't good enough yet. Also, I was insane. My heart was good, but my insides had gone bad. And he said, "You're putting the cart before the horse. So—honey? Come on *down*." My family and all my closest friends came to church that day to watch as James dipped his hand into the font, bathed my forehead with cool water, and spoke the words of Langston Hughes:

Gather out of star-dust
Earth-dust,
Cloud-dust,
Storm-dust,
And splinters of hail,

One handful of dream-dust
Not for sale.

In the next slide, two years later, I'm pregnant by a man I was dating, who really didn't want to be a father at the time. I was still poor, but friends and the people at my church convinced me that if I decided to have a child, we would be provided for every step of the way. Pammy really wanted the kid. She had been both trying to conceive and waiting to adopt for years. She said, "Let me put it this way, Annie. We're going to have this baby."

In the next slide, in August of 1989, my son is born. I named him Sam. He had huge eyes and his father's straight hair. Three months later he was baptized at St. Andrew.

Then, six months later, there would be a slide of me nursing Sam, holding the phone to my ear with a look of shock on my face, because Pammy had just been diagnosed with metastatic breast cancer. She had a lumpectomy and then aggressive chemotherapy. All that platinum hair fell out, and she took to wearing beautiful scarves and soft cotton caps. I would show you a slide of her dancing in a ballet group for breast cancer survivors. I would show you a slide of her wading in the creek at Samuel P. Taylor Park, her jeans rolled up and Sam, on her shoulders, holding on to the ends of her scarf like reins. There was joy and there were many setbacks, and she played it way down: two days after she'd finally begun to complain mildly about a cough that wouldn't go away, a doctor aspirated a *liter* of fluid from her lungs. More chemo, and the hair that had grown back fell out again. "Come shave it all off for me," she asked over the phone. "As it is, it looks like hair I found in the trash can and tried to glue back on." I gently brushed almost all of it off. She loved visits with Sam, grieved that she wouldn't get to watch him grow older. The cancer went into remission. A few months later, a slide would show her in a soft pink cotton cap with a look of supreme joy on her face, because her adoption lawyer had finally called and asked if she and her husband wanted to adopt. They did. They were given a baby girl named Rebecca, my darling goddaughter.

But the cancer came back. Not long before she died, my favorite slide would show her lying on a chaise in her lush and overgrown garden, beaming. Out of a storage room that we used for changing Rebecca, we had just fashioned a guest room for her sister, who was coming in from Italy to take care of her. She'd been up and around all morning, trying out the guest bed here and then there, putting it near the window, wanting the sun to fall on her sister just so. We found a place for all the extra junk, and a little rug for the floor, a tiny chest of drawers, and pictures for the wall. So then she went outside to rest, dressed, happy, looking once more like a citizen of the world. It was sunny and blue, a perfect day, and she had the radiance of someone who has been upright and really moving for one last time, so happy and light that even without hair, wearing a scarf, she seemed like a blonde again.

She was thirty-seven when she died. We scattered her ashes one sunny day from a boat out near the Farallon Islands—white-gold sunlight, mild breezes, baskets and bags of roses.

Then there would be some fabulous slides of Rebecca growing up. In many of these photos, she is dressed in bright saris and veils, as she and her dad go to India quite a lot to visit an ashram there. She has long brown hair, like a filly.

Meanwhile, Sam grew tall and thin and sweet, with huge brown eyes.

Then there would be thousands of slides of Sam and me at St. Andrew. I think we have missed church ten times in twelve years. Sam would be snuggled in people's arms in the earlier shots, shyly trying to wriggle free of hugs in the later ones. There would be different pastors along the way, none of them exactly right for us until a few years ago when a tall African-American woman named Veronica came to lead us. She has huge gentle doctor hands, with dimples where the knuckles should be, like a baby's fists. She stepped into us, the wonderful old worn pair of pants that is St. Andrew, and they fit. She sings to us sometimes from the pulpit and tells us stories of when she was a child. She told us this story just the other day: When she was about seven, her best friend got lost one day. The little girl ran up and down the streets of the big town where they lived, but she couldn't find a single landmark. She was very frightened. Finally a policeman stopped to help her. He put her in the passenger seat of his car, and they drove around until she finally saw her church. She pointed it out to the policeman, and then she told him firmly, "You could let me out now. This is my church, and I can always find my way home from here."

And that is why I have stayed so close to mine—because no matter how bad I am feeling, how lost or lonely or frightened, when I see the faces of the people at my church, and hear their tawny voices, I can always find my way home.

from

A PORTRAIT OF THE ARTIST AS A YOUNG MAN

JAMES JOYCE

For some, the strict paths of organized religion do not take them toward the light, but away from it. Stephen Dedalus believes he has a calling to the Church, but it is the glory of Art that truly allows his soul to fly.

The Reverend Stephen Dedalus, S.J.

His name in that new life leaped into characters before his eyes and to it there followed a mental sensation of an undefined face or colour of a face. The colour faded and became strong like a changing glow of pallid brick red. Was it the raw reddish glow he had so often seen on wintry mornings on the shaven gills of the priests? The face was eyeless and sour-favoured and devout, shot with pink tinges of suffocated anger. Was it not a mental spectre of the face of one of the jesuits whom some of the boys called Lantern Jaws and others Foxy Campbell?

He was passing at that moment before the jesuit house in Gardiner Street, and wondered vaguely which window would be his if he ever joined the order. Then he wondered at the vagueness of his wonder, at the remoteness of his soul from what he had hitherto imagined her sanctuary, at the frail hold which so many years of order and obedience had of him when once a definite and irrevocable act of his threatened to end for ever, in time and in eternity, his freedom. The voice of the director urging upon him the proud claims of the church and the mystery and power of the priestly office repeated itself idly in his memory. His soul was not there to hear and greet it and he knew now that the exhortation he had listened to had already fallen into an idle formal tale. He would never swing the thurible before the tabernacle as priest. His destiny was to be elusive of social or religious orders. The wisdom of the priest's appeal did not touch him to the quick. He was destined to learn his own wisdom apart from others or to learn the wisdom of others himself wandering among the snares of the world.

The snares of the world were its ways of sin. He would fall. He had not yet fallen but he would fall silently, in an instant. Not to fall was too hard, too hard: and he felt the silent lapse of his soul, as it would be at some instant to come, falling, falling but not yet fallen, still unfallen but about to fall.

He crossed the bridge over the stream of the Tolka and turned his eyes coldly for an instant towards the faded blue shrine of the Blessed Virgin which stood fowlwise on a pole in the middle of a hamshaped encampment of poor cottages. Then, bending to the left, he followed the lane which led up to his house. The faint sour stink of rotted cabbages came towards him from the kitchengardens on the rising ground above the river. He smiled to think that it was this disorder, the misrule and confusion of his father's house and the stagnation of vegetable life, which was to win the day in his soul. Then a short laugh broke from his lips as he thought of that solitary farmhand in the kitchengardens behind their house whom they had nicknamed the man with the hat. A second laugh, taking rise from the first after a pause, broke from him involuntarily as he thought of how the man with the hat worked, considering in turn the four points of the sky and then regretfully plunging his spade in the earth.

He pushed open the latchless door of the porch and passed through the naked hallway into the kitchen. A group of his brothers and sisters was sitting round the table. Tea was nearly over and only the last of the second watered tea remained in the bottoms of the small glassjars and jampots which did service for teacups. Discarded crusts and lumps of sugared bread, turned brown by the tea which had been poured over them, lay scattered on the table. Little wells of tea lay here and there on the board and a knife with a broken ivory handle was stuck through the pith of a ravaged turnover.

The sad quiet greyblue glow of the dying day came through the window and the open door, covering over and allaying quietly a sudden instinct of remorse in Stephen's heart. All that had been denied them had been freely given to him, the eldest: but the quiet glow of evening showed him in their faces no sign of rancour.

He sat near them at the table and asked where his father and mother were. One answered:

—Goneboro toboro lookboro atboro aboro houseboro.

Still another removal! A boy named Fallon in Belvedere had often asked him with a silly laugh why they moved so often. A frown of scorn darkened quickly his forehead as he heard again the silly laugh of the questioner.

He asked:

—Why are we on the move again, if it's a fair question?

The same sister answered:

—Becauseboro theboro landboro lordboro willboro putboro usboro outboro.

The voice of his youngest brother from the farther side of the fireplace began to sing the air *Oft in the Stilly Night*. One by one the others took up the air until a full choir of voices was singing. They would sing so for hours, melody after melody, glee after glee, till the last pale light died down on the horizon, till the first dark nightclouds came forth and night fell.

He waited for some moments, listening, before he too took up the air with them. He was listening with pain of spirit to the overtone of weariness behind their frail fresh innocent voices. Even before they set out on life's journey they seemed weary already of the way.

He heard the choir of voices in the kitchen echoed and multiplied through an endless reverberation of the choirs of endless generations of children: and heard in all the echoes an echo also of the recurring note of weariness and pain. All seemed weary of life even before entering upon it. And he remembered that Newman had heard this note also in the broken lines of Virgil *giving utterance, like the voice of Nature herself, to that pain and weariness yet hope of better things which has been the experience of her children in every time.*

• • •

He could wait no longer.

From the door of Byron's publichouse to the gate of Clontarf Chapel, from the gate of Clontarf Chapel to the door of Byron's publichouse and then back again to the chapel and then back again to the publichouse he had paced slowly at first, planting his steps scrupulously in the spaces of the patchwork of the footpath, then timing their fall to the fall of verses. A full hour had passed since his father had gone in with Dan Crosby, the tutor, to find out for him something about the university. For a full hour he had paced up and down, waiting: but he could wait no longer.

He set off abruptly for the Bull, walking rapidly lest his father's shrill whistle might call him back; and in a few moments he had rounded the curve at the police barrack and was safe.

Yes, his mother was hostile to the idea, as he had read from her listless silence. Yet her mistrust pricked him more keenly than his father's pride and he thought coldly how he had watched the faith which was fading down in his soul aging and strengthening in her eyes. A dim antagonism gathered force within him and darkened his mind as a cloud against her disloyalty: and when it passed, cloudlike, leaving his mind serene and dutiful towards her again, he was made aware dimly and without regret of a first noiseless sundering of their lives.

The university! So he had passed beyond the challenge

of the sentries who had stood as guardians of his boyhood and had sought to keep him among them that he might be subject to them and serve their ends. Pride after satisfaction uplifted him like long slow waves. The end he had been born to serve yet did not see had led him to escape by an unseen path: and now it beckoned to him once more and a new adventure was about to be opened to him. It seemed to him that he heard notes of fitful music leaping upwards a tone and downwards a diminished fourth, upwards a tone and downwards a major third, like triplebranching flames leaping fitfully, flame after flame, out of a midnight wood. It was an elfin prelude, endless and formless; and, as it grew wilder and faster, the flames leaping out of time, he seemed to hear from under the boughs and grasses wild creatures racing, their feet pattering like rain upon the leaves. Their feet passed in pattering tumult over his mind, the feet of hares and rabbits, the feet of harts and hinds and antelopes, until he heard them no more and remembered only a proud cadence from Newman: *Whose feet are as the feet of harts and underneath the everlasting arms.*

The pride of that dim image brought back to his mind the dignity of the office he had refused. All through his boyhood he had mused upon that which he had so often thought to be his destiny and when the moment had come for him to obey the call he had turned aside, obeying a wayward instinct. Now time lay between: the oils of ordination would never anoint his body. He had refused. Why?

He turned seaward from the road at Dollymount and as he passed on to the thin wooden bridge he felt the planks shaking with the tramp of heavily shod feet. A squad of christian brothers was on its way back from the Bull and had begun to pass, two by two, across the bridge. Soon the whole bridge was trembling and resounding. The uncouth faces passed him two by two, stained yellow or red or livid by the sea, and as he strove to look at them with ease and indifference, a faint stain of personal shame and commiseration rose to his own face. Angry with himself he tried to hide his face from their eyes by gazing down sideways into the shallow swirling water under the bridge but he still saw a reflection therein of their topheavy silk hats, and humble tapelike collars and loosely hanging clerical clothes.

—Brother Hickey.

Brother Quaid.

Brother MacArdle.

Brother Keogh.

Their piety would be like their names, like their faces, like their clothes, and it was idle for him to tell himself that their humble and contrite hearts, it might be, paid a far richer tribute of devotion than his had ever been, a gift tenfold more acceptable than his elaborate adoration. It was idle for him to move himself to be generous towards them, to tell himself that if he ever came to their gates, stripped of his pride, beaten and in beggar's weeds, that they would be generous towards him, loving him as themselves. Idle and embittering, finally, to argue, against his own dispassionate certitude, that the commandment of love bade us not to love our neighbour as ourselves with the same amount and intensity of love but to love him as ourselves with the same kind of love.

He drew forth a phrase from his treasure and spoke it softly to himself:

—A day of dappled seaborne clouds.

The phrase and the day and the scene harmonised in a chord. Words. Was it their colours? He allowed them to glow and fade, hue after hue: sunrise gold, the russet and green of apple orchards, azure of waves, the greyfringed fleece of clouds. No, it was not their colours: it was the poise and balance of the period itself. Did he then love the rhythmic rise and fall of words better than their associations of legend and colour? Or was it that, being as weak of sight as he was shy of mind, he drew less pleasure from the reflection of the glowing sensible world through the prism of a language manycoloured and richly storied than from the contemplation of an inner world of individual emotions mirrored perfectly in a lucid supple periodic prose?

He passed from the trembling bridge on to firm land again. At that instant, as it seemed to him, the air was chilled and looking askance towards the water he saw a flying squall darkening and crisping suddenly the tide. A faint click at his heart, a faint throb in his throat told him once more of how his flesh dreaded the cold infrahuman odour of the sea: yet he did not strike across the downs on his left but held straight on along the spine of rocks that pointed against the river's mouth.

A veiled sunlight lit up faintly the grey sheet of water where the river was embayed. In the distance along the course of the slowflowing Liffey slender masts flecked the sky and, more distant still, the dim fabric of the city lay prone in haze. Like a scene on some vague arras, old as man's weariness, the image of the seventh city of christendom was visible to him across the timeless air, no older nor more weary nor less patient of subjection than in the days of the thingmote.

Disheartened, he raised his eyes towards the slowdrifting clouds, dappled and seaborne. They were voyaging across the deserts of the sky, a host of nomads on the march, voyaging high over Ireland, westward bound. The Europe they had come from lay out there beyond the Irish Sea, Europe of strange tongues and valleyed and woodbegirt and citadelled and of entrenched and marshalled races. He heard a confused music within him as of memories and names which he was almost conscious of but could not capture even for an instant; then the music seemed to recede, to recede, to recede: and from each receding trail of nebulous music there fell always one longdrawn calling note, piercing like a star the dusk of silence. Again! Again! Again! A voice from beyond the world was calling.

—Hello, Stephanos!

—Here comes The Dedalus!

—Ao! . . . Eh, give it over, Dwyer, I'm telling you or I'll give you a stuff in the kisser for yourself . . . . Ao!

—Good man, Towser! Duck him!

—Come along, Dedalus! Bous Stephanoumenos! Bous Stephaneforos!

—Duck him! Guzzle him now, Towser!

—Help! Help! . . . Ao!

He recognised their speech collectively before he distinguished their faces. The mere sight of that medley of wet nakedness chilled him to the bone. Their bodies, corpsewhite or suffused with a pallid golden light or rawly tanned by the sun, gleamed with the wet of the sea. Their divingstone, poised on its rude supports and rocking under their plunges, and the roughhewn stones of the sloping breakwater over which they scrambled in their horseplay, gleamed with cold wet lustre. The towels with which they smacked their bodies were heavy with cold seawater: and drenched with cold brine was their matted hair.

He stood still in deference to their calls and parried their banter with easy words. How characterless they looked: Shuley without his deep unbuttoned collar, Ennis without his scarlet belt with the snaky clasp, and Connolly without his Norfolk coat with the flapless sidepockets! It was a pain to see them and a swordlike pain to see the signs of adolescence that made repellent their pitiable nakedness. Perhaps they had taken refuge in number and noise from the secret dread in their souls. But he, apart from them and in silence, remembered in what dread he stood of the mystery of his own body.

—Stephanos Dedalos! Bous Stephanoumenos! Bous Stephaneforos!

Their banter was not new to him and now it flattered his mild proud sovereignty. Now, as never before, his strange name seemed to him a prophecy. So timeless seemed the grey warm air, so fluid and impersonal his own mood, that all ages were as one to him. A moment before the ghost of the ancient kingdom of the Danes had looked forth through the vesture of the hazewrapped city. Now, at the name of the fabulous artificer, he seemed to hear the noise of dim waves and to see a winged form flying above the waves and slowly climbing the air. What did it mean? Was it a quaint device opening a page of some medieval book of prophecies and symbols, a hawklike man flying sunward above the sea, a prophecy of the end he had been born to serve and had been following through the mists of childhood and boyhood, a symbol of the artist forging anew in his workshop out of the sluggish matter of the earth a new soaring impalpable imperishable being?

His heart trembled; his breath came faster and a wild spirit passed over his limbs as though he were soaring sunward. His heart trembled in an ecstasy of fear and his soul was in flight. His soul was soaring in an air beyond the world and the body he knew was purified in a breath and delivered of incertitude and made radiant and commingled with the element of the spirit. An ecstasy of flight made radiant his eyes and wild his breath and tremulous and wild and radiant his windswept limbs.

—One! Two! . . . Look out!

—O, cripes, I'm drownded!

—One! Two! Three and away!

—Me next! Me next!

—One! . . . Uk!

—Stephaneforos!

His throat ached with a desire to cry aloud, the cry of a hawk or eagle on high, to cry piercingly of his deliverance to the winds. This was the call of life to his soul not the dull gross voice of the world of duties and despair, not the inhuman voice that had called him to the pale service of the altar. An instant of wild flight had delivered him and the cry of triumph which his lips withheld cleft his brain.

—Stephaneforos!

What were they now but cerements shaken from the body of death—the fear he had walked in night and day, the incertitude that had ringed him round, the shame that had abased him within and without—cerements, the linens of the grave?

His soul had arisen from the grave of boyhood, spurning her graveclothes. Yes! Yes! Yes! He would create proudly out of the freedom and power of his soul, as the great artificer whose name he bore, a living thing, new and soaring and beautiful, impalpable, imperishable.

He started up nervously from the stoneblock for he could no longer quench the flame in his blood. He felt his cheeks aflame and his throat throbbing with song. There was a lust of wandering in his feet that burned to set out for the ends of the earth. On! On! his heart seemed to cry. Evening would deepen above the sea, night fall upon the plains, dawn glimmer before the wanderer and show him strange fields and hills and faces. Where?

He looked northward towards Howth. The sea had fallen below the line of seawrack on the shallow side of the breakwater and already the tide was running out fast along the foreshore. Already one long oval bank of sand lay warm and dry amid the wavelets. Here and there warm isles of sand gleamed above the shallow tide, and about the isles and around the long bank and amid the shallow currents of the beach were lightclad gayclad figures, wading and delving.

In a few moments he was barefoot, his stockings folded in his pockets and his canvas shoes dangling by their knotted laces over his shoulders: and, picking a pointed salteaten stick out of the jetsam among the rocks, he clambered down the slope of the breakwater.

There was a long rivulet in the strand: and, as he waded slowly up its course, he wondered at the endless drift of seaweed. Emerald and black and russet and olive, it moved beneath the current, swaying and turning. The water of the rivulet was dark with endless drift and mirrored the high-drifting clouds. The clouds were drifting above him silently and silently the seatangle was drifting below him; and the grey warm air was still: and a new wild life was singing in his veins.

Where was his boyhood now? Where was the soul that had hung back from her destiny, to brood alone upon the shame of her wounds and in her house of squalor and subterfuge to queen it in faded cerements and in wreaths that withered at the touch? Or where was he?

He was alone. He was unheeded, happy and near to the wild heart of life. He was alone and young and wilful and wildhearted, alone amid a waste of wild air and brackish waters and the seaharvest of shells and tangle and veiled grey sunlight and gayclad lightclad figures, of children and girls and voices childish and girlish in the air.

A girl stood before him in midstream, alone and still, gazing out to sea. She seemed like one whom magic had changed into the likeness of a strange and beautiful seabird. Her long slender bare legs were delicate as a crane's and pure save where an emerald trail of seaweed had fashioned itself as a sign upon the flesh. Her thighs, fuller and softhued as ivory, were bared almost to the hips where the white fringes of her drawers were like featherings of soft white down. Her slateblue skirts were kilted boldly about her waist and dovetailed behind her. Her bosom was as a bird's soft and slight, slight and soft as the breast of some darkplumaged dove. But her long fair hair was girlish: and girlish, and touched with the wonder of mortal beauty, her face.

She was alone and still, gazing out to sea; and when she felt his presence and the worship of his eyes her eyes turned to him in quiet sufferance of his gaze, without shame or wantonness. Long, long she suffered his gaze and then quietly withdrew her eyes from his and bent them towards the stream, gently stirring the water with her foot hither and thither. The first faint noise of gently moving water broke the silence, low and faint and whispering, faint as the bells of sleep; hither and thither, hither and thither: and a faint flame trembled on her cheek.

—Heavenly God! cried Stephen's soul, in an outburst of profane joy.

He turned away from her suddenly and set off across the strand. His cheeks were aflame; his body was aglow; his limbs were trembling. On and on and on and on he strode, far out over the sands, singing wildly to the sea, crying to greet the advent of the life that had cried to him.

Her image had passed into his soul for ever and no word had broken the holy silence of his ecstasy. Her eyes had called him and his soul had leaped at the call. To live, to err, to fall, to triumph, to recreate life out of life! A wild angel had appeared to him, the angel of mortal youth and beauty, an envoy from the fair courts of life, to throw open before him in an instant of ecstasy the gates of all the ways of error and glory. On and on and on and on!

He halted suddenly and heard his heart in the silence. How far had he walked? What hour was it?

There was no human figure near him nor any sound borne to him over the air. But the tide was near the turn and already the day was on the wane. He turned landward and ran towards the shore and, running up the sloping beach, reckless of the sharp shingle, found a sandy nook amid a ring of tufted sandknolls and lay down there that the peace and silence of the evening might still the riot of his blood.

He felt above him the vast indifferent dome and the calm processes of the heavenly bodies; and the earth beneath him, the earth that had borne him, had taken him to her breast.

He closed his eyes in the languor of sleep. His eyelids trembled as if they felt the vast cyclic movement of the earth and her watchers, trembled as if they felt the strange light of some new world. His soul was swooning into some new world, fantastic, dim, uncertain as under sea, traversed by cloudy shapes and beings. A world, a glimmer, or a flower? Glimmering and trembling, trembling and unfolding, a breaking light, an opening flower, it spread in endless succession to itself, breaking in full crimson and unfolding and fading to palest rose, leaf by leaf and wave of light by wave of light, flooding all the heavens with its soft flushes, every flush deeper than the other.

Evening had fallen when he woke and the sand and arid grasses of his bed glowed no longer. He rose slowly and, recalling the rapture of his sleep, sighed at its joy.

He climbed to the crest of the sandhill and gazed about

him. Evening had fallen. A rim of the young moon cleft the pale waste of sky like the rim of a silver hoop embedded in grey sand; and the tide was flowing in fast to the land with a low whisper of her waves, islanding a few last figures in distant pools.

THE BEAST IN THE JUNGLE

HENRY JAMES

Awakening is not always a matter of pure bliss. As John Marcher learns in this story, it can also bring the painful realization of things undone.

What determined the speech that startled him in the course of their encounter scarcely matters, being probably but some words spoken by himself quite without intention—spoken as they lingered and slowly moved together after their renewal of acquaintance. He had been conveyed by friends, an hour or two before, to the house at which she was staying; the party of visitors at the other house, of whom he was one, and thanks to whom it was his theory, as always, that he was lost in the crowd, had been invited over to luncheon. There had been after luncheon much dispersal, all in the interest of the original motive, a view of Weatherend itself and the fine things, intrinsic features, pictures, heirlooms, treasures of all the arts, that made the place almost famous; and the great rooms were so numerous that guests could wander at their will, hang back from the principal group, and, in cases where they took such matters with the last seriousness, give themselves up to mysterious appreciations and measurements. There were persons to be observed, singly or in couples, bending toward objects in out-of-the-way corners with their hands on their knees and their heads nodding quite as with the emphasis of an excited sense of smell. When they were two they either mingled their sounds of ecstasy or melted into silences of even deeper import, so that there were aspects of the occasion that gave it for Marcher much the air of the "look round," previous to a sale highly advertised, that excites or quenches, as may be, the dream of acquisition. The dream of acquisition at Weatherend would have had to be wild indeed, and John Marcher found himself, among such suggestions, disconcerted almost equally by the presence of those who knew too much and by that of those who knew nothing. The great rooms caused so much poetry and history to press upon him that he needed to wander apart to feel in a proper relation with them, though his doing so was not, as happened, like the gloating of some of his companions, to be compared to the movements of a dog sniffing a cupboard. It had an issue promptly enough in a direction that was not to have been calculated.

It led, in short, in the course of the October afternoon, to his closer meeting with May Bartram, whose face, a reminder, yet not quite a remembrance, as they sat, much separated, at a very long table, had begun merely by troubling him rather pleasantly. It affected him as the sequel of something of which he had lost the beginning. He knew it, and for the time quite welcomed it, as a continuation, but didn't know what it continued, which was an interest, or an amusement, the greater as he was also somehow aware—yet without a direct sign from her—that the young woman herself had not lost the thread. She had not lost it, but she wouldn't give it back to him, he saw, without some putting forth of his hand for it; and he not only saw that, but saw several things more, things odd enough in the light of the fact that at the moment some accident of grouping brought them face to face he was still merely fumbling with the idea that any contact between them in the past would have had no importance. If it had had no importance he scarcely knew why his actual impression of her should so seem to have so much; the answer to which, however, was that in such a life as they all appeared to be leading for the moment one could but take things as they came. He was satisfied, without in the least being able to say why, that this young lady might roughly have ranked in the house as a poor relation; satisfied also that she was not there on a brief visit, but was more or less a part of the establishment—almost a working, a remunerated part. Didn't she enjoy at periods a protection that she paid for by helping, among other services, to show the place and explain it, deal with the tiresome people, answer questions about the dates of the buildings, the styles of the furniture, the authorship of the pictures, the favourite haunts of the ghost? It wasn't that she looked as if you could have given her shillings—it was impossible to look less so. Yet when she finally drifted toward him, distinctly handsome, though ever so much older—older than when he had seen her before—it might have been as an effect of her guessing that he had, within the couple of hours, devoted more imagination to her than to all the others put together, and had thereby penetrated to a kind of truth that the others were too stupid for. She *was* there on harder terms than anyone; she was there as a consequence of things suffered, in one way and another, in the interval of years; and she remembered him very much as she was remembered—only a good deal better.

By the time they at last thus came to speech they were alone in one of the rooms—remarkable for a fine portrait over the chimney place—out of which their friends had passed, and the charm of it was that even before they had spoken they had practically arranged with each other to stay behind for talk. The charm, happily, was in other things too; it was partly in there being scarce a spot at Weatherend without something to stay behind for. It was in the way the autumn day looked into the high windows as it waned; in the way the red light, breaking at the close from under a low, sombre sky, reached out in a long shaft and played over old wainscots, old tapestry, old gold, old colour. It was most of all perhaps in the way she came to him as if, since she had been turned on to deal with the simpler sort, he might, should he choose to keep the whole thing down, just take her mild attention for a part of her general business. As soon as he heard her voice, however, the gap was filled up and the missing link supplied; the slight irony he divined in her attitude lost its advantage. He almost jumped at it to get there before her. "I met you years and years ago in Rome. I remember all about it." She confessed to disappointment—she had been so sure he didn't; and to prove how well he did he began to pour forth the particular recollections that popped up as he called for them.

Her face and her voice, all at his service now, worked the miracle—the impression, operating like the torch of a lamplighter who touches into flame, one by one, a long row of gas jets. Marcher flattered himself that the illumination was brilliant, yet he was really still more pleased on her showing him, with amusement, that in his haste to make everything right he had got most things rather wrong. It hadn't been at Rome—it had been at Naples; and it hadn't been seven years before—it had been more nearly ten. She hadn't been either with her uncle or aunt, but with her mother and her brother; in addition to which it was not with the Pembles that *he* had been, but with the Boyers, coming down in their company from Rome—a point on which she insisted, a little to his confusion, and as to which she had her evidence in hand. The Boyers she had known, but she didn't know the Pembles, though she had heard of them, and it was the people he was with who had made them acquainted. The incident of the thunderstorm that had raged round them with such violence as to drive them for refuge into an excavation—this incident had not occurred at the Palace of the Cæsars, but at Pompeii, on an occasion when they had been present there at an important find.

He accepted her amendments, he enjoyed her corrections, though the moral of them was, she pointed out, that he *really* didn't remember the least thing about her; and he only felt it as a drawback that when all was made conformable to the truth there didn't appear much of anything left. They lingered together still, she neglecting her office—for from the moment he was so clever she had no proper right to him—and both neglecting the house, just waiting as to see if a memory or two more wouldn't again breathe upon them. It had not taken them many minutes, after all, to put down on the table, like the cards of a pack, those that constituted their respective hands; only what came out was that the pack was unfortunately not perfect—that the past, invoked, invited, encouraged, could give them, naturally, no more than it had. It had made them meet—her at twenty, him at twenty-five; but nothing was so strange, they seemed to say to each other, as that, while so occupied, it hadn't done a little more for them. They looked at each other as with the feeling of an occasion missed; the present one would have been so much better if the other, in the far distance, in the foreign land, hadn't been so stupidly meagre. There weren't, apparently, all counted, more than a dozen little old things that had succeeded in coming to pass between them; trivialities of youth, simplicities of freshness, stupidities of ignorance, small possible germs, but too deeply buried—too deeply (didn't it seem?) to sprout after so many years. Marcher said to himself that he ought to have rendered her some service—saved her from a capsized boat in the Bay, or at least recovered her dressing-bag, filched from her cab, in the streets of Naples, by a lazzarone with a stiletto. Or it would have been nice if he could have been taken with fever, alone, at his hotel, and she could have come to look after him, to write to his people, to drive him out in convalescence. *Then* they would be in possession of the something or other that their actual show seemed to lack. It yet somehow presented itself, this show, as too good to be spoiled; so that they were reduced for a few minutes more to wondering a little helplessly why—since they seemed to know a certain number of the same people—their reunion had been so long averted. They didn't use that name for it, but their delay from minute to minute to join the others was a kind of confession that they didn't quite want it to be a failure. Their attempted supposition of reasons for their not having met but showed how little they knew of each other. There came in fact a moment when Marcher felt a positive pang. It was vain to pretend she was an old friend, for all the communities were wanting, in spite of which it was as an old friend that he saw she would have suited him. He had new ones enough—was surrounded with them, for instance, at that hour at the other house; as a new one he probably wouldn't have so much as noticed her. He would have liked to invent something, get her to make-believe with him that some passage of a romantic or critical kind *had* originally occurred. He was really almost reaching out in imagination—as against time—for something that would do, and saying to himself that if it didn't come this new incident would simply and rather awkwardly close. They would separate, and now for no second or for no third chance. They would have tried and not succeeded. Then it was, just at the turn, as he afterwards made it out to himself, that, everything else failing, she herself decided to take up the case and, as it were, save the situation. He felt as soon as she spoke that she had been consciously keeping back what she said and hoping to get on without it; a scruple in her that immensely touched him when, by the end of three or four minutes more, he was able to measure it. What she brought out, at any rate, quite cleared the air and supplied the link—the link it was such a mystery he should frivolously have managed to lose.

"You know you told me something that I've never forgotten and that again and again has made me think of you since; it was that tremendously hot day when we went to Sorrento, across the bay, for the breeze. What I allude to was what you said to me, on the way back, as we sat, under the awning of the boat, enjoying the cool. Have you forgotten?"

He had forgotten, and he was even more surprised than ashamed. But the great thing was that he saw it was no vulgar reminder of any "sweet" speech. The vanity of women had long memories, but she was making no claim on him of a compliment or a mistake. With another woman, a totally different one, he might have feared the recall possibly even some imbecile "offer." So, in having to say that he had indeed forgotten, he was conscious rather of a loss than of a gain; he already saw an interest in the matter of her reference. "I try to think—but I give it up. Yet I remember the Sorrento day."

"I'm not very sure you do," May Bartram after a moment said; "and I'm not very sure I ought to want you to. It's dreadful to bring a person back, at any time, to what he was ten years before. If you've lived away from it," she smiled, "so much the better."

"Ah, if *you* haven't why should I?" he asked.

"Lived away, you mean, from what I myself was?"

"From what *I* was. I was of course an ass," Marcher went on; "but I would rather know from you just the sort of ass I was than—from the moment you have something in your mind—not know anything."

Still, however, she hesitated. "But if you've completely ceased to be that sort—?"

"Why, I can then just so all the more bear to know. Besides, perhaps I haven't."

"Perhaps. Yet if you haven't," she added. "I should suppose you would remember. Not indeed that *I* in the least connect with my impression the invidious name you use. If I had only thought you foolish," she explained, "the thing I speak of wouldn't so have remained with me. It was about yourself." She waited, as if it might come to him; but as, only meeting her eyes in wonder, he gave no sign, she burnt her ships. "Has it ever happened?"

Then it was that, while he continued to stare, a light

broke for him and the blood slowly came to his face, which began to burn with recognition. "Do you mean I told you—?" But he faltered, lest what came to him shouldn't be right, lest he should only give himself away.

"It was something about yourself that it was natural one shouldn't forget—that is if one remembered you at all. That's why I ask you," she smiled, "if the thing you then spoke of has ever come to pass?"

Oh, then he saw, but he was lost in wonder and found himself embarrassed. This, he also saw, made her sorry for him, as if her allusion had been a mistake. It took him but a moment, however, to feel that it had not been, much as it had been a surprise. After the first little shock of it her knowledge on the contrary began, even if rather strangely, to taste sweet to him. She was the only other person in world then who would have it, and she had had it all these years, while the fact of his having so breathed his secret had unaccountably faded from him. No wonder they couldn't have met as if nothing had happened. "I judge," he finally said, "that I know what you mean. Only I had strangely enough lost the consciousness of having taken you so far into my confidence."

"Is it because you've taken so many others as well?"

"I've taken nobody. Not a creature since then."

"So that I'm the only person who knows?"

"The only person in the world."

"Well," she quickly replied, "I myself have never spoken.

I've never, never repeated of you what you told me." She looked at him so that he perfectly believed her. Their eyes met over it in such a way that he was without a doubt. "And I never will."

She spoke with an earnestness that, as if almost excessive, put him at ease about her possible derision. Somehow the whole question was a new luxury to him—that is, from the moment she was in possession. If she didn't take the ironic view she clearly took the sympathetic, and that was what he had had, in all the long time, from no one whomsoever. What he felt was that he couldn't at present have begun to tell her and yet could profit perhaps exquisitely by the accident of having done so of old. "Please don't then. We're just right as it is."

"Oh, I am," she laughed, "if you are!" To which she added: "Then you do still feel in the same way?"

It was impossible to him not to take to himself that she was really interested, and it all kept coming as a sort of revelation. He had thought of himself so long as abominably alone, and, lo, he wasn't alone a bit. He hadn't been, it appeared, for an hour—since those moments on the Sorrento boat. It was *she* who had been, he seemed to see as he looked at her—she who had been made so by the graceless fact of his lapse of fidelity. To tell her what he had told her—what had it been but to ask something of her? something that she had given, in her charity, without his having, by a remembrance, by a return of the spirit, failing another encounter, so much as thanked her. What he had asked of her had been simply at first not to laugh at him. She had beautifully not done so for ten years, and she was not doing so now. So he had endless gratitude to make up. Only for that he must see just how he had figured to her. "What, exactly, was the account I gave—?"

"Of the way you did feel? Well, it was very simple. You said you had had from your earliest time, as the deepest thing within you, the sense of being kept for something rare and strange, possibly prodigious and terrible that was sooner or later to happen to you, that you had in your bones the foreboding and the conviction of, and that would perhaps overwhelm you."

"Do you call that very simple?" John Marcher asked.

She thought a moment. "It was perhaps because I seemed, as you spoke, to understand it."

"You do understand it?" he eagerly asked.

Again she kept her kind eyes on him. "You still have the belief?"

"Oh!" he exclaimed helplessly. There was too much to say.

"Whatever it is to be," she clearly made out, "it hasn't yet come."

He shook his head in complete surrender now. "It hasn't yet come. Only, you know, it isn't anything I'm to *do*, to achieve in the world, to be distinguished or admired for. I'm not such an ass as *that*. It would be much better, no doubt, if I were."

"It's to be something you're merely to suffer?"

"Well, say to wait for—to have to meet, to face, to see suddenly break out in my life; possibly destroying all further consciousness, possibly annihilating me; possibly, on the other hand, only altering everything, striking at the root of all my world and leaving me to the consequences, however they shape themselves."

She took this in, but the light in her eyes continued for him not to be that of mockery. "Isn't what you describe perhaps but the expectation—or, at any rate, the sense of danger, familiar to so many people—of falling in love?"

John Marcher thought. "Did you ask me that before?"

"No—I wasn't so free-and-easy then. But it's what strikes me now."

"Of course," he said after a moment, "it strikes you. Of course it strikes *me*. Of course what's in store for me may be no more than that. The only thing is," he went on, "that I think that if it had been that, I should by this time know."

"Do you mean because you've *been* in love?" And then as he but looked at her in silence: "You've been in love, and it hasn't meant such a cataclysm, hasn't proved the great affair?"

"Here I am, you see. It hasn't been overwhelming."

"Then it hasn't been love," said May Bartram.

"Well, I at least thought it was. I took it for that—I've

taken it till now. It was agreeable, it was delightful, it was miserable," he explained. "But it wasn't strange. It wasn't what *my* affair's to be."

"You want something all to yourself—something that nobody else knows or *has* known?"

"It isn't a question of what I 'want'—God knows I don't want anything. It's only a question of the apprehension that haunts me—that I live with day by day."

He said this so lucidly and consistently that, visibly, it further imposed itself. If she had not been interested before she would have been interested now. "Is it a sense of coming violence?"

Evidently now too, again, he liked to talk of it. "I don't think of it as—when it does come—necessarily violent. I only think of it as natural and as of course, above all, unmistakable. I think of it simply as *the* thing. *The* thing will of itself appear natural."

"Then how will it appear strange?"

Marcher bethought himself. "It won't—to *me*."

"To whom then?"

"Well," he replied, smiling at last, "say to you."

"Oh then, I'm to be present?"

"Why, you *are* present—since you know."

"I see." She turned it over. "But I mean at the catastrophe."

At this, for a minute, their lightness gave way to their gravity; it was as if the long look they exchanged held them together. "It will only depend on yourself—if you'll watch with me."

"Are you afraid?" she asked.

"Don't leave me *now*," he went on.

"Are you afraid?" she repeated.

"Do you think me simply out of my mind?" he pursued instead of answering. "Do I merely strike you as a harmless lunatic?"

"No," said May Bartram. "I understand you. I believe you."

"You mean you feel how my obsession—poor old thing!—may correspond to some possible reality?"

"To some possible reality."

"Then you *will* watch with me?"

She hesitated, then for the third time put her question. "Are you afraid?"

"Did I tell you I was—at Naples?"

"No, you said nothing about it."

"Then I don't know. And I should *like* to know," said John Marcher. "You'll tell me yourself whether you think so. If you'll watch with me you'll see."

"Very good then." They had been moving by this time across the room, and at the door, before passing out, they paused as if for the full wind-up of their understanding. "I'll watch with you," said May Bartram.

• • •

The fact that she "knew"—knew and yet neither chaffed him nor betrayed him—had in a short time begun to constitute between them a sensible bond, which became more marked when, within the year that followed their afternoon at Weatherend, the opportunities for meeting multiplied. The event that thus promoted these occasions was the death of the ancient lady, her great-aunt, under whose wing, since losing her mother, she had to such an extent found shelter, and who, though but the widowed mother of the new successor to the property, had succeeded—thanks to a high tone and a high temper—in not forfeiting the supreme position at the great house. The deposition of this personage arrived but with her death, which, followed by many changes, made in particular a difference for the young woman in whom Marcher's expert attention had recognised from the first a dependent with a pride that might ache though it didn't bristle. Nothing for a long time had made him easier than the thought that the aching must have been much soothed by Miss Bartram's now finding herself able to set up a small home in London. She had acquired property, to an amount that made that luxury just possible, under her aunt's extremely complicated will, and when the whole matter began to be straightened out, which indeed took time, she let him know that the happy issue was at last in view. He had seen her again before that day, both because she had more than once accompanied the ancient lady to town and because he had paid another visit to the friends who so conveniently made of Weatherend one of the charms of their own hospitality. These friends had taken him back there; he had achieved there again with Miss Bartram some quiet detachment; and he had in London succeeded in persuading her to more than one brief absence from her aunt. They went together, on these latter occasions to the National Gallery and the South Kensington Museum, where, among vivid reminders, they talked of Italy at large—not now attempting to recover, as at first, the taste of their youth and their ignorance. That recovery, the first day at Weatherend, had served its purpose well, had given them quite enough; so that they were, to Marcher's sense, no longer hovering about the head-waters of their stream, but had felt their boat pushed sharply off and down the current.

They were literally afloat together; for our gentleman this was marked, quite as marked as that the fortunate cause of it was just the buried treasure of her knowledge. He had with his own hands dug up this little hoard, brought to light—that is to within reach of the dim day constituted by their discretions and primacies—the object of value the hiding-place of which he had, after putting it into the ground himself, so strangely, so long forgotten. The exquisite luck of having again just stumbled on the spot made him indifferent to any other question; he would doubtless have devoted more time to the odd accident of his lapse of memory if he had not been moved to devote so much to the sweetness, the comfort, as he felt, for the future, that this accident itself had helped to keep fresh. It had never entered into his plan that anyone should "know," and mainly for the reason that it was not in him to tell anyone. That would have been impossible, since nothing but the amusement of a cold world would have waited on it. Since, however, a mysterious fate had opened his mouth in youth, in spite of him, he would count that a compensation and profit by it to the utmost. That the right person *should* know tempered the asperity of his secret more even than his shyness had permitted him to imagine; and May Bartram was clearly right, because—well, because there she was. Her knowledge simply settled it; he would have been sure enough by this time had she been wrong. There was that in his situation, no doubt, that disposed him too much to see her as a mere confidant, taking all her light for him from the fact—the fact only—of her interest in his predicament, from her mercy, sympathy, seriousness, her consent not to regard him as the funniest of the funny. Aware, in fine, that her price for him was just in her giving him this constant sense of his being admirably spared, he was careful to remember that she had, after all, also a life of her own, with things that might happen to *her,* things that in friendship one should likewise take account of. Something fairly remarkable came to pass with him, for that matter, in this connection—something represented by a certain passage of his consciousness, in the suddenest way, from one extreme to the other.

He had thought himself, so long as nobody knew, the most disinterested person in the world, carrying his concentrated burden, his perpetual suspense, ever so quietly, holding his tongue about it, giving others no glimpse of it nor of its effect upon his life, asking of them no allowance and only making on his side all those that were asked. He had disturbed nobody with the queerness of having to know a haunted man, though he had had moments of rather special temptation on hearing people say that they were "unsettled." If they were as unsettled as he was—he who had never been settled for an hour in his life—they would know what it meant. Yet it wasn't, all the same, for him to make them, and he listened to them civilly enough. This was why he had such good—though possibly such rather colourless—manners; this was why, above all, he could regard himself, in a greedy world, as decently—as, in fact, perhaps even a little sublimely—unselfish. Our point is accordingly that he valued this character quite sufficiently to measure his present danger of letting it lapse, against which he promised himself to be much on his guard. He was quite ready, none the less, to be selfish just a little, since, surely, no more charming occasion for it had come to him. "Just a little," in a word, was just as much as Miss Bartram, taking one day with another, would let him. He never would be in the least coercive, and he would keep well before him the lines on which consideration for her—the very highest—ought to proceed. He would thoroughly establish the heads under which her affairs, her requirements, her peculiarities—he went so far as to give them the latitude of that name—would come into their intercourse. All this naturally was a sign of how much he took the intercourse itself for granted. There was nothing more to be done about *that.* It simply existed; had sprung into being with her first penetrating question to him in the autumn light there at Weatherend. The real form it should have taken on the basis that stood out large was the form of their marrying. But the devil in this was that the very basis itself put marrying out of the question. His conviction, his apprehension, his obsession, in short, was not a condition he could invite a woman to share; and that consequence of it was precisely what was the matter with him. Something or other lay in wait for him, amid the twists and the turns of the months and the years, like a crouching beast in the jungle. It signified little whether the crouching beast were destined to slay him or to be slain. The definite point was the inevitable spring of the creature; and the definite lesson from that was that a man of feeling didn't cause himself to be accompanied by a lady on a tiger-hunt. Such was the image under which he had ended by figuring his life.

They had at first, none the less, in the scattered hours spent together, made no allusion to that view of it; which was a sign he was handsomely ready to give that he didn't expect, that he in fact didn't care always to be talking about it. Such a feature in one's outlook was really like a hump on one's back. The difference it made every minute of the day existed quite independently of discussion. One discussed, of course, *like* a hunchback, for there was always, if nothing else, the hunchback face. That remained, and she was watching him; but people watched best, as a general thing, in silence, so that such would be predominantly the manner of their vigil. Yet he didn't want, at the same time, to be solemn; solemn was what he imagined he too much tended to be with other people. The thing to be, with the one person who knew, was easy and natural—to make the reference rather than be seeming to avoid it, to avoid it rather than be seeming to make it, and to keep it, in any case, familiar, facetious even, rather than pedantic and portentous. Some such consideration as the latter was doubtless in his mind, for instance, when he wrote pleasantly to Miss Bartram that perhaps the great thing he had so long felt as in the lap of the gods was no more than this circumstance, which touched him so nearly, of her acquiring a house in London. It was the first allusion they had yet again made, needing any other hitherto so little; but when she replied, after having given him the news, that she was by no means satisfied with such a trifle, as the climax to so special a suspense, she almost set him wondering if she hadn't even a larger conception of singularity for him than he had for himself. He was at all events destined to become aware little by little, as time went by, that she was all the while looking at his life, judging it, measuring it, in the light of the thing she knew, which grew to be at last, with the consecration of the years, never mentioned between them save as "the real truth" about him. That had always been his own form of reference to it, but she adopted the form so quietly that, looking back at the end of a period, he knew there was no moment at which it was traceable that she had, as he might say, got inside his condition, or exchanged the attitude of beautifully indulging for that of still more beautifully believing him.

It was always open to him to accuse her of seeing him but as the most harmless of maniacs, and this, in the long run—since it covered so much ground—was his easiest description of their friendship. He had a screw loose for her, but she liked him in spite of it, and was practically, against the rest of the world, his kind, wise keeper, unremunerated, but fairly amused and, in the absence of other near ties, not disreputably occupied. The rest of the world of course thought him queer, but she, she only, knew, how, and above all why, queer; which was precisely what enabled her to dispose the concealing veil in the right folds. She took his gaiety from him—since it had to pass with them for gaiety—as she took everything else; but she certainly so far justified by her unerring touch his finer sense of the degree to which he had ended by convincing her. *She* at least never spoke of the secret of his life except as "the real truth about you," and she had in fact a wonderful way of making it seem, as such, the secret of her own life too. That was in fine how he so constantly felt her as allowing for him; he couldn't on the whole call it anything else. He allowed for himself, but she, exactly, allowed still more; partly because, better placed for a sight of the matter, she traced his unhappy perversion through portions of its course into which he could scarce follow it. He knew how he felt, but, besides knowing that, she knew how he *looked* as well; he knew each of the things of importance he was insidiously kept from doing, but she could add up the amount they made, understand how much, with a lighter weight on his spirit, he might have done, and thereby establish how, clever as he was, he fell short. Above all she was in the secret of the difference between the forms he went through—those of his little office under Government, those of caring for his modest patrimony, for his library, for his garden in the country, for the people in London whose invitations he accepted and repaid—and the detachment that reigned beneath them and that made of all behaviour, all that could in the least be called behaviour, a long act of dissimulation. What it had come to was that he wore a mask painted with the social simper, out of the eye-holes of which there looked eyes of an expression not in the least matching the other features. This the stupid world, even after years, had never more than half discovered. It was only May Bartram who had, and she achieved, by an art indescribable, the feat of at once—or perhaps it was only alternately—meeting the eyes from in front and mingling her own vision, as from over his shoulder, with their peep through the apertures.

So, while they grew older together, she did watch with him, and so she let this association give shape and colour to her own existence. Beneath *her* forms as well detachment had learned to sit, and behaviour had become for her, in the social sense, a false account of herself. There was but one account of her that would have been true all the while, and that she could give, directly, to nobody, least of all to John Marcher. Her whole attitude was a virtual statement, but the perception of that only seemed destined to take its place for him as one of the many things necessarily crowded out of his consciousness. If she had, moreover, like himself, to make sacrifices to their real truth, it was to be granted that her compensation might have affected her as more prompt and more natural. They had long periods, in this London time, during which, when they were together, a stranger might have listened to them without in the least pricking up his ears; on the other hand, the real truth was equally liable at any moment to rise to the surface, and the auditor would then have wondered indeed what they were talking about. They had from an early time made up their mind that society was, luckily, unintelligent, and the margin that this gave them had fairly become one of their commonplaces. Yet there were still moments when the situation turned almost fresh—usually under the effect of some expression drawn from herself. Her expressions doubtless repeated themselves, but her intervals were generous. "What saves us, you know, is that we answer so completely to so usual an appearance: that of the man and woman whose friendship has become such a daily habit, or almost, as to be at least indispensable." That, for instance, was a remark she had frequently enough had occasion to make, though she had given it at different times different developments. What we are especially concerned with is the turn it happened to take from her one afternoon when he had come to see her in honour of her birthday. This anniversary had fallen on a Sunday, at a season of thick fog and general outward gloom; but he had brought her his customary offering, having known her now long enough to have established a hundred little customs. It was one of his proofs to himself, the present he made her on her birthday, that he had not sunk into real selfishness. It was mostly nothing more than a small trinket, but it was always fine of its kind, and he was regularly careful to pay for it more than he thought he could afford. "Our habit saves you, at least, don't you see? because it makes you, after all, for the vulgar, indistinguishable from other men. What's the most inveterate mark of men in general? Why, the capacity to spend endless time with dull women—to spend it, I won't say without being bored, but without minding that they are, without being driven off at a tangent by it; which comes to the same thing. I'm your dull woman, a part of the daily bread for which you pray at church. That covers your tracks more than anything."

"And what covers yours?" asked Marcher, whom his

dull woman could mostly to this extent amuse. "I see of course what you mean by your saving me, in one way and another, so far as other people are concerned—I've seen it all along. Only, what is it that saves *you*? I often think, you know, of that."

She looked as if she sometimes thought of that too, but in rather a different way. "Where other people, you mean, are concerned?"

"Well, you're really so in with me, you know—as a sort of result of my being so in with yourself. I mean of my having such an immense regard for you, being so tremendously grateful for all you've done for me. I sometimes ask myself if it's quite fair. Fair I mean to have so involved and—since one may say it—interested you. I almost feel as if you hadn't really had time to do anything else."

"Anything else but be interested?" she asked. "Ah, what else does one ever want to be? If I've been 'watching' with you, as we long ago agreed that I was to do, watching is always in itself an absorption."

"Oh, certainly," John Marcher said, "if you hadn't had your curiosity—! Only, doesn't it sometimes come to you, as time goes on, that your curiosity is not being particularly repaid?"

May Bartram had a pause. "Do you ask that, by any chance, because you feel at all that yours isn't? I mean because you have to wait so long."

Oh, he understood what she meant. "For the thing to happen that never does happen? For the beast to jump out? No, I'm just where I was about it. It isn't a matter as to which I can *choose,* I can decide for a change. It isn't one as to which there *can* be a change. It's in the lap of the gods. One's in the hands of one's law—there one is. As to the form the law will take, the way it will operate, that's its own affair."

"Yes," Miss Bartram replied; "of course one's fate is coming, of course it *has* come, in its own form and its own way, all the while. Only, you know, the form and the way in your case were to have been—well, something so exceptional and, as one may say, so particularly *your* own."

Something in this made him look at her with suspicion. "You say 'were to *have* been,' as if in your heart you had begun to doubt."

"Oh!" she vaguely protested.

"As if you believed," he went on, "that nothing will now take place."

She shook her head slowly, but rather inscrutably. "You're far from my thought."

He continued to look at her. "What then is the matter with you?"

"Well," she said after another wait, "the matter with me is simply that I'm more sure than ever my curiosity, as you call it, will be but too well repaid."

They were frankly grave now; he had got up from his

seat, had turned once more about the little drawing-room to which, year after year, he brought his inevitable topic; in which he had, as he might have said, tasted their intimate community with every sauce, where every object was as familiar to him as the things of his own house and the very carpets were worn with his fitful walk very much as the desks in old counting-houses are worn by the elbows of generations of clerks. The generations of his nervous moods had been at work there, and the place was the written history of his whole middle life. Under the impression of what his friend had just said he knew himself, for some reason, more aware of these things, which made him, after a moment, stop again before her. "Is it, possibly, that you've grown afraid?"

"Afraid?" He thought, as she repeated the word, that his question had made her, a little, change colour; so that, lest he should have touched on a truth, he explained very kindly, "You remember that that was what you asked *me* long ago—that first day at Weatherend."

"Oh yes, and you told me you didn't know—that I was to see for myself. We've said little about it since, even in so long a time."

"Precisely," Marcher interposed—"quite as if it were too delicate a matter for us to make free with. Quite as if we might find, on pressure, that I *am* afraid. For then," he said, "we shouldn't, should we? quite know what to do."

She had for the time no answer to this question. "There have been days when I thought you were. Only, of course," she added, "there have been days when we have thought almost anything."

"Everything. Oh!" Marcher softly groaned as with a gasp, half spent, at the face, more uncovered just then than it had been for a long while, of the imagination always with them. It had always had its incalculable moments of glaring out, quite as with the very eyes of the very Beast, and, used as he was to them, they could still draw from him the tribute of a sigh that rose from the depths of his being. All that they had thought, first and last, rolled over him; the past seemed to have been reduced to mere barren speculation. This in fact was what the place had just struck him as so full of—the simplification of everything but the state of suspense. That remained only by seeming to hang in the void surrounding it. Even his original fear, if fear it had been, had lost itself in the desert. "I judge, however," he continued, "that you see I'm not afraid now."

"What I see is, as I make it out, that you've achieved something almost unprecedented in the way of getting used to danger. Living with it so long and so closely, you've lost your sense of it; you know it's there, but you're indifferent, and you cease even, as of old, to have to whistle in the dark. Considering what the danger is," May Bartram wound up, "I'm bound to say that I don't think your attitude could well be surpassed."

John Marcher faintly smiled. "It's heroic?"

"Certainly—call it that."

He considered. "I *am*, then, a man of courage?"

"That's what you were to show me."

He still, however, wondered. "But doesn't the man of courage know what he's afraid of—or *not* afraid of? I don't know *that*, you see. I don't focus it. I can't name it. I only know I'm exposed."

"Yes, but exposed—how shall I say?—so directly. So intimately. That's surely enough."

"Enough to make you feel, then—at what we may call the end of our watch—that I'm not afraid?"

"You're not afraid. But it isn't," she said, "the end of our watch. That is it isn't the end of yours. You've everything still to see."

"Then why haven't *you*?" he asked. He had had, all along, to-day, the sense of her keeping something back, and he still had it. As this was his first impression of that, it made a kind of date. The case was the more marked as she didn't at first answer; which in turn made him go on. "You know something I don't." Then his voice, for that of a man of courage, trembled a little. "You know what's to happen." Her silence, with the face she showed, was almost a confession—it made him sure. "You know; and you're afraid to tell me. It's so bad that you're afraid I'll find out."

All this might be true, for she did look as if, unexpectedly to her, he had crossed some mystic line that she had secretly drawn round her. Yet she might, after all, not have worried; and the real upshot was that he himself, at all events, needn't. "You'll never find out."

It was all to have made, none the less, as I have said, a date; as came out in the fact that again and again, even after long intervals, other things that passed between them wore, in relation to this hour, but the character of recalls and results. Its immediate effect had been indeed rather to lighten insistence—almost to provoke a reaction; as if their topic had dropped by its own weight and as if moreover, for that matter, Marcher had been visited by one of his occasional warnings against egotism. He had kept up, he felt, and very decently on the whole, his consciousness of the importance of not being selfish, and it was true that he had never sinned in that direction without promptly enough trying to press the scales the other way. He often repaired his fault, the season permitting, by inviting his friend to accompany him to the opera; and it not infrequently thus happened that, to show he didn't wish her to have but one sort of food for her mind, he was the cause of her appearing there with him a dozen nights in the month. It even happened that, seeing her home at such times, he occasionally went in with her to finish, as he called it, the evening, and, the better to make his point, sat down to the frugal but always careful little supper that awaited his pleasure. His point was made, he thought, by his not eternally insisting with her on himself; made for instance, at such hours, when it befell that, her piano at hand and each of them familiar with it, they went over passages of the opera together. It chanced to be on one of these occasions, however, that he reminded her of her not having answered a certain question he had put to her during the talk that had taken place between them on her last birthday. "What is it that saves *you*?"—saved her, he meant, from that appearance of variation from the usual human type. If he had practically escaped remark, as she pretended, by doing, in the most important particular, what most men do—find the answer to life in patching up an alliance of a sort with a woman no better than himself—how had she escaped it, and how could the alliance, such as it was, since they must suppose it had been more or less noticed, have failed to make her rather positively talked about?

"I never said," May Bartram replied, "that it hadn't made me talked about."

"Ah well then, you're not 'saved.' "

"It has not been a question for me. If you've had your woman, I've had," she said, "my man."

"And you mean that makes you all right?"

She hesitated. "I don't know why it shouldn't make me—humanly, which is what we're speaking of—as right as it makes you."

"I see," Marcher returned. "'Humanly,' no doubt, as

showing that you're living for something. Not, that is, just for me and my secret."

May Bartram smiled. "I don't pretend it exactly shows that I'm not living for you. It's my intimacy with you that's in question."

He laughed as he saw what she meant. "Yes, but since, as you say, I'm only, so far as people make out, ordinary, you're—aren't you—no more than ordinary either. You help me to pass for a man like another. So if I *am*, as I understand you, you're not compromised. Is that it?"

She had another hesitation, but she spoke clearly enough. "That's it. It's all that concerns me—to help you to pass for a man like another."

He was careful to acknowledge the remark handsomely. "How kind, how beautiful, you are to me! How shall I ever repay you?"

She had her last grave pause, as if there might be a choice of ways. But she chose. "By going on as you are."

It was into this going on as he was that they relapsed, and really for so long a time that the day inevitably came for a further sounding of their depths. It was as if these depths, constantly bridged over by a structure that was firm enough in spite of its lightness and of its occasional oscillation in the somewhat vertiginous air, invited on occasion, in the interest of their nerves, a dropping of the plummet and a measurement of the abyss. A difference had been made moreover, once for all, by the fact that she had, all the while, not appeared to feel the need of rebutting his charge of an idea within her that she didn't dare to express, uttered just before one of the fullest of their later discussions ended. It had come up for him then that she "knew" something and that what she knew was bad—too bad to tell him. When he had spoken of it as visibly so bad that she was afraid he might find it out, her reply had left the matter too equivocal to be let alone and yet, for Marcher's special sensibility, almost too formidable again to touch. He circled about it at a distance that alternately narrowed and widened and that yet was not much affected by the consciousness in him that there was nothing she could "know," after all, better than he did. She had no source of knowledge that he hadn't equally—except of course that she might have finer nerves. That was what women had where they were interested; they made out things, where people were concerned, that the people often couldn't have made out for themselves. Their nerves, their sensibility, their imagination, were conductors and revealers, and the beauty of May Bartram was in particular that she had given herself so to his case. He felt in these days what, oddly enough, he had never felt before, the growth of a dread of losing her by some catastrophe—some catastrophe that yet wouldn't at all be *the* catastrophe: partly because she had, almost of a sudden, begun to strike him as useful to him as never yet, and partly by reason of an appearance of uncertainty in her health, coincident and equally new.

It was characteristic of the inner detachment he had hitherto so successfully cultivated and to which our whole account of him is a reference, it was characteristic that his complications, such as they were, had never yet seemed so as at this crisis to thicken about him, even to the point of making him ask himself if he were, by any chance, of a truth, within sight or sound, within touch or reach, within the immediate jurisdiction of the thing that waited.

When the day came, as come it had to, that his friend confessed to him her fear of a deep disorder in her blood, he felt somehow the shadow of a change and the chill of a shock. He immediately began to imagine aggravations and disasters, and above all to think of her peril as the direct menace for himself of personal privation. This indeed gave him one of those partial recoveries of equanimity that were agreeable to him—it showed him that what was still first in his mind was the loss she herself might suffer. "What if she should have to die before knowing, before seeing—?" It would have been brutal, in the early stages of her trouble, to put that question to her; but it had immediately sounded for him to his own concern, and the possibility was what most made him sorry for her. If she did "know," moreover, in the sense of her having had some—what should he think?—mystical, irresistible light, this would make the matter not better, but worse, inasmuch as her original adoption of his own curiosity had quite become the basis of her life. She had been living to see what would *be* to be seen, and it would be cruel to her to have to give up before the accomplishment of the vision. These reflections, as I say, refreshed his generosity; yet, make them as he might, he saw himself, with the lapse of the period, more and more disconcerted. It lapsed for him with a strange, steady sweep, and the oddest oddity was that it gave him, independently of the threat of much inconvenience, almost the only positive surprise his career, if career it could be called, had yet offered him. She kept the house as she had never done; he had to go to her to see her—she could meet him nowhere now, though there was scarce a corner of their loved old London in which she had not in the past, at one time or another, done so; and he found her always seated by her fire in the deep, old-fashioned chair she was less and less able to leave. He had been struck one day, after an absence exceeding his usual measure, with her suddenly looking much older to him than he had ever thought of her being; then he recognised that the suddenness was all on his side—he had just been suddenly struck. She looked older because inevitably, after so many years, she *was* old, or almost; which was of course true in still greater measure of her companion. If she was old, or almost, John Marcher assuredly was, and yet it was her showing of the lesson, not his own, that brought the truth home to him. His surprises began here; when once they had begun they multiplied; they came rather with a rush: it was as if, in the oddest way in the world, they had all been kept back, sown in a thick cluster, for the late afternoon of life, the time at which, for people in general, the unexpected has died out.

One of them was that he should have caught himself—for he *had* so done—*really* wondering if the great accident would take form now as nothing more than his being condemned to see this charming woman, this admirable friend, pass away from him. He had never so unreservedly qualified her as while confronted in thought with such a possibility; in spite of which there was small doubt for him that as an answer to his long riddle the mere effacement of even so fine a feature of his situation would be an abject anticlimax. It would represent, as connected with his past attitude, a drop of dignity under the shadow of which his existence could only become the most grotesque of failures. He had been far from holding it a failure—long as he had waited for the appearance that was to make it a success. He had waited for a quite other thing, not for such a one as that. The breath of his good faith came short, however, as he recognized how long he had waited, or how long, at least, his companion had. That she, at all events, might be recorded as having waited in vain—this affected him sharply, and all the more because of his at first having done little more than amuse himself with the idea. It grew more grave as the gravity of her condition grew, and the state of mind it produced in him, which he ended by watching, himself, as if it had been some definite disfigurement of his outer person, may pass for another of his surprises. This conjoined itself still with another, the really stupefying consciousness of a question that he would have allowed to shape itself had he dared. What did everything mean—what, that is, did *she* mean, she and her vain waiting and her probable death and the soundless admonition of it all—unless that, at this time of day, it was simply, it was overwhelmingly too late? He had never, at any stage of his queer consciousness, admitted the whisper of such a correction; he had never, till within these last few months, been so false to his conviction as not to hold that what was to come to him had time, whether *he* struck himself as having it or not. That at last, at last, he certainly hadn't it, to speak of, or had it but in the scantiest measure—such, soon enough, as things went with him, became the inference with which his old obsession had to reckon: and this it was not helped to do by the more and more confirmed appearance that the great vagueness casting the long shadow in which he had lived had, to attest itself, almost no margin left. Since it was in Time that he was to have met his fate, so it was in Time that his fate was to have acted; and as he waked up to the sense of no longer being young, which was exactly the sense of being stale, just as that in turn, was the sense of being weak, he waked up to another matter beside. It all hung together; they were subject, he and the great vagueness, to an equal and indivisible law. When the possibilities themselves had, accordingly, turned stale, when the secret of the gods had grown faint, had perhaps even quite evaporated, that, and that only, was failure. It wouldn't have been failure to be bankrupt, dishonoured, pilloried, hanged; it was failure not to be anything. And so, in the dark valley into which his path had taken its unlooked-for twist, he wondered not a little as he groped. He didn't care what awful crash might overtake him, with what ignominy or what monstrosity he might yet be associated—since he wasn't, after all, too utterly old to suffer—if it would only be decently proportionate to the posture he had kept, all his life, in the promised presence of it. He had but one desire left—that he shouldn't have been "sold."

Then it was that one afternoon, while the spring of the year was young and new, she met, all in her own way, his frankest betrayal of these alarms. He had gone in late to see her, but evening had not settled, and she was presented to him in that long, fresh light of waning April days which affects us often with a sadness sharper than the greyest hours of autumn. The week had been warm, the spring was supposed to have begun early, and May Bartram sat, for the first time in the year, without a fire, a fact that, to Marcher's sense, gave the scene of which she formed part a smooth and ultimate look, an air of knowing, in its immaculate order and its cold, meaningless cheer, that it would never see a fire again. Her own aspect—he could scarce have said why—intensified this note. Almost as white as wax, with the marks and signs in her face as numerous and as fine as if they had been etched by a needle, with soft white draperies relieved by a faded green scarf, the delicate tone of which had been consecrated by the years, she was the picture of a serene, exquisite, but impenetrable sphinx, whose head, or indeed all whose person, might have been powdered with silver. She was a sphinx, yet with her white petals and green fronds she might have been a lily too—only an artificial lily, wonderfully imitated and constantly kept, without dust or stain, though not exempt from a slight droop and a complexity of faint creases, under some clear glass bell. The perfection of household care, of high polish and finish, always reigned in her rooms, but they especially looked to Marcher at present as if everything had been wound up, tucked in, put away, so that she might sit with folded hands and with nothing more to do. She was "out of it," to his vision; her work was over; she communicated with him as across some gulf, or from some island of rest that she had already reached, and it made him feel strangely abandoned. Was it—or, rather, wasn't it—that if for so long she had been watching with him the answer to their question had swum into her ken and taken on its name, so that her occupation was verily gone? He had as much as charged her with this in saying to her, many months before, that she even then knew something she was keeping from him. It was a point he had never since ventured to press, vaguely fearing, as he did, that it might become a difference, perhaps a disagreement, between them. He had in short, in this later time, turned nervous, which was what, in all the other years, he had never been; and the oddity was that his nervousness should have waited till he had begun to doubt, should have held off so long as he was sure. There was something, it seemed to him, that the wrong word would bring down on his head, something that would so at least put an end to his suspense. But he wanted not to speak the wrong word; that would make everything ugly. He wanted the knowledge he lacked to drop on him, if drop it could, by its own august weight. If she was to forsake him it was surely for her to take leave. This was why he didn't ask her again, directly, what she knew; but it was also why, approaching the matter from another side, he said to her in the course of his visit: "What do you regard as the very worst that, at this time of day, *can* happen to me?"

He had asked her that in the past often enough; they had, with the odd, irregular rhythm of their intensities and avoidances, exchanged ideas about it and then had seen the ideas washed away by cool intervals, washed like figures traced in sea-sand. It had ever been the mark of their talk that the oldest allusions in it required but a little dismissal and reaction to come out again, sounding for the hour as new. She could thus at present meet his inquiry quite freshly and patiently. "Oh yes, I've repeatedly thought, only it always seemed to me of old that I couldn't quite make up my mind. I thought of dreadful things, between which it was difficult to choose; and so must you have done."

"Rather! I feel now as if I had scarce done anything else. I appear to myself to have spent my life in thinking of nothing *but* dreadful things. A great many of them I've at different times named to you, but there were others I couldn't name."

"They were too, too dreadful?"

"Too, too dreadful—some of them."

She looked at him a minute, and there came to him as he met it an inconsequent sense that her eyes, when one got their full clearness, were still as beautiful as they had been in youth, only beautiful with a strange, cold light—a light that somehow was a part of the effect, if it wasn't rather a part of the cause, of the pale, hard sweetness of the season and the hour. "And yet," she said at last, "there are horrors we have mentioned."

It deepened the strangeness to see her, as such a figure in such a picture, talk of "horrors," but she was to do, in a few minutes, something stranger yet—though even of this he was to take the full measure but afterwards—and the note of it was already in the air. It was, for the matter of that, one of the signs that her eyes were having again such a high flicker of their prime. He had to admit, however, what she said. "Oh yes, there were times when we did go far." He caught himself in the act of speaking as if it all were over. Well, he wished it were; and the consummation depended, for him, clearly, more and more on his companion.

But she had now a soft smile. "Oh, far—!"

It was oddly ironic. "Do you mean you're prepared to go further?"

She was frail and ancient and charming as she continued to look at him, yet it was rather as if she had lost the thread. "Do you consider that we went so far?"

"Why, I thought it the point you were just making—that we *had* looked most things in the face."

"Including each other?" She still smiled. "But you're quite right. We've had together great imaginations, often great fears; but some of them have been unspoken."

"Then the worst—we haven't faced that. I *could* face it, I believe, if I knew what you think it. I feel," he explained, "as if I had lost my power to conceive such things." And he wondered if he looked as blank as he sounded. "It's spent."

"Then why do you assume," she asked, "that mine isn't?"

"Because you've given me signs to the contrary. It isn't a question for you of conceiving, imagining, comparing. It isn't a question now of choosing." At last he came out with it. "You know something that I don't. You've shown me that before."

These last words affected her, he could see in a moment, remarkably, and she spoke with firmness. "I've shown you, my dear, nothing."

He shook his head. "You can't hide it."

"Oh, oh!" May Bartram murmured over what she couldn't hide. It was almost a smothered groan.

"You admitted it months ago, when I spoke of it to you as of something you were afraid I would find out. Your answer was that I couldn't, that I wouldn't, and I don't pretend I have. But you had something therefore in mind, and I see now that it must have been, that it still is, the possibility that, of all possibilities, has settled itself for you as the worst. This," he went on, "is why I appeal to you. I'm only afraid of ignorance now—I'm not afraid of knowledge." And then as for a while she said nothing: "What makes me sure is that I see in your face and feel here, in this air and amid these appearances, that you're out of it. You've done. You've had your experience. You leave me to my fate."

Well, she listened, motionless and white in her chair, as if she had in fact a decision to make, so that her whole manner was a virtual confession, though still with a small, fine, inner stiffness, an imperfect surrender. "It *would* be the worst," she finally let herself say. "I mean the thing that I've never said."

It hushed him a moment. "More monstrous than all the monstrosities we've named?"

"More monstrous. Isn't that what you sufficiently express," she asked, "in calling it the worst?"

Marcher thought. "Assuredly—if you mean, as I do, something that includes all the loss and all the shame that are thinkable."

"It would if it *should* happen," said May Bartram. "What we're speaking of, remember, is only my idea."

"It's your belief," Marcher returned. "That's enough for me. I feel your beliefs are right. Therefore if, having this one, you give me no more light on it, you abandon me."

"No, no!" she repeated. "I'm with you—don't you see?—still." And as if to make it more vivid to him she rose from her chair—a movement she seldom made in these days—and showed herself, all draped and all soft, in her fairness and slimness. "I haven't forsaken you."

It was really, in its effort against weakness, a generous assurance, and had the success of the impulse not, happily, been great, it would have touched him to pain more than to pleasure. But the cold charm in her eyes had spread, as she hovered before him, to all the rest of her person, so that it was, for the minute, almost like a recovery of youth. He couldn't pity her for that; he could only take her as she showed—as capable still of helping him. It was as if, at the sane time, her light might at any instant go out; wherefore he must make the most of it. There passed before him with intensity the three or four things he wanted most to know; but the question that came of itself to his lips really covered the others. "Then tell me if I shall consciously suffer."

She promptly shook her head. "Never!"

It confirmed the authority he imputed to her, and it produced on him an extraordinary effect. "Well, what's better than that? Do you call that the worst?"

"You think nothing is better?" she asked.

She seemed to mean something so special that he again sharply wondered, though still with the dawn of a prospect of relief. "Why not, if one doesn't *know?*" After which, as their eyes, over his question, met in a silence, the dawn deepened and something to his purpose came, prodigiously, out of her very face. His own, as he took it in, suddenly flushed to the forehead, and he gasped with the force of a perception to which, on the instant, everything fitted. The sound of his gasp filled the air; then he became articulate. "I see—if I don't suffer!"

In her own look, however, was doubt. "You see what?"

"Why, what you mean—what you've always meant."

She again shook her head. "What I mean isn't what I've always meant. It's different."

"It's something new?"

She hesitated. "Something new. It's not what you think. I see what you think."

His divination drew breath then; only her correction might be wrong. "It isn't that I *am* a donkey?" he asked between faintness and grimness. "It isn't that it's all a mistake?"

"A mistake?" she pityingly echoed. *That* possibility, for her, he saw, would be monstrous; and if she guaranteed him the immunity from pain it would accordingly not be what she had in mind. "Oh, no," she declared; "it's nothing of that sort. You've been right."

Yet he couldn't help asking himself if she weren't, thus pressed, speaking but to save him. It seemed to him he should be most lost if his history should prove all a platitude. "Are you telling me the truth, so that I sha'n't have been a bigger idiot than I can bear to know? I *haven't* lived with a vain imagination, in the most besotted illusion? I haven't waited but to see the door shut in my face?"

She shook her head again. "However the case stands *that* isn't the truth. Whatever the reality, it *is* a reality. The door isn't shut. The door's open," said May Bartram.

"Then something's to come?"

She waited once again, always with her cold, sweet eyes on him. "It's never too late." She had, with her gliding step, diminished the distance between them, and she stood nearer to him, close to him, a minute, as if still full of the unspoken. Her movement might have been for some finer emphasis of what she was at once hesitating and deciding to say. He had been standing by the chimney-piece, fireless and sparely adorned, a small, perfect old French clock and two morsels of rosy Dresden constituting all its furniture; and her hand grasped the shelf while she kept him waiting, grasped it a little as for support and encouragement. She only kept him waiting, however; that is he only waited. It had become suddenly, from her movement and attitude, beautiful and vivid to him that she had something more to give him; her wasted face delicately shone with it, and it glittered, almost as with the white lustre of silver, in her expression. She was right, incontestably, for what he saw in her face was the truth, and strangely, without consequence, while their talk of it as dreadful was still in the air, she appeared to present it as inordinately soft. This, prompting bewilderment, made him but gape the more gratefully for her revelation, so that they continued for some minutes silent, her face shining at him, her contact imponderably pressing, and his stare all kind, but all expectant. The end, none the less, was that what he had expected failed to sound. Something else took place instead, which seemed to consist at first in the mere closing of her eyes. She gave way at the same instant to a slow, fine shudder, and though he remained staring—though he stared, in fact, but the harder—she turned off and regained her chair. It was the end of what she had been intending, but it left him thinking only of that.

"Well, you don't say—?"

She had touched in her passage a bell near the chimney and had sunk back, strangely pale. "I'm afraid I'm too ill."

"Too ill to tell me?" It sprang up sharp to him, and almost to his lips, the fear that she would die without giving him light. He checked himself in time from so expressing his question, but she answered as if she had heard the words.

"Don't you know—now?"

"'Now'—?" She had spoken as if something that had made a difference had come up within the moment. But her maid, quickly obedient to her bell, was already with them. "I know nothing." And he was afterwards to say to himself that he must have spoken with odious impatience, such an impatience as to show that, supremely disconcerted, he washed his hands of the whole question.

"Oh!" said May Bartram.

"Are you in pain?" he asked, as the woman went to her.

"No," said May Bartram.

Her maid, who had put an arm round her as if to take her to her room, fixed on him eyes that appealingly contradicted her; in spite of which, however, he showed once more his mystification. "What then has happened?"

She was once more, with her companion's help, on her feet, and, feeling withdrawal imposed on him, he had found, blankly, his hat and gloves and had reached the door. Yet he waited for her answer. "What *was* to," she said.

He came back the next day, but she was then unable to see him, and as it was literally the first time this had occurred in the long stretch of their acquaintance he turned away, defeated and sore, almost angry—or feeling at least that such a break in their custom was really the beginning of the end—

and wandered alone with his thoughts, especially with one of them that he was unable to keep down. She was dying, and he would lose her; she was dying, and his life would end. He stopped in the park, into which he had passed, and stared before him at his recurrent doubt. Away from her the doubt pressed again; in her presence he had believed her, but as he felt his forlornness he threw himself into the explanation that, nearest at hand, had most of a miserable warmth for him and least of a cold torment. She had deceived him to save him—to put him off with something in which he should be able to rest. What could the thing that was to happen to him be, after all, but just this thing that had begun to happen? Her dying, her death, his consequent solitude—*that* was what he had figured as the beast in the jungle, that was what had been in the lap of the gods. He had had her word for it as he left her; for what else, on earth, could she have meant? It wasn't a thing of a monstrous order; not a fate rare and distinguished; not a stroke of fortune that overwhelmed and immortalized; it had only the stamp of the common doom. But, poor Marcher, at this hour, judged the common doom sufficient. It would serve his turn, and even as the consummation of infinite waiting he would bend his pride to accept it. He sat down on a bench in the twilight. He hadn't been a fool. Something had *been*, as she had said, to come. Before he rose indeed it had quite struck him that the final fact really matched with the long avenue through which he had had to reach it. As sharing his suspense, and as giving herself all, giving her life, to bring it to an end, she had come with him every step of the way. He had lived by her aid, and to leave her behind would be cruelly, damnably to miss her. What could be more overwhelming than that?

Well, he was to know within the week, for though she kept him a while at bay, left him restless and wretched during a series of days on each of which he asked about her only again to have to turn away, she ended his trial by receiving him where she had always received him. Yet she had been brought out at some hazard into the presence of so many of the things that were consciously, vainly, half their past, and there was scant service left in the gentleness of her mere desire, all too visible, to check his obsession and wind up his long trouble. That was clearly what she wanted; the one thing more, for her own peace, while she could still put out her hand. He was so affected by her state that, once seated by her chair, he was moved to let everything go; it was she herself therefore who brought him back, took up again, before she dismissed him, her last word of the other time. She showed how she wished to leave their affair in order. "I'm not sure you understood. You've nothing to wait for more. It *has* come."

Oh, how he looked at her! "Really?"

"Really."

"The thing that, as you said, *was* to?"

"The thing that we began in our youth to watch for."

Face to face with her once more he believed her; it was a claim to which he had so abjectly little to oppose. "You mean that it has come as a positive, definite occurrence, with a name and a date?"

"Positive. Definite. I don't know about the 'name,' but, oh, with a date!"

He found himself again too helplessly at sea. "But come in the night—come and passed me by?"

May Bartram had her strange, faint smile. "Oh no, it hasn't passed you by!"

"But if I haven't been aware of it, and it hasn't touched me—?"

"Ah, your not being aware of it," and she seemed to hesitate an instant to deal with this—"your not being aware of it is the strangeness *in* the strangeness. It's the wonder *of* the wonder." She spoke as with the softness almost of a sick child, yet now at last, at the end of all, with the perfect straightness of a sibyl. She visibly knew that she knew, and the effect on him was of something co-ordinate, in its high character, with the law that had ruled him. It was the true voice of the law; so on her lips would the law itself have sounded. "It *has* touched you," she went on. "It has done its office. It has made you all its own."

"So utterly without my knowing it?"

"So utterly without your knowing it." His hand as he leaned to her, was on the arm of her chair, and, dimly smiling always now, she placed her own on it. "It's enough if *I* know it."

"Oh!" he confusedly sounded, as she herself of late so often had done.

"What I long ago said is true. You'll never know now, and I think you ought to be content. You've *had* it," said May Bartram.

"But had what?"

"Why, what was to have marked you out. The proof of your law. It has acted. I'm too glad," she then bravely added, "to have been able to see what it's *not*."

He continued to attach his eyes to her, and with the sense that it was all beyond him, and that *she* was too, he would still have sharply challenged her, had he not felt it an abuse of her weakness to do more than take devoutly what she gave him, take it as hushed as to a revelation. If he did speak, it was out of the foreknowledge of his loneliness to come. "If you're glad of what it's 'not,' it might then have been worse?"

She turned her eyes away, she looked straight before her with which, after a moment: "Well, you know our fears."

He wondered. "It's something then we never feared?"

On this, slowly, she turned to him. "Did we ever dream, with all our dreams, that we should sit and talk of it thus?"

He tried for a little to make out if they had; but it was as if their dreams, numberless enough, were in solution in some thick, cold mist, in which thought lost itself. "It might have been that we couldn't talk?"

"Well"—she did her best for him—"not from this side. This, you see," she said, "is the *other* side."

"I think," poor Marcher returned, "that all sides are the same to me." Then, however, as she softly shook her head in correction: "We mightn't, as it were, have got across—?"

"To where we are—no. We're *here*"—she made her weak emphasis.

"And much good does it do us!" was her friend's frank comment.

"It does us the good it can. It does us the good that *it* isn't here. It's past. It's behind," said May Bartram. "Before—" but her voice dropped.

He had got up, not to tire her, but it was hard to combat his yearning. She after all told him nothing but that his light had failed—which he knew well enough without her. "Before—?" he blankly echoed.

"Before, you see, it was always to *come*. That kept it present."

"Oh, I don't care what comes now! Besides," Marcher added, "it seems to me I liked it better present, as you say, than I can like it absent with *your* absence."

"Oh, mine!"—and her pale hands made light of it.

"With the absence of everything." He had a dreadful sense of standing there before her for—so far as anything but this proved, this bottomless drop was concerned—the last time of their life. It rested on him with a weight he felt he could scarce bear, and this weight it apparently was that still pressed out what remained in him of speakable protest. "I believe you; but I can't begin to pretend I understand. *Nothing*, for me, is past; nothing *will* pass until I pass myself, which I pray my stars may be as soon as possible. Say, however," he added, "that I've eaten my cake, as you contend, to the last crumb—how can the thing I've never felt at all be the thing I was marked out to feel?"

She met him, perhaps, less directly, but she met him unperturbed. "You take your 'feelings' for granted. You were to suffer your fate. That was not necessarily to know it."

"How in the world—when what is such knowledge but suffering?"

She looked up at him a while, in silence. "No—you don't understand."

"I suffer," said John Marcher.

"Don't, don't!"

"How can I help at least *that*?"

"*Don't!*" May Bartram repeated.

She spoke it in a tone so special, in spite of her weakness, that he stared an instant—stared as if some light, hitherto hidden, had shimmered across his vision. Darkness again closed over it, but the gleam had already become for him an idea. "Because I haven't the right—?"

"Don't *know*—when you needn't," she mercifully urged. "You needn't—for we shouldn't."

"Shouldn't?" If he could but know what she meant!

"No—it's too much."

"Too much?" he still asked—but with a mystification that was the next moment, of a sudden, to give way. Her words, if they meant something, affected him in this light—the light also of her wasted face—as meaning *all*, and the sense of what knowledge had been for herself came over him with a rush which broke through into a question. "Is it of that, then, you're dying?"

She but watched him, gravely at first, as if to see, with this, where he was, and she might have seen something, or feared something, that moved her sympathy. "I would live for you still—if I could." Her eyes closed for a little, as if, withdrawn into herself, she were, for a last time, trying. "But I can't!" she said as she raised them again to take leave of him.

She couldn't indeed, as but too promptly and sharply appeared, and he had no vision of her after this that was anything but darkness and doom. They had parted forever in that strange talk; access to her chamber of pain, rigidly guarded, was almost wholly forbidden him; he was feeling now moreover, in the face of doctors, nurses, the two or three relatives attracted doubtless by the presumption of what she had to "leave," how few were the rights, as they were called in such cases, that he had to put forward, and how odd it might even seem that their intimacy shouldn't have given him more of them. The stupidest fourth cousin had more, even though she had been nothing in such a person's life. She had been a feature of features in *his*, for what else was it to have been so indispensable? Strange beyond saying were the ways of existence, baffling for him the anomaly of his lack, as he felt it to be, of producible claim. A woman might have been, as it were, everything to him, and it might yet present him in no connection that anyone appeared obliged to recognise. If this was the case in these closing weeks it was the case more sharply on the occasion of the last offices rendered, in the great grey London cemetery, to what had been mortal, to what had been precious, in his friend. The concourse at her grave was not numerous, but he saw himself treated as scarce more nearly concerned with it than if there had been a thousand others. He was in short from this moment face to face with the fact that he was to profit extraordinarily little by the interest May Bartram had taken in him. He couldn't quite have said what he expected, but he had somehow not expected this approach to a double privation. Not only had her interest failed him, but he seemed to feel himself unattended—and for a reason he couldn't sound—by the distinction, the dignity, the propriety, if nothing else, of the man markedly bereaved. It was as if, in the view of society, he had not *been* markedly bereaved, as if there still failed some sign or proof of it, and as if, none the less, his character could never be affirmed, nor the deficiency ever made up. There were moments, as the weeks went by, when he would have liked, by some almost aggressive act, to take his stand on the intimacy of his loss, in order that it *might* be questioned and his retort, to the relief of his spirit, so recorded; but the moments of an irritation more helpless followed fast on these, the moments during which, turning things over with a good conscience but with a bare horizon, he found himself wondering if he oughtn't to have begun, so to speak, further back.

He found himself wondering indeed at many things, and this last speculation had others to keep it company. What could he have done, after all, in her lifetime, without giving them both, as it were, away? He couldn't have made it known she was watching him, for that would have published the superstition of the Beast. This was what closed his mouth now—now that the Jungle had been threshed to vacancy and that the Beast had stolen away. It sounded too foolish and too flat; the difference for him in this particular, the extinction in his life of the element of suspense, was such in fact as to surprise him. He could scarce have said what the effect resembled; the abrupt cessation, the positive prohibition, of music perhaps, more than anything else, in some place all adjusted and all accustomed to sonority and to attention. If he could at any rate have conceived lifting the veil from his image at some moment of the past (what had he done, after all, if not lift it to *her*?), so to do this to-day, to talk to people at large of the jungle cleared and confide to them that he now felt it as safe, would have been not only to see them listen as to a goodwife's tale, but really to hear himself tell one. What it presently came to in truth was that poor Marcher waded through his beaten grass, where no life stirred, where no breath sounded, where no evil eye seemed to gleam from a possible lair, very much as if vaguely looking for the Beast, and still more as if missing it. He walked about in an existence that had grown strangely more spacious, and, stopping fitfully in places where the undergrowth of life struck him as closer, asked himself yearningly, wondered secretly and sorely, if it would have lurked here or there. It would have at all events *sprung;* what was at least complete was his belief in the truth itself of the assurance given him. The change from his old sense to his new was absolute and final: what was to happen *had* so absolutely and finally happened that he was as little able to know a fear for his future as to know a hope; so absent in short was any question of anything still to come. He was to live entirely with the other question, that of his unidentified past, that of his having to see his fortune impenetrably snuffled and masked.

The torment of this vision became then his occupation; he couldn't perhaps have consented to live but for the possibility of guessing. She had told him, his friend, not to guess; she had forbidden him, so far as he might, to know, and she had even in a sort denied the power in him to learn: which were so many things, precisely, to deprive him of rest. It wasn't that he wanted, he argued for fairness, that anything that had happened to him should happen over again; it was only that he shouldn't, as an anticlimax, have been taken sleeping so sound as not to be able to win back by an effort of thought the lost stuff of consciousness. He declared to himself at moments that he would either win it back or have done with consciousness for ever; he made this idea his one motive, in fine, made it so much his passion that none other, to compare with it, seemed ever to have touched him. The lost stuff of consciousness became thus for him as a strayed or stolen child to an unappeasable father; he hunted it up and down very much as if he were knocking at doors and inquiring of the police. This was the spirit in which, inevitably, he set himself to travel; he started on a journey that was to be as long as he could make it; it danced before him that, as the other side of the globe couldn't possibly have less to say to him, it might, by a possibility of suggestion, have more. Before he quitted London, however, he made a pilgrimmage to May Bartram's grave, took his way to it through the endless avenues of the grim suburban necropolis, sought it out in the wilderness of tombs, and, though he had come but for the renewal of the act of farewell, found himself, when he had at last stood by it, beguiled into long intensities. He stood for an hour, powerless to turn away and yet powerless to penetrate the darkness of death; fixing with his eyes her inscribed name and date, beating his forehead against the fact of the secret they kept, drawing his breath, while he waited as if, in pity of him, some sense would rise from the stones. He kneeled on the stones, however, in vain; they kept what they concealed; and if the face of the tomb did become a face for him it was because her two names were like a pair of eyes that didn't know him. He gave them a last long look, but no palest light broke.

He stayed away, after this, for a year; he visited the depths of Asia, spending himself on scenes of romantic interest, of superlative sanctity; but what was present to him everywhere was that for a man who had known what *he* had known the world was vulgar and vain. The state of mind in which he had lived for so many years shone out to him, in reflection, as a light that coloured and refined, a light beside which the glow of the East was garish, cheap and thin. The terrible truth was that he had lost—with everything else—a distinction as well; the things he saw couldn't help being common when he had become common to look at them. He was simply now one of them himself—he was in the dust, without a peg for the sense of difference; and there were hours when, before the temples of gods and the sepulchres of kings, his spirit turned, for nobleness of association, to the barely discriminated slab in the London suburb. That had become for him, and more intensely with time and distance, his one witness of a past glory. It was all that was left to him for proof or pride, yet the past glories of Pharaohs were nothing to him as he thought of it. Small wonder then that he came back to it on the morrow of his return. He was drawn there this time as irresistibly as the other, yet with a confidence, almost, that was doubtless the effect of the many months that had elapsed. He had lived, in spite of himself, into his change of feeling, and in wandering over the earth had wandered, as might be said, from the circumference to the centre of his desert. He had settled to his safety and accepted perforce his extinction; figuring to himself, with some colour, in the likeness of certain little old men he remembered to have seen, of whom, all meagre and wizened as they might look, it was related that they had in their time fought twenty duels or been loved by ten princesses. They indeed had been wondrous for others, while he was but wondrous for himself; which, however, was exactly the cause of his haste to renew the wonder by getting back, as he might put it, into his own presence. That had quickened his steps and checked his delay. If his visit was prompt it was because he had been separated so long from the part of himself that alone he now valued.

It is accordingly not false to say that he reached his goal with a certain elation and stood there again with a certain assurance. The creature beneath the sod *knew* of his rare experience, so that, strangely now, the place had lost for him its mere blankness of expression. It met him in mildness—not, as before, in mockery; it wore for him the air of conscious greeting that we find, after absence, in things that have closely belonged to us and which seem to confess of themselves to the connection. The plot of ground, the graven tablet, the tended flowers affected him so as belonging to him that he quite felt for the hour like a contented landlord reviewing a piece of property. Whatever had happened—well, had happened. He had not come back this time with the vanity of that question, his former worrying, "What, *what*?" now practically so spent. Yet he would, none the less, never again so cut himself off from the spot; he would come back to it every month, for if he did nothing else by its aid he at least held up his head. It thus grew for him, in the oddest way, a positive resource; he carried out his idea of periodical returns, which took their place at last among the most inveterate of his habits. What it all amounted to, oddly enough, was that, in his now so simplified world, this garden of death gave him the few square feet of earth on which he could still most live. It was as if, being nothing anywhere else for anyone, nothing even for himself, he were just everything here, and if not for a crowd of witnesses, or indeed for any witness but John Marcher, then by clear right of the register that he could scan like an open page. The open page was the tomb of his friend, and *there* were the facts of the past, there the truth of his life, there the backward reaches in which he could lose himself. He did this, from time to time, with such effect that he seemed to wander through the old years with his hand in the arm of a companion who was, in the most extraordinary manner, his other, his younger self; and to wander, which was more extraordinary yet, round and round a third presence—not wandering she, but stationary, still, whose eyes, turning with his revolution, never ceased to follow him and whose seat was his point, so to speak, of orientation. Thus in short he settled to live—feeding only on the sense that he once *had* lived, and dependent on it not only for a support but for an identity.

It sufficed him, in its way, for months, and the year elapsed; it would doubtless even have carried him further but for an accident, superficially slight, which moved him, in a quite other direction, with a force beyond any of his impressions of Egypt or of India. It was a thing of the merest chance—the turn, as he afterwards felt, of a hair, though he was indeed to live to believe that if light hadn't come to him in this particular fashion it would still have come in another. He was to live to believe this, I say, though he was not to live, I may not less definitely mention, to do much else. We allow him at any rate the benefit of the conviction, struggling up for him at the end, that, whatever might have happened or not happened, he would have come round of himself to the light. The incident of an autumn day had put the match to the train laid from of old by his misery. With the light before him he knew that even of late his ache had only been smothered. It was strangely drugged, but it throbbed; at the touch it began to bleed. And the touch, in the event, was the face of a fellow-mortal. This face, one grey afternoon when the leaves were thick in the alleys, looked into Marcher's own, at the cemetery, with an expression like the cut of a blade. He felt it, that is, so deep down that he winced at the steady thrust. The person who so mutely assaulted him was a figure he had noticed, on reaching his own goal, absorbed by a grave a short distance away, a grave apparently fresh, so that the emotion of the visitor would probably match it for frankness. This fact alone forbade further attention, though during the time he stayed he remained vaguely conscious of his neighbour, a middle-aged man apparently, in mourning, whose bowed back, among the clustered monuments and mortuary yews, was constantly presented. Marcher's theory that these were elements in contact with which he himself revived, had suffered, on this occasion, it may be granted, a sensible though inscrutable check. The autumn day was dire for him as none had recently been, and he rested with a heaviness he had not yet known on the low stone table that bore May Bartram's name. He rested without power to move, as if some spring in him, some spell vouchsafed, had suddenly been broken forever. If he could have done that moment as he wanted he would simply have stretched himself on the slab that was ready to take him, treating it as a place prepared to receive his last sleep. What in all the wide world had he now to keep awake for? He stared before him with the question, and it was then that, as one of the cemetery walks passed near him, he caught the shock of the face.

His neighbour at the other grave had withdrawn, as he himself, with force in him to move, would have done by now, and was advancing along the path on his way to one of the gates. This brought him near, and his pace was slow, so that—and all the more as there was a kind of hunger in his look—the two men were for a minute directly confronted. Marcher felt him on the spot as one of the deeply stricken—a perception so sharp that nothing else in the picture lived for it, neither his dress, his age, nor his presumable character and class; nothing lived but the deep ravage of the features that he showed. He *showed* them—that was the point; he was moved, as he passed, by some impulse that was either a signal for sympathy or, more possibly, a challenge to another sorrow. He might already have been aware of our friend, might, at some previous hour, have noticed in him the smooth habit of the scene, with which the state of his own senses so scantly consorted, and might thereby have been stirred as by a kind of overt discord. What Marcher was at all events conscious of was, in the first place, that the image of scarred passion presented to him was conscious too—of something that profaned the air; and, in the second, that, roused, startled, shocked, he was yet the next moment looking after it, as it went, with envy. The most extraordinary thing that had happened to him—though he had given that name to other matters as well—took place, after his immediate vague stare, as a consequence of this impression. The stranger passed, but the raw glare of his grief remained, making our friend wonder in pity what wrong, what wound it expressed, what injury not to be healed. What had the man *had* to make him, by the loss of it, so bleed and yet live?

Something—and this reached him with a pang—that *he*, John Marcher, hadn't; the proof of which was precisely John Marcher's arid end. No passion had ever touched him, for this was what passion meant; he had survived and maundered and pined, but where had been *his* deep ravage? The extraordinary thing we speak of was the sudden rush of the result of this question. The sight that had just met his eyes named to him, as in letters of quick flame, something he had utterly, insanely missed, and what he had missed made these things a train of fire, made them mark themselves in an anguish of inward throbs. He had seen *outside* of his life, not learned it within, the way a woman was mourned when she had been loved for herself; such was the force of his conviction of the meaning of the stranger's face, which still flared for him like a smoky torch. It had not come to him, the knowledge, on the wings of experience; it had brushed him, jostled him, upset him, with the disrespect of chance, the insolence of an accident. Now that the illumination had begun, however, it blazed to the zenith, and what he presently stood there gazing at was the sounded void of his life. He gazed, he drew breath, in pain; he turned in his dismay, and, turning, he had before him in sharper incision than ever the open page of his story. The name on the table smote him as the passage of his neighbour had done, and what it said to him, full in the face, was that *she* was what he had missed. This was the awful thought, the answer to all the past, the vision at the dread clearness of which he turned as cold as the stone beneath him. Everything fell together, confessed, explained, overwhelmed; leaving him most of all stupefied at the blindness he had cherished. The fate he had been marked for he had met with a vengeance—he had emptied the cup to the lees; he had been the man of his time, *the* man, to whom nothing on earth was to have happened. That was the rare stroke—that was his visitation. So he saw it, as we say, in pale horror, while the pieces fitted and fitted. So *she* had seen it, while he didn't, and so she served at this hour to drive the truth home. It was the truth, vivid and monstrous, that all the while he had waited the wait was itself his portion. This the companion of his vigil had at a given moment perceived, and she had then offered him the chance to baffle his doom. One's doom, however, was never baffled, and on the day she had told him that his own had come down, she had seen him but stupidly stare at the escape she offered him.

The escape would have been to love her; then, *then* he would have lived. *She* had lived—who could say now with what passion?—since she had loved him for himself; whereas he had never thought of her (ah, how it hugely glared at him!) but in the chill of his egotism and the light of her use. Her spoken words came back to him, and the chain stretched and stretched. The beast had lurked indeed, and the beast, at its hour, had sprung; it had sprung in that twilight of the cold April when, pale, ill, wasted, but all beautiful, and perhaps even then recoverable, she had risen from her chair to stand before him and let him imaginably guess. It had sprung as he didn't guess; it had sprung as she hopelessly turned from him, and the mark, by the time he left her, had fallen where it *was* to fall. He had justified his fear and achieved his fate; he had failed, with the last exactitude, of all he was to fail of; and a moan now rose to his lips as he remembered she had prayed he mightn't know. This horror of waking—*this* was knowledge, knowledge under the breath of which the very tears in his eyes seemed to freeze. Through them, none the less, he tried to fix it and hold it; he kept it there before him so that he might feel the pain. That at least, belated and bitter, had something of the taste of life. But the bitterness suddenly sickened him, and it was as if, horribly, he saw, in the truth, in the cruelty of his image, what had been appointed and done. He saw the Jungle of his life and saw the lurking Beast; then, while he looked, perceived it, as by a stir of the air, rise, huge and hideous, for the leap that was to settle him. His eyes darkened—it was close; and, instinctively turning, in his hallucination, to avoid it, he flung himself, on his face, on the tomb.

from

IN GOD WE TRUST: ALL OTHERS PAY CASH

JEAN SHEPHERD

At its most fundamental, coming awake is an act of profound self-knowledge. Though the painful little anecdote of teenage embarrassment Jean Shepherd recounts here does not include any visions of the Godhead or singing Angels, it surely transformed him.

Mewling, puking babes. That's the way we all start. Damply clinging to someone's shoulder, burping weakly, clawing our way into life. *All* of us. Then gradually, surely, we begin to divide into two streams, all marching together up that long yellow brick road of life, but on opposite sides of the street. One crowd goes on to become the Official people, peering out at us from television screens; magazine covers. They are forever appearing in newsreels, carrying attaché cases, surrounded by banks of microphones while the world waits for their decisions and statements. And the rest of us go on to become . . . just us.

They are the Prime Ministers, the Presidents, Cabinet members, Stars, dynamic molders of the Universe, while we remain forever the onlookers, the applauders of their real lives.

Forever down in the dark dungeons of our souls we ask ourselves:

"How did they get away from me? When did I make that first misstep that took me forever to the wrong side of the street, to become eternally part of the accursed, anonymous Audience?"

It seems like one minute we're all playing around back of the garage, kicking tin cans and yelling at girls, and the next instant you find yourself doomed to exist as an office boy in the Mail Room of Life, while another ex-mewling, puking babe sends down Dicta, says "No comment" to the Press, and lives a real, genuine *Life* on the screen of the world.

Countless sufferers at this hour are spending billions of dollars and endless man hours lying on analysts' couches, trying to pinpoint the exact moment that they stepped off the track and into the bushes forever.

It all hinges on one sinister reality that is rarely mentioned, no doubt due to its implacable, irreversible inevitability. These decisions cannot be changed, no matter how many brightly cheerful, buoyantly optimistic books on HOW TO ACHIEVE A RICHER, FULLER, MORE BOUNTIFUL LIFE or SEVEN MAGIC GOLDEN KEYS TO INSTANT DYNAMIC SUCCESS or THE SECRET OF HOW TO BECOME A BILLIONAIRE we read, or how many classes are attended for instruction in handshaking, back-slapping, grinning, and making After-Dinner speeches. Joseph Stalin was not a Dale Carnegie graduate. He went all the way. It is an unpleasant truth that is swallowed, if at all, like a rancid, bitter pill. A star is a star; a numberless cipher is a numberless cipher.

Even more eerie a fact is that the Great Divide is rarely a matter of talent or personality. Or even luck. Adolf Hitler had a notoriously weak handshake. His smile was, if anything, a vapid mockery. But inevitably his star zoomed higher and higher. Cinema luminaries of the first order are rarely blessed with even the modicum of Talent, and often their physical beauty leaves much to be desired. What is the difference between Us and

Them, We and They, the Big Ones and the great, teeming rabble?

There are about four times in a man's life, or a woman's, too, for that matter, when unexpectedly, from out of the darkness, the blazing carbon lamp, the cosmic searchlight of Truth shines full upon them. It is how we react to those moments that forever seals our fate. One crowd simply puts on its sunglasses, lights another cigar, and heads for the nearest plush French restaurant in the jazziest section of town, sits down and orders a drink, and ignores the whole thing. While we, the Doomed, caught in the brilliant glare of illumination, see ourselves inescapably for what we are, and from that day on sulk in the weeds, hoping no one else will spot us.

Those moments happen when we are least able to fend them off. I caught the first one full in the face when I was fourteen. The fourteenth summer is a magic one for all kids. You have just slid out of the pupa stage, leaving your old baby skin behind, and have not yet become a grizzled, hardened, tax-paying beetle. At fourteen you are made of cellophane. You curl easily and everyone can see through you.

When I was fourteen, Life was flowing through me in a deep, rich torrent of Castoria. How did I know that the first rocks were just ahead, and I was about to have my keel ripped out on the reef? Sometimes you feel as though you are alone in a rented rowboat, bailing like mad in the darkness with a leaky bailing can. It is important to know that there are at least two billion other ciphers in the same boat, bailing with the same leaky can. They all think they are alone and are crossed with an evil star. They are right.

I'm fourteen years old, in my sophomore year at high school. One day Schwartz, my purported best friend, sidled up to me edgily outside of school while we were waiting on the steps to come in after lunch. He proceeded to outline his plan:

"Helen's old man won't let me take her out on a date on Saturday night unless I get a date for her girlfriend. A double date. The old coot figures, I guess, that if there are four of us there won't be no monkey business. Well, how about it? Do you want to go on a blind date with this chick? I never seen her."

Well. For years I had this principle—absolutely *no* blind dates. I was a man of perception and taste, and life was short. But there is a time in your life when you have to stop taking and begin to give just a little. For the first time the warmth of sweet Human Charity brought the roses to my cheeks. After all, Schwartz was my friend. It was little enough to do, have a blind date with some no doubt skinny, pimply girl for your best friend. I would do it for Schwartz. He would do as much for me.

"Okay. Okay, Schwartz."

Then followed the usual ribald remarks, feckless boasting, and dirty jokes about dates in general and girls in particular. It was decided that next Saturday we would go all the way. I had a morning paper route at the time, and my life savings stood at about $1.80. I was all set to blow it on one big night.

I will never forget that particular Saturday as long as I live. The air was as soft as the finest of spun silk. The scent of lilacs hung heavy. The catalpa trees rustled in the early evening breeze from off the Lake. The inner Me itched in that nameless way, that indescribable way that only the fourteen-year-old Male fully knows.

All that afternoon I had carefully gone over my wardrobe to select the proper symphony of sartorial brilliance. That night I set out wearing my magnificent electric blue sport coat, whose shoulders were so wide that they hung out over my frame like vast, drooping eaves, so wide I had difficulty going through an ordinary door head-on. The electric blue sport coat that draped voluminously almost to my knees, its wide lapels flapping soundlessly in the slightest breeze. My pleated gray flannel slacks began just below my breastbone and indeed chafed my armpits. High-belted, cascading down finally to grasp my ankles in a vise-like grip. My tie, indeed one of my most prized possessions, had been a gift from my Aunt Glenn upon the state occasion of graduation from eighth grade. It was of a beautiful silky fabric, silvery pearly colored, four inches wide at the fulcrum, and of such a length to endanger occasionally my zipper in moments of haste. Hand-painted upon it was a magnificent blood-red snail.

I had spent fully two hours carefully arranging and rearranging my great mop of wavy hair, into which I had rubbed fully a pound and a half of Greasy Kid Stuff.

Helen and Schwartz waited on the corner under the streetlight at the streetcar stop near Junie Jo's home. Her name was Junie Jo Prewitt. I won't forget it quickly, although she has, no doubt, forgotten mine. I walked down the dark street alone, past houses set back off the street, through the darkness, past privet hedges, under elm trees, through air rich and ripe with promise. Her house stood back from the street even farther than the others. It sort of crouched in the darkness, looking out at me, kneeling. Pregnant with Girldom. A real Girlfriend house.

The first faint touch of nervousness filtered through the marrow of my skullbone as I knocked on the door of the screen-enclosed porch. No answer. I knocked again, louder. Through the murky screens I could see faint lights in the house itself. Still no answer. Then I found a small doorbell button buried in the sash. I pressed. From far off in the bowels of the house I heard two chimes "Bong" politely. It sure didn't sound like our doorbell. We had a real ripper that went off like a broken buzz saw, more of a BRRRAAAAKKK than a muffled Bong. This was a rich people's doorbell.

The door opened and there stood a real, genuine, gold-plated Father: potbelly, underwear shirt, suspenders, and all.

"Well?" he asked.

For one blinding moment of embarrassment I couldn't remember her name. After all, she was a blind date. I couldn't just say:

"I'm here to pick up some girl."

He turned back into the house and hollered:

"JUNIE JO! SOME KID'S HERE!"

"Heh, heh . . . ." I countered.

He led me into the living room. It was an itchy house, sticky stucco walls of a dull orange color, and all over the floor this Oriental rug with the design crawling around, making loops and sworls. I sat on an overstuffed chair covered in stiff green mohair that scratched even through my slacks. Little twisty bridge lamps stood everywhere. I instantly began to sweat down the back of my clean white shirt. Like I said, it was a very itchy house. It had little lamps sticking out of the walls that looked like phony candles, with phony glass orange flames. The rug started moaning to itself.

I sat on the edge of the chair and tried to talk to this Father. He was a Cub fan. We struggled under water for what seemed like an hour and a half, when suddenly I heard someone coming down the stairs. First the feet; then those legs, and there she was. She was magnificent! The greatest-looking girl I ever saw in my life! I have hit the double jackpot! And on a blind date! Great Scot!

My senses actually reeled as I clutched the arm of that bilge-green chair for support. Junie Jo Prewitt made Cleopatra look like a Girl Scout!

Five minutes later we are sitting in the streetcar, heading toward the bowling alley. I am sitting next to the most fantastic creation in the Feminine department known to Western man. There are the four of us in that long, yellow-lit streetcar. No one else was aboard; just us four. I, naturally, being a trained gentleman, sat on the aisle to protect her from candy wrappers and cigar butts and such. Directly ahead of me, also on the aisle, sat Schwartz, his arm already flung affectionately is a death grip around Helen's neck as we boomed and rattled through the night.

I casually flung my right foot up onto my left knee so that she could see my crepe-soled, perforated, wing-toed, Scotch bluchers with the two-toned laces. I started to work my famous charm on her. Casually, with my practiced offhand, cynical, cutting, sardonic humor I told her about how my Old Man had cracked the block in the Oldsmobile, how the White Sox were going to have a good year this year, how my kid brother wet his pants when he saw a snake, how I figured it was going to rain, what a great guy Schwartz was, what a good second baseman I was, how I figured I might go out for football. On and on I rolled, like Old Man River, pausing significantly for her to pick up the conversation. Nothing.

Ahead of us Schwartz and Helen were almost indistinguishable one from the other. They giggled, bit each other's ears, whispered, clasped hands, and in general made me itch even more.

From time to time Junie Jo would bend forward stiffly from the waist and say something I could never quite catch into Helen's right ear.

I told her my great story of the time that Uncle Carl lost his false teeth down the airshaft. Still nothing. Out of the corner of my eye I could see that she had her coat collar turned up, hiding most of her face as she sat silently, looking forward past Helen Weathers into nothingness.

I told her about this old lady on my paper route who chews tobacco, and roller skates in the backyard every morning. I still couldn't get through to her. Casually I inched my right arm up over the back of the seat behind her shoulders. The acid test. She leaned forward, avoiding my arm, and stayed that way.

"Heh, heh, heh . . . ."

As nonchalantly as I could, I retrieved it, battling a giant cramp in my right shoulder blade. I sat in silence for a few seconds, sweating heavily as ahead Schwartz and Helen are going at it hot and heavy.

It was then that I became aware of someone saying something to me. It was an empty car. There was no one else but us. I glanced around, and there it was. Above us a line of car cards looked down on the empty streetcar. One was speaking directly to me, to me alone.

DO YOU OFFEND?

Do I *offend?!*

With no warning, from up near the front of the car where the motorman is steering I see this thing coming down the aisle directly toward *me.* It's coming closer and closer. I can't escape it. It's this blinding, fantastic, brilliant, screaming blue light. I am spread-eagled in it. There's a pin sticking through my thorax. I see it all now.

I AM THE BLIND DATE!

ME!!

I'M the one they're being nice to!

I'm suddenly getting fatter, more itchy. My new shoes are like bowling balls with laces; thick, rubber-crepe bowling balls. My great tie that Aunt Glenn gave me is two feet wide, hanging down to the floor like some crinkly tinfoil noose. My beautiful hand-painted snail is seven feet high, sitting up on my shoulder, burping. Great Scot! It is all clear to me in the searing white light of Truth. My friend Schwartz, I can see him saying to Junie Jo:

"I got this crummy fat friend who never has a date. Let's give him a break and . . . ."

I AM THE BLIND DATE!

They are being nice to *me!* She is the one who is out on a Blind Date. A Blind Date that didn't make it.

In the seat ahead, the merriment rose to a crescendo. Helen tittered; Schwartz cackled. The marble statue next to me stared gloomily out into the darkness as our streetcar rattled on. The ride went on and on.

I AM THE BLIND DATE!

I didn't say much the rest of the night. There wasn't much to be said.

THE POT OF GOLD

JOHN CHEEVER

The search for success and meaning is what drives most of us through our travels on this earth, and as unlucky as Ralph Whittemore may seem, he is lucky for finally finding it in the one place we never seem to look.

You could not say fairly of Ralph and Laura Whittemore that they had the failings and the characteristics of incorrigible treasure hunters, but you could say truthfully of them that the shimmer and the smell, the peculiar force of money, the promise of it, had an untoward influence on their lives. They were always at the threshold of fortune; they always seemed to have something on the fire. Ralph was a fair young man with a tireless commercial imagination and an evangelical credence in the romance and sorcery of business success, and although he held an obscure job with a clothing manufacturer, this never seemed to him anything more than a point of departure.

The Whittemores were not importunate or overbearing people, and they had an uncompromising loyalty to the gentle manners of the middle class. Laura was a pleasant girl of no particular beauty who had come to New York from Wisconsin at about the same time that Ralph had reached the city from Illinois, but it had taken two years of comings and goings before they had been brought together, late one afternoon, in the lobby of a lower Fifth Avenue office building. So true was Ralph's heart, so well did it serve him then, that the moment he saw Laura's light hair and her pretty and sullen face he was enraptured. He followed her out of the lobby, pushing his way through the crowd, and since she had dropped nothing, since there was no legitimate excuse to speak to her, he shouted after her, *"Louise! Louise! Louise!"* and the urgency in his voice made her stop. He said he'd made a mistake. He said he was sorry. He said she looked just like a girl named Louise Hatcher. It was a January night and the dark air tasted of smoke, and because she was a sensible and a lonely girl, she let him buy her a drink.

This was in the thirties, and their courtship was hasty. They were married three months later. Laura moved her belongings into a walk-up on Madison Avenue, above a pants presser's and a florist's, where Ralph was living. She worked as a secretary, and her salary, added to what he brought home from the clothing business, was little more than enough to keep them going, but they never seemed touched by the monotony of a saving and gainless life. They ate dinners in drugstores. She hung a reproduction of van Gogh's "Sunflowers" above the sofa she had bought with some of the small sum of money her parents had left her. When their aunts and uncles came to town—their parents were dead—they had dinner at the Ritz and went to the theatre. She sewed curtains and shined his shoes, and on Sundays they stayed in bed until noon. They seemed to be standing at the threshold of plenty; and Laura often told people that she was terribly excited because of this wonderful job that Ralph had lined up.

In the first year of their marriage, Ralph worked nights on a plan that promised him a well-paying job in Texas, but through no fault of his own this promise was never realized. There was an opening in Syracuse a year later, but an older man was decided upon. There were many other profitable but elusive openings and projects between these two. In the third year of their marriage, a firm that was almost identical in size and character with the firm Ralph worked for underwent a change of ownership, and Ralph was approached and asked if he would be interested in joining the overhauled firm. His own job promised only meager security after a series of slow promotions and he was glad of the chance to escape. He met the new owners, and their enthusiasm for him seemed intense. They were prepared to put him in charge of a department and pay him twice what he was getting then. The arrangement was to remain tacit for a month or two, until the new owners had secured their position, but they shook hands warmly and had a drink on the deal, and that night Ralph took Laura out to dinner at an expensive restaurant.

They decided, across the table, to look for a larger apartment, to have a child, and to buy a secondhand car. They faced their good fortune with perfect calm, for it was what they had expected all along. The city seemed to them a generous place, where people were rewarded either by a sudden and deserved development like this or by the capricious bounty of lawsuits, eccentric and peripheral business ventures, unexpected legacies, and other windfalls. After dinner, they walked in Central Park in the moonlight while Ralph smoked a cigar. Later, when Laura had fallen asleep, he sat in the open bedroom window in his pajamas.

The peculiar excitement with which the air of the city seems charged after midnight, when its life falls into the hands of watchmen and drunks, had always pleased him. He knew intimately the sounds of the night street: the bus brakes, the remote sirens, and the sound of water turning high in the air—the sound of water turning a mill wheel—the sum, he supposed, of many echoes, although, often as he had heard the sound, he had never decided on its source. Now he heard all this more keenly because the night seemed to him portentous.

He was twenty-eight years old; poverty and youth were inseparable in his experience, and one was ending with the other. The life they were about to leave had not been hard, and he thought with sentiment of the soiled tablecloth in the Italian restaurant where they usually went for their celebrations, and the high spirits with which Laura on a wet night ran from the subway to the bus stop. But they were drawing away from all this. Shirt sales in department-store basements, lines at meat counters, weak drinks, the roses he brought her up from the subway in the spring, when roses were cheap—these were all unmistakably the souvenirs of the poor, and while they seemed to him good and gentle, he was glad that they would soon be memories.

Laura resigned from her job when she got pregnant. The reorganization and Ralph's new position hung fire, but the Whittemores talked about it freely when they were with friends. "We're *terribly* pleased with the way things are going," Laura would say. "All we need is patience." There were many delays and postponements, and they waited with the patience of people expecting justice. The time came when they both needed clothes, and one evening Ralph suggested that they spend some of the money they had put aside. Laura refused. When he brought up the subject, she didn't answer him and seemed not to hear him. He raised his voice and lost his temper. He shouted. She cried. He thought of all the other girls he could have married—the dark blonde, the worshipful Cuban, the rich and pretty one with a cast in her right eye. All his desires seemed to lie outside the small apartment Laura had arranged. They were still not speaking in the morning, and in order to strengthen his position he telephoned his potential employers. Their secretary told him they were both out. This made him apprehensive. He called several times from the telephone booth in the lobby of the building he worked in and was told that they were busy, they were out, they were in conference with lawyers, or they were talking long distance. This variety of excuses frightened him. He said nothing to Laura that evening and tried to call them the next day. Late in the afternoon, after many tries, one of them came to the phone. "We gave the job to somebody else, sonny," he said. Like a saddened father, he spoke to Ralph in a hoarse and gentle voice. "Don't try and get us on the telephone any more. We've got other things to do besides answer the telephone. This other fellow seemed better suited, sonny. That's all I can tell you, and don't try to get me on the telephone any more."

Ralph walked the miles from his office to his apartment that night, hoping to free himself in this way from some of the weight of his disappointment. He was so unprepared for the shock that it affected him like vertigo, and he walked with an old, high step, as if the paving were quicksand. He stood downstairs in front of the building he lived in, trying to decide how to describe the disaster to Laura, but when he went in, he told her bluntly. "Oh, I'm sorry, darling," she said softly and kissed him. "I'm terribly sorry." She wandered away from him and began to straighten the sofa cushions. His frustration was so ardent, he was such a prisoner of his schemes and expectations, that he was astonished at the serenity with which she regarded the failure. There was nothing to worry about, she said. She still had a few hundred dollars in the bank, from the money her parents had left her. There was nothing to worry about.

When the child, a girl, was born, they named her Rachel, and a week after the delivery Laura returned to the Madison Avenue walk-up. She took all the care of the baby and continued to do the cooking and the housework.

• • •

Ralph's imagination remained resilient and fertile, but he couldn't seem to hit on a scheme that would fit into his lack of time and capital. He and Laura, like the hosts of the poor everywhere, lived a simple life. They still went to the theatre with visiting relatives and occasionally they went to parties, but Laura's only continuous contact with the bright lights that surrounded them was vicarious and came to her through a friend she made in Central Park.

She spent many afternoons on a park bench during the first years of Rachel's life. It was a tyranny and a pleasure. She resented her enchainment but enjoyed the open sky and the air. One winter afternoon, she recognized a woman she had met at a party, and a little before dark, as Laura and the other mothers were gathering their stuffed animals and preparing their children for the cold journey home, the woman came across the playground and spoke to her. She was Alice Holinshed, she said. They had met at the Galvins'. She was pretty and friendly, and walked with Laura to the edge of the Park. She had a boy of about Rachel's age. The two women met again the following day. They became friends.

Mrs. Holinshed was older than Laura, but she had a more youthful and precise beauty. Her hair and her eyes were black, her pale and perfectly oval face was delicately colored, and her voice was pure. She lighted her cigarettes with Stork Club matches and spoke of the inconvenience of living with a child in a hotel. If Laura had any regrets about her life, they were expressed in her friendship for this pretty woman, who moved so freely through expensive stores and restaurants.

It was a friendship circumscribed, with the exception of the Galvins', by the sorry and touching countryside of Central Park. The women talked principally about their husbands, and this was a game that Laura could play with an empty purse. Vaguely, boastfully, the two women discussed the irons their men had in the fire. They sat together with their children through the sooty twilights, when the city to the south burns like a Bessemer furnace, and the air smells of coal, and the wet boulders shine like slag, and the Park itself seems like a strip of woods on the edge of a coal town. Then Mrs. Holinshed would remember that she was late—she was always late for something mysterious and splendid—and the two women would walk together to the edge of the woods. This vicarious contact with comfort pleased Laura, and the pleasure would stay with her as she pushed the baby carriage over to Madison Avenue and then began to cook supper, hearing the thump of the steam iron and smelling the cleaning fluid from the pants presser's below.

One night, when Rachel was about two years old, the frustration of Ralph's search for the goat track that would let him lead his family to a realm of reasonable contentment kept him awake. He needed sleep urgently, and when this blessing eluded him, he got out of bed and sat in the dark. The charm and excitement of the street after midnight escaped him. The explosive brakes of a Madison Avenue bus made him jump. He shut the window, but the noise of traffic continued to pass through it. It seemed to him that the penetrating voice of the city had a mortal effect on the precious lives of the city's inhabitants and that it should be muffled.

He thought of a Venetian blind whose outer surfaces would be treated with a substance that would deflect or absorb sound waves. With such a blind, friends paying a call on a spring evening would not have to shout to be heard above the noise of trucks in the street below. Bedrooms could be silenced that way—bedrooms, above all, for it seemed to him then that sleep was what everyone in the city sought and only half captured. All the harried faces on the streets at dusk, when even the pretty girls talk to themselves, were looking for sleep. Night-club singers and their amiable customers, the people waiting for taxis in front of the Waldorf on a wet night, policemen, cashiers, window washers—sleep eluded them all.

He talked over this Venetian blind with Laura the following night, and the idea seemed sensible to her. He bought a blind that would fit their bedroom window, and experimented with various paint mixtures. At last he stumbled on one that dried to the consistency of felt and was porous. The paint had a sickening smell, which filled their apartment during the four days it took him to coat and recoat the outer surface of the slats. When the paint had dried, he hung the blind, and they opened the window for a test. Silence—a relative silence—charmed their ears. He wrote down his formula, and took it during his lunch hour to a patent attorney. It took the lawyer several weeks to discover that a similar formula had been patented some years earlier. The patent owner—a man named Fellows—had a New York address, and the lawyer suggested that Ralph get in touch with him and try to reach some agreement.

The search for Mr. Fellows began one evening when Ralph had finished work, and took him first to the attic of a Hudson Street rooming house, where the landlady showed Ralph a pair of socks that Mr. Fellows had left behind when he moved out. Ralph went south from there to another rooming house and then west to the neighborhood of ship chandlers and marine boarding houses. The nocturnal search went on for a week. He followed the thread of Mr. Fellows' goings south to the Bowery and then to the upper West Side. He climbed stairs past the open doors of rooms where lessons in Spanish dancing were going on, past whores, past women practicing the "Emperor" Concerto, and one evening he found Mr. Fellows sitting on the edge of his bed in an attic room, rubbing the spots out of his necktie with a rag soaked in gasoline.

Mr. Fellows was greedy. He wanted a hundred dollars in cash and fifty per cent of the royalties. Ralph got him to agree to twenty per cent of the royalties, but he could not get him to reduce the initial payment. The lawyer drew up a paper defining Ralph's and Mr. Fellows' interests, and a few nights later Ralph went over to Brooklyn and got to a Venetian-blind factory after its doors had closed but while the lights of the office were still burning. The manager agreed to manufacture some blinds to Ralph's specifications, but he would not take an order of less than a hundred dollars. Ralph agreed to this and to furnish the compound for the outer surface of the slats. These expenditures had taken more than three-fourths of the Whittemores' capital, and now the problem of money was joined by the element of time. They put a small advertisement in the paper for a housewares salesman, and for a week Ralph interviewed candidates in the living room after supper. He chose a young man who was leaving at the end of the week for the Midwest. He wanted a fifty-dollar advance, and pointed out to them that Pittsburgh and Chicago were just as noisy as New York. A department-store collection agency was threatening to bring them into the small-claims court at this time, and they had come to a place where any illness, any fall, any damage to themselves or to the few clothes they owned would be critical. Their salesman promised to write them from Chicago at the end of the week, and they counted on good news, but there was no news from Chicago at all. Ralph wired the salesman twice, and the wires must have been forwarded, for he replied to them from Pittsburgh: "Can't merchandise blinds. Returning samples express." They put another advertisement for a salesman in the paper and took the first one who rang their bell, an old gentleman with a cornflower in his button-hole. He had a number of other lines—mirror wastebaskets, orange-juicers—and he said that he knew all the Manhattan housewares buyers intimately. He was garrulous, and when he was unable to sell the blinds, he came to the Whittemores' apartment and discussed their product at length, and with a blend of criticism and charity that we usually reserve for human beings.

Ralph was to borrow money, but neither his salary nor his patent was considered adequate collateral for a loan at anything but ruinous rates, and one day, at his office, he was served a summons by the department-store collection agency. He went out to Brooklyn and offered to sell the Venetian blinds back to the manufacturer. The man gave him sixty dollars for what had cost a hundred, and Ralph was able to pay the collection agency. They hung the samples in their windows and tried to put the venture out of their minds.

Now they were poorer than ever, and they ate lentils for dinner every Monday and sometimes again on Tuesday. Laura washed the dishes after dinner while Ralph read to Rachel. When the girl had fallen asleep, he would go to his desk in the living room and work on one of his projects. There was always something coming. There was a job in Dallas and a job in Peru. There were the plastic arch preserver, the automatic closing device for icebox doors, and the scheme to pirate marine specifications and undersell Jane's. For a month, he was going to buy some fallow acreage in upstate New York and plant Christmas trees on it, and then, with one of his friends, he projected a luxury mail-order business, for which they could never get backing. When the Whittemores met Uncle George and Aunt Helen at the Ritz, they seemed delighted with the way things were going. They were terribly excited, Laura said, about a sales agency in Paris that had been offered to Ralph but that they had decided against, because of the threat of war.

The Whittemores were apart for two years during the war. Laura took a job. She walked Rachel to school in the morning and met her at the end of the day. Working and saving, Laura was able to buy herself and Rachel some clothes. When Ralph returned at the end of the war, their affairs were in good order. The experience seemed to have refreshed him, and while he took up his old job as an anchor to windward, as an ace in the hole, there had never been more talk about jobs—jobs in Venezuela and jobs in Iran. They resumed all their old habits and economies. They remained poor.

Laura gave up her job and returned to the afternoons with Rachel in Central Park. Alice Holinshed was there. The talk was the same. The Holinsheds were living in a hotel. Mr. Holinshed was vice-president of a new firm manufacturing a soft drink, but the dress that Mrs. Holinshed wore day after day was one that Laura recognized from before the war. Her son was thin and bad-tempered. He was dressed in serge, like an English schoolboy, but his serge, like his mother's dress, looked worn and outgrown. One afternoon when Mrs. Holinshed and her son came into the Park, the boy was crying. "I've done a dreadful thing," Mrs. Holinshed told Laura. "We've been to the doctor's and I forgot to bring any money, and I wonder if you could lend me a few dollars, so I can take a taxi back to the hotel." Laura said she would be glad to. She had only a five-dollar bill with her, and she gave Mrs. Holinshed this. The boy continued to cry, and his mother dragged him off toward Fifth Avenue. Laura never saw them in the Park again.

Ralph's life was, as it had always been, dominated by anticipation. In the years directly after the war, the city appeared to be immensely rich. There seemed to be money everywhere, and the Whittemores, who slept under their worn overcoats in the winter to keep themselves warm, seemed separated from their enjoyment of this prosperity by only a little patience, resourcefulness, and luck. On Sunday, when the weather was fine, they walked with the prosperous crowds on upper Fifth Avenue. It seemed to Ralph that it might only be another month, at the most another year, before he found the key to the prosperity they deserved. They would walk on Fifth Avenue until the afternoon was ended and then go home and eat a can of beans for dinner and, in order to balance the meal, an apple for dessert.

They were returning from such a walk one Sunday when, as they climbed the stairs to their apartment, the telephone began to ring. Ralph went on ahead and answered it.

He heard the voice of his Uncle George, a man of the generation that remains conscious of distance, who spoke into the telephone as if he were calling from shore to a passing boat. "This is Uncle George, Ralphie!" he shouted, and Ralph supposed that he and Aunt Helen were paying a surprise visit to the city, until he realized that his uncle was calling from Illinois. "Can you hear me?" Uncle George shouted. "Can you hear me, Ralphie? . . . I'm calling you about a job, Ralphie. Just in case you're looking for a job. Paul Hadaam came through—can you hear me, Ralphie?—Paul Hadaam came through here on his way East last week and he stopped off to pay me a visit. He's got a lot of money, Ralphie—he's rich—and he's starting this business out in the West to manufacture synthetic wool. Can you hear me, Ralphie? . . . I told him about you, and he's staying at the Waldorf, so you go and see him. I saved his life once. I pulled him out of Lake Erie. You go and see him tomorrow at the Waldorf, Ralphie. You know where that is? The Waldorf Hotel . . . . Wait a minute, here's Aunt Helen. She wants to talk with you."

Now the voice was a woman's, and it came to him faintly. All his cousins had been there for dinner, she told him. They had had a turkey for dinner. All the grandchildren were there and they behaved very well. George took them all for a walk after dinner. It was hot, but they sat on the porch, so they didn't feel the heat. She was interrupted in her account of Sunday by her husband, who must have seized the instrument from her to continue his refrain about going to see Mr. Hadaam at the Waldorf. "You go see him tomorrow, Ralphie—the nineteenth—at the Waldorf. He's expecting you. Can you hear me? . . . The Waldorf Hotel. He's a millionaire. I'll say goodbye now."

Mr. Hadaam had a parlor and a bedroom in the Waldorf Towers, and when Ralph went to see him, late the next afternoon, on his way home from work, Mr. Hadaam was alone. He seemed to Ralph a very old man, but an obdurate one, and in the way he shook hands, pulled at his earlobes, stretched himself, and padded around the parlor on his bandy legs Ralph recognized a spirit that was unimpaired, independent, and canine. He poured Ralph a strong drink and himself a weak one. He was undertaking the manufacture of synthetic wool on the West Coast, he explained, and had come East to find men who were experienced in merchandising wool. George had given him Ralph's name, and he wanted a man with Ralph's experience. He would find the Whittemores a suitable house, arrange for their transportation, and begin Ralph at a salary of fifteen thousand. It was the size of the salary that made Ralph realize that the proposition was an oblique attempt to repay his uncle for having saved Mr.

Hadaam's life, and the old man seemed to sense what he was feeling. "This hasn't got anything to do with your uncle's saving my life," he said roughly. "I'm grateful to him—who wouldn't be?—but this hasn't got anything to do with your uncle, if that's what you're thinking. When you get to be as old and as rich as I am, it's hard to meet people. All my old friends are dead—all of them but George. I'm surrounded by a cordon of associates and relatives that's damned near impenetrable, and if it wasn't for George giving me a name now and then, I'd never get to see a new face. Last year, I got into an automobile accident. It was my fault. I'm a terrible driver. I hit this young fellow's car and I got right out and went over to him and introduced myself. We had to wait about twenty minutes for the wreckers and we got to talking. Well, he's working for me today and he's one of the best friends I've got, and if I hadn't run into him, I'd never have met him. When you get to be as old as me, that's the only way you can meet people—automobile accidents, fires, things like that."

He straightened up against the back of his chair and tasted his drink. His rooms were well above the noise of traffic and it was quiet there. Mr. Hadaam's breath was loud and steady, and it sounded, in a pause, like the heavy breath of someone sleeping. "Well, I don't want to rush you into this," he said. "I'm going back to the Coast the day after tomorrow. You think it over and I'll telephone you." He took out an engagement book and wrote down Ralph's name and telephone number. "I'll call you on Tuesday evening, the twenty-seventh, about nine o'clock—nine o'clock your time. George tells me you've got a nice wife, but I haven't got time to meet her now. I'll see her on the Coast." He started talking about baseball and then brought the conversation back to Uncle George. "He saved my life. My damned boat capsized and then righted herself and sunk right from underneath me. I can still feel her going down under my feet. I couldn't swim. Can't swim today. Well, goodbye." They shook hands, and as soon as the door closed, Ralph heard Mr. Hadaam begin to cough. It was the profane, hammering cough of an old man, full of bitter complaints and distempers, and it hit him pitilessly for all the time that Ralph was waiting in the hallway for the elevator to take him down.

On the walk home, Ralph felt that this might be it, that this preposterous chain of contingencies that had begun with his uncle's pulling a friend out of Lake Erie might be the one that would save them. Nothing in his experience made it seem unlikely. He recognized that the proposition was the vagary of an old man and that it originated in the indebtedness Mr. Hadaam felt to his uncle—an indebtedness that age seemed to have deepened. He gave Laura the details of the interview when he came in, and his own views on Mr. Hadaam's conduct, and, to his mild surprise, Laura said that it looked to her like the bonanza. They were both remarkably calm, considering the change that confronted them. There was no talk of celebrating, and he helped her wash the dishes. He looked up the site of Mr. Hadaam's factory in an atlas, and the Spanish place name on the coast north of San Francisco gave them a glimpse of a life of reasonable contentment.

Eight days lay between Ralph's interview and the telephone call, and he realized that nothing would be definite until Tuesday, and that there was a possibility that old Mr. Hadaam, while crossing the country, might, under the subtle influence of travel, suffer a change of heart. He might be poisoned by a fish sandwich and be taken off the train in Chicago, to die in a nursing home there. Among the people meeting him in San Francisco might be his lawyer, with the news that he was ruined or that his wife had run away. But eventually Ralph was unable to invent any new disasters or to believe in the ones he had invented.

This inability to persevere in doubting his luck showed some weakening of character. There had hardly been a day when he had not been made to feel the power of money, but he found that the force of money was most irresistible when it took the guise of a promise, and that years of resolute self-denial, instead of rewarding him with reserves of fortitude, had left him more than ordinarily susceptible to temptation. Since the change in their lives still depended upon a telephone call, he refrained from talking—from thinking, so far as possible—about the life they might have in California. He would go so far as to say that he would like some white shirts, but he would not go beyond this deliberately contrite wish, and here, where he thought he was exercising restraint and intelligence, he was, instead, beginning to respect the bulk of superstition that is supposed to attend good fortune, and when he wished for white shirts, it was not a genuinely modest wish so much as it was a memory—he could not have put it into words himself—that the gods of fortune are jealous and easily deceived by false modesty. He had never been a superstitious man, but on Tuesday he scooped the money off his coffee table and was elated when he saw a ladybug on the bathroom window sill. He could not remember when he had heard money and this insect associated, but neither could he have explained any of the other portents that he had begun to let govern his movements.

Laura watched this subtle change that anticipation worked on her husband, but there was nothing she could say. He did not mention Mr. Hadaam or California. He was quiet; he was gentle with Rachel; he actually grew pale. He had his hair cut on Wednesday. He wore his best suit. On Saturday, he had his hair cut again and his nails manicured. He took two baths a day, put on a fresh shirt for dinner, and frequently went into the bathroom to wash his hands, brush his teeth, and wet down his cowlick. The preternatural care he gave his body and his appearance reminded her of an adolescent surprised by early love.

The Whittemores were invited to a party for Monday

night and Laura insisted that they go. The guests at the party were the survivors of a group that had coalesced ten years before, and if anyone had called the roll of the earliest parties in the same room, like the retreat ceremony of a breached and decimated regiment, "Missing . . . . Missing . . . . Missing" would have been answered for the squad that had gone into Westchester; "Missing . . . . Missing . . . . Missing" would have been spoken for the platoon that divorce, drink, nervous disorders, and adversity had slain or wounded. Because Laura had gone to the party in indifferent spirits, she was conscious of the missing.

She had been at the party less than an hour when she heard some people coming in, and, looking over her shoulder, saw Alice Holinshed and her husband. The room was crowded and she put off speaking to Alice until later. Much later in the evening, Laura went into the toilet, and when she came out of it into the bedroom, she found Alice sitting on the bed. She seemed to be waiting for Laura. Laura sat down at the dressing table to straighten her hair. She looked at the image of her friend in the glass.

"I hear you're going to California," Alice said.

"We hope to. We'll know tomorrow."

"Is it true that Ralph's uncle saved his life?"

"That's true."

"You're lucky."

"I suppose we are."

"You're lucky, all right." Alice got up from the bed and crossed the room and closed the door, and came back across the room again and sat on the bed. Laura watched her in the glass, but she was not watching Laura. She was stooped. She seemed nervous. "You're lucky," she said. "You're so lucky. Do you know how lucky you are? Let me tell you about this cake of soap," she said. "I have this cake of soap. I mean I had this cake of soap. Somebody gave it to me when I was married, fifteen years ago. I don't know who. Some maid, some music teacher—somebody like that. It was good soap, good English soap, the kind I like, and I decided to save it for the big day when Larry made a killing, when he took me to Bermuda. First, I was going to use it when he got the job in Bound Brook. Then I thought I could use it when we were going to Boston, and then Washington, and then when he got this new job, I thought maybe this is it, maybe *this* is the time when I get to take the boy out of that rotten school and pay the bills and move out of those bum hotels we've been living in. For fifteen years I've been planning to use this cake of soap. Well, last week I was looking through my bureau drawers and I saw this cake of soap. It was all cracked. I threw it out. I threw it out because I knew I was never going to have a chance to use it. Do you realize what that means? Do you know what that feels like? To live for fifteen years on promises and expectations and loans and credits in hotels that aren't fit to live in, never for a single day to be out of debt, and yet to pretend, to feel that every year, every winter, every job, every meeting is going to be the one. To live like this for fifteen years and then to realize that it's never going to end. Do you know what that feels like?" She got up and went over to the dressing table and stood in front of Laura. Tears had risen into her large eyes, and her voice was harsh and loud. "I'm never going to get to Bermuda," she said. "I'm never even going to get to Florida. I'm never going to get out of hock, ever, ever, *ever*. I know that I'm never going to have a decent home and that everything I own that is worn and torn and no good is going to stay that way. I know that for the rest of my life, for the rest of my life, I'm going to wear ragged slips and torn nightgowns and torn underclothes and shoes that hurt me. I know that for the rest of my life nobody is going to come up to me and tell me that I've got on a pretty dress, because I'm not going to be able to afford that kind of a dress. I know that for the rest of my life every taxi driver and doorman and headwaiter in this town is going to know in a minute that I haven't got five bucks in that black imitation-suede purse that I've been brushing and brushing and brushing and carrying around for ten years. How do you get it? How do you rate it? What's so wonderful about you that you get a break like this?" She ran her fingers down Laura's bare arm. The dress she was wearing smelled of benzine. "Can I rub it off you? Will that make me lucky? I swear to Jesus I'd murder somebody if I thought it would bring us in any money. I'd wring somebody's neck—yours, anybody's—I swear to Jesus I would—"

Someone began knocking on the door. Alice strode to the door, opened it, and went out. A woman came in, a stranger looking for the toilet. Laura lighted a cigarette and waited in the bedroom for about ten minutes before she went back to the party. The Holinsheds had gone. She got a drink and sat down and tried to talk, but she couldn't keep her mind on what she was saying.

The hunt, the search for money that had seemed to her natural, amiable, and fair when they first committed themselves to it, now seemed like a hazardous and piratical voyage. She had thought, earlier in the evening, of the missing. She thought now of the missing again. Adversity and failure accounted for more than half of them, as if beneath the amenities in the pretty room a keen race were in progress, in which the loser's forfeits were extreme. Laura felt cold. She picked the ice out of her drink with her fingers and put it in a flower vase, but the whiskey didn't warm her. She asked Ralph to take her home.

After dinner on Tuesday, Laura washed the dishes and Ralph dried them. He read the paper and she took up some sewing. At a quarter after eight, the telephone, in the bedroom, rang, and he went to it calmly. It was someone with two theatre tickets for a show that was closing. The telephone didn't ring again, and at half past nine he told Laura that he was going to call California. It didn't take long for the connection to be made, and the fresh voice of a young woman spoke to him from Mr. Hadaam's number. "Oh, yes, Mr. Whittemore," she said. "We tried to get you earlier in the evening but your line was busy."

"Could I speak to Mr. Hadaam?"

"No, Mr. Whittemore. This is Mr. Hadaam's secretary. I know he meant to call you, because he had entered this in his engagement book. Mrs. Hadaam has asked me to disappoint as few people as possible, and I've tried to take care of all the calls and appointments in his engagement book. Mr. Hadaam had a stroke on Sunday. We don't expect him to recover. I imagine he made you some kind of promise, but I'm afraid he won't be able to keep it."

"I'm very sorry," Ralph said. He hung up.

Laura had come into the bedroom while the secretary was talking. "Oh, darling!" she said. She put her sewing basket on the bureau and went toward the closet. Then she went back and looked for something in the sewing basket and left the basket on her dressing table. Then she took off her shoes, treed them, slipped her dress over her head and hung it up neatly. Then she went to the bureau, looking for her sewing basket, found it on the dressing table, and took it into the closet, where she put it on a shelf. Then she took her brush and comb into the bathroom and began to run the water for a bath.

The lash of frustration was laid on and the pain stunned Ralph. He sat by the telephone for he did not know how long. He heard Laura come out of the bathroom. He turned when he heard her speak.

"I feel dreadfully about old Mr. Hadaam," she said. "I wish there were something we could do." She was in her nightgown, and she sat down at the dressing table like a skillful and patient woman establishing herself in front of a loom, and she picked up and put down pins and bottles and combs and brushes with the thoughtless dexterity of an experienced weaver, as if the time she spent there were all part of a continuous operation. "It did look like the treasure . . ."

The word surprised him, and for a moment he saw the chimera, the pot of gold, the fleece, the treasure buried in the faint lights of a rainbow, and the primitivism of his hunt struck him. Armed with a sharp spade and a homemade divining rod, he had climbed over hill and dale, through droughts and rain squalls, digging wherever the maps he had drawn himself promised gold. Six paces east of the dead pine, five panels in from the library door, underneath the creaking step, in the roots of the pear tree, beneath the grape arbor lay the bean pot full of doubloons and bullion.

She turned on the stool and held her thin arms toward him, as she had done more than a thousand times. She was no longer young, and more wan, thinner than she might have been if he had found the doubloons to save her anxiety and unremitting work. Her smile, her naked shoulders had begun to trouble the indecipherable shapes and symbols that are the touchstones of desire, and the light from the lamp seemed to brighten and give off heat and shed that unaccountable complacency, that benevolence, that the spring sunlight brings to all kinds of fatigue and despair. Desire for her delighted and confused him. Here it was, here it all was, and the shine of the gold seemed to him then to be all around her arms.

from

SIDDHARTHA

HERMAN HESSE

As Buddhist writer Jean Smith has pointed out, Siddhartha Gautama, who became the Buddha, was the only founder of a major religion to neither claim to be God or God's messenger. His only claim was to be "awake." With this fictional account, Hesse lets us imagine the moment of this most influential awakening of all.

For a long time Siddhartha had lived the life of the world without belonging to it. His senses, which he had deadened during his ardent Samana years, were again awakened. He had tasted riches, passion and power, but for a long time he remained a Samana in his heart. Clever Kamala had recognized this. His life was always directed by the art of thinking, waiting and fasting. The people of the world, the ordinary people, were still alien to him, just as he was apart from them.

The years passed by. Enveloped by comfortable circumstances, Siddhartha hardly noticed their passing. He had become rich. He had long possessed a house of his own and his own servants, and a garden at the outskirts of the town, by the river. People liked him; they came to him if they wanted money or advice. However, with the exception of Kamala, he had no close friends.

That glorious, exalted awakening which he had once experienced in his youth, in the days after Gotama's preaching, after the parting from Govinda, that alert expectation, that pride of standing alone without teachers and doctrines, that eager readiness to hear the divine voice within his own heart had gradually become a memory, had passed. The only fountainhead which had once been near and which had once sung loudly within him, now murmured softly in the distance. However, many things which he had learned from the Samanas, which he had learned from Gotama, from his father, from the Brahmins, he still retained for a long time: a moderate life, pleasure in thinking, hours of meditation, secret knowledge of the Self, of the eternal Self, that was neither body nor consciousness. Many of these he had retained; others were submerged and covered with dust. Just as the potter's wheel, once set in motion, still turns for a long time and then turns only very slowly and stops, so did the wheel of the ascetic, the wheel of thinking, the wheel of discrimination still revolve for a long time in Siddhartha's soul; it still revolved, but slowly and hesitatingly, and it had nearly come to a standstill. Slowly, like moisture entering the dying tree trunk, slowly filling and rotting it, so did the world and inertia creep into Siddhartha's soul; it slowly filled his soul, made it heavy, made it tired, sent it to sleep. But on the other hand his senses became more awakened, they learned a great deal, experienced a great deal.

Siddhartha had learned how to transact business affairs, to exercise power over people, to amuse himself with women; he had learned to wear fine clothes, to command servants, to bathe in sweet-smelling waters. He had learned to eat sweet and carefully prepared foods, also fish and meat and fowl, spices and dainties, and to drink wine which made him lazy and forgetful. He had learned to play dice and chess, to watch dancers, to be carried in sedan chairs, to sleep on a soft bed. But he had always felt different from and superior to the others; he had always watched them a little scornfully, with a slightly mocking disdain, with that disdain which a Samana always feels towards the people of the world. If Kamaswami was upset, if he felt that he had been insulted, or if he was troubled with his business affairs, Siddhartha had always regarded him mockingly. But slowly and imperceptibly, with the passing of the seasons, his mockery and feeling of superiority diminished. Gradually, along with his growing riches, Siddhartha himself acquired some of the characteristics of the ordinary people, some of their childishness and some of their anxiety. And yet he envied them; the more he became like them, the more he envied them. He envied them the one thing that he lacked and that they had: the sense of importance with which they lived their lives, the depth of their pleasures and sorrows, the anxious but sweet happiness of their continual power to love. These people were always in love with themselves, with their children, with honor or money, with plans or hope. But these he did not learn from them, these child-like pleasures and follies; he only learned the unpleasant things from them which he despised. It happened more frequently that after a merry evening, he lay late in bed the following morning and felt dull and tired. He would become annoyed and impatient when Kamaswami bored him with his worries. He would laugh too loudly when he lost at dice. His face was still more clever and intellectual than other people's, but he rarely laughed, and gradually his face assumed the expressions which are so often found among rich people—the expressions of discontent, of sickliness, of displeasure, of idleness, of lovelessness. Slowly the soul sickness of the rich crept over him.

Like a veil, like a thin mist, a weariness settled on Siddhartha, slowly, every day a little thicker, every month a little darker, every year a little heavier. As a new dress grows old with time, loses its bright color, becomes stained and creased, the hems frayed, and here and there weak and threadbare places, so had Siddhartha's new life which he had begun after his parting from Govinda, become old. In the same way it lost its color and sheen with the passing of the years: creases and stains accumulated, and hidden in the depths, here and there already appearing, waited disillusionment and nausea. Siddhartha did not notice it. He only noticed that the bright and clear inward voice, that had once awakened in him and had always guided him in his finest hours, had become silent.

The world had caught him; pleasure, covetousness, idleness, and finally also that vice that he had always despised and scorned as the most foolish—acquisitiveness. Property, possessions and riches had also finally trapped him. They were no longer a game and a toy; they had become a chain and a burden. Siddhartha wandered along a strange, twisted path of this last and most base declivity through the game of dice. Since the time he had stopped being a Samana in his heart, Siddhartha began to play dice for money and jewels with increasing fervor, a game in which he had previously smilingly and indulgently taken part as a custom of the ordinary people. He was a formidable player; few dared play with him for his stakes were so high and reckless. He played the game as a result of a heartfelt need. He derived a passionate pleasure through the gambling away and squandering of wretched money. In no other way could he show more clearly and mockingly his contempt for riches, the false deity of businessmen. So he staked high and unsparingly, hating himself, mocking himself. He won thousands, he threw thousands away, lost money, lost jewels, lost a country house, won again, lost again. He loved that anxiety, that terrible and oppressive anxiety which he experienced during the game of dice, during the suspense of high stakes. He loved this feeling and continually sought to renew it, to increase it, to stimulate it, for in this feeling alone did he experience some kind of happiness, some kind of excitement, some heightened living in the midst of his satiated, tepid, insipid existence. And after every great loss he devoted himself to the procurement of new riches, went eagerly after business and pressed his debtors for payment, for he wanted to play again, he wanted to squander again, he wanted to show his contempt for riches again. Siddhartha became impatient at losses, he lost his patience with slow-paying debtors, he was no longer kindhearted to beggars, he no longer had the desire to give gifts and loans to the poor. He, who staked ten thousand on the throw of the dice and laughed, became more hard and mean in business, and sometimes dreamt of money at night. And whenever he awakened from this hateful spell, when he saw his face reflected in the mirror on the wall of his bedroom, grown older and uglier, whenever shame and nausea overtook him, he fled again, fled to a new game of chance, fled in confusion to passion, to wine, and from there back again to the urge for acquiring and hoarding wealth. He wore himself out in this senseless cycle, became old and sick.

Then a dream once reminded him. He had been with Kamala in the evening, in her lovely pleasure garden. They sat under a tree talking. Kamala was speaking seriously, and grief and weariness were concealed behind her words. She had asked him to tell her about Gotama, and could not hear enough about him, how clear his eyes were, how peaceful and beautiful his mouth, how gracious his smile, how peaceful his entire manner. For a long time he had to talk to her about the Illustrious Buddha and Kamala had sighed and said: "One day, perhaps soon, I will also become a follower of this Buddha. I will give him my pleasure garden and take refuge in his teachings." But then she enticed him, and in love play she clasped him to her with extreme fervor, fiercely and tearfully, as if she wanted once more to extract the last sweet drop from this fleeting pleasure. Never had it been so strangely clear to Siddhartha how closely related passion was to death. Then he lay beside her and Kamala's face was near to his, and under her eyes and near the corners of her mouth, he read clearly for the first time a sad sign—fine lines and wrinkles, a sign which gave a reminder of autumn and old age. Siddhartha himself, who was only in his forties, had noticed grey hairs here and there in his black hair. Weariness was written on Kamala's beautiful face, weariness from continuing along a long path which had no joyous goal, weariness and incipient old age, and concealed and not yet mentioned, perhaps a not yet conscious fear—fear of the autumn of life, fear of old age, fear of death. Sighing, he took leave of her, his heart full of misery and secret fear.

Then Siddhartha had spent the night at his house with dancers and wine, had pretended to be superior to his companions, which he no longer was. He had drunk much wine and late after midnight he went to bed, tired and yet agitated, nearly in tears and in despair. In vain did he try to sleep. His heart was so full of misery, he felt he could no longer endure it. He was full of a nausea which overpowered him like a distasteful wine, or music that was too sweet and superficial, or like the too sweet smile of the dancers or the too sweet perfume of their hair and breasts. But above all he was nauseated with himself, with his perfumed hair, with the smell of wine from his mouth, with the soft, flabby appearance of his skin. Like one who has eaten and drunk too much and vomits painfully and then feels better, so did the restless man wish he could rid himself with one terrific heave of these pleasures, of these habits of this entirely senseless life. Only at daybreak and at the first signs of activity outside his town house, did he doze off and had a few moments of semi-oblivion, a possibility of sleep. During that time he had a dream.

Kamala kept a small rare songbird in a small golden cage. It was about this bird that he dreamt. This bird, which usually sang in the morning, became mute, and as this surprised him, he went up to the cage and looked inside. The little bird was dead and lay stiff on the floor. He took it out, held it a moment in his hand and then threw it away on the road, and at the same moment he was horrified and his heart ached as if he had thrown away with this dead bird all that was good and of value in himself.

Awakening from this dream, he was overwhelmed by a feeling of great sadness. It seemed to him that he had spent his life in a worthless and senseless manner; he retained nothing vital, nothing in any way precious or worth while. He stood alone, like a shipwrecked man on the shore.

Sadly, Siddhartha went to a pleasure garden that belonged to him, closed the gates, sat under a mango tree, and felt horror and death in his heart. He sat, and felt himself dying, withering, finishing. Gradually, he collected his thoughts and mentally went through the whole of his life, from the earliest days which he could remember. When had he really been happy? When had he really experienced joy? Well, he had experienced this several times. He had tasted it in the days of his boyhood, when he had won praise from the Brahmins, when he far outstripped his contemporaries, when he excelled himself at the recitation of the holy verses, in argument with the learned men, when assisting at the sacrifices. Then he had felt in his heart: "A path lies before you which you are called to follow. The gods await you." And again as a youth when his continually soaring goal had propelled him in and out of the crowd of similar seekers, when he had striven hard to understand the Brahmins' teachings, when every freshly acquired knowledge only engendered a new thirst, then again, in the midst of his thirst, in the midst of his efforts, he had thought: Onwards, onwards, this is your path. He had heard this voice when he had left his home and chosen the life of the Samanas, and again when he had left the Samanas and gone to the Perfect One, and also when he had left him for the unknown. How long was it now since he had heard this voice, since he had soared to any heights? How flat and desolate his path had been! How many long years he had spent without any lofty goal, without any thirst, without any exaltation, content with small pleasures and yet never really satisfied! Without knowing it, he had endeavored and longed all these years to be like all these other people, like these children, and yet his life had been much more wretched and poorer than theirs, for their aims were not his, nor their sorrows his. This whole world of the Kamaswami people had only been a game to him, a dance, a comedy which one watches. Only Kamala was dear to him—had been of value to him—but was she still? Did he still need her—and did she still need him? Were they not playing a game without an end? Was it necessary to live for it? No. This game was called Samsara, a game for children, a game which was perhaps enjoyable played once, twice, ten times—but was it worth playing continually?

Then Siddhartha knew that the game was finished, that he could play it no longer. A shudder passed through his body; he felt as if something had died.

He sat all that day under the mango tree, thinking of his father, thinking of Govinda, thinking of Gotama. Had he left all these in order to become a Kamaswami? He sat there till night fell. When he looked up and saw the stars, he thought: I am sitting here under my mango tree, in my pleasure garden. He smiled a little. Was it necessary, was it right, was it not a foolish thing that he should possess a mango tree and a garden?

He had finished with that. That also died in him. He rose, said farewell to the mango tree and the pleasure garden. As he had not had any food that day he felt extremely hungry, and thought of his house in the town, of his room and bed, of the table with food. He smiled wearily, shook his head and said good-bye to these things.

The same night Siddhartha left his garden and the town and never returned. For a long time Kamaswami tried to find him, believing he had fallen into the hands of bandits. Kamala did not try to find him. She was not surprised when she learned that Siddhartha had disappeared. Had she not always expected it? Was he not a Samana, without a home, a pilgrim? She had felt it more than ever at their last meeting, and in the midst of her pain at her loss, she rejoiced that she had pressed him so close to her heart on that last occasion, had felt so completely possessed and mastered by him.

When she heard the first news of Siddhartha's disappearance, she went to the window where she kept a rare songbird in a golden cage. She opened the door of the cage, took the bird out and let it fly away. For a long time she looked after the disappearing bird. From that day she received no more visitors and kept her house closed. After a time, she found that she was with child as a result of her last meeting with Siddhartha.

Siddhartha wandered into the forest, already far from the town, and knew only one thing—that he could not go back, that the life he had lived for many years was past, tasted and drained to a degree of nausea. The songbird was dead; its death, which he had dreamt about, was the bird in his own heart. He was deeply entangled in Samsara; he had drawn nausea and death to himself from all sides, like a sponge that absorbs water until it is full. He was full of ennui, full of misery, full of death; there was nothing left in the world that could attract him, that could give him pleasure and solace.

He wished passionately for oblivion, to be at rest, to be dead. If only a flash of lightning would strike him! If only a tiger would come and eat him! If there were only some wine, some poison, that would give him oblivion, that would make him forget, that would make him sleep and never awaken! Was there any kind of filth with which he had not besmirched himself, any sin and folly which he had not committed, any stain upon his soul for which he alone had not been responsible? Was it then still possible to live? Was it possible to take in breath again and again, to breathe out, to feel hunger, to eat again, to sleep again, to lie with women again? Was this cycle not exhausted and finished for him?

Siddhartha reached the long river in the wood, the same river across which a ferryman had once taken him when he was still a young man and had come from Gotama's town. He stopped at this river and stood hesitatingly on the bank. Fatigue and hunger had weakened him. Why should he go any further, where, and for what purpose? There was no more purpose; there was nothing more than a deep, painful longing to shake off this whole confused dream, to spit out this stale wine, to make an end of this bitter, painful life.

There was a tree on the river bank, a cocoanut tree. Siddhartha leaned against it, placed his arm around the trunk and looked down into the green water which flowed beneath him. He looked down and was completely filled with a desire to let himself go and be submerged in the water. A chilly emptiness in the water reflected the terrible emptiness in his soul. Yes, he was at the end. There was nothing more for him but to efface himself, to destroy the unsuccessful structure of his life, to throw it away, mocked at by the gods. That was the deed which he longed to commit, to destroy the form which he hated! Might the fishes devour him, this dog of a Siddhartha, this madman, this corrupted and rotting body, this sluggish and misused soul! Might the fishes and crocodiles devour him, might the demons tear him to little pieces!

With a distorted countenance he stared into the water. He saw his face reflected, and spat at it; he took his arm away from the tree trunk and turned a little, so that he could fall headlong and finally go under. He bent, with closed eyes—towards death.

Then from a remote part of his soul, from the past of his tired life, he heard a sound. It was one word, one syllable, which without thinking he spoke indistinctly, the ancient beginning and ending of all Brahmin prayers, the holy Om, which had the meaning of "the Perfect One" or "Perfection." At that moment, when the sound of Om reached Siddhartha's ears, his slumbering soul suddenly awakened and he recognized the folly of his action.

Siddhartha was deeply horrified. So that was what he had come to; he was so lost, so confused, so devoid of all reason, that he had sought death. This wish, this childish wish had grown so strong within him: to find peace by destroying his body. All the torment of these recent times, all the disillusionment, all the despair, had not affected him so much as it did the moment the Om reached his consciousness and he recognized his wretchedness and his crime.

"Om," he pronounced inwardly, and he was conscious of Brahman, of the indestructibleness of life; he remembered all that he had forgotten, all that was divine.

But it was only for a moment, a flash. Siddhartha sank down at the foot of the cocoanut tree, overcome by fatigue. Murmuring Om, he laid his head on the tree roots and sank into a deep sleep.

His sleep was deep and dreamless; he had not slept like that for a long time. When he awakened after many hours, it seemed to him as if ten years had passed. He heard the soft rippling of the water; he did not know where he was nor what had brought him there. He looked up and was surprised to see the trees and the sky above him. He remembered where he was and how he came to be there. He felt a desire to remain there for a long time. The past now seemed to him to be covered by a veil, extremely remote, very unimportant. He only knew that his previous life (at the first moment of his return to consciousness his previous life seemed to him like a remote incarnation, like an earlier birth of his present Self) was finished, that it was so full of nausea and wretchedness that he had wanted to destroy it, but that he had come to himself by a river, under a cocoanut tree, with the holy word Om on his lips. Then he had fallen asleep, and on awakening he looked at the world like a new man. Softly he said the word Om to himself, over which he had fallen asleep, and it seemed to him as if his whole sleep had been a long deep pronouncing of Om, thinking of Om, an immersion and penetration into Om, into the nameless, into the Divine.

What a wonderful sleep it had been! Never had a sleep so refreshed him, so renewed him, so rejuvenated him! Perhaps he had really died, perhaps he had been drowned and was reborn in another form. No, he recognized himself, he recognized his hands and feet, the place where he lay and the Self in his breast, Siddhartha, self-willed, individualistic. But this Siddhartha was somewhat changed, renewed. He had slept wonderfully. He was remarkably awake, happy and curious.

Siddhartha raised himself and saw a monk in a yellow gown, with shaved head, sitting opposite him in the attitude of a thinker. He looked at the man, who had neither hair on his head nor a beard, and he did not look at him long when he recognized in this monk, Govinda, the friend of his youth, Govinda who had taken refuge in the Illustrious Buddha. Govinda had also aged, but he still showed the old characteristics in his face—eagerness, loyalty, curiosity, anxiety. But when Govinda, feeling his glance, raised his eyes and looked at him, Siddhartha saw that Govinda did not recognize him. Govinda was pleased to find him awake. Apparently he had sat there a long time waiting for him to awaken, although he did not know him.

"I was sleeping," said Siddhartha. "How did you come here?"

"You were sleeping," answered Govinda, "and it is not good to sleep in such places where there are often snakes and animals from the forest prowling about. I am one of the followers of the Illustrious Gotama, the Buddha of Sakyamuni, and I am on a pilgrimage with a number of our order. I saw you lying asleep in a dangerous place, so I tried to awaken you, and then as I saw you were sleeping very deeply, I remained behind my brothers and sat by you. Then it seems that I, who wanted to watch over you, fell asleep myself. Weariness overcame me and I kept my watch badly. But now you are awake, so I must go and overtake my brothers."

"I thank you, Samana, for guarding my sleep. The followers of the Illustrious One are very kind, but now you may go on your way."

"I am going. May you keep well."

"I thank you, Samana."

Govinda bowed and said, "Good-bye."

"Good-bye, Govinda," said Siddhartha.

The monk stood still.

"Excuse me, sir, how do you know my name?"

Thereupon Siddhartha laughed.

"I know you, Govinda, from your father's house and from the Brahmins' school, and from the sacrifices, and from our sojourn with the Samanas and from that hour in the grove of Jetavana when you swore allegiance to the Illustrious One."

"You are Siddhartha," cried Govinda aloud. "Now I recognize you and do not understand why I did not recognize you immediately. Greetings, Siddhartha, it gives me great pleasure to see you again."

"I am also pleased to see you again. You have watched over me during my sleep. I thank you once again, although I needed no guard. Where are you going, my friend?"

"I am not going anywhere. We monks are always on the way, except during the rainy season. We always move from place to place, live according to the rule, preach the gospel, collect alms and then move on. It is always the same. But where are you going, Siddhartha?"

Siddhartha said: "It is the same with me as it is with you, my friend. I am not going anywhere. I am only on the way. I am making a pilgrimage."

Govinda said: "You say you are making a pilgrimage and I believe you. But forgive me, Siddhartha, you do not look like a pilgrim. You are wearing the clothes of a rich man, you are wearing the shoes of a man of fashion, and your perfumed hair is not the hair of a pilgrim, it is not the hair of a Samana."

"You have observed well, my friend; you see everything

with your sharp eyes. But I did not tell you that I am a Samana. I said I was making a pilgrimage and that is true."

"You are making a pilgrimage," said Govinda, "but few make a pilgrimage in such clothes, in such shoes and with such hair. I, who have been wandering for many years, have never seen such a pilgrim."

"I believe you, Govinda. But today you have met such a pilgrim in such shoes and dress. Remember, my dear Govinda, the world of appearances is transitory, the style of our clothes and hair is extremely transitory. Our hair and our bodies are themselves transitory. You have observed correctly. I am wearing the clothes of a rich man. I am wearing them because I have been a rich man, and I am wearing my hair like men of the world and fashion because I have been one of them."

"And what are you now, Siddhartha?"

"I do not know; I know as little as you. I am on the way. I was a rich man, but I am no longer and what I will be tomorrow I do not know."

"Have you lost your riches?"

"I have lost them, or they have lost me—I am not sure. The wheel of appearances revolves quickly, Govinda. Where is Siddhartha the Brahmin, where is Siddhartha the Samana, where is Siddhartha the rich man? The transitory soon changes, Govinda. You know that."

For a long time Govinda looked doubtfully at the friend

of his youth. Then he bowed to him, as one does to a man of rank, and went on his way.

Smiling, Siddhartha watched him go. He still loved him, this faithful anxious friend. And at that moment, in that splendid hour, after his wonderful sleep, permeated with Om, how could he help but love someone and something. That was just the magic that had happened to him during his sleep and the Om in him—he loved everything, he was full of joyous love towards everything that he saw. And it seemed to him that was just why he was previously so ill—because he could love nothing and nobody.

With a smile Siddhartha watched the departing monk. His sleep had strengthened him, but he suffered great hunger for he had not eaten for two days, and the time was long past when he could ward off hunger. Troubled, yet also with laughter, he recalled that time. He remembered that at that time he had boasted of three things to Kamala, three noble and invincible arts: fasting, waiting and thinking. These were his possessions, his power and strength, his firm staff. He had learned these three arts and nothing else during the diligent, assiduous years of his youth. Now he had lost them, he possessed none of them any more, neither fasting, nor waiting, nor thinking. He had exchanged them for the most wretched things, for the transitory, for the pleasures of the senses, for high living and riches. He had gone along a strange path. And now, it seemed that he had indeed become an ordinary person.

Siddhartha reflected on his state. He found it difficult to think; he really had no desire to, but he forced himself.

Now, he thought, that all these transitory things have slipped away from me again, I stand once more beneath the sun, as I once stood as a small child. Nothing is mine, I know nothing, I possess nothing, I have learned nothing. How strange it is! Now, when I am no longer young, when my hair is fast growing gray, when strength begins to diminish, now I am beginning again like a child. He had to smile again. Yes, his destiny was strange! He was going backwards, and now he again stood empty and naked and ignorant in the world. But he did not grieve about it; no, he even felt a great desire to laugh, to laugh at himself, to laugh at this strange foolish world!

Things are going backwards with you, he said to himself and laughed, and as he said it, his glance lighted on the river, and he saw the river also flowing continually backwards, singing merrily. That pleased him immensely; he smiled cheerfully at the river. Was this not the river in which he had once wished to drown himself—hundreds of years ago—or had he dreamt it?

How strange his life had been, he thought. He had wandered along strange paths. As a boy I was occupied with the gods and sacrifices, as a youth with asceticism, with thinking and meditation. I was in search of Brahman and revered the eternal in Atman. As a young man I was attracted to expiation. I lived in the woods, suffered heat and cold. I learned to fast, I learned to conquer my body. I then discovered with wonder the teachings of the great Buddha. I felt knowledge and the unity of the world circulate in me like my own blood, but I also felt compelled to leave the Buddha and the great knowledge. I went and learned the pleasures of love from Kamala and business from Kamaswami. I hoarded money, I squandered money, I acquired a taste for rich food, I learned to stimulate my senses. I had to spend many years like that in order to lose my intelligence, to lose the power to think, to forget about the unity of things. Is it not true, that slowly and through many deviations I changed from a man into a child? From a thinker into an ordinary person? And yet this path has been good and the bird in my breast has not died. But what a path it has been! I have had to experience so much stupidity, so many vices, so much error, so much nausea, disillusionment and sorrow, just in order to become a child again and begin anew. But it was right that it should be so; my eyes and heart acclaim it. I had to experience despair, I had to sink to the greatest mental depths, to thoughts of suicide, in order to experience grace, to hear Om again, to sleep deeply again and to awaken refreshed again. I had to become a fool again in order to find Atman in myself. I had to sin in order to live again. Whither will my path yet lead me? This path is stupid, it goes in spirals, perhaps in circles, but whichever way it goes, I will follow it.

He was aware of a great happiness mounting within him.

Where does it come from, he asked himself? What is the reason for this feeling of happiness? Does it arise from my good long sleep which has done me so much good? Or from the word Om which I pronounced? Or because I have run away, because my flight is accomplished, because I am at last free again and stand like a child beneath the sky? Ah, how good this flight has been, this liberation! In the place from which I escaped there was always an atmosphere of pomade, spice, excess and inertia. How I hated that world of riches, carousing and playing! How I hated myself for remaining so long in that horrible world! How I hated myself, thwarted, poisoned and tortured myself, made myself old and ugly. Never again, as I once fondly imagined, will I consider that Siddhartha is clever. But one thing I have done well, which pleases me, which I must praise—I have now put an end to that self-detestation, to that foolish empty life. I commend you, Siddhartha, that after so many years of folly, you have again had a good idea, that you have accomplished something, that you have again heard the bird in your breast sing and followed it.

So he praised himself, was pleased with himself and listened curiously to his stomach which rumbled from hunger. He felt he had thoroughly tasted and ejected a portion of sorrow, a portion of misery during those past times, that he had consumed them up to a point of despair and death. But all was well. He could have remained much longer with

Kamaswami, made and squandered money, fed his body and neglected his soul; he could have dwelt for a long time yet in that soft, well-upholstered hell, if this had not happened, this moment of complete hopelessness and despair and the tense moment when he had bent over the flowing water, ready to commit suicide. This despair, this extreme nausea which he had experienced had not overpowered him. The bird, the clear spring and voice within him was still alive—that was why he rejoiced, that was why he laughed, that was why his face was radiant under his gray hair.

It is a good thing to experience everything oneself, he thought. As a child I learned that pleasures of the world and riches were not good. I have known it for a long time, but I have only just experienced it. Now I know it not only with my intellect, but with my eyes, with my heart, with my stomach. It is a good thing that I know this.

He thought long of the change in him, listened to the bird singing happily. If this bird within him had died, would he have perished? No, something else in him had died, something that he had long desired should perish. Was it not what he had once wished to destroy during his ardent years of asceticism? Was it not his Self, his small, fearful and proud Self, with which he had wrestled for so many years, but which had always conquered him again, which appeared each time again and again, which robbed him of happiness and filled him with fear? Was it not this which had finally died today in the wood by this delightful river? Was it not because of its death that he was now like a child, so full of trust and happiness, without fear?

Siddhartha now also realized why he had struggled in vain with this Self when he was a Brahmin and an ascetic. Too much knowledge had hindered him; too many holy verses, too many sacrificial rites, too much mortification of the flesh, too much doing and striving. He had been full of arrogance; he had always been the cleverest, the most eager—always a step ahead of the others, always the learned and intellectual one, always the priest or the sage. His Self had crawled into this priesthood, into this arrogance, into this intellectuality. It sat there tightly and grew, while he thought he was destroying it by fasting and penitence. Now he understood it and realized that the inward voice had been right, that no teacher could have brought him salvation. That was why he had to go into the world, to lose himself in power, women and money; that was why he had to be a merchant, a dice player, a drinker and a man of property, until the priest and Samana in him were dead. That was why he had to undergo those horrible years, suffer nausea, learn the lesson of the madness of an empty, futile life till the end, till he reached bitter despair, so that Siddhartha the pleasure-monger and Siddhartha the man of property could die. He had died and a new Siddhartha had awakened from his sleep. He also would grow old and die. Siddhartha was transitory, all forms were transitory, but today he was young, he was a child—the new Siddhartha—and he was very happy.

These thoughts passed through his mind. Smiling, he listened to his stomach, listened thankfully to a humming bee. Happily he looked into the flowing river. Never had a river attracted him as much as this one. Never had he found the voice and appearance of flowing water so beautiful. It seemed to him as if the river had something special to tell him, something which he did not know, something which still awaited him. Siddhartha had wanted to drown himself in this river; the old, tired, despairing Siddhartha was today drowned in it. The new Siddhartha felt a deep love for this flowing water and decided that he would not leave it again so quickly.

REVELATION

FLANNERY O'CONNOR

For Zen monks, it is sometimes a blow from a paddle that snaps them into enlightenment. For Mrs. Turpin, it is a book, but the result is the same.

The doctor's waiting room, which was very small, was almost full when the Turpins entered and Mrs. Turpin, who was very large, made it look even smaller by her presence. She stood looming at the head of the magazine table set in the center of it, a living demonstration that the room was inadequate and ridiculous. Her little bright black eyes took in all the patients as she sized up the seating situation. There was one vacant chair and a place on the sofa occupied by a blond child in a dirty blue romper who should have been told to move over and make room for the lady. He was five or six, but Mrs. Turpin saw at once that no one was going to tell him to move over. He was slumped down in the seat, his arms idle at his sides and his eyes idle in his head; his nose ran unchecked.

Mrs. Turpin put a firm hand on Claud's shoulder and said in a voice that included anyone who wanted to listen, "Claud, you sit in that chair there," and gave him a push down into the vacant one. Claud was florid and bald and sturdy, somewhat shorter than Mrs. Turpin, but he sat down as if he were accustomed to doing what she told him to.

Mrs. Turpin remained standing. The only man in the room besides Claud was a lean stringy old fellow with a rusty hand spread out on each knee, whose eyes were closed as if he were asleep or dead or pretending to be so as not to get up and offer her his seat. Her gaze settled agreeably on a well-dressed gray-haired lady whose eyes met hers and whose expression said: if that child belonged to me, he would have some manners and move over—there's plenty of room there for you and him too.

Claud looked up with a sigh and made as if to rise.

"Sit down," Mrs. Turpin said. "You know you're not supposed to stand on that leg. He has an ulcer on his leg," she explained.

Claud lifted his foot onto the magazine table and rolled his trouser leg up to reveal a purple swelling on a plump marble-white calf.

"My!" the pleasant lady said. "How did you do that?"

"A cow kicked him," Mrs. Turpin said.

"Goodness!" said the lady.

Claud rolled his trouser leg down.

"Maybe the little boy would move over," the lady suggested, but the child did not stir.

"Somebody will be leaving in a minute," Mrs. Turpin said. She could not understand why a doctor—with as much money as they made charging five dollars a day to just stick their head in the hospital door and look at you—couldn't afford a decent-sized waiting room. This one was hardly bigger than a garage. The table was cluttered with limp-looking magazines and at one end of it there was a big green glass ash tray full of cigarette butts and cotton wads with little blood spots on them. If she had had anything to do with the running of the place, that would have been emptied every so often. There were no chairs against the wall at the head of the room. It had a rectangular-shaped panel in it that permitted a view of the office where the nurse came and went and the secretary listened to the radio. A plastic fern in a gold pot sat in the opening and trailed its fronds down almost to the floor. The radio was softly playing gospel music.

Just then the inner door opened and a nurse with the highest stack of yellow hair Mrs. Turpin had ever seen put her face in the crack and called for the next patient. The woman sitting beside Claud grasped the two arms of her chair and hoisted herself up; she pulled her dress free from her legs and lumbered through the door where the nurse had disappeared.

Mrs. Turpin eased into the vacant chair, which held her tight as a corset. "I wish I could reduce," she said, and rolled her eyes and gave a comic sigh.

"Oh, *you* aren't fat," the stylish lady said.

"Ooooo I am too," Mrs. Turpin said. "Claud he eats all he wants to and never weighs over one hundred and seventy-five pounds, but me I just look at something good to eat and I gain some weight," and her stomach and shoulders shook with laughter. "You can eat all you want to, can't you, Claud?" she asked, turning to him.

Claud only grinned.

"Well, as long as you have such a good disposition," the stylish lady said, "I don't think it makes a bit of difference what size you are. You just can't beat a good disposition."

Next to her was a fat girl of eighteen or nineteen, scowling into a thick blue book which Mrs. Turpin saw was entitled *Human Development.* The girl raised her head and directed her scowl at Mrs. Turpin as if she did not like her looks. She appeared annoyed that anyone should speak while she tried to read. The poor girl's face was blue with acne and Mrs. Turpin thought how pitiful it was to have a face like that at that age. She gave the girl a friendly smile but the girl only scowled the harder. Mrs. Turpin herself was fat but she had always had good skin, and, though she was forty-seven years old, there was not a wrinkle in her face except around her eyes from laughing too much.

Next to the ugly girl was the child, still in exactly the same position, and next to him was a thin leathery old woman in a cotton print dress. She and Claud had three sacks of chicken feed in their pump house that was in the same print. She had seen from the first that the child belonged with the old woman. She could tell by the way they sat—kind of vacant and white-trashy, as if they would sit there until Doomsday if nobody called and told them to get up. And at right angles but next to the well-dressed pleasant lady was a lank-faced woman who was certainly the child's mother. She had on a yellow sweat shirt and wine-colored slacks, both gritty-looking, and the rims of her lips were stained with snuff. Her dirty yellow hair was tied behind with a little piece of red paper ribbon. Worse than niggers any day, Mrs. Turpin thought.

The gospel hymn playing was, "When I looked up and He looked down," and Mrs. Turpin, who knew it, supplied the last line mentally, "And wona these days I know I'll weeara crown."

Without appearing to, Mrs. Turpin always noticed people's feet. The well-dressed lady had on red and gray suede shoes to match her dress. Mrs. Turpin had on her good black patent leather pumps. The ugly girl had on Girl Scout shoes and heavy socks. The old woman had on tennis shoes and the white-trashy mother had on what appeared to be bedroom slippers, black straw with gold braid threaded through them—exactly what you would have expected her to have on.

Sometimes at night when she couldn't go to sleep, Mrs. Turpin would occupy herself with the question of who she would have chosen to be if she couldn't have been herself. If Jesus had said to her before he made her, "There's only two places available for you. You can either be a nigger or white-trash," what would she have said? "Please, Jesus, please," she would have said, "just let me wait until there's another place available," and he would have said, "No, you have to go right now and I have only those two places so make up your mind." She would have wiggled and squirmed and begged and pleaded but it would have been no use and finally she would have said, "All right, make me a nigger then—but that don't mean a trashy one." And he would have made her a neat clean respectable Negro woman, herself but black.

Next to the child's mother was a red-headed youngish woman, reading one of the magazines and working a piece of chewing gum, hell for leather, as Claud would say. Mrs. Turpin could not see the woman's feet. She was not white-trash, just common. Sometimes Mrs. Turpin occupied herself at night naming the classes of people. On the bottom of the heap were most colored people, not the kind she would have been if she had been one, but most of them; then next to them—not above, just away from—were the white-trash; then above them were the home-owners, and above them the home-and-land owners, to which she and Claud belonged. Above she and Claud were people with a lot of money and much bigger houses and much more land. But here the complexity of it would begin to bear in on her, for some of the people with a lot money were common and ought to be below she and Claud and some of the people who had good blood had lost their money and had to rent and then there were colored people who owned their homes and land as well. There was a colored dentist in town who had two red Lincolns and a swimming pool and a farm with registered white-face cattle on it. Usually by the time she had fallen asleep all the classes of people were moiling and roiling around in her head, and she would dream they were all crammed in together in a box car, being ridden off to be put in a gas oven.

"That's a beautiful clock," she said and nodded to her right. It was a big wall clock, the face encased in a brass sunburst.

"Yes, it's very pretty," the stylish lady said agreeably. "And right on the dot too," she added, glancing at her watch.

The ugly girl beside her cast an eye upward at the clock, smirked, then looked directly at Mrs. Turpin and smirked again. Then she returned her eyes to her book. She was obviously the lady's daughter because, although they didn't look anything alike as to disposition, they both had the same shape of face and the same blue eyes. On the lady they sparkled pleasantly but in the girl's seared face they appeared alternately to smolder and to blaze.

What if Jesus had said, "All right, you can be white-trash or a nigger or ugly"!

Mrs. Turpin felt an awful pity for the girl, though she thought it was one thing to be ugly and another to act ugly.

The woman with the snuff-stained lips turned around in her chair and looked up at the clock. Then she turned back and appeared to look a little to the side of Mrs. Turpin. There was a cast in one of her eyes. "You want to know wher you can get you one of themther clocks?" she asked in a loud voice.

"No, I already have a nice clock," Mrs. Turpin said.

Once somebody like her got a leg in the conversation, she would be all over it.

"You can get you one with green stamps," the woman said. "That's most likely wher he got hisn. Save you up enough, you can get you most anythang. I got me some joo'ry."

Ought to have got you a wash rag and some soap, Mrs. Turpin thought.

"I get contour sheets with mine," the pleasant lady said.

The daughter slammed her book shut. She looked straight in front of her, directly through Mrs. Turpin and on through the yellow curtain and the plate glass window which made the wall behind her. The girl's eyes seemed lit all of a sudden with a peculiar light, an unnatural light like night road signs give. Mrs. Turpin turned her head to see if there was anything going on outside that she should see, but she could not see anything. Figures passing cast only a pale shadow through the curtain. There was no reason the girl should single her out for her ugly looks.

"Miss Finley," the nurse said, cracking the door. The gum-chewing woman got up and passed in front of her and Claud and went into the office. She had on red high-heeled shoes.

Directly across the table, the ugly girl's eyes were fixed on Mrs. Turpin as if she had some very special reason for disliking her.

"This is wonderful weather, isn't it?" the girl's mother said.

"It's good weather for cotton if you can get the niggers to

pick it," Mrs. Turpin said, "but niggers don't want to pick cotton any more. You can't get the white folks to pick it and now you can't get the niggers—because they got to be right up there with the white folks."

"They gonna *try* anyways," the white-trash woman said, leaning forward.

"Do you have one of the cotton-picking machines?" the pleasant lady asked.

"No," Mrs. Turpin said, "they leave half the cotton in the field. We don't have much cotton anyway. If you want to make it farming now, you have to have a little of everything. We got a couple of acres of cotton and a few hogs and chickens and just enough white-face that Claud can look after them himself."

"One thang I don't want," the white-trash woman said, wiping her mouth with the back of her hand. "Hogs. Nasty stinking things, a-gruntin and a-rootin all over the place."

Mrs. Turpin gave her the merest edge of her attention. "Our hogs are not dirty and they don't stink," she said. "They're cleaner than some children I've seen. Their feet never touch the ground. We have a pig-parlor—that's where you raise them on concrete," she explained to the pleasant lady, "and Claud scoots them down with the hose every afternoon and washes off the floor." Cleaner by far than that child right there, she thought. Poor nasty little thing. He had not moved except to put the thumb of his dirty hand into his mouth.

The woman turned her face away from Mrs. Turpin. "I know I wouldn't scoot down no hog with no hose," she said to the wall.

You wouldn't have no hog to scoot down, Mrs. Turpin said to herself.

"A-gruntin and a-rootin and a-groanin," the woman muttered.

"We got a little of everything," Mrs. Turpin said to the pleasant lady. "It's no use in having more than you can handle yourself with help like it is. We found enough niggers to pick our cotton this year but Claud he has to go after them and take them home again in the evening. They can't walk that half a mile. No they can't. I tell you," she said and laughed merrily, "I sure am tired of buttering up niggers, but you got to love em if you want em to work for you. When they come in the morning, I run out and I say, 'Hi yawl this morning?' and when Claud drives them off to the field I just wave to beat the band and they just wave back." And she waved her hand rapidly to illustrate.

"Like you read out of the same book," the lady said, showing she understood perfectly.

"Child, yes," Mrs. Turpin said. "And when they come in from the field, I run out with a bucket of icewater. That's the way it's going to be from now on," she said. "You may as well face it."

"One thang I know," the white-trash woman said. "Two

thangs I ain't going to do: love no niggers or scoot down no hog with no hose." And she let out a bark of contempt.

The look that Mrs. Turpin and the pleasant lady exchanged indicated they both understood that you had to *have* certain things before you could *know* certain things. But every time Mrs. Turpin exchanged a look with the lady, she was aware that the ugly girl's peculiar eyes were still on her, and she had trouble bringing her attention back to the conversation.

"When you got something," she said, "you got to look after it." And when you ain't got a thing but breath and britches, she added to herself, you can afford to come to town every morning and just sit on the Court House coping and spit.

A grotesque revolving shadow passed across the curtain behind her and was thrown palely on the opposite wall. Then a bicycle clattered down against the outside of the building. The door opened and a colored boy glided in with a tray from the drugstore. It had two large red and white paper cups on it with tops on them. He was a tall, very black boy in discolored white pants and a green nylon shirt. He was chewing gum slowly, as if to music. He set the tray down in the office opening next to the fern and stuck his head through to look for the secretary. She was not in there. He rested his arms on the ledge and waited, his narrow bottom stuck out, swaying to the left and right. He raised a hand over his head and scratched the base of his skull.

"You see that button there, boy?" Mrs. Turpin said. "You can punch that and she'll come. She's probably in the back somewhere."

"Is thas right?" the boy said agreeably, as if he had never seen the button before. He leaned to the right and put his finger on it. "She sometime out," he said and twisted around to face his audience, his elbows behind him on the counter. The nurse appeared and he twisted back again. She handed him a dollar and he rooted in his pocket and made the change and counted it out to her. She gave him fifteen cents for a tip and he went out with the empty tray. The heavy door swung to slowly and closed at length with the sound of suction. For a moment no one spoke.

"They ought to send all them niggers back to Africa," the white-trash woman said. "That's wher they come from in the first place."

"Oh, I couldn't do without my good colored friends," the pleasant lady said.

"There's a heap of things worse than a nigger," Mrs. Turpin agreed. "It's all kinds of them just like it's all kinds of us."

"Yes, and it takes all kinds to make the world go round," the lady said in her musical voice.

As she said it, the raw-complexioned girl snapped her teeth together. Her lower lip turned downwards and inside out, revealing the pale pink inside of her mouth. After a second it rolled back up. It was the ugliest face Mrs. Turpin had ever seen anyone make and for a moment she was certain that the girl had made it at her. She was looking at her as if she had known and disliked her all her life—all of Mrs. Turpin's life, it seemed too, not just all the girl's life. Why, girl, I don't even know you, Mrs. Turpin said silently.

She forced her attention back to the discussion. "It wouldn't be practical to send them back to Africa," she said. "They wouldn't want to go. They got it too good here."

"Wouldn't be what they wanted—if I had anythang to do with it," the woman said.

"It wouldn't be a way in the world you could get all the niggers back over there," Mrs. Turpin said. "They'd be hiding out and lying down and turning sick on you and wailing and hollering and raring and pitching. It wouldn't be a way in the world to get them over there."

"They got over here," the trashy woman said. "Get back like they got over."

"It wasn't so many of them then," Mrs. Turpin explained.

The woman looked at Mrs. Turpin as if here was an idiot indeed but Mrs. Turpin was not bothered by the look, considering where it came from.

"Nooo," she said, "they're going to stay here where they can go to New York and marry white folks and improve their color. That's what they all want to do, every one of them, improve their color."

"You know what comes of that, don't you?" Claud asked.

"No, Claud, what?" Mrs. Turpin said.

Claud's eyes twinkled. "White-faced niggers," he said with never a smile.

Everybody in the office laughed except the white-trash and the ugly girl. The girl gripped the book in her lap with white fingers. The trashy woman looked around her from face to face as if she thought they were all idiots. The old woman in the feed sack dress continued to gaze expressionless across the floor at the high-top shoes of the man opposite her, the one who had been pretending to be asleep when the Turpins came in. He was laughing heartily, his hands still spread out on his knees. The child had fallen to the side and was lying now almost face down in the old woman's lap.

While they recovered from their laughter, the nasal chorus on the radio kept the room from silence.

"You go to blank blank
And I'll go to mine
But we'll all blank along
To-geth-ther,
And all along the blank
We'll hep each other out
Smile-ling in any kind of
Weath-ther!"

Mrs. Turpin didn't catch every word but she caught enough to agree with the spirit of the song and it turned her thoughts sober. To help anybody out that needed it was her philosophy of life. She never spared herself when she found somebody in need, whether they were white or black, trash or decent. And of all she had to be thankful for, she was most thankful that this was so. If Jesus had said, "You can be high society and have all the money you want and be thin and svelte-like, but you can't be a good woman with it," she would have had to say, "Well don't make me that then. Make me a good woman and it don't matter what else, how fat or how ugly or how poor!" Her heart rose. He had not made her a nigger or white-trash or ugly! He had made her herself and given her a little of everything. Jesus, thank you! she said. Thank you thank you thank you! Whenever she counted her blessings she felt as buoyant as if she weighed one hundred and twenty-five pounds instead of one hundred and eighty.

"What's wrong with your little boy?" the pleasant lady asked the white-trashy woman.

"He has a ulcer," the woman said proudly. "He ain't give me a minute's peace since he was born. Him and her are just alike," she said, nodding at the old woman, who was running her leathery fingers through the child's pale hair. "Look like I can't get nothing down them two but Co' Cola and candy."

That's all you try to get down em, Mrs. Turpin said to herself. Too lazy to light the fire. There was nothing you could tell her about people like them that she didn't know already. And it was not just that they didn't have anything. Because if you gave them everything, in two weeks it would all be broken or filthy or they would have chopped it up for lightwood. She knew all this from her own experience. Help them you must, but help them you couldn't.

All at once the ugly girl turned her lips inside out again. Her eyes fixed like two drills on Mrs. Turpin. This time there was no mistaking that there was something urgent behind them.

Girl, Mrs. Turpin exclaimed silently, I haven't done a thing to you! The girl might be confusing her with somebody else. There was no need to sit by and let herself be intimidated. "You must be in college," she said boldly, looking directly at the girl. "I see you reading a book there."

The girl continued to stare and pointedly did not answer.

Her mother blushed at this rudeness. "The lady asked you a question, Mary Grace," she said under her breath.

"I have ears," Mary Grace said.

The poor mother blushed again. "Mary Grace goes to Wellesley College," she explained. She twisted one of the buttons on her dress. "In Massachusetts," she added with a grimace. "And in the summer she just keeps right on studying. Just reads all the time, a real book worm. She's done real well at Wellesley; she's taking English and Math and History and Psychology and Social Studies," she rattled on, "and I think it's too much. I think she ought to get out and have fun."

The girl looked as if she would like to hurl them all through the plate glass window.

"Way up north," Mrs. Turpin murmured and thought, well, it hasn't done much for her manners.

"I'd almost rather to have him sick," the white-trash woman said, wrenching the attention back to herself. "He's so mean when he ain't. Look like some children just take natural to meanness. It's some gets bad when they get sick but he was the opposite. Took sick and turned good. He don't give me no trouble now. It's me waitin to see the doctor," she said.

If I was going to send anybody back to Africa, Mrs. Turpin thought, it would be your kind, woman. "Yes, indeed," she said aloud, but looking up at the ceiling, "it's a heap of things worse than a nigger." And dirtier than a hog, she added to herself.

"I think people with bad dispositions are more to be pitied than anyone on earth," the pleasant lady said in a voice that was decidedly thin.

"I thank the Lord he has blessed me with a good one," Mrs. Turpin said. "The day has never dawned that I couldn't find something to laugh at."

"Not since she married me anyways," Claud said with a comical straight face.

Everybody laughed except the girl and the white-trash.

Mrs. Turpin's stomach shook. "He's such a caution," she said, "that I can't help but laugh at him."

The girl made a loud ugly noise through her teeth.

Her mother's mouth grew thin and tight. "I think the

worst thing in the world," she said, "is an ungrateful person. To have everything and not appreciate it. I know a girl," she said, "who has parents who would give her anything, a little brother who loves her dearly, who is getting a good education, who wears the best clothes, but who can never say a kind word to anyone, who never smiles, who just criticizes and complains all day long."

"Is she too old to paddle?" Claud asked.

The girl's face was almost purple.

"Yes," the lady said, "I'm afraid there's nothing to do but leave her to her folly. Some day she'll wake up and it'll be too late."

"It never hurt anyone to smile," Mrs. Turpin said. "It just makes you feel better all over."

"Of course," the lady said sadly, "but there are just some people you can't tell anything to. They can't take criticism."

"If it's one thing I am," Mrs. Turpin said with feeling, "it's grateful. When I think who all I could have been besides myself and what all I got, a little of everything, and a good disposition besides, I just feel like shouting, 'Thank you, Jesus, for making everything the way it is!' It could have been different!" For one thing, somebody else could have got Claud. At the thought of this, she was flooded with gratitude and a terrible pang of joy ran through her. "Oh thank you, Jesus, Jesus, thank you!" she cried aloud.

The book struck her directly over her left eye. It struck

almost at the same instant that she realized the girl was about to hurl it. Before she could utter a sound, the raw face came crashing across the table toward her, howling. The girl's fingers sank like clamps into the soft flesh of her neck. She heard the mother cry out and Claud shout, "Whoa!" There was an instant when she was certain that she was about to be in an earthquake.

All at once her vision narrowed and she saw everything as if it were happening in a small room far away, or as if she were looking at it through the wrong end of a telescope. Claud's face crumpled and fell out of sight. The nurse ran in, then out, then in again. Then the gangling figure of the doctor rushed out of the inner door. Magazines flew this way and that as the table turned over. The girl fell with a thud and Mrs. Turpin's vision suddenly reversed itself and she saw everything large instead of small. The eyes of the white-trashy woman were staring hugely at the floor. There the girl, held down on one side by the nurse and on the other by her mother, was wrenching and turning in their grasp. The doctor was kneeling astride her, trying to hold her arm down. He managed after a second to sink a long needle into it.

Mrs. Turpin felt entirely hollow except for her heart which swung from side to side as if it were agitated in a great empty drum of flesh.

"Somebody that's not busy call for the ambulance," the

doctor said in the off-hand voice young doctors adopt for terrible occasions.

Mrs. Turpin could not have moved a finger. The old man who had been sitting next to her skipped nimbly into the office and made the call, for the secretary still seemed to be gone.

"Claud!" Mrs. Turpin called.

He was not in his chair. She knew she must jump up and find him but she felt like some one trying to catch a train in a dream, when everything moves in slow motion and the faster you try to run the slower you go.

"Here I am," a suffocated voice, very unlike Claud's, said.

He was doubled up in the corner on the floor, pale as paper, holding his leg. She wanted to get up and go to him but she could not move. Instead, her gaze was drawn slowly downward to the churning face on the floor, which she could see over the doctor's shoulder.

The girl's eyes stopped rolling and focused on her. They seemed a much lighter blue than before, as if a door that had been tightly closed behind them was now open to admit light and air.

Mrs. Turpin's head cleared and her power of motion returned. She leaned forward until she was looking directly into the fierce brilliant eyes. There was no doubt in her mind that the girl did know her, knew her in some intense and personal way, beyond time and place and condition. "What you got to say to me?" she asked hoarsely and held her breath, waiting, as for a revelation.

The girl raised her head. Her gaze locked with Mrs. Turpin's. "Go back to hell where you came from, you old wart hog," she whispered. Her voice was low but clear. Her eyes burned for a moment as if she saw with pleasure that her message had struck its target.

Mrs. Turpin sank back in her chair.

After a moment the girl's eyes closed and she turned her head wearily to the side.

The doctor rose and handed the nurse the empty syringe. He leaned over and put both hands for a moment on the mother's shoulders, which were shaking. She was sitting on the floor, her lips pressed together, holding Mary Grace's hand in her lap. The girl's fingers were gripped like a baby's around her thumb. "Go on to the hospital," he said. "I'll call and make the arrangements."

"Now let's see that neck," he said in a jovial voice to Mrs. Turpin. He began to inspect her neck with his first two fingers. Two little moon-shaped lines like pink fish bones were indented over her windpipe. There was the beginning of an angry red swelling above her eye. His fingers passed over this also.

"Lea' me be," she said thickly and shook him off. "See about Claud. She kicked him."

"I'll see about him in a minute," he said and felt her pulse. He was a thin gray-haired man, given to pleasantries.

"Go home and have yourself a vacation the rest of the day," he said and patted her on the shoulder.

Quit your pattin me, Mrs. Turpin growled to herself.

"And put an ice pack over that eye," he said. Then he went and squatted down beside Claud and looked at his leg. After a moment he pulled him up and Claud limped after him into the office.

Until the ambulance came, the only sounds in the room were the tremulous moans of the girl's mother, who continued to sit on the floor. The white-trash woman did not take her eyes off the girl. Mrs. Turpin looked straight ahead at nothing. Presently the ambulance drew up, a long dark shadow, behind the curtain. The attendants came in and set the stretcher down beside the girl and lifted her expertly onto it and carried her out. The nurse helped the mother gather up her things. The shadow of the ambulance moved silently away and the nurse came back in the office.

"That ther girl is going to be a lunatic, ain't she?" the white-trash woman asked the nurse, but the nurse kept on to the back and never answered her.

"Yes, she's going to be a lunatic," the white-trash woman said to the rest of them.

"Po' critter," the old woman murmured. The child's face was still in her lap. His eyes looked idly out over her knees. He had not moved during the disturbance except to draw one leg up under him.

"I thank Gawd," the white-trash woman said fervently, "I ain't a lunatic."

Claud came limping out and the Turpins went home.

As their pick-up truck turned into their own dirt road and made the crest of the hill, Mrs. Turpin gripped the window ledge and looked out suspiciously. The land sloped gracefully down through a field dotted with lavender weeds and at the start of the rise their small yellow frame house, with its little flower beds spread out around it like a fancy apron, sat primly in its accustomed place between two giant hickory trees. She would not have been startled to see a burnt wound between two blackened chimneys.

Neither of them felt like eating so they put on their house clothes and lowered the shade in the bedroom and lay down, Claud with his leg on a pillow and herself with a damp wash-cloth over her eye. The instant she was flat on her back, the image of a razor-backed hog with warts on its face and horns coming out behind its ears snorted into her head. She moaned, a low quiet moan.

"I am not," she said tearfully, "a wart hog. From hell." But the denial had no force. The girl's eyes and her words, even the tone of her voice, low but clear, directed only to her, brooked no repudiation. She had been singled out for the message, though there was trash in the room to whom it might justly have been applied. The full force of this fact struck her only now. There was a woman there who was neglecting her own child but she had been overlooked. The message had been given to Ruby Turpin, a respectable, hard-working, church-going woman. The tears dried. Her eyes began to burn instead with wrath.

She rose on her elbow and the washcloth fell into her hand. Claud was lying on his back, snoring. She wanted to tell him what the girl had said. At the same time, she did not wish to put the image of herself as a wart hog from hell into his mind.

"Hey, Claud," she muttered and pushed his shoulder.

Claud opened one pale baby blue eye.

She looked into it warily. He did not think about anything. He just went his way.

"Wha, whasit?" he said and closed the eye again.

"Nothing," she said. "Does your leg pain you?"

"Hurts like hell," Claud said.

"It'll quit terreckly," she said and lay back down. In a moment Claud was snoring again. For the rest of the afternoon they lay there. Claud slept. She scowled at the ceiling. Occasionally she raised her fist and made a small stabbing motion over her chest as if she was defending her innocence to invisible guests who were like the comforters of Job, reasonable-seeming but wrong.

About five-thirty Claud stirred. "Got to go after those niggers," he sighed, not moving.

She was looking straight up as if there were unintelligible handwriting on the ceiling. The protuberance over her eye had turned a greenish-blue. "Listen here," she said.

"What?"

"Kiss me."

Claud leaned over and kissed her loudly on the mouth. He pinched her side and their hands interlocked. Her expression of ferocious concentration did not change. Claud got up, groaning and growling, and limped off. She continued to study the ceiling.

She did not get up until she heard the pick-up truck coming back with the Negroes. Then she rose and thrust her feet in her brown oxfords, which she did not bother to lace, and stumped out onto the back porch and got her red plastic bucket. She emptied a tray of ice cubes into it and filled it half full of water and went out into the back yard. Every afternoon after Claud brought the hands in, one of the boys helped him put out hay and the rest waited in the back of the truck until he was ready to take them home. The truck was parked in the shade under one of the hickory trees.

"Hi yawl this evening?" Mrs. Turpin asked grimly, appearing with the bucket and the dipper. There were three women and a boy in the truck.

"Us doin nicely," the oldest woman said. "Hi you doin?" and her gaze stuck immediately on the dark lump on Mrs. Turpin's forehead. "You done fell down, ain't you?" she asked in a solicitous voice. The old woman was dark and almost toothless. She had on an old felt hat of Claud's set back on her head. The other two women were younger and lighter and they both had new bright green sunhats. One of them had hers on her head; the other had taken hers off and the boy was grinning beneath it.

Mrs. Turpin set the bucket down on the floor of the truck. "Yawl hep yourselves," she said. She looked around to make sure Claud had gone. "No, I didn't fall down," she said, folding her arms. "It was something worse than that."

"Ain't nothing bad happen to you!" the old woman said. She said it as if they all knew that Mrs. Turpin was protected in some special way by Divine Providence. "You just had you a little fall."

"We were in town at the doctor's office for where the cow kicked Mr. Turpin," Mrs. Turpin said in a flat tone that indicated they could leave off their foolishness. "And there was this girl there. A big fat girl with her face all broke out. I could look at that girl and tell she was peculiar but I couldn't tell how. And me and her mama was just talking and going along and all of a sudden WHAM! She throws this big book she was reading at me and . . ."

"Naw!" the old woman cried out.

"And then she jumps over the table and commences to choke me."

"Naw!" they all exclaimed, "naw!"

"Hi come she do that?" the old woman asked. "What ail her?"

Mrs. Turpin only glared in front of her.

"Somethin ail her," the old woman said.

"They carried her off in an ambulance," Mrs. Turpin continued, "but before she went she was rolling on the floor and they were trying to hold her down to give her a shot and she said something to me." She paused. "You know what she said to me?"

"What she say?" they asked.

"She said," Mrs. Turpin began, and stopped, her face very dark and heavy. The sun was getting whiter and whiter, blanching the sky overhead so that the leaves of the hickory tree were black in the face of it. She could not bring forth the words. "Something real ugly," she muttered.

"She sho shouldn't said nothin ugly to you," the old woman said. "You so sweet. You the sweetest lady I know."

"She pretty too," the one with the hat on said.

"And stout," the other one said. "I never knowed no sweeter white lady."

"That's the truth befo' Jesus," the old woman said. "Amen! You des as sweet and pretty as you can be."

Mrs. Turpin knew exactly how much Negro flattery was worth and it added to her rage. "She said," she began again and finished this time with a fierce rush of breath, "that I was an old wart hog from hell."

There was an astounded silence.

"Where she at?" the youngest woman cried in a piercing voice.

"Lemme see her. I'll kill her!"

"I'll kill her with you!" the other one cried.

"She b'long in the sylum," the old woman said emphatically. "You the sweetest white lady I know."

"She pretty too," the other two said. "Stout as she can be and sweet. Jesus satisfied with her!"

"Deed he is," the old woman declared.

Idiots! Mrs. Turpin growled to herself. You could never say anything intelligent to a nigger. You could talk at them but not with them. "Yawl ain't drunk your water," she said shortly. "Leave the bucket in the truck when you're finished with it. I got more to do than just stand around and pass the time of day," and she moved off and into the house.

She stood for a moment in the middle of the kitchen. The dark protuberance over her eye looked like a miniature tornado cloud which might any moment sweep across the horizon of her brow. Her lower lip protruded dangerously. She squared her massive shoulders. Then she marched into the front of the house and out the side door and started down the road to the pig parlor. She had the look of a woman going single-handed, weaponless, into battle.

The sun was a deep yellow now like a harvest moon and was riding westward very fast over the far tree line as if it meant to reach the hogs before she did. The road was rutted and she kicked several good-sized stones out of her path as she strode along. The pig parlor was on a little knoll at the end of a lane that ran off from the side of the barn. It was a square of concrete as large as a small room, with a board fence about four feet high around it. The concrete floor sloped slightly so that the hog wash could drain off into a trench where it was carried to the field for fertilizer. Claud was standing on the outside, on the edge of the concrete, hanging onto the top board, hosing down the floor inside. The hose was connected to the faucet of a water trough nearby.

Mrs. Turpin climbed up beside him and glowered down at the hogs inside. There were seven long-snouted bristly shoats in it—tan with liver-colored spots—and an old sow a few weeks off from farrowing. She was lying on her side grunting. The shoats were running about shaking themselves like idiot children, their little slit pig eyes searching the floor for anything left. She had read that pigs were the most intelligent animal. She doubted it. They were supposed to be smarter than dogs. There had even been a pig astronaut. He had performed his assignment perfectly but died of a heart attack afterwards because they left him in his electric suit, sitting upright throughout his examination when naturally a hog should be on all fours.

A-gruntin and a-rootin and a-groanin.

"Gimme that hose," she said, yanking it away from Claud. "Go on and carry them niggers home and then get off that leg."

"You look like you might have swallowed a mad dog," Claud observed, but he got down and limped off. He paid no attention to her humors.

Until he was out of earshot, Mrs. Turpin stood on the side of the pen, holding the hose and pointing the stream of water at the hind quarters of any shoat that looked as if it might try to lie down. When he had had time to get over the hill, she turned her head slightly and her wrathful eyes scanned the path. He was nowhere in sight. She turned back again and seemed to gather herself up. Her shoulders rose and she drew in her breath.

"What do you send me a message like that for?" she said in a low fierce voice, barely above a whisper but with the force of a shout in its concentrated fury. "How am I a hog and me both? How am I saved and from hell too?" Her free fist was knotted and with the other she gripped the hose, blindly pointing the steam of water in and out of the eye of the old sow whose outraged squeal she did not hear.

The pig parlor commanded a view of the back pasture where their twenty beef cows were gathered around the hay-bales Claud and the boy had put out. The freshly cut pasture sloped down to the highway. Across it was their cotton field and beyond that a dark green dusty wood which they owned as well. The sun was behind the wood, very red, looking over the paling of trees like a farmer inspecting his own hogs.

"Why me?" she rumbled. "It's no trash around here, black or white, that I haven't given to. And break my back to the bone every day working. And do for the church."

She appeared to be the right size woman to command the arena before her. "How am I a hog?" she demanded. "Exactly how am I like them?" and she jabbed the stream of water at the shoats. "There was plenty of trash there. It didn't have to be me.

"If you like trash better, go get yourself some trash then," she railed. "You could have made me trash. Or a nigger. If trash is what you wanted why didn't you make me trash?" She shook her fist with the hose in it and a watery snake appeared momentarily in the air. "I could quit working and take it easy and be filthy," she growled. "Lounge about the sidewalks all day drinking root beer. Dip snuff and spit in every puddle and have it all over my face. I could be nasty.

"Or you could have made me a nigger. It's too late for me to be a nigger," she said with deep sarcasm, "but I could act like one. Lay down in the middle of the road and stop traffic. Roll on the ground."

In the deepening light everything was taking on a mysterious hue. The pasture was growing a peculiar glassy green and the streak of highway had turned lavender. She braced herself for a final assault and this time her voice rolled out over the pasture. "Go on," she yelled, "call me a hog! Call me a hog again. From hell. Call me a wart hog from hell. Put that bottom rail on top. There'll still be a top and bottom!"

A garbled echo returned to her.

A final surge of fury shook her and she roared, "Who do you think you are?"

The color of everything, field and crimson sky, burned for a moment with a transparent intensity. The question carried over the pasture and across the highway and the cotton field and returned to her clearly like an answer from beyond the wood.

She opened her mouth but no sound came out of it.

A tiny truck, Claud's, appeared on the highway, heading rapidly out of sight. Its gears scraped thinly. It looked like a child's toy. At any moment a bigger truck might smash into it and scatter Claud's and the niggers' brains all over the road.

Mrs. Turpin stood there, her gaze fixed on the highway, all her muscles rigid, until in five or six minutes the truck reappeared, returning. She waited until it had had time to turn into their own road. Then like a monumental statue coming to life, she bent her head slowly and gazed, as if through the very heart of mystery, down into the pig parlor at the hogs. They had settled all in one corner around the old sow who was grunting softly. A red glow suffused them. They appeared to pant with a secret life.

Until the sun slipped finally behind the tree line, Mrs. Turpin remained there with her gaze bent to them as if she were absorbing some abysmal life-giving knowledge. At last she lifted her head. There was only a purple streak in the sky, cutting through a field of crimson and leading, like an extension of the highway, into the descending dusk. She raised her hands from the side of the pen in a gesture hieratic and profound. A visionary light settled in her eyes. She saw the streak as a vast swinging bridge extending upward from the earth through a field of living fire. Upon it a vast horde of souls were rumbling toward heaven. There were whole companies of white-trash, clean for the first time in their lives, and bands of black niggers in white robes, and battalions of freaks and lunatics shouting and clapping and leaping like frogs. And bringing up the end of the procession was a tribe of people whom she recognized at once as those who, like herself and Claud, had always had a little of everything and the God-given wit to use it right. She leaned forward to observe them closer. They were marching behind the others with great dignity, accountable as they had always been for good order and common sense and respectable behavior. They alone were on key. Yet she could see by their shocked and altered faces that even their virtues were being burned away. She lowered her hands and gripped the rail of the hog pen, her eyes small but fixed unblinkingly on what lay ahead. In a moment the vision faded but she remained where she was, immobile.

At length she got down and turned off the faucet and made her slow way on the darkening path to the house. In the woods around her the invisible cricket choruses had struck up, but what she heard were the voices of the souls climbing upward into the starry field and shouting hallelujah.

from

SALVATION ON SAND MOUNTAIN

DENNIS COVINGTON

Writer Dennis Covington most certainly did not imagine he would find revelation among the snake handling sects of Alabama when he began researching a book about them, but instead of pushing a man out of the Garden, this time the snake pulled one back in.

And a vision appeared to Paul in the night; There stood a man of Macedonia, and prayed him, saying, Come over into Macedonia, and help us.

—Acts 16:9

That spring, Charles McGlocklin told me that Glenn Summerford's cousins, Billy and Jimmy, had started a new church on top of Sand Mountain, near a place called Macedonia. Charles didn't worship with them, though.

"Why not?" I asked.

Brother Charles took a deep breath and surveyed the land around him, yellow and gray in the afternoon light. We were on the deck behind his and Aline's trailer in New Hope, Alabama. Beside the trailer was a doghouse for their blue tick hound named Smokey, and behind it was a corral for their horse, a buckskin mare named Dixie Honeydew.

"I know enough about some of those people to know I ought not to worship anymore with them," Charles said. As a snake handler, he had set himself apart from the world, and sometimes he even set himself apart from other snake handlers. It was part of the Southern character, I thought, to be always turning away like that toward some secret part of oneself.

"You know how much I love you," Charles said. He put

one of his big hands on my shoulder and shook it. "You're my brother. But anytime you go up there on Sand Mountain, you be careful."

We could hear the sound of the wind through trees, a soughing, dry and hesitant, and then Dixie Honeydew neighed.

"You might be anointed when you take up a serpent," Charles continued, "but if there's a witchcraft spirit in the church, it could zap your anointing and you'd be left cold turkey with a serpent in your hand and the spirit of God gone off of you. That's when you'll get bit."

We walked around the corner of the trailer, where Jim Neel was waiting for me in a truck that had belonged to his brother.

"So you really watch and remember what Brother Charles tells you," Charles whispered. "Always be careful who you take a rattlesnake from."

This sounded like solid advice.

I got into Jim's truck, and Charles motioned for us to roll a window down. "Y'all come back any time," he yelled. "And, hey, it's not us that's messed up, Brother Dennis. It's the world."

My journey had come back around to the congregation on Sand Mountain, the remnant of Glenn Summerford's flock that had left the converted service station on Wood's Cove

Road in Scottsboro and then met under a brush arbor in back of J.L. Dyal's house until the weather got too cold. After worshiping for a while in the basement of an old motel, they finally found a church for sale on the mountain. It was miles from nowhere, in the middle of a hay field south of Section, Alabama, home of Tammy Little, Miss Alabama 1984. The nearest dot on the map, though, was Macedonia, a crossroads consisting of a filling station, a country store, and a junk emporium. It was not the kind of place you'd visit of your own accord. You'd have to be led there. In fact, Macedonia had gotten its name from the place in the Bible that Paul had been called to go to in a dream. Paul's first European converts to Christianity had been in Macedonia. But that was, you know, a long time ago and in another place.

Glenn Summerford's cousins, Billy and Jimmy, negotiated the deal for the church. Billy was friendly and loose limbed, with a narrow red face and buck teeth. He'd worked mostly as a carpenter, but he'd also sold coon dogs. Jimmy was less amiable but more compact. Between them, they must have been persuasive. They got the church for two thousand dollars. A guy down the road had offered five thousand, Billy said, but the owner had decided to sell it to them. "God was working in that one," he concluded.

It was called the Old Rock House Holiness Church, in spite of the fact that it wasn't made of rock. But it was old in contrast to the brick veneer churches out on highway 35, the ones with green indoor-outdoor carpet in the vestibules and blinking U-Haul It signs out front.

The Old Rock House Holiness Church had been built in 1916, a few years before Dozier Edmonds first saw people take up serpents in Jackson County, at a church in Sauty Bottom, down by Saltpeter Cave. I'd met Dozier during the brush-arbor meetings. A rail-thin old man with thick glasses and overalls, he was the father-in-law of J.L. Dyal and the husband of Burma, the snake-handling twin. Dozier said he'd seen men get bit in that church in Sauty Bottom. They didn't go to a doctor, just swelled up a little bit. He also remembered a Holiness boy at the one-room school who would fall into a trance, reach into the potbellied stove, and get himself a whole handful of hot coals. The teacher would have to tell the boy to put them back. There was a Baptist church in those days called Hell's Half Acre, Dozier said. They didn't take up serpents, but they'd do just about anything else. They were called Buckeye Baptists. They'd preach and pray till midnight, then gamble and fight till dawn. One time a man rode a horse into the church, right up to the pulpit. Out of meanness, Dozier said. Everything was different then. "They used to tie the mules up to a white mulberry bush in the square," he said. Why, he remembered when Scottsboro itself was nothing but a mud hole. When the carnival came through, the elephants were up to their bellies in mud. There wasn't even a road up Sand Mountain until Dozier helped build one. And it seemed like the Civil War had just occurred.

Dozier came from a family of sharecroppers who lived on the property of a famous Confederate veteran named Mance. He had a bullet hole through his neck. He'd built his own casket. Every Easter, Colonel Mance invited the children of the families who lived on his property to come to the big house for an egg hunt. One Easter, he wanted the children to see what he'd look like when he was dead, so he lay down in the casket and made the children march around it. Some of the grown-ups had to help get him out. It was a pine casket with metal handles on it, Dozier said. Colonel Mance eventually died, but he wasn't buried in the casket he'd made. He'd taken that thing apart years before and given the handles to the families who lived on his property, to use as knockers on the doors of their shacks.

That was the kind of place Sand Mountain had been when the Old Rock House Holiness Church was in its heyday. By the time the Summerford brothers bought it in the winter of 1993, it had fallen onto hard times. Didn't even have a back door. Paper wasps had built nests in the eaves. The green shingles on the outside were cracked, and the paint on the window sills had just about peeled off. Billy Summerford and some of the other men from the congregation repaired and restored the church as best they could. It'd be another year, though, before they could get around to putting in a bathroom. In the meantime, there would be an outhouse for the women and a bunch of trees for the men. The church happened to be sited in the very center of a grove of old oak trees. Fields of hay surrounded the grove and stretched to the horizon. As you approached the church along a dirt road during summer heat, the oak grove looked like a dark island in the middle of a shimmering sea of gold and green.

That's the way it looked to me, anyway, on a bright Sunday morning in late June, six months after the Summerfords had bought the church, when Jim and I drove up from Birmingham for their first annual homecoming. Brother Carl had invited us by phone and given us directions. He was scheduled to preach at the homecoming. Other handlers were coming from all over—from East Tennessee and South Georgia, from the mountains of Kentucky and the scrublands of the Florida panhandle. If we hadn't had Carl's directions, we'd never have found the place. The right turn off the paved road from Macedonia was unmarked. It was one of several gravel roads that angled off into the distance. Where it crossed another paved road, there finally was a sign, made of cardboard and mounted at waist level on a wooden stake. After that, the gravel turned to dirt. Dust coated the jimsonweed. The passionflowers were in bloom, and the blackberries had begun to ripen in the heat. There were no houses on this road, and no sound except for cicadas, a steady din, like the sound of approaching rain.

from SALVATION ON SAND MOUNTAIN

For once, Jim and I were early. We stepped up on a cement block to get through the back doorway of the church. The door itself was off its hinges, and none of the windows in the church had screens. There were no cushions on the pews and no ornaments of any kind, except a portrait of Jesus etched into a mirror behind the pulpit and a vase of plastic flowers on the edge of the piano bench, where a boy with a withered hand sat staring at the keys. We took our places on a back pew and watched the handlers arrive. They greeted each other with the holy kiss, women with women, men with men, as prescribed by Paul in Romans 16. Among them was the legendary Punkin Brown, the evangelist who I'd been told would wipe the sweat off his brow with rattlesnakes. Jamie Coots from Kentucky and Allen Williams from Tennessee were also there. They sat beside Punkin on the deacons' bench. All three were young and heavyset, the sons of preachers, and childhood friends. Punkin and Jamie both wore scowls, as though they were waiting for somebody to cross their paths in an unhappy way. Allen Williams, though, looked serene. Allen's father had died drinking strychnine in 1973, and his brother had died of snakebite in 1991. Maybe he thought he didn't have anything more to lose. Or maybe he was just reconciled to losing everything he had. Within six months of sitting together on the deacons' bench at the Old Rock House Church, Jamie, Allen, and Punkin would all be bit.

The church continued to fill with familiar faces, many from what used to be The Church of Jesus with Signs Following in Scottsboro, and the music began without an introduction of any kind. James Hatfield of Old Straight Creek, a Trinitarian church on the mountain, was on drums. My red-haired friend Cecil Esslinder from Scottsboro was on guitar, grinning and tapping his feet. Cecil's wife, Carolyn, stood in the very middle of the congregation, facing backward, as was her habit, to see who might come in the back way. Also in the congregation were Bobbie Sue Thompson, twins Burma and Erma, J.L. Dyal and his wife and in-laws, and just about the whole Summerford clan. The only ones missing were Charles and Aline McGlocklin. Charles was still recovering from neck surgery on an old injury, but I knew from the conversation we'd had in New Hope that even if he'd been well, he wouldn't have come.

One woman I didn't recognize told me she was from Detroit, Michigan. This came as some surprise, and her story seemed equally improbable. She said her husband used to work in the casinos in Las Vegas, and when he died she moved to Alabama and started handling rattlesnakes at the same church on Lookout Mountain where the lead singer of the group Alabama used to handle. "Didn't you see the photo?" she asked. "It was in the *National Enquirer*."

I told her I'd missed that one.

Children were racing down the aisles. High foreheads.

Eyes far apart. Gaps between their front teeth. They all looked like miniature Glenn Summerfords. Maybe they were. He had at least seven children by his first wife, and all of them were old enough to have children of their own. I started to wonder if there were any bad feelings among the Summerfords about the way Brother Carl Porter had refused to let them send the church offerings to Glenn in prison.

About that time, Brother Carl himself walked in with a serpent box containing the biggest rattlesnake I'd ever seen. Carl smelled of Old Spice and rattlesnake and something else underneath: a pleasant smell, like warm bread and apples. I associated it with the Holy Ghost. The handlers had told me that the Holy Ghost had a smell, a "sweet savor," and I had begun to think I could detect it on people and in churches, even in staid, respectable churches like the one I went to in Birmingham. Anyway, that was what I smelled on Brother Carl that day as he talked about the snake in the box. "I just got him today," he said. "He's never been in church before." Carl looked over his glasses at me and smiled. He held the serpent box up to my face and tapped the screen until the snake started rattling good.

"Got your name on him," he said to me.

A shiver went up my spine, but I just shook my head and grinned.

"Come on up to the front," he said. I followed him and sat on the first pew next to J.L. Dyal, but I made a mental note to avoid Carl's eyes during the service and to stay away from that snake of his.

Billy Summerford's wife, Joyce, led the singing. She was a big woman with a voice that wouldn't quit. "*Remember how it felt, when you walked out of the wilderness, walked out of the wilderness, walked out of the wilderness. Remember how it felt, when you walked out of the wilderness . . .* " It was one of my favorite songs because it had a double meaning now. There was the actual wilderness in the Old Testament that the Israelites were led out of, and the spiritual wilderness that was its referent, the condition of being lost. But there was also the wilderness that the New World became for my father's people. I don't mean the mountains. I mean the America that grew up around them, that tangled thicket of the heart.

"*Remember how it felt, when you walked out of the wilderness . . .* " My throat tightened as I sang. I remembered how it had felt when I'd sobered up in 1983. It's not often you get a second chance at life like that. And I remembered the births of my girls, the children Vicki and I had thought we'd never be able to have. Looking around at the familiar faces in the congregation, I figured they were thinking about their own wildernesses and how they'd been delivered out of them. I was still coming out of mine. It was a measure of how far I'd come, that I'd be moved nearly to tears in a rundown Holiness church on Sand Mountain. But my restless and stubborn intellect was still intact. It didn't like what it saw, a crowd of men dancing up to the serpent boxes, unclasping the lids, and taking out the poisonous snakes. Reason told me it was too early in the service. The snakes hadn't been prayed over enough. There hadn't even been any preaching yet, just Billy Summerford screaming into a microphone while the music swirled around us like a fog. But the boys from Tennessee and Kentucky had been hungry to get into the boxes. Soon, Punkin Brown was shouting at his snake, a big black-phase timber rattler that he had draped around his neck. Allen Williams was offering his copperhead up like a sacrifice, hands outstretched. But Brother Carl had the prize, and everyone seemed to know it. It was a yellow-phase timber, thick and melancholy, as big as timber rattlers come. Carl glanced at me, but I wouldn't make eye contact with him. I turned away. I walked to the back of the church and took a long drink of water from the bright yellow cooler propped up against a portrait of Jesus with his head on fire.

"Who knows what this snake is thinking?" Carl shouted. "God knows! God understands the mind of this snake!" And when I turned back around, Carl had laid the snake down and was treading barefoot on it from tail to head, as though he were walking a tightrope. Still, the snake didn't bite. I had heard about this, but never seen it before. The passage was from Luke: *Behold, I give unto you power to tread on serpents and scorpions, and over all the power of the enemy: and nothing shall by any means hurt you.* Then Carl picked the snake back up and draped it around his neck. The snake seemed to be looking for a way out of its predicament. Carl let it nuzzle into his shirt. Then the snake pulled back and cocked its head, as if in preparation to strike Carl's chest. Its head was as big as a child's hand.

Help him, Jesus! someone yelled above the din. Instead of striking, the snake started to climb Carl's sternum toward his collarbone. It went up the side of his neck and then lost interest and fell back against his chest.

The congregation was divided into two camps now, the men to the left, with the snakes, the women to the right, with each other. In front of Carl, one of the men suddenly began jumping straight up and down, as though he were on a pogo stick. Down the aisle he went and around the sanctuary. When he returned, he collapsed at Carl's feet. One of the Summerford brothers attended to him there by soaking his handkerchief with olive oil and dabbing it against the man's forehead until he sat up and yelled, "Thank God!"

In the meantime, in the corner where the women had gathered, Joyce Summerford's sister, Donna, an attractive young woman in a lime green dress, was laboring in the spirit with a cataleptic friend. She circled the friend, eyeing her contortions carefully, and then, as if fitting her into an imaginary dress, she clothed her in the spirit with her hands, an invisible tuck here, an invisible pin there, making sure the spirit draped well over the flailing arms. It took her a while. Both of the women were drenched in sweat and stuttering in tongues by the time they finished.

"They say we've gone crazy!" Brother Carl shouted above the chaos. He was pacing in front of the pulpit, the enormous rattlesnake balanced now across his shoulder. "Well, they're right!" he cried. "I've gone crazy! I've gone Bible crazy! I've got the papers here to prove it!" And he waved his worn Bible in the air. "Some people say we're just a bunch of fanatics!"

Amen. Thank God.

"Well, we are! *Hai-i-salemos-ah-cahn-ne-hi-yee!* Whew! That last one nearly took me out of here!"

It's not true that you become used to the noise and confusion of a snake-handling Holiness service. On the contrary, you become enmeshed in it. It is theater at its most intricate—improvisational, spiritual jazz. The more you experience it, the more attentive you are to the shifts in the surface and the dark shoals underneath. For every outward sign, there is a spiritual equivalent. When somebody falls to his knees, a specific problem presents itself, and the others know exactly what to do, whether it's oil for a healing, or a prayer cloth thrown over the shoulders, or a devil that needs to be cast out. The best, of course, the simplest and cleanest, is when someone gets the Holy Ghost for the first time. The younger the worshiper, the easier it seems to be for the Holy Ghost to descend and speak—lips loosened, tongue flapping, eyes rolling backward in the head. It transcends the erotic when a thirteen-year-old girl gets the Holy Ghost. The older ones often take time. I once saw an old man whose wife had gotten the Holy Ghost at a previous service. He wanted it bad for himself, he said. Brother Charles McGlocklin started praying with him before the service even started, and all through it, the man was in one attitude or another at the front of the church—now lying spread-eagled on the floor, while a half dozen men prayed over him and laid on hands, now up and running from one end of the sanctuary to the other, now twirling, now swooning, now collapsing once again on the floor, his eyes like the eyes of a horse that smells smoke, the unknown tongue spewing from his mouth. He got the Holy Ghost at last! He got the Holy Ghost! you think, until you see him after the service eating a pimiento cheese sandwich downstairs. His legs are crossed. He's brushing the crumbs from his lap. He agrees it was a good service all right, but it sure would have been better if he'd only gotten the Holy Ghost. You can never get enough of the Holy Ghost. Maybe that's what he means. You can never exhaust the power when the Spirit comes down, not even when you take up a snake, not even when you take up a dozen of them. The more faith you expend, the more power is released. It's an inexhaustible, eternally renewable resource. It's the only power some of these people have.

So the longer you witness it, unless you just don't get into the spontaneous and unexpected, the more you become a part of it. *I* did, and the handlers could tell. They knew before I did what was going to happen. They saw me angling in. They were already making room for me in front of the deacons' bench. As I said, I'd always been drawn to danger. Alcohol. Psychedelics. War. If it made me feel good, I'd do it. I was always up for a little trip. I figured if I could trust my guide, I'd be all right. I'd come back to earth in one piece. I wouldn't really lose my mind. That's what I thought, anyway. I couldn't be an astronaut, but there were other things I could do and be. So I got up there in the middle of the handlers. J.L. Dyal, dark and wiry, was standing on my right; a clean-cut boy named Steve Frazier on my left. Who was it going to be? Carl's eyes were saying, you. And yes, it was the big rattler, the one with my name on it, acrid-smelling, carnal, alive. And the look in Carl's eyes seemed to change as he approached me. He was embarrassed. The snake was all he had, his eyes seemed to say. But as low as it was, as repulsive, if I took it, I'd be possessing the sacred. Nothing was required except obedience. Nothing had to be given up except my own will. This was the moment. I didn't stop to think about it. I just gave in. I stepped forward and took the snake with both hands. Carl released it to me. I turned to face the congregation and lifted the rattlesnake up toward the light. It was moving like it wanted to get up even higher, to climb out of that church and into the air. And it was exactly as the handlers had told me. I felt no fear. The snake seemed to be an extension of myself. And suddenly there seemed to be nothing in the room but me and the snake. Everything else had disappeared. Carl, the congregation, Jim—all gone, all faded to white. And I could not hear the earsplitting music. The air was silent and still and filled with that strong, even light. And I realized that I, too, was fading into the white. I was losing myself by degrees, like the incredible shrinking man. The snake would be the last to go, and all I could see was the way its scales shimmered one last time in the light, and the way its head moved from side to side, searching for a way out. I knew then why the handlers took up serpents. There is power in the act of disappearing; there is victory in the loss of self. It must be close to our conception of paradise, what it's like before you're born or after you die.

I came back in stages, first with the recognition that the shouting I had begun to hear was coming from my own mouth. Then I realized I was holding a rattlesnake, and the church rushed back with all its clamor, heat, and smell. I remembered Carl and turned toward where I thought he might be. I lowered the snake to waist level. It was an enormous animal, heavy and firm. The scales on its side were as rough as calluses. I could feel its muscles rippling beneath the skin. I was aware it was not a part of me now and that I couldn't predict what it might do. I extended it toward

Carl. He took it from me, stepped to the side, and gave it in turn to J.L.

"Jesus," J.L. said. "Oh, Jesus." His knees bent, his head went back. I knew it was happening to him too.

Then I looked around and saw that I was in a semicircle of handlers by the deacons' bench. Most had returned their snakes to the boxes, but Billy Summerford, Glenn's buck-toothed cousin, still had one, and he offered it to me, a medium-sized canebrake that was rattling violently. I took the snake in one hand without thinking. It was smaller than the first, but angrier, and I realized circumstances were different now. I couldn't seem to steer it away from my belt line. Fear had started to come back to me. I remembered with sudden clarity what Brother Charles had said about being careful who you took a snake from. I studied the canebrake as if I were seeing it for the first time and then gave it back to Billy Summerford. He passed it to Steve Frazier, the young man on my left. I watched Steve cradle it, curled and rattling furiously in his hands, and then I walked out the side door of the church and onto the steps, where Bobbie Sue Thompson was clutching her throat and leaning against the green shingles of the church.

"Jesus," she said. "Jesus, Jesus."

It was a sunny, fragrant day, with high-blown clouds. I looked into Bobbie Sue's face. Her eyes were wide and her mouth hooked at the corner. "Jesus," she said.

I thought at first she was in terrible pain, but then I realized she wasn't. "Yes. I know. Jesus," I said.

At the conclusion of the service, Brother Carl reminded everyone there would be dinner on the grounds. Most of the women had already slipped out, to arrange their casseroles and platters of ham on the butcher paper that covered the tables the men had set up under the trees. Jim and I waited silently in line for fried chicken, sweet potatoes, and black bottom pie, which we ate standing up among a knot of men who were discussing the merits of various coon dogs they'd owned. "The next time you handle a snake," Jim whispered, "try to give me a little warning. I ran out of film."

I told him I'd try, but that it was not something I'd be likely to do in the future, or be able to predict even if I did. There was more I wanted to tell him, but I didn't know how, and besides, I figured he knew. We'd lain in a ditch together thinking we were dead men. It was pretty much the same thing, I guessed. That kind of terror and joy.

"This one I had, it was a cur," said Gene Sherbert, a handler with a flattop and a scar. "He treed two coons at the same time."

"Same tree?" one of the other men asked.

"Naw," Gene said. "It was two separate trees, and that fool dog nearly run himself to death going back and forth."

The men laughed. "Was that Sport?" another man asked.

"Sport was Brother Glenn's dog," Gene said, and he turned his attention back to his plate.

I remembered then that Gene Sherbert was the man Glenn Summerford had accused Darlene of running with. I tried to imagine them in bed together—his flattop, her thick auburn hair. Gene was also Brother Carl's cousin. He'd kept the church in Kingston going while Carl did drugs and chased women on the Coast. Where was Brother Carl? I found a trash bag for my paper plate and went off to find him. I still felt like I had not come back all the way from the handling. My feet were light, my head still encased in an adrenaline cocoon. The air in the oak grove was golden. A breeze moved in the leaves and sent a stack of paper plates tumbling across the grass. On the breeze I heard snatches of a sweet and gentle melody. It was coming from a circle of handlers at the edge of the grove. Some were standing, some leaning against cars, some squatting on their heels in the dirt. As I got closer, I saw that Cecil Esslinder, the redheaded guitar player from Scottsboro, was sitting in the center of the circle. He was playing a dulcimer under the trees.

I stopped and listened. I'd never heard music more beautiful. It was filled with remorse and desire. When it ended, I asked Cecil what song he'd been playing. He shrugged. A hymn about Jesus. I asked how long he'd been playing the dulcimer.

"Never played one before in my life," he said.

His wife, Carolyn, was leaning into the fender of a battered Dodge Dart behind him. "Come on, Cecil," she said. "I want to go. My head is killing me."

Cecil smiled up at me, but he was talking to Carolyn. "You ought to go up and get anointed with oil. Let 'em lay hands on you. Ask for a healing. God'll heal you."

"I know that," Carolyn said. "But you've got to have faith."

"You've *got* faith," Cecil said, still smiling at me.

"My faith's been a little poorly." She took a pill bottle from the pocket of her dress. "I'm putting my faith in here," she said.

Cecil just laughed, and so did the other men. He handed the dulcimer back to its owner and stood up from the grass. "There's something I forgot to tell you," he said to me, although I couldn't even remember the last time we'd talked.

"You have to be careful when you're casting out demons," he said. "An evil spirit can come right from that person into *you*."

That's when it washed over me, the memory of the story I'd written when I was nineteen. "Salvation on Sand Mountain." About a church like the Old Rock House Holiness Church, and two brothers, family men, who pretend to get saved, so they can fake their own rapture, caught up like Elijah in the air, when what they're really doing is running off to live with their girlfriends in Fort Payne. I'd never been on

Sand Mountain when I wrote the story, but twenty-five years later, I knew that this was the place. This was the church, in a grove of oak trees, surrounded on all sides by fields of hay. I don't mean it resembled the church in my story. What I mean is that this was the church *itself*.

At the heart of the impulse to tell stories is a mystery so profound that even as I begin to speak of it, the hairs on the back of my hand are starting to stand on end. I believe that the writer has another eye, not a literal eye, but an eye on the inside of his head. It is the eye with which he sees the imaginary, three-dimensional world where the story he is writing takes place. But it is also the eye with which the writer beholds the connectedness of things, of past, present, and future. The writer's literal eyes are like vestigial organs, useless except to record physical details. The only eye worth talking about is the eye in the middle of the writer's head, the one that casts its pale, sorrowful light backward over the past and forward into the future, taking everything in at once, the whole story, from beginning to end.

I found Brother Carl by his pickup truck. He was talking to J.L. Dyal. They'd just loaded the big yellow-phase rattler into the bed of the truck, and they were giving him one last look.

Carl hugged me when I walked up. "I sure am proud of you," he said.

I asked if he was leaving for Georgia already.

"I've got to get back to God's country," he said.

While Carl went to say goodbye to some of the others, J.L. and I stared at the snake in the back of the truck. I told J.L. I just couldn't believe that we'd taken it up.

"It's something, all right," he said.

I asked what it had been like for him.

"It's love, that's all it is," he said. "You love the Lord, you love the Word, you love your brother and sister. You're in one mind, one accord, you're all combined together. The Bible says we're each a part of the body, and when it all comes together . . . Hey!" He whistled through his teeth. "What was it like for you?" he asked.

I didn't know what to say.

It's hard for me to talk about myself. As a journalist, I've always tried to keep out of the story. But look what had happened to me. I loved Brother Carl, but sometimes I suspected he was crazy. Sometimes I thought he was intent on getting himself, and maybe the rest of us, killed. Half the time I walked around saying to myself, "This thing is real! This thing is real!" The other half of the time, I walked around thinking that nothing was real, and that if there really was a God, we must have been part of a dream he was having, and when he woke up . . . *poof!* Either way, I worried I'd gone off the edge, and nobody would be able to pull me back. One of my uncles by marriage was a Baptist minister, one of the kindest men I've ever known. I was fifteen, though, when he killed himself, and

I didn't know the whole story. I just knew that he sent his family and friends a long, poignant, and some have said beautiful letter about how he was ready to go meet Abraham, Isaac, and Jacob. I believe he ran a high-voltage line from his basement to a ground-floor bedroom. He put "How Great Thou Art" on the record player. Then he lay down on the bed, reached up, and grabbed the live wire. He left a widow and two sons. My uncle's death confirmed a suspicion of mine that madness and religion were a hair's breadth away. My beliefs about the nature of God and man have changed over the years, but that one never has. Feeling after God is dangerous business. And Christianity without passion, danger, and mystery may not really be Christianity at all.

from THE DEATH OF IVAN ILYICH

LEO TOLSTOY

Awakening, enlightenment, epiphany: all of these concepts involve the light necessary not to see with our eyes, but with the spirit that binds creation, and it is light that the suffering Ivan Ilyich finally receives at the end of his regrettable life.

In the large building housing the Law Courts, during a recess in the Melvinsky proceedings, members of the court and the public prosecutor met in the office of Ivan Egorovich Shebek, where the conversation turned on the celebrated Krasov case. Fyodor Vasilyevich vehemently denied that it was subject to their jurisdiction, Ivan Egorovich clung to his own view, while Pyotr Ivanovich, who had taken no part in the dispute from the outset, glanced through a copy of the *News* that had just been delivered.

"Gentlemen!" he said. "Ivan Ilyich is dead."

"Really?"

"Here, read this," he said to Fyodor Vasilyevich, handing him the fresh issue, still smelling of printer's ink.

Framed in black was the following announcement: "With profound sorrow Praskovya Fyodorovna Golovina informs relatives and acquaintances that her beloved husband, Ivan Ilyich Golovin, Member of the Court of Justice, passed away on the 4th of February, 1882. The funeral will be held on Friday at one o'clock."

Ivan Ilyich had been a colleague of the gentlemen assembled here and they had all been fond of him. He had been ill for some weeks and his disease was said to be incurable. His post had been kept open for him, but it had been speculated that in the event of his death Alekseev might be appointed to his place and either Vinnikov or Shtabel succeed Alekseev. And so the first thought that occurred to each of the gentlemen in this office, learning of Ivan Ilyich's death, was what effect it would have on their own transfers and promotions or those of their acquaintances.

"Now I'm sure to get Shtabel's post or Vinnikov's," thought Fyodor Vasilyevich. "It was promised to me long ago, and the promotion will mean an increase of eight hundred rubles in salary plus an allowance for office expenses."

"I must put in a request to have my brother-in-law transferred from Kaluga," thought Pyotr Ivanovich. "My wife will be very happy. Now she won't be able to say I never do anything for her family."

"I had a feeling he'd never get over it," said Pyotr Ivanovich. "Sad."

"What, exactly, was the matter with him?"

"The doctors couldn't decide. That is, they decided, but in different ways. When I last saw him, I thought he would recover."

"And I haven't been there since the holidays. I kept meaning to go."

"Was he a man of any means?"

"His wife has a little something, I think, but nothing much."

"Well, there's no question but that we'll have to go and see her. They live so terribly far away."

"From you, that is. From your place, everything's far away."

"You see, he just can't forgive me for living on the other side of the river," said Pyotr Ivanovich, smiling at Shebek. And with that they began talking about relative distances in town and went back to the courtroom.

In addition to the speculations aroused in each man's mind about the transfers and likely job changes this death might occasion, the very fact of the death of a close acquaintance evoked in them all the usual feeling of relief that it was someone else, not they, who had died.

"Well, isn't that something—he's dead, but I'm not," was what each of them thought or felt. The closer acquaintances, the so-called friends of Ivan Ilyich, involuntarily added to themselves that now they had to fulfill the tedious demands of propriety by attending the funeral service and paying the widow a condolence call.

Fyodor Vasilyevich and Pyotr Ivanovich had been closest to him. Pyotr Ivanovich had studied law with Ivan Ilyich and considered himself indebted to him. At dinner that evening he told his wife the news of Ivan Ilyich's death, conjectured about the possibility of having her brother transferred to their district, and then, dispensing with his usual nap, he put on a dress coat and drove to Ivan Ilyich's home.

A carriage and two cabs were parked before the entrance. Downstairs in the hallway, next to the coat stand, a coffin lid decorated with silk brocade, tassels, and highly polished gilt braid was propped against the wall. Two women in black were taking off their fur coats. One of them he recognized as Ivan Ilyich's sister; the other was a stranger. Schwartz, his colleague, was just starting down the stairs, but on seeing Pyotr Ivanovich enter, he paused at the top step and winked at him as if to say: "Ivan Ilyich has really bungled—not the sort of thing you and I would do."

There was, as usual, an air of elegant solemnity about Schwartz, with his English side-whiskers and his lean figure in a dress coat, and this solemnity, always such a marked contrast to his playful personality, had a special piquancy here. So, at least, Pyotr Ivanovich thought.

Pyotr Ivanovich stepped aside to let the ladies pass and slowly followed them up the stairs. Schwartz did not proceed downward but remained on the landing. Pyotr Ivanovich understood why; obviously, he wanted to arrange where they should play whist that evening. The ladies went upstairs to the widow's quarters, while Schwartz, his lips compressed into a serious expression and his eyes gleaming playfully, jerked his brows to the right to indicate the room where the dead man lay.

Pyotr Ivanovich went in bewildered, as people invariably are, about what he was expected to do there. The one thing he knew was that on such occasions it never did any harm to cross oneself. He was not quite certain whether he ought also to bow and so he adopted a middle course: on entering the room he began to cross himself and make a slight movement resembling a bow. At the same time, to the extent that the motions of his hands and head permitted, he glanced about the room. Two young people, apparently nephews, one of them a gymnasium student, were crossing themselves as they left the room. An old woman was standing motionless. And a lady with peculiarly arched brows was whispering something to her. A church reader in a frock coat—a vigorous, resolute fellow—was reading something in a loud voice and in a tone that brooked no contradiction. The pantry boy, Gerasim, stepped lightly in front of Pyotr Ivanovich, sprinkling something about the floor. Seeing this, Pyotr Ivanovich immediately became aware of a faint odor of decomposition. On his last visit Pyotr Ivanovich had seen this peasant boy in Ivan Ilyich's study; he had acted as a sick nurse to the dying man and Ivan Ilyich had been particularly fond of him.

Pyotr Ivanovich went on crossing himself and bowing slightly in a direction midway between the coffin, the church reader, and the icons on a table in the corner. Then, when he felt he had overdone the crossing, he paused and began to examine the dead man.

The body lay, as the dead invariably do, in a peculiarly heavy manner, with its rigid limbs sunk into the bedding of the coffin and its head eternally bowed on the pillow, exhibiting, as do all dead bodies, a yellow waxen forehead (with bald patches gleaming on the sunken temples), the protruding nose beneath seeming to press down against the upper lip. Ivan Ilyich had changed a great deal, grown even thinner since Pyotr

Ivanovich had last seen him, and yet, as with all dead men, his face had acquired an expression of greater beauty—above all, of greater significance—than it had in life. Its expression implied that what needed to be done had been done and done properly. Moreover, there was in this expression a reproach or a reminder to the living. This reminder seemed out of place to Pyotr Ivanovich, or at least inapplicable to him. He began to feel somewhat uncomfortable and so he crossed himself hurriedly (all too hurriedly, he felt, from the standpoint of propriety), turned, and headed for the door.

In the adjoining room Schwartz was waiting for him, his feet planted solidly apart, his hands toying with the top hat he held behind his back. One glance at his playful, well-groomed, elegant figure was enough to revive Pyotr Ivanovich. He felt that Schwartz was above all this and would not succumb to mournful impressions. His very appearance seemed to say: "In no way can the incident of this funeral service for Ivan Ilyich be considered sufficient grounds for canceling the regular session; that is, nothing can prevent us from meeting tonight and flipping through a new deck of cards while a footman places four fresh candles around the table. There is, in fact, no reason to assume this incident can keep us from spending a pleasant evening." And he said as much to Pyotr Ivanovich in a whisper, proposing they meet for a game at Fyodor Vasilyevich's.

But Pyotr Ivanovich was not destined to play cards that

evening. Praskovya Fyodomvna, a short, stocky woman (far broader at the hips than at the shoulders, despite all her efforts to the contrary), dressed all in black, with a lace shawl on her head and with the same peculiarly arched brows as the woman facing the coffin, emerged from her chambers with some other ladies whom she showed to the door of the room where the dead man lay, and said:

"The service is about to begin, do go in."

Schwartz made a vague sort of bow, then stopped, neither accepting nor rejecting the invitation. Recognizing Pyotr Ivanovich, Praskovya Fyodorovna sighed, went right up to him, took his hand, and said: "I know you were a true friend of Ivan Ilyich's . . ." and looked at him, awaiting a fitting response. Pyotr Ivanovich knew that just as he had to cross himself in there, here he had to press her hand, sigh, and say: "I assure you!" And so he did. And having done so felt he had achieved the desired effect: he was touched and so was she.

"Come, before it begins, I must have a talk with you," said the widow. "Give me your arm."

He gave her his arm and they proceeded toward the inner rooms, past Schwartz, who threw Pyotr Ivanovich a wink of regret that said: "So much for your card game. Don't be offended if we find another player. Perhaps you can make a fifth when you get away."

Pyotr Ivanovich sighed even more deeply and plaintively, and Praskovya Fyodorovna squeezed his hand gratefully. On entering her drawing room, decorated in pink cretonne and lit with a dim lamp, they sat down beside a table: she on a sofa, Pyotr Ivanovich on a low ottoman with broken springs that shifted under his weight. Praskovya Fyodorovna wanted to warn him against sitting there but felt such a warning was not in keeping with her situation and decided against it. As he sat down on the ottoman Pyotr Ivanovich recalled how, in decorating the room, Ivan Ilyich had consulted him about this pink cretonne with the green leaves. The whole room was crammed with furniture and knickknacks, and as the widow stepped past the table to seat herself on the sofa, she entangled the lace of her black shawl in a bit of carving. Pyotr Ivanovich rose slightly to untangle it, and as he did the springs of the ottoman, freed of pressure, surged and gave him a little shove. The widow started to disentangle the lace herself and Pyotr Ivanovich sat down again, suppressing the rebellious springs beneath him. But the widow had not fully disentangled herself and Pyotr Ivanovich rose once again, and again the ottoman rebelled and even creaked. When all this was over, the widow took out a clean cambric handkerchief and began to weep. The episode with the lace and the battle with the ottoman had chilled Pyotr Ivanovich's emotions and he sat there scowling. The strain of the situation was broken when Sokolov, Ivan Ilyich's footman, came to report that the plot Praskovya Fyodorovna had selected in the cemetery would cost two hundred rubles. She stopped weeping and, glancing at Pyotr Ivanovich with a victimized air, told him in French how hard this was for her. He responded with a silent gesture indicating he had no doubt this was so.

"Please feel free to smoke," she said in a magnanimous yet crushed tone of voice and turned to Sokolov to discuss the price of the grave. As he lit his cigarette Pyotr Ivanovich heard her make detailed inquiries about the prices of various plots and arrive at a very sound decision. Moreover, when she had settled that matter, she made arrangements about the choristers. Then Sokolov left.

"I attend to everything myself," she said to Pyotr Ivanovich, moving aside some albums on the table. And noticing that the ashes of his cigarette were in danger of falling on the table, she quickly passed him an ashtray and said: "I believe it would be sheer pretense for me to say that I am unable, because of grief, to attend to practical matters. On the contrary, if anything can . . . I won't say console but . . . distract me, it is seeing to all these things about him." Again she took out a handkerchief as if about to weep but suddenly seemed to have mastered her emotion, and with a little toss of her head she began to speak calmly.

"But there is a matter I wish to discuss with you."

Pyotr Ivanovich bowed his head in response, taking care not to allow the springs of the ottoman, which immediately grew restive, to have their way.

"He suffered terribly the last few days."

"Did he?" asked Pyotr Ivanovich.

"Oh, frightfully! He screamed incessantly, not for minutes but for hours on end. He screamed for three straight days without pausing for breath. It was unbearable. I don't know how I bore up through it all. You could hear him three rooms away. Oh, what I've been through!"

"And was he really conscious through it all?" asked Pyotr Ivanovich.

"Yes," she whispered, "to the very last. He took leave of us a quarter of an hour before he died and even asked us to take Volodya away."

Despite a distasteful awareness of his own hypocrisy as well as hers, Pyotr Ivanovich was overcome with horror as he thought of the suffering of someone he had known so well, first as a carefree boy, then as a schoolmate, later as a grown man, his colleague. Once again he saw that forehead, that nose pressing down on the upper lip, and fear for himself took possession of him.

"Three days of terrible suffering and death. Why, the same thing could happen to me at anytime now," he thought and for a moment felt panic-stricken. But at once, he himself did not know how, he was rescued by the customary reflection that all this had happened to Ivan Ilyich, not to him, that it could not and should not happen to him; and that if he were to grant such a possibility, he would succumb to depression which, as Schwartz's expression had made abundantly clear, he ought not to do. With this line of reasoning Pyotr Ivanovich set his mind at rest and began to press for details about Ivan Ilyich's death, as though death were a chance experience that could happen only to Ivan Ilyich, never to himself.

After giving him various details about the truly horrible physical suffering Ivan Ilyich had endured (details which Pyotr Ivanovich learned strictly in terms of their unnerving effect upon Praskovya Fyodorovna), the widow evidently felt it necessary to get down to business.

"Ah, Pyotr Ivanovich, how hard it is, how terribly, terribly hard," she said and again began weeping.

Pyotr Ivanovich sighed and waited for her to blow her nose. When she had, he said: "I assure you! . . ." and again she began to talk freely and got down to what was obviously her chief business with him: to ask how, in connection with her husband's death, she could obtain a grant of money from the government. She made it appear that she was asking Pyotr Ivanovich's advice about a pension, but he saw that she already knew more about this than he did, knew exactly, down to the finest detail, how much could be had from the government, but wanted to know if there was any possibility of extracting a bit more. Pyotr Ivanovich tried to think of some means of doing so, but after giving the matter a little thought and, for the sake of propriety, condemning the government for its stinginess, said he thought no more could be had. Whereupon she sighed and evidently tried to find some pretext for getting rid of her visitor. He surmised as much, put out his cigarette, stood up, shook her hand, and went out into the hall.

In the dining room with the clock which Ivan Ilyich had been so happy to have purchased at an antique shop, Pyotr Ivanovich met a priest and a few acquaintances who had come for the service, and he caught sight of a handsome young woman, Ivan Ilyich's daughter. She was dressed all in black, which made her slender waist appear even more so. She had a gloomy, determined, almost angry expression and bowed to Pyotr Ivanovich as if he were to blame for something. Behind her, with the same offended look, stood a rich young man Pyotr Ivanovich knew—an examining magistrate who, he had heard, was her fiancé. Pyotr Ivanovich gave them a mournful bow and was about to enter the dead man's room when Ivan Ilyich's son, a schoolboy who had an uncanny resemblance to his father, appeared from behind the stairwell. He was a small replica of the Ivan Ilyich whom Pyotr Ivanovich remembered from law school. His eyes were red from crying and had the look common to boys of thirteen or fourteen whose thoughts are no longer innocent. Seeing Pyotr Ivanovich, he frowned in a shamefaced way. Pyotr Ivanovich nodded to him and entered the room where the body lay. The service began: candles, groans, incense, tears, sobs. Pyotr Ivanovich stood with his brows knitted, staring at the feet of people in front of him. Never once did he look at the dead man or succumb to depression, and he was one of the first to leave. There was no one in the hallway, but Gerasim, the pantry boy, darted out of the dead man's room, rummaged with his strong hands through the mound of fur coats to find Pyotr Ivanovich's and helped him on with it.

"Well, Gerasim, my boy," said Pyotr Ivanovich in order to say something. "It's sad, isn't it?"

"It's God's will, sir. We all have to die someday," said Gerasim, displaying an even row of healthy white peasant teeth. And then, like a man in the thick of work, he briskly opened the door, shouted to the coachman, seated Pyotr Ivanovich in the carriage, and sprang back up the porch steps as though wondering what to do next.

After the smell of incense, the corpse, and the carbolic acid, Pyotr Ivanovich found it particularly pleasant to breathe in the fresh air.

"Where to, sir?" asked the coachman.

"It's not that late, I'll drop in at Fyodor Vasilyevich's."

And so he went. And when he arrived, he found they were just finishing the first rubber, so that it was convenient for him to make a fifth for the next.

Ivan Ilyich's life had been most simple and commonplace—and most horrifying.

He died at the age of forty-five, a member of the Court of Justice. He was the son of an official who, in various Petersburg ministries and departments, had established the sort of career whereby men reach a stage at which, owing to their rank and years of service, they cannot be dismissed, even though they are clearly unfit for any responsible work; and therefore they receive fictitious appointments, especially designed for them, and by no means fictitious salaries of from six to ten thousand on which they live to a ripe old age.

Such was the Privy Councillor Ilya Efimovich Golovin, superfluous member of various superfluous institutions.

He had three sons, of whom Ivan Ilyich was the second. The eldest had established the same type of career as his father, except in a different ministry, and was rapidly approaching the stage where men obtain sinecures. The third son was a failure. He had ruined his prospects in a number of positions and was now serving in the Railway Division. His father and brothers, and especially their wives, not only hated meeting him but, unless compelled to do otherwise, managed to forget his existence. The sister had married Baron Greff, the same sort of Petersburg official as his father-in-law. Ivan Ilyich, as they said, was *le phénix de la famille.* He was neither as cold and punctilious as his elder brother nor as reckless as his younger. He was a happy mean between the two—a clever, lively, pleasant, and respectable man. He and his younger brother had both attended the school of jurisprudence. The younger brother never graduated, for he was expelled when he reached the fifth course. On the other hand, Ivan Ilyich completed the program creditably. As a law student he had become exactly what he was to remain the rest of his life: a capable, cheerful, good-natured, and sociable man but one strict to carry out whatever he considered his duty, and he considered his duty all things that were so designated by people in authority. Neither as a boy nor as an adult had he been a toady, but from his earliest youth he had been drawn to people of high standing in society as a moth is to light; he had adopted their manners and their views on life and had established friendly relations with them. All the enthusiasms of childhood and youth passed, leaving no appreciable impact on him; he had succumbed to sensuality and vanity and, in his last years at school, to liberalism, but strictly within the limits his instinct unerringly prescribed.

As a student he had done things which, at the time, seemed to him extremely vile and made him feel disgusted with himself; but later, seeing that people of high standing had no qualms about doing these things, he was not quite able to consider them good but managed to dismiss them and not feel the least perturbed when he recalled them.

When he graduated from law school with a degree qualifying him for the tenth rank of the civil service, and had obtained money from his father for his outfit, he ordered some suits at Sharmer's, the fashionable tailor, hung a medallion inscribed *respice finem* on his watch chain, took leave of his mentor and prince, who was patron of the school, dined in state with his friends at Donon's, and then, with fashionable new luggage, linen, clothes, shaving and other toilet articles, and a traveling rug (all ordered and purchased at the finest shops), he set off for one of the provinces to assume a post his father had secured for him there as assistant on special commissions to the governor.

Ivan Ilyich immediately made his life in the provinces as easy and pleasant as it had been at law school. He worked, saw to his career, and, at the same time, engaged in proper and pleasant forms of diversion. When from time to time he traveled to country districts on official business, he maintained his dignity with both his superiors and inferiors and fulfilled the duties entrusted to him (primarily cases involving a group of religious sectarians) with an exactitude and incorruptibility in which he could only take pride.

In his official duties, despite his youth and love of light forms of amusement, he was exceedingly reserved, punctilious, and even severe; but in society he was often playful and witty, always good-humored and polite—a *bon enfant*, as the governor and his wife, with whom he was like one of the family, used to say of him.

In the provinces he had an affair with one of the ladies who threw themselves at the chic young lawyer; there was also a milliner: there were drinking bouts with visiting aides-de-camp and after-supper trips to a certain street on the outskirts of town; there were also attempts to curry favor with his chief and even with his chief's wife. But all this had such a heightened air of respectability that nothing bad could be said about it. It could all be summed up by the French saying: '*Il faut que jeunesse se passe.*" It was all done with clean hands, in clean shirts, and with French phrases, and, most importantly, among people of the best society—consequently, with the approval of those in high rank.

Ivan Ilyich spent five years of his service career in this manner, and at the end of that time there was a change in his official life. New judicial institutions had been formed and new men were needed.

Ivan Ilyich became such a new man.

He was offered a post as examining magistrate and he accepted it, even though it meant moving to another province, giving up the connections he had formed, and establishing new ones. His friends met to bid him farewell: they had a group photograph taken and presented him with a silver cigarette case, and he set off to assume his new position.

As an examining magistrate, Ivan Ilyich was just as *comme il faut* and respectable, just as capable of separating his official duties from his private life and of inspiring general respect as he had been while acting as assistant on special commissions. He found the work of a magistrate far more interesting and appealing than his former duties. In his previous position he had enjoyed the opportunity to stride freely and easily in his Sharmer uniform past the crowd of anxious, envious petitioners and officials waiting to be heard by the governor, to go straight into his chief's office and sit with him over a cup of tea and a cigarette. But few people had been directly under his control then—only the district police officers and religious sectarians he encountered when sent out on special commissions. And he loved to treat these people courteously, almost as comrades, loved to make them feel that he who had the power to crush them was dealing with them in such a friendly, unpretentious manner. But there had been few such people. Now, as an examining magistrate, Ivan Ilyich felt that all, without exception—including the most important and self-satisfied people—all were in his power, and that he had only to write certain words on a sheet of paper with an official heading and this or that important, self-satisfied person would be brought to him as a defendant or a witness, and if Ivan Ilyich did not choose to have him sit, he would be forced to stand and answer his questions. Ivan Ilyich never abused his power; on the contrary, he tried to exercise it leniently; but the awareness of that power and the opportunity to be lenient constituted the chief interest and appeal of his new post. In the work itself—that is, in conducting investigations—Ivan Ilyich soon mastered the technique of dispensing with all considerations that did not pertain to his job as examining magistrate, and of writing up even the most complicated cases in a style that reduced them to their externals, bore no trace of his personal opinion, and, most importantly, adhered to all the prescribed for formalities. This type of work was new, and he was one of the first men to give practical application to the judicial reforms instituted by the Code of 1864.

On taking up the post of examining magistrate in the new town, Ivan Ilyich made new acquaintances and connections, adopted a new stance, and assumed a somewhat different tone. He put a suitable amount of distance between himself and the provincial authorities, chose his friends from among the best circle of lawyers and wealthy gentry in the town, and assumed an air of mild dissatisfaction with the government, of moderate liberalism, of enlightened civic responsibility. And though he remained as fastidious as ever about his attire, he stopped shaving his chin and allowed his beard to grow freely.

In the new town, too, life turned out to be very pleasant for Ivan Ilyich. The people opposed to the governor were friendly and congenial, his salary was higher, and he began to play whist, which added considerably to the pleasure of his life, for he had an ability to maintain his good spirits while playing and to reason quickly and subtly, so that he usually came out ahead.

After he had been working in the town for two years, Ivan Ilyich met his future wife. Praskovya Fyodorovna Mikhel was the most attractive, intelligent, and outstanding young lady of the set in which Ivan Ilyich moved. In addition to the other amusements and relaxations that provided relief from his work as an examining magistrate, Ivan Ilyich began a light flirtation with Praskovya Fyodorovna.

As an assistant on special commissions Ivan Ilyich had, as a rule, danced; as an examining magistrate he danced as an exception. He danced to show that although he was a representative of the reformed legal institutions and an official of the fifth rank, when it came to dancing, he could also excel at that. So he occasionally danced with Praskovya Fyodorovna at the end of an evening, and it was mainly during the time they danced together that he conquered her. She fell in love with him. Ivan Ilyich had no clear and definite intention of marrying, but when the girl fell in love with him, he asked himself: "Really, why shouldn't I get married?"

Praskovya Fyodorovna came from a good family and was quite attractive; she also had a little money. Ivan Ilyich could have counted on a more illustrious match, but even this one was quite good. He had his salary, and her income, he hoped, would bring in an equal amount. It would be a good alliance: she was a sweet, pretty, and extremely well-bred young woman. To say that Ivan Ilyich married because he fell in love with his fiancée and found her sympathetic to his views on life would be as mistaken as to say that he married because the people in his circle approved of the match. Ivan Ilyich married for both reasons: in acquiring such a wife he did something that gave him pleasure and, at the same time, did what people of the highest standing considered correct.

And so Ivan Ilyich got married.

The preparations for marriage and the first period of married life, with its conjugal caresses, new furniture, new dishes, new linen—the period up to his wife's pregnancy—went very well, so that Ivan Ilyich began to think that marriage would not disrupt the easy, pleasant, cheerful, and respectable life approved of by society (a pattern he believed to be universal); that it would even enhance such a life. But during the first months of his wife's pregnancy, something new, unexpected, and disagreeable manifested itself, something painful and unseemly, which he had no way of anticipating and could do nothing to avoid.

For no reason at all, so it seemed to Ivan Ilyich—*de gaîté de cœur*, as he told himself—his wife began to undermine the pleasure and propriety of their life: she became jealous without cause, demanded he be more attentive to her, found fault with everything, and created distasteful and ill-mannered scenes.

At first Ivan Ilyich hoped to escape from this unpleasant state of affairs by preserving the same carefree and proper approach to life that had served him in the past. He tried to ignore his wife's bad moods, went on living in a pleasant and easygoing fashion, invited friends over for cards, and made an effort to get away to his club or his friends' homes. But on one occasion his wife lashed out at him with such fury and such foul language, and persisted in attacking him every time he failed to satisfy her demands (apparently having resolved not to let up until he submitted—that is, until he stayed home and moped as she did) that Ivan Ilyich was horrified. He realized that married life—at least with his wife—was not always conducive to the pleasures and proprieties of life but, on the contrary, frequently disrupted them, and for that reason he must guard against such disruptions. Ivan Ilyich tried to find some means of doing this. His work was the one thing that made any impression on Praskovya Fyodorovna, and so he began to use his work and the obligations it entailed as a way of combating his wife and safeguarding his independence.

With the birth of the baby, the attempts to feed it and the various difficulties, the real and imaginary illnesses of mother and child, which Ivan Ilyich was supposed to sympathize with but failed to understand, his need to fence off a world for himself outside the family became even more imperative.

To the degree that his wife became more irritable and demanding, Ivan Ilyich increasingly made work the center of gravity in his life. He grew more attached to his job and more ambitious than before.

Very soon, within a year after his wedding, Ivan Ilyich realized that married life, though it offered certain conveniences, was in fact a very complex and difficult business, and that to do one's duty to it—that is, to lead a proper, socially acceptable life—one had to develop a clearly defined attitude to it, just as one did with respect to work.

And Ivan Ilyich developed such an attitude. Of married life he demanded only the conveniences it could provide—dinners at home, a well-run household, a partner in bed, and, above all, a veneer of respectability which public opinion required. As for the rest, he tried to find enjoyment in family life, and, if he succeeded, was very grateful; but if he met with resistance and querulousness, he immediately withdrew into his separate, entrenched world of work and found pleasure there.

Ivan Ilyich was esteemed for his diligent service, and after three years he was made assistant public prosecutor. His new duties, the importance of them, the possibility of indicting and imprisoning anyone he chose, the publicity his speeches received and the success they brought him—all this further enhanced the appeal of his work.

Other children were born. His wife became more and more petulant and irascible, but the attitude Ivan Ilyich had adopted toward domestic life made him almost impervious to her carping.

After serving for seven years in this town, Ivan Ilyich was transferred to another province as public prosecutor. They moved, they were short of money, and his wife disliked the new town. Although his salary was higher, the cost of living was greater; moreover, two of their children had died, and so family life became even more unpleasant for Ivan Ilyich.

Praskovya Fyodorovna blamed her husband for every setback they experienced in the new town. Most of the topics of conversation between husband and wife, especially the children's education, brought up issues on which they remembered having quarreled, and these quarrels were apt to flare up again at any moment. All they had left were the rare periods of amorousness that came over them, but these did not last long. They were merely little islands at which the couple anchored for a while before setting out again on a sea of veiled hostility, which took the form of estrangement from one another. This estrangement might have distressed Ivan Ilyich had he felt it should not exist, but by now he not only regarded it as a normal state of affairs, but as a goal he sought to achieve in family life. That goal was to free himself more and more from these disturbances, to make them appear innocuous and respectable. He managed to do this by spending less and less time with his family and, when obliged to be at home, tried to safeguard his position through the presence of outsiders. But what mattered most was that Ivan Ilyich had his work. His entire interest in life was centered in the world of official duties and that interest totally absorbed him. The awareness of his power, the chance to ruin whomever he chose, the importance attached even to his entry into the courtroom and manner of conferring with his subordinates, the success he enjoyed both with them and his superiors, and, above all, his own recognition of the skill with which he handled cases—all this gave him cause for rejoicing and, together with chats with his colleagues, dinner invitations, and whist, made his life full. So that on the whole Ivan Ilyich's life proceeded as he felt it should—pleasantly and properly.

He went on living this way for another seven years. His daughter was then sixteen years old, another child had died, and one son remained, a schoolboy, the subject of dissension. Ivan Ilyich wanted to send him to the school of jurisprudence, but out of spite Praskovya Fyodorovna enrolled him in the gymnasium. The daughter had studied at home and made good progress; the boy, too, was a rather good student.

Ivan Ilyich spent seventeen years of his married life this way. He was already an experienced public prosecutor who had declined several positions in the hope of obtaining a more desirable one, when an unforeseen and unpleasant circumstance virtually disrupted the peaceful course of his life. He expected to be appointed presiding judge in a university town, but Hoppe managed to move in ahead and get the appointment. Ivan Ilyich was infuriated, made accusations, and quarreled with Hoppe and his immediate superiors. They began to treat him with disdain and during the next round of appointments again passed him by.

This happened in 1880, the most difficult year in Ivan

Ilyich's life. For one thing, it turned out that he could not make ends meet on his salary; for another, that he had been neglected, and that what he considered the most outrageous, heartless injustice appeared to others as quite commonplace. Even his father did not consider it his duty to help him. Ivan Ilyich felt that everyone had abandoned him, convinced that the position of a man earning three thousand five hundred rubles was entirely normal and even fortunate. He alone knew that what with the injustices he had suffered, his wife's incessant nagging, and the debts he had incurred by living above his means, his position was far from normal.

That summer, in order to save money, he took a leave of absence and went to the country with his wife to live at her brother's place. In the country, with no work to do, Ivan Ilyich for the first time in his life experienced not only boredom but intolerable anguish; he decided that he simply could not go on living this way, that he had to take some decisive measures.

After a sleepless night spent pacing the terrace, he made up his mind to go to Petersburg and punish *those people*—those who had failed to appreciate him—by trying to get himself transferred to another ministry.

The next day, despite all the efforts of his wife and his brother-in-law to dissuade him, he set off for Petersburg. He had only one purpose in going: to obtain a post with a salary of five thousand rubles. He was no longer bent on any particular ministry, field, or type of work. He only wanted a post that would pay him five thousand; it could be a post with the administration, the banks, the railways, the Dowager Empress Maria's charitable institutions, or even the customs office, but it had to pay five thousand and allow him to stop working for a ministry that failed to appreciate him.

And his trip was crowned with amazing and unexpected success. At Kursk an acquaintance of his, F. S. Ilyin, boarded the train, sat down in the first-class carriage, and told Ivan Ilyich that the governor of Kursk had just received a telegram announcing an important change of staff that was about to take place in the ministry: Ivan Semyonovich was to replace Pyotr Ivanovich.

The proposed change, in addition to the significance it had for Russia, was of particular significance for Ivan Ilyich, since it brought to power a new man, Pyotr Petrovich, and, it appeared, his friend Zakhar Ivanovich—a circumstance that was highly favorable for Ivan Ilyich. Zakhar Ivanovich was a colleague and friend of his.

In Moscow the news was confirmed, and on reaching Petersburg, Ivan Ilyich looked up Zakhar Ivanovich, who guaranteed him an appointment in the Ministry of Justice where he had served before.

A week later he telegraphed his wife: "Zakhar in Miller's place. With first report I receive appointment."

Thanks to this change of staff, Ivan Ilyich unexpectedly received an appointment in his former ministry that placed him two ranks above his colleagues, paid him a salary of five thousand rubles, and provided an additional three thousand five hundred for the expenses of relocation. His resentment against his former enemies and the whole ministry vanished completely and he was perfectly happy.

Ivan Ilyich returned to the country more cheerful and contented than he had been in some time. Praskovya Fyodorovna's spirits also picked up, and they concluded a truce. Ivan Ilyich told her how he had been honored in Petersburg, how all his enemies had been disgraced and fawned on him now and envied his position; and he made a point of telling her how much everyone in Petersburg had liked him.

Praskovya Fyodorovna listened, pretended to believe all of this, never once contradicted him, and devoted herself exclusively to making plans for their life in the city to which they were moving. And Ivan Ilyich was delighted to see that her plans were his, that he and his wife were in agreement, and that after a little stumble his life was resuming its genuine and natural quality of carefree pleasure and propriety.

Ivan Ilyich had come back for only a brief stay. On the tenth of September he had to assume his new position; moreover, he needed time to get settled in the new place, to move all their belongings from the provinces, to buy and order a great many more things. In short, to arrange their life in the style he had set his mind to (which corresponded almost exactly to the style Praskovya Fyodorovna had set her heart on).

Now that everything had worked out so well and he and his wife were at one in their aims and, in addition, saw very little of each other, they were closer than they had been since the first years of their married life. Ivan Ilyich had intended to take his family with him at once, but at the urging of his sister-in-law and brother-in-law, who suddenly became unusually amiable and warm to Ivan Ilyich and his family, he set off alone.

He set off, and the happy frame of mind induced by his success and the understanding with his wife, the one intensifying the other, never once deserted him. He found a charming apartment, exactly what he and his wife had dreamed of. Spacious reception rooms with high ceilings in the old style, a magnificent and comfortable study, rooms for his wife and daughter, a study room for his son—all as though it had been designed especially for them. Ivan Ilyich himself undertook the decorating, selecting the wallpaper and the upholstery, purchasing more furniture, mostly antiques, which he thought particularly *comme il faut*, and everything progressed until it began to approach the ideal he had set himself. When only half the decorating had been completed, the result exceeded his expectations. He sensed how elegant and refined an atmosphere, free of vulgarity, the whole place would acquire when it was finished. As he fell asleep he pictured to himself how the reception room would look. When he glanced at the unfinished drawing room he conjured up an image of the fireplace, the screen, the what-not, the little chairs scattered here and there, the plates and china on the walls, and the bronzes, as they would appear when everything was in place. He was thrilled to think how he would surprise Pasha and Lizanka, who also had good taste in these matters. They had no idea what was in store for them. He had been particularly successful at finding and making inexpensive purchases of old furniture, which added a decidedly aristocratic tone to the whole place. In his letters to his family he deliberately understated everything in order to surprise them. All this was so engrossing that even his new post, work he loved, absorbed him less than he had expected. During court sessions he sometimes became distracted, wondering whether he should have straight or curved cornices for the draperies. He was so preoccupied with these matters that he often did some of the work himself—rearranged the furniture, rehung the draperies. Once, when he mounted a stepladder to show a perplexed upholsterer how he wanted the draperies hung, he missed a step and fell, but being a strong and agile man, he held on to the ladder and merely banged his side against the knob of the window frame. The bruise hurt for a while, but the pain soon disappeared. All through this period Ivan Ilyich felt particularly well and cheerful. "I feel fifteen years younger," he wrote his family. He expected to finish in September, but the work dragged on until mid-October. Yet the result was stunning—an opinion voiced not only by him but by everyone else who saw the place.

In actuality, it was like the homes of all people who are not really rich but who want to look rich, and therefore end up looking like one another: it had damasks, ebony, plants, carpets, and bronzes, everything dark and gleaming—all the effects a certain class of people produce so as to look like people of a certain class. And his place looked so much like the others that it would never have been noticed, though it all seemed quite exceptional to him. When he met his family at the station and brought them back to their brightly lit furnished apartment, and a footman in a white tie opened the door to a flower-bedecked entrance hall, from which they proceeded to the drawing room and the study, gasping with delight, he was very happy, showed them everywhere, drank in their praises and beamed with satisfaction. At tea that evening when, among other things, Praskovya Fyodorovna asked him about his fall, he laughed and gave them a comic demonstration of how he had gone flying off the stepladder and frightened the upholsterer.

"It's a good thing I'm so agile. Another man would have killed himself, but I got off with just a little bump here; it hurts when I touch it, but it's already beginning to clear up—it's just a bruise."

And so they began to live in their new quarters which, as always happens when people get settled, was just one room too small, and on their new income which, as is always the case, was just a bit less—about five hundred rubles—than they needed. But it was all very nice. It was particularly nice in the beginning, before the apartment was fully arranged and some work still had to be done: this thing bought, that thing ordered, another thing moved, still another adjusted. And while there were some disagreements between husband and wife, both were so pleased and had so much to do that it all passed off without any major quarrels. When there was no work left to be done, it became a bit dull and something seemed to be lacking, but by then they were making acquaintances, forming new habits, and life was full.

Ivan Ilyich spent his mornings in court and came home for dinner, and at first he was in fine spirits, though it was precisely the apartment that caused him some distress. (Every spot on the tablecloth or the upholstery, every loose cord on the draperies irritated him; he had gone to such pains with the decorating that any damage to it upset him.) But on the whole Ivan Ilyich's life moved along as he believed life should: easily, pleasantly, and properly. He got up at nine, had his coffee, read the newspapers, then put on his uniform and went to court. There the harness in which he worked had already been worn into shape and he slipped right into it: petitioners, inquiries sent to the office, the office itself, the court sessions—preliminary and public. In all this one had to know how to exclude whatever was fresh and vital, which always disrupted the course of official business: one could have only official relations with people, and only on official grounds, and the relations themselves had to be kept purely official. For instance, a man would come and request some information. As an official who was charged with other duties, Ivan Ilyich could not have any dealings with such a man; but if the man approached him about a matter that related to his function as a court member, then within the limits of this relationship Ivan Ilyich would do everything, absolutely everything he could for him and, at the same time, maintain a semblance of friendly, human relations—that is, treat him with civility. As soon as the official relations ended, so did all the rest. Ivan Ilyich had a superb ability to detach the official aspect of things from his real life, and thanks to his talent and years of experience, he had cultivated it to such a degree that occasionally, like a virtuoso, he allowed himself to mix human and official relations, as if for fun. He allowed himself this liberty because he felt he had the strength to isolate the purely official part of the relationship again, if need be, and discard the human. And he did so not only in an easy, pleasant, and proper manner, but with style. In between times he smoked, had tea, talked a little about politics, a little about general matters, but most of all about appointments. And then tired, but with the feeling of a virtuoso—one of the first violinists in an orchestra who had played his part superbly—he would return home. There he would find that his wife and daughter had been out paying calls or had a visitor; that his son had been to the gymnasium, had gone over his lessons with a tutor, and was diligently learning all that students are taught in the gymnasium. Everything was just fine. After dinner, if there were no guests, Ivan Ilyich sometimes read a book that was the talk of the day and in the evening settled down to work—that is, read official papers, checked laws, compared depositions, and classified them according to the legal statutes. He found such work neither boring nor engaging. It was a bore if it meant foregoing a card game, but if there was no game on, it was better than sitting home alone or with his wife. Ivan Ilyich derived pleasure from giving small dinner parties to which he invited men and women of good social standing; and the dinners he gave resembled the ones they usually gave as much as his drawing room looked like all the other drawing rooms.

Once they even had an evening party with dancing. Ivan Ilyich was in fine spirits and everything went off well except that he had an enormous fight with his wife over the pastries and bonbons. Praskovya Fyodorovna had her own plans about these, but Ivan Ilyich insisted on ordering everything from an expensive confectioner; he ordered a great many pastries, and the quarrel broke out because some of the pastries were left over and the bill came to forty-five rubles. It was such an enormous, nasty fight that Praskovya Fyodorovna called him an "imbecile" and a "spoiler," while he clutched his head and inwardly muttered something about a divorce. But the party itself was gay. The best people came and Ivan

Ilyich danced with Princess Trufonova, sister of the Trufonova who had founded the charitable society called "Take My Grief Upon Thee."

The pleasures Ivan Ilyich derived from his work were those of pride; the pleasures he derived from society those of vanity; but it was genuine pleasure that he derived from playing whist. He confessed that no matter what happened, regardless of all the unhappiness he might experience, there was one pleasure which, like a bright candle, outshone all the others in his life: that was to sit down with some good players, quiet partners, to a game of whist, definitely a four-handed game (with five players it was painful to sit out, even though one pretended not to mind), to play a clever, serious game (when the cards permitted), then have supper and drink a glass of wine. After a game of whist, especially if he had won a little (winning a lot was distasteful), Ivan Ilyich went to bed in a particularly good mood.

So they lived. They moved in the best circles and their home was frequented by people of importance and by the young. There was complete accord between husband, wife, and daughter about their set of acquaintances and, without discussing the matter, they were equally adept at brushing off and escaping from various shabby friends and relations who, with a great show of affection, descended on them in their drawing room with the Japanese plates on the walls. Soon these shabby friends stopped intruding and the Golovins' set included only the best. Young men courted Lizanka, and the examining magistrate Petrishchev, the son and sole heir of Dmitry Ivanovich Petrishchev, was so attentive that Ivan Ilyich talked to Praskovya Fyodorovna about having a sleighing party for them or arranging some private theatricals.

So they lived. Everything went along without change and everything was fine.

They were all in good health. Ivan Ilyich sometimes complained of a strange taste in his mouth and some discomfort in his left side, but this could hardly be called ill health.

Yet the discomfort increased, and although it had not developed into real pain, the sense of a constant pressure in his side made Ivan Ilyich ill-tempered. His irritability became progressively more marked and began to spoil the pleasure of the easy and proper life that had only recently been established in the Golovin family. Husband and wife began to quarrel more often, and soon the ease and pleasure disappeared and even the propriety was barely maintained. Scenes became more frequent. Once again there were only little islands, very few at that, on which husband and wife could meet without an explosion.

Praskovya Fyodorovna had good reason now for saying that her husband had a trying disposition. With her characteristic tendency to exaggerate, she said he had always had such a horrid disposition and that only someone with her goodness of heart could have put up with it for twenty years. It was true that he was the one now who started the arguments. He invariably began cavilling when he sat down to dinner—often just as he was starting on his soup. Either he noticed that a dish was chipped, or the food was not good, or his son had put his elbow on the table, or his daughter had not combed her hair properly. And for all this he blamed Praskovya Fyodorovna. At first she fought back and said nasty things to him, but once or twice at the start of dinner he flew into such a rage that she realized it was due to some physical discomfort provoked by eating, and so she restrained herself and did not answer back but merely tried to get dinner over with as quickly as possible. Praskovya Fyodorovna regarded her self-restraint as a great virtue. Having concluded that her husband had a horrid disposition and had made her life miserable, she began to pity herself. And the more she pitied herself, the more she hated her husband. She began to wish he would die, yet she could not really wish that, for then there would be no income. This made her even more incensed with him. She considered herself supremely unhappy because even his death could not save her. She was exasperated yet concealed it, and her suppressed exasperation only heightened his exasperation.

After a scene in which Ivan Ilyich had been particularly unjust and, by way of explanation, admitted being irritable but attributed this to illness, she told him that if he was ill he must be treated, and she insisted he go and consult a celebrated physician.

He did. The whole procedure was just what he expected, just what one always encounters. There was the waiting, the doctor's exaggerated air of importance (so familiar to him since it was the very air he assumed in court), the tapping, the listening, the questions requiring answers that were clearly superfluous since they were foregone conclusions, and the significant look that implied: "Just put yourself in our hands and we'll take care of everything; we know exactly what has to be done—we always use one and the same method for every patient, no matter who." Everything was just as it was in court. The celebrated doctor dealt with him in precisely the manner he dealt with men on trial.

The doctor said: such and such indicates that you have such and such, but if an analysis of such and such does not confirm this, then we have to assume you have such and such. On the other hand, if we assume such and such is the case, then . . . and so on. To Ivan Ilyich only one question mattered: was his condition serious or not? But the doctor ignored this inappropriate question. From his point of view it was an idle question and not worth considering. One simply had to weigh the alternatives: a floating kidney, chronic catarrh, or a disease of the caecum. It was not a matter of Ivan Ilyich's life but a conflict between a floating kidney and a disease of the caecum.

And in Ivan Ilyich's presence the doctor resolved that conflict brilliantly in favor of the caecum, with the reservation that if an analysis of the urine yielded new evidence, the case would be reconsidered. This was exactly what Ivan Ilyich had done a thousand times, and in the same brilliant manner, with prisoners in the dock. The doctor summed up just as brilliantly, glancing triumphantly, even jovially, over his glasses at the prisoner. From the doctor's summary Ivan Ilyich concluded that things were bad, but that to the doctor and perhaps everyone else, it was of no consequence, even though for him it was bad. And this conclusion, which came as a painful shock to Ivan Ilyich, aroused in him a feeling of great self-pity and equally great resentment toward the doctor for being so indifferent to a matter of such importance.

But he made no comment, he simply got up, put his fee on the table, heaved a sigh, and said: "No doubt we sick people often ask inappropriate questions. But, in general, would you say my illness is serious or not?"

The doctor cocked one eye sternly at him over his glasses as if to say: "Prisoner, if you do not confine yourself to the questions allowed, I shall be obliged to have you expelled from the courtroom."

"I have already told you what I consider necessary and suitable," said the doctor. "Anything further will be revealed by the analysis." And with a bow the doctor brought the visit to a close.

Ivan Ilyich went out slowly, seated himself despondently in his sledge and drove home. All the way home he kept going over in his mind what the doctor had said, trying to translate all those vague, confusing scientific terms into simple language and find an answer to his question: "Is my condition serious? Very serious? Or nothing much to worry about?" And it seemed to him that the essence of what the doctor had said was that it was very serious. Everything in the streets seemed dismal to Ivan Ilyich. The cab drivers looked dismal, the houses looked dismal, the passersby, the shops—everything looked dismal. And in light of the doctor's obscure remarks, that pain—that dull, nagging pain which never let up for a second—acquired a different, a more serious implication. Ivan Ilyich focused on it now with a new sense of distress.

He reached home and began telling his wife about the visit. She listened, but in the middle of his account his daughter came in with her hat on—she and her mother were preparing to go out. She forced herself to sit and listen to this tedious stuff but could not stand it for long, and his wife, too, did not hear him out.

"Well, I'm very glad," she said. "Now see to it you take your medicine regularly. Give me the prescription, I'll send Gerasim to the apothecary's." And she went off to dress.

While she was in the room Ivan Ilyich had scarcely paused for breath, but he heaved a deep sigh when she left.

"Well," he said, "maybe there's nothing much to worry about."

He began to take the medicine and follow the doctor's instructions, which were changed after the analysis of his urine. But then it appeared that there was some confusion between the results of the analysis and what should have followed from it. It was impossible to get any information out of the doctor, but somehow things were not working out as he had said they should. Either the doctor had overlooked something, or lied, or concealed something from him. Nonetheless, Ivan Ilyich followed his instructions explicitly and at first derived some comfort from this.

After his visit to the doctor, Ivan Ilyich was preoccupied mainly with attempts to carry out the doctor's orders about hygiene, medicine, observation of the course of his pain, and all his bodily functions. His main interests in life became human ailments and human health. Whenever there was any talk in his presence of people who were sick, or who had died or recuperated, particularly from an illness resembling his own, he would listen intently, trying to conceal his agitation, ask questions, and apply what he learned to his own case.

The pain did not subside, but Ivan Ilyich forced himself to think he was getting better. And he managed to deceive himself as long as nothing upset him. But no sooner did he have a nasty episode with his wife, a setback at work, or a bad hand at cards, than he immediately became acutely aware of his illness. In the past he had been able to cope with such adversities, confident that in no time at all he would set things right, get the upper hand, succeed, have a grand slam. Now every setback knocked the ground out from under him and reduced him to despair. He would say to himself: "There, just as I was beginning to get better and the medicine was taking effect, this accursed misfortune or trouble had to happen." And he raged against misfortune or against the people who were causing him trouble and killing him, for he felt his rage was killing him but could do nothing to control it. One would have expected him to understand that the anger he vented on people and circumstances only aggravated his illness and that, consequently, the thing to do was to disregard unpleasant occurrences. But his reasoning took just the opposite turn: he said he needed peace, was on the lookout for anything that might disturb it, and at the slightest disturbance became exasperated. What made matters worse was that he read medical books and consulted doctors. His condition deteriorated so gradually that he could easily deceive himself when comparing one day with the next—the difference was that slight. But when he consulted doctors, he felt he was not only deteriorating but at a very rapid rate. And in spite of this he kept on consulting them.

That month he went to see another celebrated physician. This celebrity told him practically the same thing as the first but posed the problem somewhat differently. And the consultation with this celebrity only reinforced Ivan Ilyich's doubts and fears. A friend of a friend—a very fine doctor—diagnosed the case quite differently, and though he assured Ivan Ilyich that he would recover, his questions and suppositions only made him more confused and heightened his suspicions. A homeopath offered still another diagnosis and prescribed certain medicine, and for about a week Ivan Ilyich took it without telling anyone. But when a week passed with no sign of relief, he lost faith in both this and the previous types of treatment and became even more despondent.

Once a lady he knew told him about a cure effected with wonder-working icons. Ivan Ilyich caught himself listening intently and believing in the possibility. This incident alarmed him. "Have I really become so gullible?" he asked himself. "Nonsense! It's all rubbish. Instead of giving in to these nervous fears, I've got to choose one doctor and stick to his method of treatment. That's just what I'll do. Enough! I'll stop thinking about it and follow the doctor's orders strictly until summer and then see what happens. No more wavering!"

It was an easy thing to say but impossible to do. The pain in his side exhausted him, never let up, seemed to get worse all the time; the taste in his mouth became more and more peculiar; he felt his breath had a foul odor; his appetite diminished and he kept losing strength. There was no deceiving himself: something new and dreadful was happening to him, something of such vast importance that nothing in his life could compare with it. And he alone was aware of this. Those about him either did not understand or did not wish to understand and thought that nothing in the world had changed. It was precisely this which tormented Ivan Ilyich most of all. He saw that the people in his household—particularly his wife and daughter, who were caught up in a whirl of social activity—had no understanding of what was happening and were vexed with him for being so disconsolate and demanding, as though he were to blame. Although they tried to conceal this, he saw that he was an obstacle to them, and that his wife had adopted a certain attitude toward his illness and clung to it regardless of what he said or did. Her attitude amounted to this: "You know," she would say to her acquaintances, "Ivan Ilyich, like most people, simply cannot adhere to the course of treatment prescribed for him. One day he takes his drops, sticks to his diet, and goes to bed on time. But if I don't keep an eye on him, the next day he'll forget to take his medicine, eat sturgeon—which is forbidden—and sit up until one o'clock in the morning playing cards."

"Oh, when was that?" Ivan Ilyich retorted peevishly. "Only once at Pyotr Ivanovich's."

"And last night with Shebek."

"What difference did it make? I couldn't sleep anyway because of the pain."

"Well, it really doesn't matter why you did it, but if you go on like this, you'll never get well and just keep on torturing us."

From the remarks she made to both him and others, Praskovya Fyodorovna's attitude toward her husband's illness was that he himself was to blame for it, and that the whole thing was simply another way of making her life unpleasant. Ivan Ilyich felt that these remarks escaped her involuntarily, but this did not make things any easier for him.

In court, too, Ivan Ilyich noticed, or thought he noticed, a strange attitude toward himself. At times he felt people were eyeing him closely as a man whose post would soon be vacant; at other times his friends suddenly began teasing him, in a friendly way, about his nervous fears, as though that horrid, appalling, unheard-of something that had been set in motion within him and was gnawing away at him day and night, ineluctably dragging him off somewhere, was a most agreeable subject for a joke. He was particularly irritated by Schwartz, whose playfulness, vivacity, and *comme il faut* manner reminded him of himself ten years earlier.

Friends came over to make up a set and sat down to a game of cards with him. They dealt, bending the new cards to soften them; Ivan Ilyich sorted the diamonds in his hand and found he had seven. His partner said: "No trumps," and supported him with two diamonds. What more could he have wished for? He ought to have felt cheered, invigorated—they would make a grand slam. But suddenly Ivan Ilyich became aware of that gnawing pain in his side, that taste in his mouth, and under the circumstances it seemed preposterous to him to rejoice in a grand slam.

He saw his partner, Mikhail Mikhailovich, rapping the table with a vigorous hand, courteously and indulgently refraining from snatching up the tricks, pushing them over to him, so that he could have the pleasure of picking them up without having to exert himself. "Does he think I'm so weak I can't stretch my hand out?" Ivan Ilyich thought, and forgetting what he was doing, he overtrumped his partner, missing the grand slam by three tricks. And worst of all, he saw how upset Mikhail Mikhailovich was while he himself did not care. And it was dreadful to think why he did not care.

They could see that he was in pain and said: "We can stop if you're tired. Rest for a while." Rest? Why, he wasn't the least bit tired, they'd finish the rubber. They were all gloomy and silent. Ivan Ilyich knew he was responsible for the gloom that had descended but could do nothing to dispel it. After supper his friends went home, leaving Ivan Ilyich alone with the knowledge that his life had been poisoned and was poisoning the lives of others, and that far from diminishing, that poison was penetrating deeper and deeper into his entire being.

And with this knowledge and the physical pain and the horror as well, he had to go to bed, often to be kept awake by pain the greater part of the night. And the next morning he had to get up again, dress, go to court, talk and write, or if he did not go, put in those twenty-four hours at home, every one of them a torture. And he had to go on living like this, on the brink of disaster, without a single person to understand and pity him.

One month went by this way, then another. Just before the New Year his brother-in-law came to town and stayed with them. Ivan Ilyich was at court when he arrived. Praskovya Fyodorovna was out shopping. On his return home Ivan Ilyich found his brother-in-law—a robust, ebullient fellow—in the study unpacking his suitcase. The latter raised his head on hearing Ivan Ilyich's step and looked at him for a moment in silence. That look told Ivan Ilyich everything. His brother-in-law opened his mouth to gasp but checked himself. That movement confirmed it all.

"What is it—have I changed?"

"Y-yes . . . you have."

After that, try as he might to steer the conversation back to his appearance, Ivan Ilyich could not get a word out of his brother-in-law. When Praskovya Fyodorovna came back, her brother went in to see her. Ivan Ilyich locked the door of his room and began to examine himself in the mirror—first full face, then in profile. He picked up a photograph he had taken with his wife and compared it to what he saw in the mirror. The change was enormous. Then he bared his arms to the elbow, examined them, pulled down his sleeves, sat down on an ottoman, and fell into a mood blacker than night.

"I mustn't! I mustn't!" he said to himself. He jumped up, went to his desk, opened a case file, started to read but could not go on. He unlocked his door and went into the hall. The door to the drawing room was shut. He tiptoed over and began listening.

"No, you're exaggerating," said Praskovya Fyodorovna.

"Exaggerating? Can't you see for yourself? He's a dead man. Just look at his eyes. Not a spark of life in them. What's wrong with him?"

"No one knows. Nikolaev (another doctor) said something, but I don't understand. Leshchetitsky (the celebrated doctor) said just the opposite."

Ivan Ilyich walked away, went to his room, lay down and began thinking. "A kidney, a floating kidney." He remembered everything the doctors had told him about how the kidney had come loose and was floating about. And by force of imagination he tried to catch that kidney and stop it, to hold it in place. It took so little effort, it seemed. "I'll go and see Pyotr Ivanovich again" (the friend with the doctor friend). He rang, ordered the carriage, and got ready to leave.

"Where are you going, *Jean*?" asked his wife in a particularly sad and unusually kind tone of voice.

This unusual kindness on her part infuriated him. He gave her a somber look.

"I've got to go and see Pyotr Ivanovich."

He went to his friend with the doctor friend and together they went to the doctor. They found him in, and Ivan Ilyich had a long talk with him.

As he went over the anatomical and physiological details of what, in the doctor's view, was going on in him, Ivan Ilyich understood everything.

There was just one thing, a tiny little thing in the caecum. It could be remedied entirely. Just stimulate the energy of one organ, depress the activity of another, then absorption would take place and everything would be fine.

Ivan Ilyich was somewhat late getting home to dinner. He conversed cheerfully after dinner but for some time could not bring himself to go to his room and work. At last he went to his study and immediately set to work. He read through some cases, concentrated, but was constantly aware that he had put off an important, private matter which he would attend to once he was through. When he finished his work he remembered that this private matter involved some thoughts about his caecum. But instead of devoting himself to them he went into the drawing room to have tea. Guests were there talking, playing the piano, and singing; among them was the examining magistrate, a desirable fiancé for their daughter. Ivan Ilyich, as Praskovya Fyodorovna observed, was more cheerful that evening than usual, but never for a moment did he forget that he had put off that important business about his caecum. At eleven o'clock he took leave of everyone and went to his room. Ever since his illness he had slept alone in a little room adjoining his study. He went in, undressed, and picked up a novel by Zola, but instead of reading he lapsed into thought. And in his imagination that longed-for cure of his caecum took place: absorption, evacuation, and a restoration of normal functioning. "Yes, that's the way it works," he told himself. "One need only give nature a hand." He remembered his medicine, raised himself, took it, then lay on his back observing what a beneficial effect the medicine was having, how it was killing the pain. "Only I must take it regularly and avoid anything that could have a bad effect on me. I feel somewhat better already, much better." He began probing his side—it was not painful to the touch. "I really can't feel anything there, it's much better already." He put out the candle and lay on his side—his caecum was improving, absorbing. Suddenly he felt the old, familiar, dull, gnawing pain—quiet, serious, insistent. The same familiar bad taste in his mouth. His heart sank, he felt dazed. "My God, my God!" he muttered. "Again and again, and it will never end." And suddenly he saw things in an entirely different light. "A caecum! A kidney!" he exclaimed inwardly. "It's not a question of a caecum or a kidney, but of life and . . . death. Yes, life was there and now it's going, going, and I can't hold on to it.

Yes. Why deceive myself? Isn't it clear to everyone but me that I'm dying, that it's only a question of weeks, days—perhaps minutes? Before there was light, now there is darkness. Before I was here, now I am going there. Where?" He broke out in a cold sweat, his breathing died down. All he could hear was the beating of his heart.

"I'll be gone. What will there be then? Nothing. So where will I be when I'm gone? Can this really be death? No! I don't want this!" He jumped up, wanted to light the candle, groped for it with trembling hands, dropped the candle and candlestick on the floor and sank back on the pillow again. "Why bother? It's all the same," he thought, staring into the darkness with wide-open eyes. "Death. Yes . . . death. And they don't know and don't want to know and have no pity for me. They're playing." (Through the door of his room he caught the distant, intermittent sound of a voice and its accompaniment.) "It's all the same to them, but they'll die too. Fools! I'll go first, then they, but it will be just the same for them. Now they're enjoying themselves, the beasts!" His resentment was choking him. He felt agonizingly, unspeakably miserable. It seemed inconceivable to him that all men invariably had been condemned to suffer this awful horror. He raised himself.

"Something must be wrong. I must calm down, think it all through from the beginning." And he began thinking. "Yes. The beginning of my illness. I banged my side, but I was perfectly all right that day and the next; it hurt a little, then got worse; then came the doctors, then the despondency, the anguish, then more doctors; and all the while I was moving closer and closer to the abyss. Had less and less strength. Kept moving closer and closer. And now I've wasted away, haven't a spark of life in my eyes. It's death, yet I go on thinking about my caecum. I think about how to mend my caecum, whereas this is death. But can it really be death?" Once again he was seized with terror; he gasped for breath, leaned over, began groping for the matches, pressing his elbow for support on the bedside table. It was in his way and it hurt him; he became furious with it, pressed even harder, and knocked it over. And then breathless, in despair, he slumped down on his back, expecting death to strike him that very moment.

Just then the guests were leaving, Praskovya Fyodorovna was seeing them off. Hearing something fall, she came in.

"What is it?"

"Nothing. I accidentally knocked it over."

She went out and came back with a candle. He lay there, breathing heavily and rapidly like a man who has just run a mile, and stared at her with a glazed look.

"What is it, *Jean*?"

"N-nothing. I kn-nocked it over." (What's the point of telling her? She won't understand, he thought.)

And she really did not understand. She picked up the

stand, lit the candle for him, and hurried away—she had to see another guest off.

When she returned he was still lying on his back, staring upward.

"What is it? Do you feel worse?"

"Yes."

She shook her head and sat down.

"I wonder, *Jean,* if we shouldn't send for Leshchetitsky."

That meant calling in the celebrated doctor, regardless of the expense. He smiled vindictively and said: "No." She sat there a while longer, then went up and kissed him on the forehead.

As she was kissing him, he hated her with every inch of his being, and he had to restrain himself from pushing her away.

"Good night. God willing, you'll fall asleep."

"Yes."

Ivan Ilyich saw that he was dying, and he was in a constant state of despair.

In the depth of his heart he knew he was dying, but not only was he unaccustomed to such an idea, he simply could not grasp it, could not grasp it at all.

The syllogism he had learned from Kiesewetter's logic—"Caius is a man, men are mortal, therefore Caius is mortal"—had always seemed to him correct as applied to Caius, but by no means to himself. That man Caius represented man in the abstract, and so the reasoning was perfectly sound; but he was not Caius, not an abstract man; he had always been a creature quite, quite distinct from all the others. He had been little Vanya with a mama and a papa, with Mitya and Volodya, with toys, a coachman, and a nurse, and later with Katenka—Vanya, with all the joys, sorrows, and enthusiasms of his childhood, boyhood, and youth. Had Caius ever known the smell of that little striped leather ball Vanya had loved so much? Had Caius ever kissed his mother's hand so dearly, and had the silk folds of her dress ever rustled so for him? Had Caius ever rioted at school when the pastries were bad? Had he ever been so much in love? Or presided so well over a court session?

Caius really was mortal, and it was only right that he should die, but for him, Vanya, Ivan Ilyich, with all his thoughts and feelings, it was something else again. And it simply was not possible that he should have to die. That would be too terrible.

So his feelings went.

"If I were destined to die like Caius, I would have known it; an inner voice would have told me. But I was never aware of any such thing; and I and all my friends—we knew our situation was quite different from Caius's. Yet now look what's happened! It can't be. It just can't be, and yet it is. How is it possible? How is one to understand it?"

He could not understand it and tried to dismiss the

thought as false, unsound, and morbid, to force it out of his mind with other thoughts that were sound and healthy. But the thought—not just the thought but, it seemed, the reality itself—kept coming back and confronting him.

And one after another, in place of that thought, he called up others, hoping to find support in them. He tried to revert to a way of thinking that had obscured the thought of death from him in the past. But, strangely, everything that had once obscured, hidden, obliterated the awareness of death no longer had that effect. Ivan Ilyich spent most of this latter period trying to recapture habits of feeling that had screened death from him. He would say to himself: "I'll plunge into my work; after all, it was my whole life." And driving his doubts away, he would go to court, enter into conversation with his colleagues and, in his habitually distracted way, take his seat, eyeing the crowd with a pensive look, resting both his emaciated arms on those of his oaken chair, bending over as usual to a colleague, moving the papers over to him, exchanging remarks in a whisper, and then suddenly raising his eyes, holding himself erect, would utter the well-known words that began the proceedings. But suddenly, in the middle of the session, the pain in his side, disregarding the stage the proceedings had reached, would begin its gnawing proceedings. Ivan Ilyich would focus on it, then try to drive the thought of it away, but the pain went right on with its work. And then *It* would come back and stand there and stare at him, and he would be petrified, the light would go out of his eyes, and again he would begin asking himself: "Can *It* alone be true?" And his colleagues and subordinates, amazed and distressed, saw that he who was such a brilliant, subtle judge had become confused, was making mistakes. He would rouse himself, try to regain his composure, somehow bring the session to a close, and return home sadly aware that his judicial work could no longer hide what he wanted it to hide; that his judicial work could not rescue him from *It*. And the worst thing was that *It* drew his attention not so that he would do anything, but merely so that he would look at *It*, look *It* straight in the face and, doing nothing, suffer unspeakable agony.

And to escape from this situation Ivan Ilyich sought relief—other screens—and other screens turned up and for a while seemed to offer some escape; but then they immediately collapsed or rather became transparent, as though *It* penetrated everything and nothing could obscure *It*.

Sometimes during this latter period he went into the drawing room he had furnished—the very drawing room where he had fallen, for the sake of which, he would think with bitter humor, he had sacrificed his life, for he was certain that his illness had begun with that injury. He went in and saw that a deep scratch had cut through the varnished surface of a table. He tried to find the cause of the damage and discovered that the bronze ornament on an album had become bent. He picked up the album, a costly one that he had put together with loving care, and became indignant with his daughter and her friends for being so careless: in some places the album was torn, in others the photographs were upside down. Painstakingly he put everything in order and bent the ornament back into place.

Later on it would occur to him to transfer the whole *établissement* with the albums to another corner of the room, next to the plants. He would call the footman. Either his wife or daughter would come in to help; they would disagree, contradict one another; he would argue, get angry. But that was all to the good, because it kept him from thinking about *It*. *It* was nowhere in sight.

But when he began moving the table himself, his wife said: "Let the servants do it, you'll only hurt yourself again." And suddenly *It* flashed through the screen and he saw *It*. *It* had only appeared as a flash, so he hoped *It* would disappear, but involuntarily he became aware of his side: the pain was still there gnawing away at him and he could no longer forget—*It* was staring at him distinctly from behind the plants. What was the point of it all?

"Can it be true that here, on this drapery, as at the storming of a bastion, I lost my life? How awful and how stupid! It just can't be! It can't be, yet it is."

He went to his study, lay down, and once again was left alone with *It*. Face to face with *It*, unable to do anything with *It*. Simply look at *It* and grow numb with horror.

• • •

It is impossible to say how it happened, for it came about gradually, imperceptibly, but in the third month of Ivan Ilyich's illness his wife, his daughter, his son, his acquaintances, the servants, the doctors, and—above all—he himself knew that the only interest he had for others was whether he would soon vacate his place, free the living at last from the constraint of his presence and himself from his sufferings.

He slept less and less. They gave him opium and began morphine injections. But this brought no relief. At first the muffled sense of anguish he experienced in this semiconscious state came as a relief in that it was a new sensation, but then it became as agonizing, if not more so, than the raw pain.

Special foods were prepared for him on the doctors' orders, but these became more and more unpalatable, more and more revolting.

Special arrangements, too, were made for his bowel movements. And this was a regular torture—a torture because of the filth, the unseemliness, the stench, and the knowledge that another person had to assist in this.

Yet it was precisely through this unseemly business that Ivan Ilyich derived some comfort. The pantry boy, Gerasim, always came to carry out the chamber pot. Gerasim was a clean, ruddy-faced young peasant who was thriving on town food. He was always bright and cheerful. At first it embarrassed Ivan Ilyich to see this young fellow in his clean Russian peasant clothes performing such a revolting task.

Once, when he got up from the pot too weak to draw up his trousers, he collapsed into an armchair and, horrified, gazed at his naked thighs with the muscles clearly etched on his wasted flesh. Just then Gerasim entered the room with a light, vigorous step, exuding a pleasant smell of tar from his heavy boots and of fresh winter air. He was wearing a clean hemp apron and a clean cotton shirt with the sleeves rolled up over his strong arms; obviously trying to suppress the joy of life that his face radiated, and thereby not offend the sick man, he avoided looking at Ivan Ilyich and went over to get the pot.

"Gerasim," said Ivan Ilyich in a feeble voice.

Gerasim started, fearing he had done something wrong, and quickly turned his fresh, good-natured, simple, young face, which was showing the first signs of a beard, to the sick man.

"Yes, sir?"

"This must be very unpleasant for you. You must forgive me. I can't help it."

"Oh no, sir!" said Gerasim as he broke into a smile, his eyes and strong white teeth gleaming. "Why shouldn't I help you? You're a sick man."

And with strong, deft hands he performed his usual task, walking out of the room with a light step. Five minutes later, with just as light a step, he returned.

Ivan Ilyich was still sitting in the armchair in the same position.

"Gerasim," he said when the latter had replaced the freshly washed pot. "Please come and help me." Gerasim went over to him. "Lift me up. It's hard for me to get up, and I've sent Dmitry away."

Gerasim took hold of him with his strong arms and with a touch as light as his step, deftly, gently lifted and supported him with one hand, while with the other he pulled up his trousers. He was about to set him down again, but Ivan Ilyich asked that he help him over to the sofa. With no effort and no apparent pressure, Gerasim led—almost carried—him to the sofa and seated him there.

"Thank you. How skillfully . . . how well you do everything."

Gerasim smiled again and turned to leave, but Ivan Ilyich felt so good with him there that he was reluctant to have him go.

"Oh, one thing more. Please move that chair over here. No, the other one, to put under my feet. I feel better with my legs raised."

Gerasim carried the chair over and in one smooth motion set it down gently in place and lifted Ivan Ilyich's legs onto it. It seemed to Ivan Ilyich that he felt better when Gerasim lifted his legs up.

"I feel better with my legs raised," said Ivan Ilyich. "Bring that pillow over and put it under them."

Gerasim did so. He lifted his legs up again and placed the pillow under them. Again Ivan Ilyich felt better while Gerasim raised his legs. When he let them down he seemed to feel worse.

"Gerasim," he said. "Are you busy now?"

"Not at all, sir," said Gerasim, who had learned from the working people in town how to speak to the masters.

"What else do you have to do?"

"What else? I've done everything except chop wood for tomorrow."

"Then could you hold my legs up a bit higher?"

"Why of course I can." Gerasim lifted his legs higher, and it seemed to Ivan Ilyich that in this position he felt no pain at all.

"But what about the firewood?"

"Don't worry yourself about it, sir. I'll get it done."

Ivan Ilyich had Gerasim sit down and hold his legs up, and he began talking to him. And, strangely enough, he thought he felt better while Gerasim was holding his legs.

After that, Ivan Ilyich would send for Gerasim from time to time and have him hold his feet on his shoulders. And he loved to talk to him. Gerasim did everything easily, willingly, simply, and with a goodness of heart that moved Ivan Ilyich. Health, strength, and vitality in other people offended Ivan Ilyich, whereas Gerasim's strength and vitality had a soothing effect on him.

Ivan Ilyich suffered most of all from the lie, the lie which, for some reason, everyone accepted: that he was not dying but was simply ill, and that if he stayed calm and underwent treatment he could expect good results. Yet he knew that regardless of what was done, all he could expect was more agonizing suffering and death. And he was tortured by this lie, tortured by the fact that they refused to acknowledge what he and everyone else knew, that they wanted to lie about his horrible condition and to force him to become a party to that lie. This lie, a lie perpetrated on the eve of his death, a lie that was bound to degrade the awesome, solemn act of his dying to the level of their social calls, their draperies, and the sturgeon they ate for dinner, was an excruciating torture for Ivan Ilyich. And, oddly enough, many times when they were going through their acts with him he came within a hair-breadth of shouting: "Stop your lying! You and I know that I'm dying, so at least stop lying!" But he never had the courage to do it. He saw that the awesome, terrifying act of his dying had been degraded by those about him to the level of a chance unpleasantness, a bit of unseemly behavior (they reacted to him as they would to a man who emitted a foul odor on entering a drawing room); that it had been degraded by that very "propriety" to which he had devoted his entire life. He saw that no one pitied him because no one even cared to understand his situation. Gerasim was the only one who understood and pitied him. And for that reason Ivan Ilyich felt comfortable only with Gerasim. It was a comfort to him when Gerasim sat with him sometimes the whole night through, holding his legs, refusing to go to bed, saying: "Don't worry, Ivan Ilyich, I'll get a good sleep later on"; or when he suddenly addressed him in the familiar form and said: "It would be a different thing if you weren't sick, but as it is, why shouldn't I do a little extra work?" Gerasim was the only one who did not lie; everything he did showed that he alone understood what was happening, saw no need to conceal it, and simply pitied his feeble, wasted master. Once, as Ivan Ilyich was sending him away, he came right out and said: "We all have to die someday, so why shouldn't I help you?" By this he meant that he did not find his work a burden because he was doing it for a dying man, and he hoped that someone would do the same for him when his time came.

In addition to the lie, or owing to it, what tormented Ivan Ilyich most was that no one gave him the kind of compassion he craved. There were moments after long suffering when what he wanted most of all (shameful as it might be for him to admit) was to be pitied like a sick child. He wanted to be caressed, kissed, cried over, as sick children are caressed and comforted. He knew that he was an important functionary with a graying beard, and so this was impossible; yet all the same he longed for it. There was something approaching this in his relationship with Gerasim, and so the relationship was a comfort to him. Ivan Ilyich wanted to cry, wanted to be caressed and cried over, yet his colleague Shebek, a member of the court, would come, and instead of crying and getting some affection, Ivan Ilyich would assume a serious, stern, profound expression and, by force of habit, offer his opinion about a decision by the Court of Appeals and stubbornly defend it. Nothing did so much to poison the last days of Ivan Ilyich's life as this falseness in himself and in those around him.

It was morning. He knew it was morning simply because Gerasim had gone and Pyotr, the footman, had come, snuffed out the candles, drawn back one of the curtains, and quietly begun to tidy up the room. Morning or night, Friday or Sunday, made no difference, everything was the same: that gnawing, excruciating, incessant pain; that awareness of life irrevocably passing but not yet gone; that dreadful, loathsome death, the only reality, relentlessly closing in on him; and that same endless lie. What did days, weeks, or hours matter?

"Will you have tea, sir?"

"He wants order, so the masters should drink tea in the morning," thought Ivan Ilyich. But he merely replied: "No."

"Would you care to move to the sofa, sir?"

"He wants to tidy up the room and I'm in the way. I represent filth and disorder," thought Ivan Ilyich. But he merely replied: "No, leave me alone."

The footman busied himself a while longer. Ivan Ilyich stretched out his hand. Pyotr went up to him obligingly.

"What would you like, sir?"

"My watch."

Pyotr picked up the watch, which was lying within Ivan Ilyich's reach, and gave it to him.

"Half-past eight. Are they up?"

"No, sir. Vasily Ivanovich (the son) went to school and Praskovya Fyodorovna left orders to awaken her if you asked. Shall I, sir?"

"No, don't bother," he said. "Perhaps I should have some tea," he thought, and said: "Yes, tea . . . bring me some."

Pyotr headed for the door. Ivan Ilyich was terrified at the thought of being left alone. "What can I do to keep him here?" he thought. "Oh, of course, the medicine."

"Pyotr, give me my medicine," he said. "Why not?" he thought. "Maybe the medicine will still do some good." He took a spoonful and swallowed it. "No, it won't help. It's just nonsense, a hoax," he decided as soon as he felt that familiar, sickly, hopeless taste in his mouth. "No, I can't believe in it anymore. But why this pain, this pain? If only it would let up for a minute!" He began to moan. Pyotr came back.

"No, go. Bring me some tea."

Pyotr went out. Left alone Ivan Ilyich moaned less from the pain, agonizing as it was, than from anguish. "The same thing, on and on, the same endless days and nights. If only it would come quicker! If only *what* would come quicker? Death, darkness. No! No! Anything is better than death!"

When Pyotr returned with the tea, Ivan Ilyich looked at him in bewilderment for some time, unable to grasp who and what he was. Pyotr was disconcerted by that look. Seeing his confusion, Ivan Ilyich came to his senses.

"Yes," he said. "Tea . . . good. Put it down. Only help me wash up and put on a clean shirt."

And Ivan Ilyich began to wash himself. Pausing now and then to rest, he washed his hands and face, brushed his teeth, combed his hair, and looked in the mirror. He was horrified, particularly horrified to see the limp way his hair clung to his pale brow. He knew he would be even more horrified by the sight of his body, and so while his shirt was being changed he avoided looking at it. Finally it was all over. He put on a dressing gown, wrapped himself in a plaid, and sat down in an armchair to have his tea. For a brief moment he felt refreshed, but as soon as he began to drink his tea he sensed that same taste again, that same pain. He forced himself to finish the tea and then lay down, stretched out his legs, and sent Pyotr away.

The same thing again and again. One moment a spark of hope gleams, the next a sea of despair rages; and always the pain, the pain, always the anguish, the same thing on and on. Left alone he feels horribly depressed, wants to call someone, but knows beforehand that with others present it will be even worse. "Oh, for some morphine again—to sink into oblivion. I'll tell the doctor he must think of something to give me."

One hour then another pass this way. Then there is a ring in the entranceway. The doctor perhaps? The doctor indeed—fresh, hearty, stocky, cheerful, and with a look on his face that seems to say: "Now, now, you've had yourself a bad scare, but we're going to fix everything right away." The doctor knows this expression is inappropriate here, but he has put it on once and for all and can't take it off—like a man who has donned a frock coat in the morning to make a round of social calls.

The doctor rubs his hands briskly, reassuringly. "I'm chilled. Freezing cold outside. Just give me a minute to warm up," he says in a tone implying that one need only wait a moment until he warmed up and he would set everything right.

"Well, now, how are you?"

Ivan Ilyich feels the doctor wants to say: "How goes it?" but that even he knows this won't do, and so he says: "What sort of night did you have?"

Ivan Ilyich looks at the doctor inquisitively as if to say: "Won't you ever be ashamed of your lying?" But the doctor does not wish to understand such a question.

"Terrible. Just like all the others," Ivan Ilyich said. "The pain never leaves, never subsides. If only you'd give me something!"

"Yes, you sick people are always carrying on like this. Well, now, I seem to have warmed up. Even Praskovya Fyodorovna, who's so exacting, couldn't find fault with my temperature. Well, now I can say good morning." And the doctor shakes his hand.

Then, dispensing with all the banter, the doctor assumes a serious air and begins to examine the patient, taking his pulse, his temperature, sounding his chest, listening to his heart and lungs.

Ivan Ilyich knows for certain, beyond any doubt, that this is all nonsense, sheer deception, but when the doctor gets down on his knees, bends over him, placing his ear higher, then lower, and with the gravest expression on his face goes through all sorts of contortions, Ivan Ilyich is taken in by it, just as he used to be taken in by the speeches of lawyers, even though he knew perfectly well they were lying and why they were lying.

The doctor is still kneeling on the sofa, tapping away at him, when there is a rustle of silk at the doorway and Praskovya Fyodorovna can be heard reproaching Pyotr for not informing her of the doctor's arrival.

She comes in, kisses her husband, and at once tries to demonstrate that she has been up for some time, and owing simply to a misunderstanding failed to be in the room when the doctor arrived.

Ivan Ilyich looks her over from head to toe and resents her for the whiteness, plumpness, and cleanliness of her arms and neck, the luster of her hair, and the spark of vitality that gleams in her eyes. He hates her with every inch of his being. And her touch causes an agonizing well of hatred to surge up in him.

Her attitude toward him and his illness is the same as ever. Just as the doctor had adopted a certain attitude toward his patients, which he could not change, so she had adopted one toward him: that he was not doing what he should and was himself to blame, and she could only reproach him tenderly for this. And she could no longer change this attitude.

"He just doesn't listen, you know. He doesn't take his medicine on time. And worst of all, he lies in a position that is surely bad for him—with his legs up."

And she told him how he made Gerasim hold his legs up.

The doctor smiled disdainfully, indulgently, as if to say: "What can you do? Patients sometimes get absurd ideas into their heads, but we have to forgive them."

When he had finished his examination the doctor glanced at his watch, and then Praskovya Fyodorovna announced to Ivan Ilyich that whether he liked it or not, she had called in a celebrated physician, and that he and Mikhail Danilovich (the regular doctor) would examine him together that day and discuss his case.

"So no arguments, please. I'm doing this for my sake," she said ironically, letting him know that she was doing it all for his sake and had said this merely to deny him the right to protest. He scowled and said nothing. He felt that he was trapped in such a mesh of lies that it was difficult to make sense out of anything.

Everything she did for him was done strictly for her sake;

and she told him she was doing for her sake what she actually was, making this seem so incredible that he was bound to take it to mean just the reverse.

At half-past eleven the celebrated doctor did indeed arrive. Again there were soundings and impressive talk in his presence and in the next room about the kidney and the caecum, and questions and answers exchanged with such an air of importance that once again, instead of the real question of life and death, the only one confronting Ivan Ilyich, the question that had arisen concerned a kidney or a caecum that was not behaving properly, and that would soon get a good trouncing from Mikhail Danilovich and the celebrity and be forced to mend its ways.

The celebrated doctor took leave of him with a grave but not hopeless air. And when Ivan Ilyich looked up at him, his eyes glistening with hope and fear, and timidly asked whether there was any chance of recovery, he replied that he could not vouch for it but there was a chance. The look of hope Ivan Ilyich gave the doctor as he watched him leave was so pathetic that, seeing it, Praskovya Fyodorovna actually burst into tears as she left the study to give the celebrated doctor his fee.

The improvement in his morale prompted by the doctor's encouraging remarks did not last long. Once again the same room, the same pictures, draperies, wallpaper, medicine bottles, and the same aching, suffering body. Ivan Ilyich began to moan. They gave him an injection and he lost consciousness.

When he came to, it was twilight; his dinner was brought in. He struggled to get down some broth. Then everything was the same again, and again night was coming on.

After dinner, at seven o'clock, Praskovya Fyodorovna came into his room in evening dress, her full bosom drawn up tightly by her corset, and traces of powder showing on her face. She had reminded him in the morning that they were going to the theater. Sarah Bernhardt had come to town, and at his insistence they had reserved a box. He had forgotten about this and was hurt by the sight of her elaborate attire. But he concealed his indignation when he remembered that he himself had urged them to reserve a box and go, because the aesthetic enjoyment would be edifying for the children.

Praskovya Fyodorovna had come in looking self-satisfied but guilty. She sat down and asked how he was feeling—merely for the sake of asking, as he could see, not because she wanted to find out anything, for she knew there was nothing to find out; and she went on to say what she felt was necessary: that under no circumstances would she have gone except that the box was reserved, and that Helene and their daughter and Petrishchev (the examining magistrate, their daughter's fiancé) were going, and it was unthinkable to let them go alone, but that she would much prefer to sit home with him, and would he promise to follow the doctor's orders while she was away.

"Oh, and Fyodor Petrovich (the fiancé) would like to come in. May he? And Liza?"

"All right."

His daughter came in all decked out in a gown that left much of her young flesh exposed; she was making a show of that very flesh which, for him, was the cause of so much agony. Strong, healthy, and obviously in love, she was impatient with illness, suffering, and death, which interfered with her happiness.

Fyodor Petrovich came in, too, in evening dress, his hair curled *à la Capoul*, a stiff white collar encircling his long, sinewy neck, an enormous white shirtfront over his chest, narrow black trousers hugging his strong thighs, a white glove drawn tightly over one hand, an opera hat clasped in the other.

Behind him the schoolboy son crept in unnoticed, all decked out in a new uniform, poor fellow, with gloves on and those awful dark circles under his eyes, whose meaning Ivan Ilyich understood only too well. He had always felt sorry for his son. And he found the boy's frightened, pitying look terrifying to behold. It seemed to Ivan Ilyich that, except for Gerasim, Vasya was the only one who understood and pitied him.

They all sat down and again asked how he was feeling. Then silence. Liza asked her mother about the opera glasses. This led to an argument between mother and daughter about who had mislaid them. It occasioned some unpleasantness.

Fyodor Petrovich asked Ivan Ilyich if he had ever seen

Sarah Bernhardt. Ivan Ilyich did not understand the question at first, but then he said: "No, have you?"

"Yes, in *Adrienne Lecouvreur.*"

Praskovya Fyodorovna said she had been particularly good in something or other. The daughter disagreed. They started a conversation about the charm and naturalness of her acting—precisely the kind of conversation people always have on the subject.

In the middle of the conversation Fyodor Petrovich glanced at Ivan Ilyich and stopped talking. The others also looked at him and stopped talking. Ivan Ilyich was staring straight ahead with glittering eyes, obviously infuriated with them. The situation had to be rectified, but there was no way to rectify it. The silence had to be broken. No one ventured to break it, and they began to fear that the lie dictated by propriety suddenly would be exposed and the truth become clear to all. Liza was the first who ventured to break the silence. She wanted to conceal what they were feeling but, in going too far, she divulged it.

"Well, *if we're going*, it's time we left," she said, glancing at her watch, a gift from her father. And smiling at her young man in a significant but barely perceptible way about something only they understood, she stood up, rustling her dress.

They all got up, said goodbye, and left.

When they had gone, Ivan Ilyich thought he felt better: the lie was gone—it had left with them. But the pain remained.

That same pain, that same fear that made nothing harder, nothing easier. Everything was getting worse.

Again time dragged on, minute by minute, hour by hour, on and on without end, with the inevitable end becoming more and more horrifying.

"Yes, send Gerasim," he said in reply to a question Pyotr asked him.

His wife returned late that night. She tip-toed into the room, but he heard her; he opened his eyes and quickly closed them again. She wanted to send Gerasim away and sit with him herself, but he opened his eyes and said:

"No, go away."

"Are you in very great pain?"

"It doesn't matter."

"Take some opium."

He consented and drank some. She went away.

Until about three in the morning he was in an agonizing delirium. It seemed to him that he and his pain were being thrust into a narrow black sack—a deep one—were thrust farther and farther in but could not be pushed to the bottom. And this dreadful business was causing him suffering. He was afraid of that sack, yet wanted to fall through; struggled, yet cooperated. And then suddenly he lost his grip and fell—and regained consciousness. Gerasim was still sitting at the foot of the bed, dozing quietly, patiently, while Ivan Ilyich lay with his emaciated, stockinged feet on his shoulders. The same shaded candle was there and the same incessant pain.

"Go, Gerasim," he whispered.

"It's all right, sir. I'll stay awhile."

"No; go."

He lowered his legs, turned sideways with his arm nestled under his cheek, and began to feel terribly sorry for himself. He waited until Gerasim had gone into the next room, and then, no longer able to restrain himself, cried like a baby. He cried about his helplessness, about his terrible loneliness, about the cruelty of people, about the cruelty of God, about the absence of God.

"Why hast Thou done all this? Why hast Thou brought me to this? Why dost Thou torture me so? For what?"

He did not expect an answer, and he cried because there was no answer and there could be none. The pain started up again, but he did not stir, did not call out. He said to himself: "Go on then! Hit me again! But what for? What for? What have I done to Thee?"

Then he quieted down and not only stopped crying but held his breath and became all attention: he seemed to be listening—not to an audible voice, but to the voice of his soul, to the flow of thoughts surging within him.

"What do you want?" was the first thought sufficiently intelligible to be expressed in words. "What do you want?

What do you want?" he repeated inwardly. "What? Not to suffer. To live," he replied.

And once again he listened with such rapt attention that even the pain did not distract him.

"To live? How?" asked the voice of his soul.

"Why, to live as I did before—happily and pleasantly."

"As you lived before, happily and pleasantly?" asked the voice.

And in his imagination he called to mind the best moments of his pleasant life. Yet, strangely enough, all the best moments of his pleasant life now seemed entirely different than they had in the past—all except the earliest memories of childhood. Way back in his childhood there had been something really pleasant, something he could live with were it ever to recur. But the person who had experienced that happiness no longer existed. It was as though he were recalling the memories of another man.

As soon as he got to the period that had produced the present Ivan Ilyich, all the seeming joys of his life vanished before his sight and turned into something trivial and often nasty.

And the farther he moved from childhood, the closer he came to the present, the more trivial and questionable these joyful experiences appeared. Beginning with the years he had spent in law school. A little of what was genuinely good had still existed then: there had been playfulness and friendship and hope. But by the time he reached the upper classes, the good moments in his life had become rarer. After that, during the period he worked for the governor, there had also been some good moments—memories of his love for a woman. But then everything became more and more mixed, and less of what was good remained. Later on there was even less, and the farther he went, the less there was.

His marriage—a mere accident—and his disillusionment with it, and his wife's bad breath, and the sensuality, and the pretense! And that deadly service, and those worries about money; and so it had gone for a year, two years, ten years, twenty years—on and on in the same way. And the longer it lasted, the more deadly it became. "It's as though I had been going steadily downhill while I imagined I was going up. That's exactly what happened. In public opinion I was moving uphill, but to the same extent life was slipping away from me. And now it's gone and all I can do is die!

"What does it all mean? Why has it happened? It's inconceivable, inconceivable that life was so senseless and disgusting. And if it really was so disgusting and senseless, why should I have to die, and die in agony? Something must be wrong. Perhaps I did not live as I should have," it suddenly occurred to him. "But how could that be when I did everything one is supposed to?" he replied and immediately dismissed the one solution to the whole enigma of life and death, considering it utterly impossible.

"Then what do you want now? To live? Live how? Live as you did in court when the usher proclaimed: 'The court is open!' The court is open, open," he repeated inwardly. "Now comes the judgment! But I'm not guilty!" he cried out indignantly. "What is this for?" And he stopped crying and, turning his face to the wall, began to dwell on one and the same question: "Why all this horror? What is it for?"

But think as he might, he could find no answer. And when it occurred to him, as it often did, that he had not lived as he should have, he immediately recalled how correct his whole life had been and dismissed this bizarre idea.

Another two weeks passed. Ivan Ilyich no longer got off the sofa. He did not want to lie in bed and so he lay on the sofa. And as he lay there, facing the wall most of the time, he suffered, all alone, the same inexplicable suffering and, all alone, brooded on the same inexplicable question: "What is this? Is it true that this is death?" And an inner voice answered: "Yes, it is true." "Then why these torments?" And the voice answered: "For no reason—they just are." Above and beyond this there was nothing.

From the start of his illness, from the time he first went to a doctor, Ivan Ilyich's life had been divided into two contradictory and fluctuating moods: one a mood of despair and expectation of an incomprehensible and terrible death; the other a mood of hope filled with intent observation of the course of his bodily functions. At times he was confronted with nothing but a kidney or an intestine that was temporarily evading its duty; at others nothing but an unfathomable, horrifying death from which there was no escape.

These two moods had fluctuated since the onset of his illness, but the farther that illness progressed, the more unlikely and preposterous considerations about his kidney became and the more real his sense of impending death.

He had merely to recall what he had been like three months earlier and what he was now, to remember how steadily he had gone downhill, for all possibility of hope to be shattered.

During the last days of the isolation in which he lived, lying on the sofa with his face to the wall, isolation in the midst of a populous city among numerous friends and relatives, an isolation that could not have been greater anywhere, either in the depths of the sea or the bowels of the earth—during the last days of that terrible isolation, Ivan Ilyich lived only with memories of the past. One after another images of his past came to mind. His recollections always began with what was closest in time and shifted back to what was most remote, to his childhood, and lingered there. If he thought of the stewed prunes he had been served that day, he remembered the raw, shrivelled French prunes he had eaten as a child, the special taste they had, the way his mouth watered when he got down to the pit; and along with the memory of that taste came a whole series of memories of those days: of his nurse, his brother, his toys. "I mustn't think about them—it's too painful," he would tell himself and shift back to the present. He would look at the button on the back of the sofa and the crease in the morocco. "Morocco is expensive, doesn't wear well; we had a quarrel over it. But there had been another morocco and another quarrel—the time we tore papa's briefcase and got punished, but mama brought us some tarts." And again his memories centered on his childhood, and again he found them painful and tried to drive them away by thinking about something else.

And together with this train of recollections, another flashed through his mind—recollections of how his illness had progressed and become more acute. Here, too, the farther back in time he went, the more life he found. There had been more goodness in his life earlier and more of life itself. And the one fused with the other. "Just as my torments are getting worse and worse, so my whole life got worse and worse," he thought. There was only one bright spot back at the beginning of life; after that things grew blacker and blacker, moved faster and faster. "In inverse ratio to the square of the distance from death," thought Ivan Ilyich. And the image of a stone hurtling downward with increasing velocity became fixed in his mind. Life, a series of increasing sufferings, falls faster and faster toward its end—the most frightful suffering. "I am falling . . ." He shuddered, shifted back and forth, wanted to resist, but by then knew there was no resisting. And again, weary of contemplating but unable to tear his eyes away from what was right there before him, he stared at the back of the sofa and waited—waited for that dreadful fall, shock, destruction. "Resistance is impossible," he said to himself. "But if only I could understand the reason for this agony. Yet even that is impossible. It would make sense if one could say I had not lived as I should have. But such an admission is impossible," he uttered inwardly, remembering how his life had conformed to all the laws, rules, and proprieties. "That is a point I cannot grant," he told himself, smiling ironically, as though someone could see that smile of his and be taken in by it. "There is no explanation. Agony. Death. Why?"

Two more weeks went by this way. During that time the event Ivan Ilyich and his wife had hoped for occurred: Petrishchev made a formal proposal. It happened in the evening. The next day Praskovya Fyodorovna went into her husband's room thinking over how she would announce the proposal, but during the night Ivan Ilyich had undergone a change for the worse. Praskovya Fyodorovna found him on the same sofa but in a different position. He was lying flat on his back, moaning, and staring straight ahead with a fixed look in his eyes.

She started to say something about his medicine. He shifted his gaze to her. So great was the animosity in that look—animosity toward her—that she broke off without finishing what she had to say.

"For Christ's sake, let me die in peace!" he said.

She wanted to leave, but at that moment their daughter came in and went over to say good morning to him. He looked at her as he had at his wife, and when she asked how he was feeling coldly replied that they would soon be rid of him. Both of them were silent, sat there for a while, and then went away.

"Is it our fault?" Liza asked her mother. "You'd think we were to blame. I'm sorry for papa, but why should he torture us like this?"

The doctor came at his usual time. Ivan Ilyich merely answered Yes or No to his questions, glowered at him throughout the visit, and toward the end said:

"You know perfectly well you can do nothing to help me, so leave me alone."

"We can ease your suffering," said the doctor.

"You can't even do that; leave me alone."

The doctor went into the drawing room and told Praskovya Fyodorovna that his condition was very bad and that only one remedy, opium, could relieve his pain, which must be excruciating.

The doctor said his physical agony was dreadful, and that was true; but even more dreadful was his moral agony, and it was this that tormented him most.

What had induced his moral agony was that during the night, as he gazed at Gerasim's broad-boned, sleepy, good-natured face, he suddenly asked himself: "What if my entire life, my entire conscious life, simply was *not the real thing?*"

It occurred to him that what had seemed utterly inconceivable before—that he had not lived the kind of life he should have—might in fact be true. It occurred to him that those scarcely perceptible impulses of his to protest what people of high rank considered good, vague impulses which he had always suppressed, might have been precisely what mattered, and all the rest not been the real thing. His official duties, his manner of life, his family, the values adhered to by people in society and in his profession—all these might not have been the real thing. He tried to come up with a defense of these things and suddenly became aware of the insubstantiality of them all. And there was nothing left to defend.

"But if that is the case," he asked himself, "and I am taking leave of life with the awareness that I squandered all I was given and have no possibility of rectifying matters—what then?" He lay on his back and began to review his whole life in an entirely different light.

When, in the morning, he saw first the footman, then his wife, then his daughter, and then the doctor, their every gesture, their every word, confirmed the horrible truth revealed to him during the night. In them he saw himself, all he had lived by, saw clearly that all this was not the real thing but a dreadful, enormous deception that shut out both life and death. This awareness intensified his physical sufferings, magnified them tenfold. He moaned and tossed and clutched at his bedclothes. He felt they were choking and suffocating him, and he hated them on that account.

He was given a large dose of opium and lost consciousness, but at dinnertime it all started again. He drove everyone away and tossed from side to side.

His wife came to him and said:

"*Jean,* dear, do this for me." (For me?) "It can't do you any harm, and it often helps. Really, it's such a small thing. And even healthy people often . . ."

He opened his eyes wide.

"What? Take the sacrament? Why? I don't want to! And yet . . ."

She began to cry.

"Then you will, dear? I'll send for our priest, he's such a nice man."

"Fine, very good," he said.

When the priest came and heard his confession, he relented, seemed to feel relieved of his doubts and therefore of his agony, and experienced a brief moment of hope. Again he began to think about his caecum and the possibility of curing it. As he took the sacrament, there were tears in his eyes.

When they laid him down afterward, he felt better for a second and again held out hope of living. He began to think of the operation the doctors had proposed doing. "I want to live, to live!" he said to himself. His wife came in to congratulate him on taking the sacrament; she said the things people usually do, and then added:

"You really do feel better, don't you?"

"Yes," he said without looking at her.

Her clothes, her figure, the expression of her face, the sound of her voice—all these said to him: "*Not the real thing.* Everything you lived by and still live by is a lie, a deception that blinds you from the reality of life and death." And no sooner had he thought this than hatred welled up in him, and with the hatred, excruciating physical pain, and with the pain, an awareness of inevitable, imminent destruction. The pain took a new turn: it began to grind and shoot and constrict his breathing.

The expression on his face when he uttered that "Yes" was dreadful. Having uttered it, he looked his wife straight in the eye, and with a rapidity extraordinary for one so weak, flung himself face downward and shouted:

"Go away! Go away! Leave me alone!"

• • •

That moment started three days of incessant screaming, screaming so terrible that even two rooms away one could not hear it without trembling. The moment he had answered his wife, he realized that he was lost, that there was no return, that the end had come, the very end, and that his doubts, still unresolved, remained with him.

"Oh! Oh! No!" he screamed in varying tones. He had begun by shouting: "I don't want it! I don't!" and went on uttering screams with that "O" sound.

For three straight days, during which time ceased to exist for him, he struggled desperately in that black sack into which an unseen, invincible force was thrusting him. He struggled as a man condemned to death struggles in the hands of an executioner, knowing there is no escape. And he felt that with every minute, despite his efforts to resist, he was coming closer and closer to what terrified him. He felt he was in agony because he was being shoved into that black hole, but even more because he was unable to get right into it. What prevented him from getting into it was the belief that his life had been a good one. This justification of his life held him fast, kept him from moving forward, and caused him more agony than anything else.

Suddenly some force struck him in the chest and the side and made his breathing even more constricted: he plunged into the hole and there at the bottom, something was shining.

What had happened to him was what one frequently experiences in a railway car when one thinks one is going forward but is actually moving backward, and suddenly becomes aware of the actual direction.

"Yes, all of it was simply *not the real thing.* But no matter. I can still make it *the real thing*—I can. But what *is* the real thing?" Ivan Ilyich asked himself and suddenly grew quiet.

This took place at the end of the third day, an hour before his death. Just then his son crept quietly into the room and went up to his bed. The dying man was still screaming desperately and flailing his arms. One hand fell on the boy's head. The boy grasped it, pressed it to his lips, and began to cry. At that very moment Ivan Ilyich fell through and saw a light, and it was revealed to him that his life had not been what it should have but that he could still rectify the situation. "But what *is* the real thing?" he asked himself and grew quiet, listening. Just then he felt someone kissing his hand. He opened his eyes and looked at his son. He grieved for him. His wife came in and went up to him. He looked at her. She gazed at him with an open mouth, with unwiped tears on her nose and cheeks, with a look of despair on her face. He grieved for her.

"Yes, I'm torturing them," he thought. "They feel sorry for me, but it will be better for them when I die." He wanted to tell them this but lacked the strength to speak. "But why speak—I must do something," he thought. He looked at his wife and, indicating his son with a glance, said:

"Take him away . . . sorry for him . . . and you." He wanted to add: "Forgive" but instead said "Forget," and too feeble to correct himself, dismissed it, knowing that He who needed to understand would understand.

And suddenly it became clear to him that what had been oppressing him and would not leave him suddenly was vanishing all at once—from two sides, ten sides, all sides. He felt sorry for them, he had to do something to keep from hurting them. To deliver them and himself from this suffering. "How good and how simple!" he thought. "And the pain?" he asked himself. "Where has it gone? Now, then, pain, where are you?"

He waited for it attentively.

"Ah, there it is. Well, what of it? Let it be."

"And death? Where is it?"

He searched for his accustomed fear of death and could not find it. Where was death? What death? There was no fear because there was no death.

Instead of death there was light.

"So that's it!" he exclaimed. "What bliss!"

All this happened in a single moment, but the significance of that moment was lasting. For those present, his agony continued for another two hours. Something rattled in his chest; his emaciated body twitched. Then the rattling and wheezing gradually diminished.

"It is all over," said someone standing beside him.

He heard these words and repeated them in his soul.

"Death is over," he said to himself. "There is no more death."

He drew in a breath, broke off in the middle of it, stretched himself out, and died.

from

WINDING THE GOLDEN STRING

BEDE GRIFFITHS

There is life after the moment of enlightenment and in this essay, Catholic monk Bede Griffiths describes the challenge of living fully awake. For him, the Catholic Church became his vehicle for implementing in his daily life what he had seen.

I give you the end of a golden string;
Only wind it into a ball,
It will lead you in at heaven's gate,
Built in Jerusalem's wall.

—William Blake

One day during my last term at school I walked out alone in the evening and heard the birds singing in that full chorus of song, which can only be heard at that time of the year at dawn or at sunset. I remember now the shock of surprise with which the sound broke on my ears. It seemed to me that I had never heard the birds singing before and I wondered whether they sang like this all the year round and I had never noticed it. As I walked on I came upon some hawthorn trees in full bloom and again I thought that I had never seen such a sight or experienced such sweetness before. If I had been brought suddenly among the trees of the Garden of Paradise and heard a choir of angels singing I could not have been more surprised. I came then to where the sun was setting over the playing fields. A lark rose suddenly from the ground beside the tree where I was standing and poured out its song above my head, and then sank still singing to rest. Everything then grew still as the sunset faded and the veil of dusk began to cover the earth. I remember now the feeling of awe which came over me. I felt inclined to kneel on the ground, as though I had been standing in the presence of an angel; and I hardly dared to look on the face of the sky, because it seemed as though it was but a veil before the face of God.

These are the words with which I tried many years later to express what I had experienced that evening, but no words can do more than suggest what it meant to me. It came to me quite suddenly, as it were out of the blue, and now that I look back on it, it seems to me that it was one of the decisive events of my life. Up to that time I had lived the life of a normal schoolboy, quite content with the world as I found it. Now I was suddenly made aware of another world of beauty and mystery such as I had never imagined to exist, except in poetry. It was as though I had begun to see and smell and hear for the first time. The world appeared to me as Wordsworth describes it with "the glory and the freshness of a dream." The sight of a wild rose growing on a hedge, the scent of lime tree blossoms caught suddenly as I rode down a hill on a bicycle, came to me like visitations from another world. But it was not only that my senses were awakened. I experienced an overwhelming emotion in the presence of nature, especially at evening. It began to wear a kind of sacramental character for me. I approached it with a sense of almost religious awe, and in the hush which comes before sunset, I felt again the presence of an unfathomable mystery. The song of the birds, the shapes of the trees, the colors of the sunset, were so many signs of this presence, which seemed to be drawing me to itself.

As time went on this kind of worship of nature began to take the place of any other religion. I would get up before dawn to hear the birds singing and stay out late at night to watch the stars appear, and my days were spent, whenever I was free, in long walks in the country. No religious service could compare with the effect which nature had upon me, and I had no religious faith which could influence me so deeply. I had begun to read the Romantic poets, Wordsworth, Shelley, and Keats, and I found in them the record of an experience like my own. They became my teachers and my guides, and I gradually gave up my adherence to any form of Christianity. The religion in which I had been brought up seemed to be empty and meaningless in comparison with that which I had found, and all my reading led me to believe that Christianity was a thing of the past.

An experience of this kind is probably not at all uncommon, especially in early youth. Something breaks suddenly into our lives and upsets their normal pattern, and we have to begin to adjust ourselves to a new kind of existence. This experience may come, as it came to me, through nature and poetry, or through art or music; or it may come through the adventure of flying or mountaineering, or of war; or it may come simply through falling in love, or through some apparent accident, an illness, the death of a friend, a sudden loss of fortune. Anything which breaks through the routine of daily life may be the bearer of this message to the soul. But however it may be, it is as though a veil has been lifted and we see for the first time behind the facade which the world has built round us. Suddenly we know that we belong to another world, that there is another dimension to existence. It is impossible to put what we have seen into words; it is something beyond all words which has been revealed.

There can be few people to whom such an experience does not come at some time, but it is easy to let it pass, and to lose its significance. The old habits of thought reassert themselves; our world returns to its normal appearance and the vision which we have seen fades away. But these are the moments when we really come face to face with reality; in the language of theology they are moments of grace. We see our life for a moment in its true perspective in relation to eternity. We are freed from the flux of time and see something of the eternal order which underlies it. We are no longer isolated individuals in conflict with our surroundings; we are parts of a whole, elements in a universal harmony.

This, as I understand it, is the "golden string" of Blake's poem. It is the grace which is given to every soul, hidden under the circumstances of our daily life, and easily lost if we choose not to attend to it. To follow up the vision which we have seen, to keep it in mind when we are thrown back again on the world, to live in its light and to shape our lives by its law, is to wind the string into a ball, and to find our way out of the labyrinth of life.

But this is no easy matter. It involves a readjustment to reality which is often a long and painful process. The first effect of such an experience is often to lead to the abandonment of all religion. Wordsworth himself was to spend many years in the struggle to bring his mystical experience into relation with orthodox Christianity and it may be doubted whether he was ever quite successful. But the experience is a challenge at the same time to work out one's religion for oneself. For most people today this has become almost a necessity. For many people the very idea of God has ceased to have any meaning. It is like the survival from a half-forgotten mythology. Before it can begin to have any meaning for them they have to experience his reality in their lives. They will not be converted by words or arguments, for God is not merely an idea or a concept in philosophy; he is the very ground of existence. We have to encounter him as a fact of our existence before we can really be persuaded to believe in him. To discover God is not to discover an idea but to discover oneself. It is to awake to that part of one's existence which has been hidden from sight and which one has refused to recognize. The discovery may be very painful; it is like going through a kind of death. But it is the one thing which makes life worth living.

• • •

I was led to make this discovery myself by the experience which I have recorded at school. This was the beginning for me of a long adventure which ended in a way for which nothing in my previous life had prepared me. If anyone had told me when I was at school or at Oxford that I should end my life as a monk, I should have doubted his sanity. I had no idea that any such thing as a monastery existed in the modern world, and the idea of it would have been without meaning to me. I have tried to show, however, that the steps which led to this revolution in my life, though they were in some ways exceptional, nevertheless followed a logical course, and I hope therefore that they may be found to have more than a personal interest.

I was one of those who came of age in the period after the first world war, and I shared its sense of disillusionment at the apparent failure of our civilization. In an effort to escape from the situation in which we found ourselves I was led, with two Oxford friends, to make an attempt to "return to nature," and to get behind the industrial revolution. The attempt was, of course, in one sense, a failure, but it led to the unexpected result that I made the discovery of Christianity. I read the Bible seriously for the first time, and found that the facts were quite different from what I had supposed and that Christianity was just as much a living power now as it had ever been. I then had to find a Church in which I could learn to practice my new-found faith, and after a long struggle, which cost me more than anything else in my life, I found my way to the Catholic Church. From that it was but a short step to the monastic life, and so by successive stages a radical change in my life was effected.

That search for God which began for me on that evening at school has gone on ever since. For the more one discovers of God, the more one finds one has to learn. Every step in advance is a return to the beginning, and we shall not really know him as he is, until we have returned to our beginning, and learned to know him as both the beginning and the end of our journey. We are all, like the Prodigal Son, seeking our home, waiting to hear the Father's voice say: "This my son was dead and is alive again; was lost and is found."

It is only now after thirty years that the full meaning of that which was revealed to me that day at school has become clear to me. That mysterious Presence which I felt in all the forms of nature has gradually disclosed itself as the infinite and eternal Being, of whose beauty all the forms of nature are but a passing reflection. Even when I was at school I had been fascinated by that passage of Plato in the Symposium, where he describes the soul's ascent on the path of love; how we should pass from the love of fair forms to the love of fair conduct, and from the love of fair conduct to the love of fair principles, until we finally come to the ultimate principle of all and learn what Beauty itself is. But I have learned what Plato could never have taught me, that the divine Beauty is not only truth but also Love, and that Love has come down from heaven and made his dwelling among men. I know now the meaning of St. Augustine's words, "O thou Beauty, so ancient and so new, too late have I loved thee, too late have I loved thee." I know now that God is present not only in the life of nature and in the mind of man, but in a still more wonderful way in the souls of those who have been formed in his image by his grace. I had sought him in the solitude of nature and in the labor of my mind, but I found him in the society of his Church and in the Spirit of Charity. And all this came to me not so much as a discovery but as a recognition. I felt that I had been wandering in a far country and had returned home; that I had been dead and was alive again; that I had been lost and was found.

ACKNOWLEDGMENTS

We gratefully acknowledge all those who gave permission for written material to appear in this book. We have made every effort to trace and contact copyright holders. If an error or omission is brought to our notice we will be pleased to correct the situation in future editions of this book. For further information, please contact the publisher.

Excerpt from *The Seven Storey Mountain* by Thomas Merton. Copyright © 1956 by The Trustees of the Merton Legacy Trust. Reprinted with permission of Harcourt Brace & Company. ✥ Excerpt from *Take Me to the River* by Al Green with Davin Seay. Copyright © 2000 by Al Green and Davin Seay. Reprinted by permission of HarperCollins Publishers. ✥ Excerpt from *Zen in the Art of Archery* by Eugen Herrigel. Copyright © 1953 by Pantheon Books, renewed 1981 by Random House, Inc. Used by permission of Pantheon Books, a division of Random House, Inc. ✥ Excerpt from *Traveling Mercies: Some Thoughts on Faith* by Anne Lamott. Copyright © 1999 by Anne Lamott. Used by permission of Pantheon Books, a division of Random House, Inc. ✥ Excerpt from *A Portrait of the Artist as a Young Man* by James Joyce.

Copyright © 1964 by The Estate of James Joyce. Reprinted by permission of Penguin Books. ✥ Excerpt from *In God We Trust: All Others Pay Cash* by Jean Shepherd. Copyright © 1966 by Jean Shepherd. Used by permission of Doubleday, a division of Random House, Inc. ✥ "The Pot of Gold" from *The Stories of John Cheever* by John Cheever. Copyright © 1978 by John Cheever. Used by permission of Alfred A. Knopf, a division Random House, Inc. ✥ Excerpt from *Siddhartha* by Herman Hesse. Copyright © 1951 by New Directions Publishing Corp. Reprinted by permission of New Directions Publishing Corp. ✥ "Revelation" from *The Complete Stories* by Flannery O'Connor. Copyright © 1971 by the Estate of Mary Flannery O'Connor. Reprinted by permission of Farrar, Straus and Giroux, LLC. ✥ Excerpt from *Salvation on Sand Mountain* by Dennis Covington. Copyright © 1995 by Dennis Covington. Reprinted by permission of Perseus Book Publishers, a member of Perseus Books, L.L.C. ✥ Excerpt from *Winding the Golden String* by Bede Griffiths. Copyright © 1954 by Bede Griffiths. Reprinted by permission of Templegate Publishers, Springfield, Illinois.

BIBLIOGRAPHY

Cheever, John. *The Stories of John Cheever.* New York: Vintage, 2000.

Covington, Dennis. *Salvation on Sand Mountain*. New York: Penguin Books, 1995.

Green, Al with Davin Seay. *Take Me to the River*. New York: HarperCollins Publishers, 2000.

Griffiths, Bede. *Winding the Golden String*. Springfield, IL: Templegate Publishers, 1980.

Hamalian, Leo and Edmond L. Volpe. *Ten Modern Short Novels*. New York: G.P. Putnam's Sons, 1958. (For *The Death of Ivan Ilyich* by Leo Tolstoy).

Herrigel, Eugen. *Zen in the Art of Archery*. New York: Vintage Books, 1971.

Hesse, Herman. *Siddhartha*. New York: New Directions Publishing Company, 1951.

James, Henry. *The Beast in the Jungle*. New York: W.W. Norton & Company, 1984.

Joyce, James. *A Portrait of the Artist as a Young Man*. New York: Penguin Books, 1992.

Lamott, Anne. *Traveling Mercies: Some Thoughts on Faith*. New

York: Anchor Books, 1999.

Merton, Thomas. *The Seven Storey Mountain*. New York: Harcourt, Brace & Company, 1998.

O'Connor, Flannery. *Revelation*. New York: Noonday Press, 1992.

Shepherd, Jean. *In God We Trust: All Others Pay Cash*. New York: Bantam Books, 1967.